The Gibraltar Incident

Cranley Harding

A Scott Rutherford thriller

To my darling Dan,
Thanks for your contribution without
which this would be unreadable
        Love you always
            Norm

Copyright © 2019 Cranley Harding

ISBN: 978-0-244-23276-4

Publish Nation

www.publishnation.co.ok

To Morley. Sadly missed.

May you never walk alone.

PROLOGUE

The wind which howled through the top sail rigging usually brought to lookout Tobias Finch's ear the melodic tune of the sea and gave him great comfort during his long weary and boring duty stuck atop the main mast in the crows' nest. But tonight, amidst the deep rumble of thunder and flashing lightning, the melodic tune of the sea was absent and a horizontal sleet-driven gale tore through the rigging as the sixty-four gun ship of the line, HMS Worcester, listed sharply to port shifting its cannons from their tethers. As it dipped into a deep depression between the frothing, foaming, restless and turbulent sea of the Bay of Gibraltar; it was all hands on deck.

Looking down from his lofty perch Tobias witnessed his fellow able-bodied seamen scuffling about like demented ants endeavouring to carry out the mid-ship officer's hollered orders as directed by Captain Mark Robinson – the words being mainly lost in the wind. As the Worcester floundered out of a depression it hit a gigantic wave causing the ship to stall and jar every New Forest oak and tar caulked joint to its limits. Had it not been for tying himself into the nest with a stout rope the jarring and listing would have torn Tobias from his eyrie. He was not a religious man but he felt the need in the circumstances to pray for safe deliverance. From long experience he knew them to be by location not more than fifteen minutes sailing from the safety of Gibraltar harbour – but the weather was worsening. He removed the cover from a leather and brass eyeglass and directed it towards where he knew the harbour to lie. He saw nothing. The eyeglass lens being rapidly covered in sleet. He removed the sleet with the sleeve of his inadequate tunic and after several unsuccessful attempts his eyeglass eventually picked up a faint glow through the murk and sleet. Without warning the ship dipped violently again and he almost lost his precious eyeglass overboard from his numb fingers. Readjusting his position he frantically managed to half-sit, half-jamb, himself into the nest to allow him to steady the eyeglass on the rim of the cage and thereby have the use of both hands. He cleaned the lens once again and trained the eyeglass towards where he had last viewed the dim glow. They could only be minutes from safety. The glow came into focus and he observed what he took to be a flag flying next to the glow. It was impossible to read as it was violently fluttering in direct line with the gale. The Worcester, in trying to manoeuvre out of the depression, came about broadside to the flag, giving Tobias time to read the signal. Surely it must be the glow of the harbour light that was causing it to glow yellow? A clean of the lens with his sleeve, a further check with the eyeglass, a period of disbelief, then the realization that what he was witnessing was indeed a yellow flag. It was a warning to stay clear – Gibraltar was once again in the grip of the deadly yellow fever. Tobias deserted his post, scrambled down the rigging in such panic that he forgot about his eyeglass and his almost frostbitten fingers. The fear of Gibraltar's St. Jago's cemetery – the cemetery hosting the last epidemic of yellow fever victims – being enough to strike the fear of God into the hardiest of men. He stumbled aft to report his bad news to a young acting fourth Lieutenant – Horatio Nelson.

***

Office of the Comptroller of the Navy London 1777

When the Worcester finally limped into Portsmouth harbour, the eighteen year old Horatio Nelson, after much research in the naval archives, sought an audience with the new Comptroller of the Navy, his uncle Sir Maurice Suckling. The audience granted, he now found himself sitting in an oak panelled ante-room. After a short period a polite cough announced the arrival of a secretary wearing the sleeve insignia braiding of captain who ushered him into a palatial office befitting a naval officer of high rank. As they entered the inner sanctum an immaculate gold braided, medal-bedecked, stately figure arose from behind his desk to greet Nelson with a warm handshake, and with an arm around his nephew's shoulder escort him to one of a pair of carver seats around a low table. Once comfortably seated he ordered afternoon tea from his secretary.

After the usual pleasantries relating to their families Sir Maurice said affably, 'Now then, young sir, I take it you're not here to enquire about your dear uncle's health, for it is I who should be enquiring about your near death escape aboard the Worcester. Nasty happening. Nearly lost the ship and all aboard. Care to refresh my memory, Horatio?'

Nelson explained to his uncle how Captain Robinson had made the brave decision to partially drop his rigging and run free with the gale. He had never witnessed such seamanship as the captain showed when he miraculously manoeuvred the Worcester into harbour with little damage and drop anchor to sit the gale out. At the first easing of the gale they upped anchor to rousing cheers from the crew for Captain Robinson and set sail for neutral Portugal and fresh water.

Suckling, who had listened intently, enquired, 'Now, Horatio, the reason for your visit please – I'm sure it's not to advise me of Captain Robinson's assured seamanship.'

Nelson nervously cleared his throat. 'Well, sir, I have spent time researching the Gibraltar navy archives and find that whatever happened to the Worcester is far from the first time this situation has occurred – the need for and the subsequent shortage of fresh water. The Navy and the regular garrison in Gibraltar, not to mention the civilians, are all vying for their share of water – and with the constant threat of war with Spain and France ever present – the need for us to take on fresh water will be of the utmost importance. I fully realize that the navy hierarchy, including your good self, sir, are aware of the strategic importance of Gibraltar – whoever controls Gibraltar controls the Mediterranean. So, pray tell uncle, why this ridiculous situation regarding water and drains is allowed to exist?'

A short silence ensued as Sir Maurice weighed up his options. He could, of course, tell his nephew, whom he thought the world of, to mind his own damned business and let his elders who know better get on with their plans but knowing Horatio's doggedness this would be to no avail – apart from which he agreed with his nephew about the abominable situation. So he took a deep breath and with a sigh gave him the facts as he knew them. Nelson who had expected a rollicking from his uncle for his cheek was instead shocked at what he heard. The basics he knew from his research: There were no rivers or streams and no successful wells. Rainwater was gathered in cisterns, earthenware pots, barrels and whatever receptacle the locals could muster. These facts he had discovered for himself. However, the further facts gleaned from Sir Maurice shocked him beyond belief. Many of the collection vessels lay next to privies and food preparation areas. There was no surplus water to clean the privies – they relied on heavy rains to clean the drains – and that was only successful in part. Regrettably, the consensus of His Majesty's Government's expert opinion was that the resultant diseases of cholera and yellow fever were caused by the "miasma" – the smell. However, there was now a strain of thought that the yellow fever might be caused by mosquitoes with the stagnant water in the various collection vessels being the ideal breeding ground. That was HMG's findings. However, the locals knew that it was proper drainage and reservoirs that were needed. HMG claimed it gave Gibraltar adequate subsidies to cover these requirements. Gibraltar claimed it did not receive enough funding to even start the work. A stand-off that could have immense consequences come war. The young Nelson also heard from a now emotional Sir Maurice that he had in his files estimates for the work going back two decades. All ignored by HMG. The Navy and the Army were constantly badgering the government to carry out these vital works. Sir Maurice reckoned it would take another war before anything was achieved – or the loss of a ship similar to the near calamitous circumstances as the Worcester.

A deflated Nelson departed his uncle's office as had many senior ranking officers of the Navy and Army before him after debating the same subject. Unfortunately, by the time of Nelson's death at Trafalgar, aged forty seven in 1805, some twenty nine years after his meeting with Sir Maurice, the sewage systems and reservoir quotations for Gibraltar remained in the Comptroller of the Navy's filing cabinet. And there had been two wars in between – the Napoleonic and American Revolution – which went against his uncle's prediction of it requiring a war before something was achieved. The work finally started in 1815..........

CHAPTER 1

Easter 1916 Dublin

Having never been outside the city limits of Belfast before the ten year old Stephen Curran stepped down off the Irish Volunteers' outing bus in Dublin. The hand of help was given by his adoring mother. The journey had seen him pass rolling meadows and lush green fields where cattle grazed, all framed in the distance by low purple-hazed hills. The views had been rural and tranquil, but as he looked around him at the urban sprawl that was Dublin he felt more at home especially with the bedlam around him – horns blaring, drums beating, and the chanting of independence slogans to the marching of boots. Had his dad, who was round the back of the bus removing his protest banner from the luggage compartment, been beside him he would have ruffled his hair and called him a townie. The call of his name by his mother shook him out of his reverie as he joined her to help his father unfurl the banner. When the banner had been unrolled his mother grasped one pole and his father the other. He was told to stand between them and not to leave his mother's side. Waiting for a break in the continuous throng of the happy singing and chanting demonstrators Stephen took the opportunity to look up at his parents' banner. It proclaimed: "A free Ireland for all – no matter religion or politics". Whilst looking upwards he took the opportunity to look further afield at other banners – they, too, read along similar lines. A few, however, announced their hatred of the British. His incredulous curiosity that had caused him to lag behind his parents was put right with a tug on his sleeve by his mother. As he adjusted his step he saw a street name – it was O'Connell Street. He had heard his father mention the name. As he recalled he had said they were marching to the General Post office in O'Connell Street to declare Irish Independence. The atmosphere around him was one of expectation. According to his father, Irish history was in the making. If what he was experiencing was history then he was all for it. It was about to become his favourite subject at school. Speaking across the top of his head to his father he heard his mother's comment that several of the marchers were carrying rifles. His father's answer was, "they are just for show." His mother then retorted, "And I suppose the boarded-up shop windows and the street barricades that we have had to swerve around are just for show also?" With no reply forthcoming she added, "To me it's beginning to look like an armed insurrection instead of *your* peaceful demonstration." His father had not replied because he was staring in delirious rapture at a banner hung from the upper floors of the Post Office declaring that an independent Irish Republic had been declared. He flung his cloth cap into the air – never to be seen again. It mattered not, as downing his banner carrying pole he grabbed his wife and did a jig – a new Irish Republic jig, of course. Young Stephen was all agog, he had never seen his parents so happy. It was then that he was suddenly aware of lethal whistling noises whipping, with little puff sighs, through the air followed by a distant rat-a-tat-tat. All around him people were screaming and running for non-existant cover as bullets ricocheted off the post office walls to be answered with salvos of muzzle flame from rifles firing over their heads from the upper storeys. As his mother grabbed at him to bring him to the ground he heard someone near at hand yelling, "The bastards are using machine guns on us." From school he knew the meaning of bastard but not to whom it was being referred. As his mother lay on top of him she looked up towards her husband in time to witness his upper body being shredded by bullets. She let out a fearful cry and after telling Stephen to close his eyes she lunged upwards with arms wide towards her collapsing husband only for her upper back to be met by the deadly returning arc of lead death from the machine gun. Her blood-drenched body fell backwards onto Stephen who screamed-and-screamed-and-screamed hysterically until he entered a vortex: into a black void. His father's blood-soaked banner gave one last waft in the wind before it blew into the gutter.

He woke up between fresh linen sheets in his Aunt Mabel's house – an orphan. The acrid smell of gun smoke still lingered in his nostrils. The day, if it was the same day, he distantly recalled, had started so marvelously. What had gone so tragically wrong?

***

Stephen's life had already been determined for him at an early age in his Protestant, middle-class parents' home. His father, a lecturer in economics and political science at Queens University, had indoctrinated him in the way of Nationalism – Home rule – through the Irish Volunteers' stated goal: *"To secure and maintain the rights and liberty common to all peoples of Ireland*

6

irrespective of religion or politics." His father had always stressed – *by peaceful means*. The young Stephen was not minded as to whether that was the actual Volunteers' goal or wishful thinking on his father's part. At the age of ten he was too young to understand the ramifications of this dogma, as with glee he was told he was going on a bus run to Dublin on a trip organized by the Irish Volunteers.

Because of the war raging in Europe there were large crowds of mainly women at the bus station waving Union Jack flags and hurling abuse. The men, including his father, were being spat upon and called "Sinn Fein bastards" and "conchies" as they boarded the bus. He was to find out later that a "conchie" was a conscientious objector – a pacifist – men looked upon as cowards for not engaging in the war against the Kaiser's Germany. However, to Stephen it was a grand day out but to his parents it was the start of something memorable. They were to join the Volunteers' march to the Dublin Post Office in O'Connell Street to declare Ireland a Republic. It was Easter, the timing of the declaration the Volunteer's thought to be perfect – a weak Britain in the midst of war – but it turned out to be a tragic error of judgement. They were cut down mercilessly by the British military.

Stephen was brutally pulled off his dead, blood-soaked, parents lying on the Post Office pavement. His mother lay with outstretched arms towards her dead Nationalist husband. An orphan at ten his recently war-widowed Aunt Mabel took him into her household. She held the very opposite views of her sister, his late mother. Her husband had been killed in some far flung field in Belgium and she was, as had been her husband, a proud Unionist. Stephen kept his Nationalist feelings hidden for many years from the aunt he adored and now looked upon her as his real mother – but his hatred of the British intensified with each passing year. He never forgave nor forgot the Post Office massacre that had left him an orphan.

Throughout the years he harboured the need for revenge but not being given to violence he felt impotent.... useless. When he left senior school he sat the Civil Service exams. He passed and chose Customs and Excise for no good reason other than it did not entail office work. He was an outdoors man. One of his postings was to the main road between Belfast and Dublin at the new border between the Irish Free State (Eire) and the Northern Ireland of British rule. His mind still full of vengeance he often turned a blind eye to cross border smuggling in the belief that every shady little bit of smuggling that helped to dent the British economy was revenge for his murdered parents. Pathetic he knew, but that was all he could see to offer. However, this relaxed attitude towards the people of Eire had not gone unnoticed. He was approached by a local commander of the recently formed Irish Republican Army – the IRA. The outcome of the meeting was that he became a member. His first major assignment for his new masters was to allow a shipment of arms, hidden under vegetables, to pass into the North successfully. With a Military presence evident it had been a nail-biting time for him and all concerned. The successful outcome delighted the IRA. They then, contradictorily, instructed him to become tough on petty smuggling – they could not risk him being considered soft by the authorities and replaced for he had become irreplaceable to them. Not only had he become irreplaceable, but he had built his own irreplaceable custom officers' team. He was now a major "plant" for the IRA in the British Home Office.

It was late January 1935 when Stephen was summoned to Brigade Headquarters, Belfast, in the dead of night. A worrying experience, especially travelling with a coarse jute sack over his head, bundled into a room and forcibly sat on a hard wooden chair. With the sack removed he came face to face with his local commander who, with no apology, introduced him to a swarthy skinned man called Eduardo of a similar age. Eduardo spoke English with a foreign accent, possibly Spanish. Eduardo informed him that due to the forthcoming retirement of an official a vacancy would occur for a customs officer in Gibraltar. Stephen nodded his head knowing it best not to ask as to what forthcoming event was about to cause the poor sod's retirement but couldn't help wondering what this had to do with him. The local commander supplied the answer. He told Stephen that he had to apply for the job. With his experience at the volatile border between Eire and Northern Ireland he perceived no problem with him securing the position. There was only one slight problem – they required a good reason for him transferring to Gibraltar. It wasn't the British Home Office they were concerned about – it was the Foreign Office, particularly the Secret Intelligence Service – Section 6 – SIS(6). The reason had to be watertight otherwise all would be lost and with it the opportunity to inflict a major blow against the British Navy. This last said for the benefit of Stephen who on hearing this news became euphoric – at last an opportunity to avenge his parents' death. Witnessing the look of pleasure crossing Stephen's face his commander smiled inwardly. He had chosen the right tactic. With pointed forefinger he indicated to Eduardo to take over. Eduardo informed Stephen he had a contact in Gibraltar named Delores that he would introduce him to. She was an attractive, Spanish born Gibratarian, who lived and worked in Gibraltar. Stephen, who was unmarried due primarily to his love of Guinness and the horses, when he asked why he needed to be introduced to this female received the shock answer – marriage. Stephen was lost for words. Seeing the look of panic on Stephen's face his brigade commander took over again. He was told that all would be pretence but during the subterfuge if he cared for sex Delores was usually amenable. Stephen had to remind himself about the opportunity to avenge his parents' death to stop running from the room. Not that he would have got far with armed men surrounding the building. His commander continued. He was to take a holiday immediately in Torremolinos, just along the coast from Gibraltar, and to become besotted with Delores to the extent of wanting to get married. It was not unheard of for people to go on holiday and meet their future spouses. Stephen knew "the drill" his commander finalised. Stephen, had no idea of "the drill" but knew he had better learn quickly if he wanted to live to avenge his parents. Before the coarse sack was placed over his head again Eduardo told him he would meet him in Torremolinos when the time was right and introduce him to his intended. He felt sick at the thought. His commander reminded him with a veiled threat that the success of the mission rested on his shoulders. All went black as the bag was put roughly over his head. During this enforced blackout he wondered where they had managed to find the Spaniard, Eduardo.

The plot, an audacious attack on the British Navy dockyard in Gibraltar that Curran had just unwittingly agreed to, had been at the planning stage for some considerable time. It had stumbled due to the IRA not having contacts in Gibraltar. That was until articles started to appear in the English press about demonstrations in Gibraltar. The name of the principal agitator in all the articles was linked to that of an Eduardo Suarez of the Spanish fascists – the Falange Party. Suarez's main agenda being the return of Gibraltar to Spain. A senior IRA member was sent to Gibraltar to make contact. Suarez had been extremely amenable with regard to helping their cause, especially when he was offered a sizeable sum of money to infiltrate the dockyard. Also included in this sum he had to supply a willing female companion. Suarez had offered the senior IRA man the services of a willing female instantly – his secretary Estelle. He was welcome to use the bedroom upstairs. The senior IRA official had in his report, allegedly, declined Suarez's offer making clear to him that the use of a female companion was to be offered at a *later* stage in the planning. In the senior man's report he noted Suarez to be, "greedy and totally untrustworthy." Unfortunately, they had no choice but to agree to the use of him. He had been left a large sum of money to cover expenses plus all necessary travel documents to and from Belfast. And, the senior man had told his Brigade commander with an imaginary finger slice across his throat that Suarez had been reminded of the consequences of any ill-considered failure to deliver. Suarez had given his assurance.

When Stephen reached home at his Aunt Mabel's comfortable end-terrace house he filled out an application form for the Gibraltar posting. The following morning during breakfast his aunt handed him an envelope that had been delivered by hand. It contained all he needed for a vacation in Torremolinos.

***

Gibraltar Early April 1935

Eduardo Suarez was Spanish and bitterly anti-British. He wanted the British out of the country of his birth. He was the local area commander of the fascist Falange Party, and operated from La Linea a small industrial town across the isthmus and border between Gibraltar and Spain. As a Spanish national, he had been allowed access to work in Gibraltar on a work permit until he had it rescinded by the police for inciting rioting and causing civil disobedience with his "Free Gibraltar from the British" demonstrations. However, this did not stop him from visiting his long time on/off girlfriend, Delores, who lived in a squalid part of the Old Town area of Gibraltar and for whom he procured work from the nightclubs of La Linea to Malaga in her chosen profession as, so she liked to fantasize, a high class escort. Today, he was on his way to visit her. Using a forged work permit and sporting a newly grown moustache to accompany a well pulled down black beret as worn by the local workforce he pushed his bicycle through the lax pedestrian customs route. He mounted his bicycle and set off for Delores. She didn't know it but she was about to become a wealthy lady – provided she played her cards right.

As he entered her apartment he was met with the greeting, 'And where have you been for the last week, arsehole?' She then pointed at his top lip and burst out laughing. 'And where in the name of Christ did you get the walrus?'

'And it's nice to see you again too, my sweet. If you must know I've been to Belfast.... Ireland.' That answer was met with a blank look. 'To make us extremely rich.'

Suddenly, her expression turned to one of understanding. With hands on hips she replied, 'What have I to do now? Get screwed by Irish leprechauns?'

With Curran being of short stature and Irish he didn't like to say, "in a sort of a way" so he tried, 'Very funny, Dolly. Now, will you please, please listen?' as he peeled off a rubber band around a brown paper parcel and laid it on a bedside table. The partly opened parcel showed stacks of high denomination peseta bank notes. 'As I said, I've been away making us rich.' Delores' eyes lit up as she grabbed the parcel and emptied the contents on the bed. She had never seen so much money. 'And that's just a start. We will receive this amount every month and I'll split what you see here fifty/fifty with you.' He didn't, of course, mention that he had the same size parcel languishing in his office safe in La Linea for himself.

'But it does include me getting screwed?'

'Well that's what usually happens when you get married.'

'Did you say, *married*? Oh! *Eduardo*. At last. I thought you would never....' she said taking a step towards him.

Suarez, in panic, held up his hand palm outwards at Delores to stop her from taking the wrong meaning. 'Unfortunately, not us this time, Dolly. But once you've done what I need you to do – we will get married... of that I *promise* you.' To a hostile silence he hastily explained the agreement he had struck in Belfast which was basically she was to "marry" an Irish guy named Curran. To further soften the deal he had made, Suarez informed Delores that when

Curran got the position as Chief Customs Officer of Gibraltar she would be entitled, as his "wife", to a new apartment in Gibraltar New Town. At this news she had clapped her hands – the luxury of an inside toilet overcoming her. But, until such times as her ersatz "husband" Curran had served his purpose he would not, unfortunately, be able to see her again for security reasons other than to give her money at the end of each month. This he felt she agreed to with too much enthusiasm and when she asked how long the job would take he wasn't sure if she was working out her future earnings or was longing for the day she would be rid of Curran and take him up on his promise of marriage. He hoped the former applied, counting her money, but he lied as he told her he couldn't wait for their happy day to arrive.

'And who is the source of all this money? I don't want to get involved in any of your crooked political shenanigans and end up in jail,' Delores threatened.

The last thing in the world he needed now was for her to renege, so he sighed off-handedly, and said, 'Ah! Well! I gave you first chance, Dolly. Now I'll just have to try Estelle.' This he was saying as he began scooping the banknotes up off the bed and trying to stuff them into the torn parcel.

'Not that fucking cow, you don't,' cried, Delores, as she knocked the money out of his hand. 'What's the guy's name again?'

'Curran. Stephen Curran. A lovely, kind, Irishman. He'll make you a fine husband. I knew I could count on you, Dolly.' He looked at his watch. 'I can spare you five minutes before my next meeting. How's about a quickie to celebrate?' She lay back on the bed lifting her skirt with one hand and joyfully throwing banknotes in the air with the other.

***

Anxious weeks passed before the mail brought Curran news of his interview. It was to be held in London. Enclosed was his travel warrant. At the interview he was confronted by officials from the British Home Office who introduced themselves. There was another person sitting on the fringe who introduced himself in a dour Scottish accent as James McKay. The dour Scot in question was, unknown to Curran, Head of the Secret Intelligence Service SIS (6) who did not usually sit-in on these interviews. However, the Embassy in Berlin had recently lost its Serjeant-at-Arms through an alleged "accidental" drowning that had caused a security scare that turned out to be murder and now the Home Office had lost their Chief Customs Officer in Gibraltar also by accidental drowning. Not a great believer in coincidences he felt obliged to pay due diligence to this application to see where it led.

The Home Office officials' questions were all relevant to the job and handled by Curran with the ease and manner of a man that knew his job thoroughly. However, the dour Scot's questions were personal and pertinent. Curran realized by the way they were phrased he was dealing with an agent from the Intelligence Service. He awaited the stumbling block question – why did he want a transfer from Belfast to Gibraltar? The dour Scot did not disappoint as he asked the question, and sat back with arms folded as if challenging him. Stephen took a deep breath and lied the lie he had practiced for weeks – he replied that he intended to get married to a Gibraltarian lady he had met on holiday in Torremolinas. One of the other panel members enquired of him when he intended to marry the lucky lady. He replied that irrespective of whether he got the job, the answer was as soon as possible. He looked towards the dour Scot whom he took to be the main man to convince. He was busy sliding his notes into a battered leather briefcase and showing no interest in Curran's answers. Stephen departed the meeting unsure if he had been successful. It was that bloody miserable Scot that had rattled him. He thought it prudent not to say anything about the man to his Belfast controller.

As the door closed after Curran, Sir James nodded his acceptance to the Home Office officials. Their reasons for Curran being the right man for the job were very different from Sir James' who now considered the game afoot. His Irish intelligence network had informed him about the sighting in Belfast of a known Spanish subversive. Eduardo Suarez.

***

A week later, Stephen received in the post notification of his suitability for the position as Chief Customs Officer, Gibraltar Station. He bade a tearful goodbye to his Aunt Mabel and promised to keep in touch by telephone. Before his departure to Gibraltar his IRA Brigade Commander told him he was to be what was known as a "sleeper". He was to keep a low profile, work hard, and not get involved in any wrong doings at the border and to earn trust until such times as he was "activated".

At work he bade his farewells and fabricated a story to his Aunt Mabel about going to Gibraltar as emergency cover for a colleague that had taken ill. He felt bad about deceiving his beloved aunt. He left Belfast within the week.

***

Stephen Curran was met at Malaga airport by Eduardo Suarez and driven to his hotel in Torremolinos to meet Delores. She was the most beautiful woman he had ever seen. She had the looks of the classic Spanish flamenco dancers he had seen at the films back home in Belfast. She was tall and slim with long black flowing hair and high cheek bones. The red dress she wore showed her ample décolletage. All these attributes *and* she spoke English. Curran was besotted. She, unfortunately, thought he was a gormless looking weed but money was money. And she knew what was required of her – the sum of money Suarez had guaranteed her per month would have taken her the rest of her life to earn on her back.

They spent Stephen's "honeymoon" in bed. He soon forgot about Guinness and horses and at the end of fourteen days of being sexually pleasured they returned to Gibraltar to set up home in a HM Government owned house in the New Town. The ground floor apartment being tenanted by the newly "married" Mr. and Mrs. Curran. The upper floor apartment was used for HMG visitors. Curran was informed that the present occupant upstairs was a Miss Yvonne Rencoule – a Ministry of Defence inspector of works.

CHAPTER 2

Berlin early January 1936

With pennants bearing the Nazi swastika insignia fluttering from their front mudguards the open-top Mercedes limousine and the escorting cavalcade of motor-cycle outriders glided to a stop outside the former art school in Prinz Albert Strasse, the now home of the secret state police – the Geheime Staats Polizei – known to all as the "Gestapo". As the limousine stopped and the heavily armed outriders formed a cordon around the vehicle, an officer in the all black uniform with silver flash runes on his collar denoting the Waffen Scutzstaffel, stepped forward from the ornate brass doors of the Gestapo Headquarters to open the limousine's rear door. He was one of Hitler's personal elite guards, commonly referred to as the SS. The officer flung a straight stiff right arm Nazi salute to the emerging passenger and his "Heil Hitler" was the signal for the guards around the car to render their orchestrated salute in reply amid a syncopated chorus of, "Heil Hitler" salutations accompanied by a clicking of heels. The insignificant moustached figure of Germany's powerful dictator Adolf Hitler stepped from the Mercedes. Immediately his gleaming jack-boots touched the ground he strutted with the gait of an angry man towards a foyer bedecked in multitudinous, massive red flags bearing the black swastika on a white circle hung from the ornately moulded ceiling and marble walls. Once inside he was further greeted with a chorus of salutations echoing off the marble walls from the SS guards lining the floor from the main entrance to the elevator. At the elevator Hitler was met by the slim figure of Reinhard Heydrich, deputy head of the SS, whose Nazi salute was dismissed by the impatient hand wave of Hitler. The elevator operator then set the latticed cage in motion for the top floor. The cage, as it rose slowly through each floor level, showed the stairs to be lined with armed SS guards.

On the top floor, pacing back and forth, anxiously awaiting Hitler's arrival was a nervous Heinrich Himmler, chief of the Gestapo and the SS who suspected that Hitler's present displeasure was about a recent overseas operation that had gone catastrophically wrong. Himmler did not know what the operation was other than what he had read in the World's Press. However, what he did know was that this was going to be an unpleasant meeting for both himself and Heydrich. The meeting had been called by Hitler at short notice and having had no previous communication with him regarding the alleged catastrophe, Himmler could only assume that the suddenly called-for meeting was associated with what he did know from his press readings; that Hitler had lost a U-boat due to a mini tsunami caused by an eruption on Mount Teide – a natural disaster that not even Hitler could blame on others. It would appear that Hitler would have got off with his subterfuge, whatever it was, had it not been for the conning tower of a U-boat somehow surviving the disaster and had been found floating off the south coast of Tenerife. This had caused great consternation at the League of Nations being as it was a direct contravention of The Treaty of Versailles. However, this was not half the consternation aroused in Hitler – he was reportedly apoplectic with rage. Himmler had, since the meeting had been called, racked his brains trying to figure out how he or Heydrich could have possibly been directly involved in the obviously ultra-secret operation. Himmler's first thoughts had been that, with it being an overseas operation, the blame lay with Canaris' Abwehr. But on casting his mind further back he was aware that they could be implicated by an indirect involvement in the past. He knew Hitler had been made aware of an enormous underwater cave in Tenerife through an article in the National Geographic Magazine back in 1934. The author of the article, a Professor von Nida, had christened the cave, "The Great Fissure", and claimed, even though it was as yet to be found, that it was, probably from his initial probes, situated at a headland known as Punta Gaunché. To Hitler's credit, should the cave ever be found, he had seen the opportunity for a strategic U-boat base in the Atlantic. Hitler had commanded Himmler and Heydrich to draw-up a list of the top men in their fields comprising, deep sea divers, surveyors, engineers and geologists. After he and Heydrich had prepared the list, they were divorced from the project as a total blanket of secrecy descended over the operation. This being all Himmler and Heydrich were aware of at the time, Himmler had given it no further thought until the wayward conning tower had bobbed up off the coast of Tenerife. However, given the short notice of today's meeting he could not help but feel that the blame for the failure was heading his and Heyrich's way.

To the thunder of jack-boots in the corridor outside, the door opened and Heydrich entered to hold it open for Hitler's entrance. Himmler sneaked a glance at Heydrich who surreptitiously shook his head in warning as Hitler, his face a mask of fury, strode to Himmler's vacated desk and swept paperwork angrily aside to lay his gloves on top of each other. With a clicking of heels Himmler gave the Nazi salute only to have it dismissed with an angry flip of Hitler's wrist and a pointed finger waving to the two chairs placed opposite the desk. Himmler sat and Heydrich followed, occupying the vacant chair alongside.

The Führer, still standing, glared penetratingly at both and with no formal niceties thumped the desk with his clenched fist and in a voice quavering in anger, growled, '*We,* have an unmitigated disaster on our hands...' with this failure to address either by their Christian names which was the accustomed greeting they realized he was in one of his maniacal moods and, from experience, caution would be the order of the day as he continued, '...Baldwin and his British government of appeasers are having a field day at my expense. So what excuses do you have as my principal SS officers, and my eyes and ears, to offer for the failure? The failure of *me,* being exposed to world ridicule.'

Himmler and Heydrich furtively glanced at each other. It was as they had expected – they were to be made the scapegoats. Himmler broke the ensuing silence. Used to Hitler's antics he calmly replied, 'I assume, Mein Führer, you refer to these scurrilous articles in the foreign papers regarding one of our U-boats? If indeed that is what you mean then all I can offer, with the *limited* information I have of the incident, is but to blame it on Mother Nature.'

Hitler, who had after his initial outburst, sat down with arms crossed, jumped to his feet once again and raising his voice to the frenzy pitch of his usual oratory, shouted, 'You say *Mother Nature* – I say she was *not* responsible for the deaths of *my* "Special Agents" – nor the hospitalization of Kreigsmarine Kommandos – *nor* the theft of the Reich's machine pistols and ammunition from a dockside warehouse in Tenerife. But...' he hesitated for effect, '...but she, Mother Nature, may.... *just may,* have been responsible for the destruction of my newly built U-boat in its berth in the underwater cave. However, I have my own volcano and geologist experts at the Humboldt University looking into why a minor eruption on the side of Mount Teide should have affected the Great Fissure. I do not trust the Harvard University report.' This was all news to an incredulous Himmler, as Hitler continued his rant, 'All separate incidents but highly suspicious – wouldn't you say, Heinrich? Your comments please.'

Himmler, moving uneasily in his chair, replied, 'It is with regret that I can shed no further light on the matter. As you are aware Mein Führer, after organizing your geologists, divers and engineers etcetera, for whatever purpose you had in mind, Heydrich and I were relieved of further responsibilities.'

Hitler immediately responded with an irritable hand gesture pointing from one to the other. 'It is truly remarkable Heinrich, that you and Rienhard here...' the finger swivelled to cover Heydrich, '....know nothing about anything that might incriminate you both when I am trying to get to the bottom of something. So, since you claim to know nothing of the events in Tenerife I will tell you about what happened and what I expect you to do about it. Firstly my "Special Agents Unit" of highly trained special operatives under the command of Colonel Maria von Reus were murdered. Secondly, the local police idiots investigating two of the deaths claim that they were accidents – crushed by a gun barrel falling from an overhead crane'.

A gun barrel? What gun barrel?' queried Himmler.

'Of no consequence to your future enquiries, Heinrich. Suffice it for you to know I am convinced it is not an accident. And as for Colonel von Reus they claim she broke her neck whilst diving off rocks – which was remarkable, considering she did not swim. Then add the Kreigsmarine Kommandos – five trained killers – disabled and robbed of crates of machine pistols. And finally, my agent in the local Tenerife Government suddenly decides to take a swim in the Atlantic – unfortunately, still in his car. One "Special Agent" down – unfortunate.' He paused for effect then thundered, 'Four unfortunates – Never! Never! Never! Never! Something is badly wrong. Why have I to be the one to find out these things? What of *my* SS, *my* Gestapo and *my* Abwehr?'

For it to be your Abwehr, you have to have your Generals on your side – and they most definitely aren't, pondered Himmler, who had also been wondering throughout Hitler's diatribe where he had gleaned his Tenerife information. He at first assumed it might have been from an Abwehr agent which he instantly dismissed as being highly unlikely given they only disclosed intelligence gathered to "The Generals". But Hitler's disclosure of the death of his spy in the Tenerife Cabildo (local government) had solved this problem, so he ventured, 'With the theft of the machine pistols couldn't it have been this local "Free

Canary Movement" lot I've read about?'

'No. They are political separatists. They want home rule and are non-violent... all the usual rubbish. Their gripe is with Spain not us.'

'Are the Kreigsmarine Kommandos still alive – and if so can they throw any light on the matter?'

'Now you're beginning to think like an investigator at last, Heinreich. I can tell you that Colonel von Reus, in her last communiqué to me before her murder, informed me that she suspected something suspicious about an employee of Cantravel she had met in their gymnasium.'

'What's Cantravel?' queried Heydrich, breaking his silence.

'An American up-market country club in Puerto de la Cruz. This employee, a diving instructor, possessed a distinctive Harley Davidson motor cycle which had been seen in the vicinity of our raided Santa Cruz warehouse. The same warehouse where the assault on the Kommandos took place and also the theft of the machine pistols and dynamite.'

The sudden thought struck Himmler as to the need for Schmeisser machine pistols on Tenerife – surely Hitler had not intended to invade the Island. However, discretion being the order of the day he elected to say nothing as Heydrich said, 'What did the local police say about the theft, Mein Führer?'

Hitler glowered at Heydrich. 'Where are your brains, Reinhard? Thankfully Commander Müeller used *his* brains, or what was left of them after receiving a savage blow to his head, and did not report the incident to the local dolts. What was he going to tell them, Reinhard? That our machine pistols imported as agricultural machinery had been stolen?' After a short pause, during which Hitler had stared malevolently at both, he continued, 'I have digressed. Unfortunately, Colonel von Reus did not know the name of the Harley Davidson driver so I would suggest you send an agent to Cantravel before they close down their operation.'

'Close? But why?'

'Because a Spanish General election is due soon and from what I gather from Abwehr reports, that they have graciously deemed to make known to me, is that an assorted rabble of socialists, communists and anarchists that have gathered together as the Popular Front Party are likely to win.'

Tiring of the need to be constantly walking on egg shells, Himmler answered bluntly, 'I ask again – why would Cantravel close down, Adolf?'

Hitler nodded at Himmler's abruptness and answered calmly, 'Because, Heinrich, if this Popular Front rabble win, the Nationalist Generals will be put out to graze. In fact Canaris informs me that that peacock General Franco is likely to be put out to graze as the Governor of Tenerife. Knowing him he will not settle for that – nor the result of the election. So I suspect a civil war in Spain to be in the offing sooner than later. Cantravel will be aware of this and will mothball their operation until things settle down. So that is the "Why" answered for you, Heinrich.'

'Thank you, Adolf. Is there anything else that you feel may be of assistance to help my enquiries?'

'Yes. But it is more to help me. I am hearing of futile sabotage attempts on the British dockyard in Gibraltar. Is it you, Heinrich, or is it Canaris that is responsible?'

'It is not the SS. Being as it is an overseas operational area we have no brief. As regards Canaris's Abwehr I do not know. They tell us nothing. They are ultra-secretive. However, hazarding a guess, I would suspect the Spanish Falangists who are indirectly financed by my department. I will look in to it.'

'I don't care who. Have it stopped immediately. I do not want the British Government upset any further. I still have high hopes of getting Baldwin on my side against the communist threat of Stalin. Now, gentlemen, I am about to see Canaris in five minutes time, so if it is he that is causing the unrest in Gibraltar I will have him stop.' *I wish you luck with that,* thought Himmler, as Hitler stood up, put on his gloves and said, 'You now have something to get your teeth into and I expect results. I want daily reports. Somebody is responsible for the deaths of my "Special Agents Unit" personnel and I want him found.'

Whilst Hitler left the office to be met by his bodyguards outside in the corridor, Himmler was musing on what he considered the real reason for Hitler's consternation – Maria von Reus. His informers had told him that Hitler had had her secreted somewhere in the Berlin countryside.

As Hitler descended in the lift he was aware that the only others apart from his "Special Agents Unit" he had told about his attempt to secure a base on Tenerife were Admiral Zeigler who he had personally put in charge of the Kreigsmarine Kommandos involved and the person he was about to meet – Admiral Wilhelm Canaris, head of the Abwehr (German Military Intelligence). He gave thought to Canaris. He had been informed by Göring that there was a constant threat of a coup from "The Generals" and that Canaris was one of the clique who would see the end of him. He would first have a word with his spy in the Abwehr.

***

Abwehr H.Q Tirpizufer Berlin

Before setting out for work that morning Manfred Adler had received a phone call from the same flat anonymous voice he had listened to many times before. It gave him his instructions.

A now extremely nervous Adler sat at his cipher machine awaiting the phone on his desk to ring. He had been waiting since he arrived at his desk some four hours previously. It had rung several times before – each call related to work matters. It rang again. He once again nervously lifted the receiver to hear the awaited flat anonymous voice. He listened and answered "No." The phone went dead. He slammed the receiver down on its cradle and with sweat breaking out on his forehead he dabbed it with a handkerchief, before he rose from his position to begin his walk to the top floor. He stopped outside a door bearing the name Admiral W. Canaris in gold lettering. He knocked and was told to enter. A pretty blonde secretary smiled knowingly at him, bid him good morning, and led him to a door behind her. She knocked and held the door open for Adler. He was in time to hear the end of a telephone conversation. *"I am ever so sorry you cannot keep our appointment, Adolf, I was so looking forward to seeing you again.......and to you too, Adolf. Auf wiedersehen."* The distinguished looking gentleman receiving the call banged the receiver down with a laugh and a broad smile as he said to Adler, 'It worked a treat, Manfred. I knew it would. Hitler has cancelled our meeting. You did excellently well young man. Keep up your good work and I can assure you that our little secret will remain a secret from Hitler and his gang of thugs.'

Adler heaved a sigh of relief. He had that morning been instructed by the anonymous voice to check his archive files for any proof that Canaris had had any communication with organizations relating to Gibraltar or Tenerife. He had immediately contacted Canaris who told him to remove any reports associating him with anything to do with Gibraltar or Tenerife.

Himmler wanted the SS to take control of the Abwehr. Canaris and his loyal band of hand-picked anti-Nazis had thwarted all attempts by Himmler to place a spy in their network. However, when Himmler had tried to place Adler, a brilliant young cryptologist graduate from Berlin's Humboldt University in the Abwehr, Canaris could not resist the temptation to implement his wish for he required such a talent for his Enigma programme. Himmler had given Adler an excellent cover story to spin at his interview with Canaris. The story went that he had been under surveillance by the Gestapo for organizing anti-fascist demonstrations against the Third Reich whilst at university. A falsified newspaper article showing him in a photograph with fellow demonstrators and backed with a police charge sheet completed the fabrication. A good Himmler fairy tale thought Canaris at the interview. Good – but not as thorough as could fool an Anwehr background check. Digging deep into the Adler family history they had discovered that the young Manfred was a Jew, passing himself off as a gentile as so many were given to do, due to Hitler's purge. *And* – as a bonus – he was also found to be a closet homosexual. With both categories being classified as undesirable in Hitler's "New Order", the young Adler was fully aware of the penalties. This had left him in a precarious situation. Canaris had made him an offer he couldn't refuse. Hitler's Abwehr spy was now a double agent.

CHAPTER 3

Gestapo Headquarters

After the slamming of his office door, signifying the departure of Hitler, Himmler took up a position at his top floor window. Once he had satisfied himself that Hitler and his entourage had departed the building he turned from his eyrie to face Heydrich. He pointed towards an arm chair, one of two either side of a low table. Heydrich settled comfortably whilst Himmler busied himself at the drinks cabinet. Himmler finished his chore and laid two crystal glasses of schnapps on the table and sat opposite Heydrich. Himmler raised his glass and toasted, 'To our success.'

'I'll drink to that,' replied Heydrich leaning over the table to chink glasses.

'Well, Reinhard, what now? The Führer seems a little upset.'

'So, what's new, Heinrich. At least we've been spared the dungeons.' This quip being reference to the basement rooms where the Gestapo carried out their reviled interview techniques.

'Don't count your chickens yet. If we don't get this right the dungeons could still await.' After a contemplative silence Himmler continued, 'Let's start with his desire to cull the activities of that blue shirted, red beret, rag-tag bunch of trouble makers – the Falange. Who do you have available?'

Heydrich took a sip of his schnapps and sank back in the comfort of his chair and after a short period of stroking his chin, he answered, 'I have the ideal man, an Otto Hertzog.'

'Didn't he have a near death experience with the Russians in Berlin?'

'Yes. They firebombed his motor. He has dreadful facial burns. But is still the same nasty thug under the surgery.'

'He has a propensity towards violence, does he not?'

'Yes, he does. So how far do I allow him to go with that self-important little shit Suarez and his local Falange rabble in La Linea?'

'Tut, tut, Reinhard that's no way to be speaking about one who considers himself the future leader of all Spanish Falangists. However, to answer your question. I would suggest you first have a word in Suarez's ear – the Führer is unhappy, etcetera, etcetera. If that doesn't work – a little persuasion – if that doesn't work, let him do as he pleases. In fact the more I think about that money grabbing-rat, Suarez, just let Hertzog do as he pleases...... How I wish our main problem – Tenerife – was as simple. Any ideas forming from what little we have to go on, Reinhard?'

'None,' replied Heydrich emphatically and as an afterthought added, 'It was only when news of that bloody U-boat conning tower was found that I even knew where Tenerife was. For, if you remember, Heinrich, I was not given the destination of the geologists and surveyors you instructed me to recruit.'

Himmler, knowing his devious deputy well, immediately realized that Heydrich was trying to distance himself from the debacle that was Tenerife so he replied, letting Heydrich know that he knew what he was up to, 'Nor did I know the destination, Reinhard. Thank God it wasn't *me* that organized the supply of explosives for Tenerife.' He paused and looked hard at Heydrich before continuing, 'So *we* had better not fail – wouldn't you agree Reinhard?'

Heydrich, realizing he had been rumbled replied tartly, 'Fail? How can we not fail, if Adolf refuses to believe that the disaster was not of nature's doing? The whole thing's a bloody farce.'

'Ah! Therein lies our dilemma. I do not believe for one moment that Adolf does not believe that it is anything other than a natural disaster because...'

'Then why does he think somebody is responsible?' interrupted Heydrich.

'Because, Reinhard,' Himmler answered calmly as he tended to do in a crisis, 'I am of the opinion that Mein Führer cares little about the loss of his U-boat or the British and French prattling on about their precious Treaty of Versailles but more about revenge for the death of Colonel von Reus, who, as you must know, he was screwing every which way and up.'

A nod from Heydrich confirmed this well-known secret among the Party's hierarchy but a "So?" slipped from his lips.

'He requires a scapegoat or goats and I don't intend it to be either of us. We will, of course, carry out our investigation diligently and give him his damned daily reports during which period I am sure we will find a scapegoat.'

A twisted smile broke out on Heydrich's face at the thought of Himmler's cunning as he lapsed into a contemplative silence only for him to break it seconds later. 'Your mentioning Colonel von Reus jogged my memory. In her report to Adolf she had mentioned a Harley Davidson motor cycle parked near the warehouse where the Kommandos were attacked. And as Adolf says it should be easy to find out the name of the person that owns the machine, after all we know he works for this American Cantravel outfit.'

'It would be easy if we had one of our agents in Tenerife but by the way Adolf was talking his "Special Agents Unit" cell appears to have been wiped out.'

'Why don't we ask Canaris for help? His Abwehr are, after all, responsible for overseas intelligence.'

'Because they are not to be trusted. As we have established they see their allegiance first and foremost to "The Generals". Truth be told I wouldn't be surprised if the Abwehr were behind this Tenerife U-boat problem. Apart from which, since Adolf blames *us* for the debacle, he expects *us* to solve it.'

'So we have nobody available to follow up our only lead,' sighed Heydrich.

'I wouldn't say that exactly. I've been thinking about that as we speak. What about those Kreigsmarine Kommandos that were attacked in that warehouse in Santa Cruz where the Harley was spotted?'

'From what Adolf implied, with the violence used we would be lucky if any of them are still on active service.'

'But, I know one of them still to be on active service. The day after the U-boat's conning tower was found in the Atlantic I was asked to organize a secret SS tribunal by Admiral Zeigler at the alleged behest of our Führer...'

'Why us? Why not a Kreigsmarine tribunal?'

'Mine was not to reason why, Reinhard...*then*. Now, I am beginning to wonder if Mein Führer really did request the tribunal. It was a farce. The panel were all hand-picked by Zeigler. The Kreigsmarine officer, whose name is Müeller, was found guilty of gross negligence and stripped of his rank. Zeigler had *his* scapegoat. Now let's see if we can add to Müeller's woes and make him *ours*. After all that he's been through don't you think he would wish to seek revenge? And, should he accept and fail, we have found *our* scapegoat. Say he, unfortunately, whilst trying to apprehend the murderer of Colonel von Reus – was shot and killed in the line of duty during a car chase. The driver of the chased car, the supposed murderer of von Reus, also being killed when his car, after being rammed by our Kreigsmarine hero, left the road and plunged down a ravine to burst into flames. Regrettably, both dead.' But on the other hand should he ....'

'Succeed...by killing the killer of von Reus, we are also heroes,' interrupted Heydrich, cackling with sinister delight.

Himmler joined in the laughter, slapping Heydrich on the shoulder as he made his way to his desk and the telephone where he put a call through to the Kreigsmarine Headquarters at Keil.

***

Krupps Works Essen.

At an interview arranged by Heydrich the three engineers sitting opposite him, who had been engaged on Hitler's secret Tenerife project, were Krupps' top ordnance engineers who specialized in large alteration projects. They had found the mutilated bodies of Hitler's "Special Agents Unit" in their workshop, a dockside warehouse in Santa Cruz. Himmler had sent Heydrich to interview them in the hope they might be able to give an overall picture of the project and add further names of people they came into contact with throughout their contract. They had apparently worked from daily sealed orders left by a female whose name they did not know. She was described to Heydrich as a slim, attractive, auburn-haired, big-busted female. Heydrich recognized the description as fitting Colonel Maria von Reus. She was the only person they saw in relation to their work. They had been lodged in a bed and breakfast in Santa Cruz near to the docks and walked to work. This news came as a disappointment to Heydrich who had hoped that the Kreigsmarine Kommandos might have lodged at the warehouse. The engineers had been upgrading and fitting a large Howitzer gun onto the modified body of a tank. They did not know what for; nor did they know its final location. His final disappointment came when they said they had never seen a Harley Davidson motor cycle near the docks. Heydrich left Krupps none the wiser.

***

Keil Naval Dockyard

Meanwhile, whilst Heydrich was busy in Essen, Himmler was feeling chilled to the bone. The journey from Berlin had been tortuous, with the fallen snow having turned to ice on the roads. This coupled with the Mercedes limousine's heater not functioning correctly, the windscreen wipers failing to cope with the heavy falls of snow and his great coat over his pristine SS uniform failing to keep out the chilled air, he was in a foul mood as his SS chauffeur/bodyguard swept them through the gates of Keil Naval Base. He was here to meet the sole surviving member of the Kreigsmarine Kommandos from the Tenerife disaster. Apparently the others had been pensioned off with severe disabilities. Whoever had been responsible for their injuries had been little more than barbarians.

The door of the requisitioned office opened brusquely without a knock and a short, squat figure with close-cropped grey hair approached and to Himmler's Nazi salute he replied with a curt salute of an officer not of the Nazi persuasion. At Himmler's motion towards a chair he sat down in an athletically fluid motion belying his appearance. However, a nervous neck tic that manifested itself every few seconds suggested a problem. Sitting opposite Himmler was the now *Captain* Wolfgang Müeller of the Kreigsmarine Kommandos. An expert in explosives. The same person that had lead his Kommandos as *Commander* Müeller in the removal of the sharp needle rocks that had obstructed entry of U-boats into the Great Fissure before his ignominious demotion to the rank of *Captain* Müeller. To add insult to injury he had also been held responsible for the theft of large quantities of Schmeisser machine pistols by subversives unknown. They were alone with no aides or secretaries present. Himmler slid written authorization from Hitler over the desk. It ordered Müeller to disclose all he knew of his involvement in the ultra-secretive project he had worked on in Tenerife.

Himmler gave Müeller time to digest the authorization before enquiring, 'Any questions, Müeller?'

A clipped curt Prussian accent replied, 'I have indeed, Herr Himmler.' There had been no introductions but Müeller had recognized Himmler from photographs he had seen in newspapers. 'I have already been before an SS tribunal and told them all I know – I was brutally attacked from behind by an assailant pretending to be one of my men. And since I got no answer at the tribunal as to why I was being tried by the SS and not the Kreigsmarine, nor an answer as to whom brought the action against me – can you, as head of the SS, enlighten me?

Himmler, shaking his head, held up a waving hand to stop Müeller. 'I know all the details *Captain* Müeller. I have read the transcript of your trial. You were found guilty of allowing your men to leave the warehouse for a smoke. An admirable gesture on your part with explosives present, but foolhardy by allowing the men to be waylaid, seriously injured, and lucky to be alive by all accounts. Not to mention thousands of marks worth of armaments stolen. And, as regards who raised the action I am not at liberty to tell you other than to inform you that the Führer has asked me to look into the matter...thus my authorization to interview you.'

The room fell silent with both men staring belligerently at each other before Müeller broke the spell – his neck tic working overtime. 'I have served my country well, kept quiet about the secret operation in Tenerife...and for this I have been reduced to the rank of *Captain,* as you have gone to great lengths to emphasize....'

Himmler interrupted again, this time with an out of character snarl, 'Fortunately for you Müeller your punishment was not handled by me. Had it been you would have been dismissed service, pension withdrawn and given a long custodial sentence.'

Or been disposed of, thought Mueller but replied, 'I am also aware that that would have been your preference, Herr Himmler,' Müeller spat out. 'So, if you are here with your authorization paper from Hitler to rescind the tribunal's decision and jail me then I demand legal representation.'

In a typical change of tack to add confusion to his victim Himmler did not answer but asked, 'Tell me Müeller, are you fit for service or have they given you a pen pushing job out of charity?'

This sudden diversion had the desired effect as a surprised Müeller faltered, 'I ....I suppose you could say I am now fully recovered from my ordeal and as fit as I was before the cowardly attack on me....and I train with my, er, the men.'

'That accounts for the physical...but what about your mental state?'

'I still suffer from severe migraine headaches but there is no lasting brain damage, the doctors assure me, and they say the nervous tic will go eventually,' he answered angrily with hatred blazing in his eyes.

Himmler, had achieved what he set out to achieve – to arouse the anger within Müeller against his unknown assailant. He let him tic away whilst he glared at him. This deliberate observation increased Müeller's anger until, with a further confusing change in his interrogation technique, Himmler said sympathetically, 'You must feel hard done by. A reduction in rank through no real fault of your own. That at your age is a severe set-back – a pension calamity. In fact were it not for the threat of communism to the Fatherland and a civil war in Spain looming you would have been dismissed service – all through no fault of your own. Don't you feel aggrieved at your treatment?'

Müeller looked suspiciously at Himmler before choosing his words carefully, 'If I could meet the bastard that caused my woes I would slit his throat.'

With a caress of his chin between forefinger and thumb Himmler pretended deep thought before saying, 'I might be in a position to give you your life back.' Müeller looked at him again but this time with narrow-eyed suspicion. Ignoring the look Himmler continued, 'I need a man of action with a knowledge of Tenerife and you seem to fit the bill. Our intelligence informs us that that a man we are seeking to answer for crimes against the Third Reich, namely the theft of armaments, was seen driving a Harley Davidson in Santa...Santa...,' he hesitated deliberately.

'Santa Cruz – the capital of Tenerife,' replied a now attentive Müeller.

With the inclusion of Müeller into his ploy now complete, he continued to the main part of his fabrication. 'Thank you. I always get mixed up with the various Spanish Santas. Santa this...Santa that. However, as I was saying, I was informed no later than yesterday that our agents believe this could also be the man involved in the cowardly attack on you.'

Müeller held his breath and breathed out slowly as his tic ran wild, then in a hoarse, excited voice said, 'I've seen a Harley in and around Santa Cruz and also Puerto de la Cruz.'

Himmler could not believe his good fortune. This had to be the motor cycle Colonel von Reus had mentioned to Hitler in her last report. 'Would you recognize the driver again?'

'No. He was always wearing a pilot's leather helmet and goggles. But there can't be that many Harleys in Tenerife and if he's the bastard responsible I want to be the one to kick the shit out of him.'

'That's the attitude I like to hear. I knew he was right when Mein Führer chose you to find this coward. Come, let us adjourn to the Officers' mess for lunch where we can discuss your reinstatement – *Commander* Müeller.'

Himmler departed the Keil Naval Base happy in the knowledge that he had found his scapegoat. Should Müeller find who attacked him he could blame that person for the death of Colonel von Reus, which after all was the real reason for the manhunt. However, if Müeller failed, it was as he had already described to Heydrich – auf wiedersehen, Müeller.

CHAPTER 4

Tenerife

After what felt to be a never ending endurance flight of refuelling stops aboard the Lufthansa holiday charter flight, a travel weary Müeller thankfully looked out the window at the Santa Cruz de Tenerife harbour below as the Dornier DO17 aeroplane started its descent into the Los Rodeos airfield. The long, cramped flight had given him time to reflect on the ignominy of his demotion that had brought him to the edge of despair. If it had not been for his constant obsession of eventually finding his assailant and wreaking his vengeance he might well have resorted to suicide. In times of lucidity he realized there was little chance of this ever happening. That was until the intervention of that Nazi idiot Himmler who had outwardly gave the impression of sophistication but inwardly had the nature of his fellow Nazi thugs as proved by his feeble recruitment story. Himmler had preyed on what he took to be a weak, mentally unstable, washed-up has been. What sort of fool would believe that the Gestapo or the SS, both under Himmler's control, could not find within their ranks someone with a more comprehensive knowledge of Tenerife than himself. Himmler was using him for some ulterior motive, possibly a scapegoat for one of his devious plans that had gone wrong. Not that it now mattered – for at long last he was on the trail of his cowardly assailant. He was brought out of his reverie with a sudden judder as the Lufthansa Dornier landed on the crushed compacted volcanic rock runway of Los Rodeos airport.

The Fokker taxied to a lava-stone building with a corrugated iron roof, passing as the terminal, and the cabin door was opened outwards by a stewardess who asked Müeller to mind his step as he was guided to a stair rolled into place by an oil-smeared mechanic. Müeller and his fellow passengers were shown into the terminal for the Guardia Civil police passport control. With his German passport only cursorily glanced at by the officer he strode off to find his off-loaded baggage stacked outside the terminal building. As he picked up the bag he was suddenly aware of a presence at his shoulder; a gentleman wearing a white linen suit with collar and tie. He had a straw hat in one hand whilst with the other he mopped his perspiring forehead with a silk handkerchief from the sweltering mid-morning sun. Recognising Müeller from a verbal description by Himmler he replaced his hat and extended his hand in greeting before he took Müeller's bag to transfer it into the back seat of an Auto Union car standing nearby. Müeller, in turn, recognized the well-dressed gent from a photograph shown to him by Himmler. He knew him to be the new manager of the Perez and Schuster warehouse that he and his Kreigsmarine Kommandos had previously operated from in Santa Cruz. He was then driven to Santa Cruz's finest hotel, The Conquistador. When they stopped outside he was informed that a suite had been prepaid, handed a bulging envelope containing large denomination peseta bank notes and the key from the ignition of the stationary Auto Union. The driver then doffed his hat to Müeller as he hailed a taxi.

Müeller did what he had not had the chance to do on his previous visit − he had a leisurely lunch at a pavement cafe and took in the pleasant sights of Spanish Colonial Santa Cruz until his evening meal at the Conquistador. After which he retired to bed but not before he had taken medication for his depression. He now doubted the need for the medication; for the first time in weeks he felt free. After breakfast he studied a map of Santa Cruz and its environs then made his way at Himmler's suggestion to a rural police station on the outskirts of La Laguna where he had enough "get-by" Spanish to communicate with the local sergeant. What he lacked in Spanish vocabulary he made up for with a small amount from his newly acquired peseta bankroll. Pocketing the money the sergeant lifted the phone and, on the pretext of investigating a road traffic accident, was able to ascertain the owner of the Harley Davidson from the vehicle licensing department. It was the only one on the island. The registered owner was a Eugene Crozier of Cantravel International inc. New York. Müeller left the police station elated. He had a name at last − the name of his possible assailant. And he knew Cantravel's address. It was high in the mountains surrounding Puerto de la Cruz − the town where he had had his operational base.

Pointing the car in the direction of Puerto, Müeller first drove through the university town and former capital of Tenerife, La Laguna, then past the small Los Rodeos airfield he had landed at yesterday before reaching Tacaronte and turning down the north coast road. Nothing had changed since he had last travelled this route − it was as exhilarating as ever − the panoramic view of the little town of Puerto de la Cruz nestling low in the distance on the glistening, rocky Atlantic shoreline. However, the sight that had dominated the landscape beyond Puerto – the majestic headland of Punta Gaunché below in which the Great Fissure had lain for millions of years – no longer existed. It had been imploded by one of the world's most devastating natural eruptions that had destroyed his hard work. Müeller knew from Speer's design drawings that the preparation he had been working on within the Great Fissure was for U-boats. He couldn't help feeling at the time that having been entrusted with this knowledge made him vulnerable should anything go wrong because he alone was responsible for the placing of the explosives that would allow the entry of U-Boats into the cave. And with Speer being Hitler's principal architect that left himself the favourite to shoulder any blame. His situation was, of course, not helped by not being a member of the Nazi party – which he detested. And his signed orders had come from Admiral Zeigler – a leading party member. Then, after the world's press had brought to Müeller's attention the finding of a U-Boat's conning tower floating off the coast of Tenerife, he knew for certain that thanks to his explosives expertise a U-Boat had obviously berthed successfully in the Great Fissure cave.

However, what nobody knew was that a British secret service agent named Rutherford had been responsible for the Chinyero vent eruption on the side of Mount Teide. It gave the impression of being the cause of the mammoth explosion that had destroyed Punta Gaunché, the U-Boat base, and set the U-Boat's conning tower adrift in the Atlantic, when actually it was his explosives placed inside the Great Fissure whilst the U-Boat was berthed that had done the damage. To cover this duplicity Rutherford, in cahoots with an American female geologist Professor Charlene (Charley) Rogers, had circulated to the world's press that the Chinyero vent had imploded because of trapped gases in its lava tubes that ignited and caused the Great Fissure to implode.

But, before this came to light and because of what Müeller was privy to, he had not been surprised to find himself charged by the SS with negligence relating to the operation. He wondered who had issued the charge ...and why? The court, if you could call it that, for he had not been allowed legal representation, had been an SS affair – therefore it would be fair to assume the order came from Himmler. Little was he to know that the culprit was the

Kreigsmarine admiral that had signed his operational orders – the Nazi Admiral Zeigler. Requiring to rid himself of any reproach attached to the debacle he had arranged for Himmler to have Müeller arrested on the trumped-up charge of negligence. After the trial and his demotion, when he had tried discreetly to find out the person in the Kreigsmarine hierarchy who had ordered his tribunal, and more importantly the reason why, he was met with a wall of silence. Then suddenly Himmler appeared with his offer – telling him that the assailant responsible for his condition and his marriage failure, an enemy of the Third Reich, was thought to be in Tenerife. This set him to wondering if the Harley owner was his real assailant or if the reinstatement to commander was just a sweetener, or both, and another of Himmler's fabrications to get him out of the way of his "who and why" enquiries? What worried him was that it was unlike Himmler to adopt an "out of the way" policy to any problem – it was usually resolved by that person's death. The master manipulator was up to something and he got the feeling he was the target. But why? He would have to tread carefully, of this he was sure. However, he must not lose sight of his real mission – to get revenge on the bastard that had stolen his life. His tic was in over drive.

* * *

Had Müeller known of a recent phone call between Himmler and Admiral Zeigler he would have made sure that his "treading carefully" would have taken him on a one-way ticket to Outer Mongolia. Zeigler had been responsible for Müeller and his Kreigsmarine Kommandos' involvement in the failed secret Tenerife operation and was furious when he was informed by an aide about Himmler's recent meeting with Müeller in Keil – it was not that he expected anything better from an ignoramus like Himmler. It was simply that when Hitler had personally appointed him to put together the diving team, including his top explosives expert Müeller, to access the Great Fissure, he had been sworn to secrecy. The fact that Himmler was asking Müeller questions could only mean that Hitler had already started his quest for a scapegoat for the Tenerife conning tower debacle. He wondered if Himmler's unannounced interview with Müeller was the first step in Hitler's blame-game because of this damned conning tower belonging to a U-Boat being part of his command. One never knew with Hitler. He lifted his phone. The outcome of the call to Himmler helped to ease his mind. He had pretended to be offended by Himmler's lack of etiquette regarding the interview with Müeller and received an instant apology. He was also given a reason for the interview. He had been informed by Himmler that Hitler required Müeller's expertise in the German West Africa gold mines and he had been sent to recruit Müeller...However, for peace of mind, he would have Müeller terminated when he returned to Keil.

Returning his phone to its cradle Himmler wondered what the hell Zeigler's call had been all about. He had been fishing. The ruthless bastard didn't give a shit about etiquette or Müeller. Suspecting the possible double dealing hand of Hitler he had told Zeigler nothing of the true cause of his interview with Müeller and had fabricated the German West Africa gold mine story. The sooner Müeller failed in his impossible quest to find Von Reus's killer or his own nemesis, the easier Himmler would feel. Either way Müeller, on his return to German soil, would be got rid of.

***

Setting aside his paranoia Müeller entered the town of Puerto along the coast road until he came to the swimming pool. Adjacent to the pool was his old operational headquarters – now a restaurant. It being lunch time he decided to eat there. On entering the familiar doorway he felt a nostalgic lump develop in his throat for it was from here that had risked his life every day for three months to lay the volatile underwater explosives to create the entry into the Great Fissure. He was attended to by a young and very attractive waitress. When he finished, he asked her in his faltering Spanish if she knew of his friend who drove an American Harley Davidson motor cycle. Her heart skipped a beat. She knew of this Harley man from her days when she had worked at the port café and he was a regular. She always made sure she served him. He was so handsome – just like the film stars she saw when she went to the moving pictures in Santa Cruz with her friends. She desperately wanted to know about him, so she answered that she knew of him. Müeller told her he was visiting Tenerife and had lost his friend's address – did she know how he could contact him? Regaining her composure she said that she had not seen him recently (sadly) but knew he worked for Cantravel. Müeller, having heard this several times, was disappointed until she said that he sometimes met the Cantravel cruise boat, "The Sea Dolphin", when it docked and she saw him associate with an American blonde lady *(jealously)* who was a stewardess aboard the boat. It usually docked around 5-00pm. Müeller thanked her and left a large tip.

With a couple of hours to go until the docking of the Sea Dolphin, Müeller decided to take a drive along the high coast road to Teno to have a close look at the devastation wrought by the implosion. What he found was a rock strewn valley along the line of the Great Fissure with an open view seawards. The force of nature was there for all to witness. But, of the majestic headland, Punta Gaunché, there was no sign.

Müeller was back in time for the arrival of the Sea Dolphin. From his position, sitting on a rusted harbour capstan, he witnessed a loud alcohol fuelled crowd disembark. The virtually impossible task of rounding up the merry rabble to manoeuvre them to their awaiting coaches fell to two harassed females, one of which was a shapely, petite blonde. Her task completed he approached her. She looked hot and bothered. Her lapel badge informed him he was in the company of Sandy – cruise facilitator. He had no trouble with his English – not fluent but like his Spanish, passable.

Sandy saw this squat figure approach her. She took an instant dislike to him which was an unusual biological experience between Sandy and the opposite sex. He spoke to her. The tongue was German accented English which did not surprise her – for if he had worn rimless spectacles his appearance would have been typical Hollywood "B" movie casting of a Nazi bad guy. He told her that he had been informed that she knew of a person that drove a Harley Davidson motor cycle. She, in her Texas twang, didn't bother to ask how he knew – she just wanted rid of this guy pronto. However, she was intrigued as well as suspicious. Müeller, sensed her suspicion and to allay her fears asked if she had heard the person he was looking for ever mention the name, Wolfgang. She shook her head. Pointing to himself, he said he was Wolfgang, the friend of – he suddenly.....sneezed.....into a brandished handkerchief, excused himself and continued that his friend and he had met in Berlin and that they had agreed to meet in the future if he ever was in Tenerife. She stared at Jordan's alleged friend. Her summing up was that he did not look Jordan's type of friend. Mind you, that could be because this guy wasn't a female, was her embittered thought as she recalled her last surprise visit to Jordan's chalet where she had caught him in flagrante delicto with that German bird. Then it suddenly clicked.

This guy was German and the tart she had caught screwing with Jordan was German. This ugly, squat, Kraut was the irate husband! Time for revenge on that two-faced yellow bellied skunk, Jordan Hill. After a pretend racking of her brain she then told Wolfgang that she did in fact know of a person that drove a Harley – he had been a diving instructor at the place she worked – Cantravel. A womanising lecher. He could be shacked-up with some poor guy's wife as they speak. Wolfgang said that was definitely the same man he knew. Where did she think this present "shacking-up" would be taking place? She was about to say possibly following that French strumpet, Yvonne, to her new posting in Gibraltar but she suddenly felt guilty about saying these terrible things about Jordan. They had had a marvellous time together and she missed him terribly – the swine. So, resorting to her first instincts of dislike for the German she answered that she did not know where he was. He thanked her for her time and, apologizing for his bad memory, asked her to remind him once again the name of her and his friend. Sandy, having noticed the deliberate sneeze when he supposedly had claimed to know Jordan's name knew something was not stacking up correctly so she told him the name of the man he sought was Jerry Hill, a fellow Texan. (*she wondered if he would see through her play on the name Jerry for German*) He thanked her again and adjourned to his car in the port car park to await the departure of the Cantravel coaches. He followed at a discreet distance.

As the rear bus entered an arched portal bearing the name "Cantravel Country Club" a security barrier was lowered. Müeller stopped at the security kiosk to ask directions to reception on the pretext of a future wedding reception. A cheery local Spanish guard assured him of a great reception and lifted the barrier. A long driveway through the pines ended at a roundabout. By-passing the sign leading to reception he took the one to the garage. He entered the garage and with nobody about started his survey. He found what he was looking for – a Harley Davidson on its stand and in gleaming showroom condition. He was examining the machine when he heard a discreet cough from behind. The pristine boiler-suited mechanic asked in American accented English if he could be of assistance. Wolfgang explained that he had obviously taken the wrong turning to reception but being interested in motor cycles he could not help but admire such a wonderfully maintained machine. On hearing this praise of his pride and joy the mechanic from wondering how this person could have made such a mistake as to end up in the garage answered Müeller's next question – that it belonged to Mr. Crozier the owner of Cantravel but he never used it – it was driven by Mr. Crozier's friend a Mr. Hill. Unfortunately, he did not know Mr. Hill's Christian name. An excited Wolfgang, already knowing Jerry to be the Christian name, asked if he knew where he could find Mr. Hill. He was informed that Mr. Hill had been transferred to Gibraltar and was not due back any time soon. Wolfgang thanked the mechanic and as he was leaving the garage a thought struck him – a photograph of the elusive Mr. Jerry Hill would come in handy.

From Müeller's knowledge of private swimming baths in Berlin they usually had a photograph and a name of the duty swimming instructor in evidence for all to see. He reckoned his theory would apply to this up-market establishment. He could but try. By-passing reception he followed signs to the sports complex. He parked in a lined bay and entered the complex to study the layout plan in the main entrance then headed off in the direction of the swimming pools. Being dinner time all was still and quiet. He found the pools graded: main, intermediate and beginners. Choosing the main pool he entered through swing doors and found what he was looking for on a wall – a photograph of the swimming instructors. A glance confirmed that the head diving instructor was a Mr. J.Hill. He had his man – Jerry Hill. A surreptitious look around showed nobody in evidence. He removed the photograph and slid it to an inside pocket of his jacket and moved quickly out of the building into the car, setting it in motion immediately. He gave the security guard a wave as he drove through the arched portals.

The following day he made passage on a German merchantman bound for Algecirus on the Spanish mainland situated in the Bay of Gibraltar along the coast from Gibraltar.

CHAPTER 5

La Linea Spain

The crunching noise of tyres on the volcanic ash parking lot outside his office window caused Suarez to rise from his desk in time to see a pale blue American Buick convertible with white wall tyres come to a stop. The tall, red haired man who showed up in Suarez's office a moment later spoke with a peculiar English accent which he recognized from his recent trip to Ireland to be a southern Irish brogue. The stranger came straight to the point regarding who he was. He claimed he was Suarez's new IRA control. He wanted an update on Suarez's plan on how he intended to breach dockyard security. A suspicious Suarez immediately suspected the Irishman of being British Intelligence and claimed to know nothing about the IRA, but answered that as the local organizer of the Falange party supporting the anti-British illegal occupancy of Gibraltar, he wished whoever intended to breach dockyard security all the best in their attempts at sabotage. The Irishman said he liked people that were suspicious but would ask him only one more time — how far had he progressed with his planning? Belfast weren't happy about Suarez's progress and had asked him to take overall control. And that, as of now, he was in charge and that included the payment of any forthcoming monthly pay cheques due to Suarez and his lady associate — Señorita Delores Castillano. At the mention of the possibility of withdrawal of monies Suarez protested that he still had to pay Señorita Castillano. Suarez's new control said that the señorita would be taken care of, in more ways than payment, if she didn't stop her whoring around. She was being paid to be Curran's obedient and *"faithful"* wife. Her infidelity was incredulous news to Suarez. The stupid bitch was endangering his newly found wealth. He was told to sort out the problem immediately. The Irishman's threat was backed with a smoothly drawn automatic from an underarm holster. The pistol aimed at Suarez's heart held steady. Suarez felt his bowels weaken. He had done precisely nothing regarding any dockyard reconnaissance for the IRA. He had been too busy spending their money. His new Auto Union saloon car parked outside bearing testament to his spending spree. Then, suddenly, without warning the Irishman brought the pistol up to Suarez head. He felt the first trickle of hot urine run down the inside of his leg as he watched agog the finger squeeze the trigger and felt the hot compressed air passage of the bullet as it creased his ear and buried itself in the wall behind him. That was the last Suarez remembered of the day. As his bowels opened he collapsed onto the floor. Finding paper and a pencil on Suarez's desk the Irishman scribbled a note giving him his precise instructions for the forthcoming race day. The main agenda being that he was to make sure that Curran was on duty come race day to allow a horsebox bearing the logo "Marbella Racing" to cross the border freely. He was to phone the given number to confirm that he clearly understood what was required of him.

He gave the crumpled body on the floor a derisory kick as he took his leave. It was a pity he had to use such a pathetic idiot but with time running short he could not risk his own men, especially with the main prize in sight.

***

La Linea   The Following Evening.

The rhythm of the tango was urgent, pulsating and the atmosphere oppressively hot and layered with cigarette smoke hanging over the entwined dancers on the nightclub floor as the band's trumpeter with a high shrill note brought the Latin number to a close. Standing at the bar as the dancers started to make their way to their respective tables, a suave, good-looking and well-dressed onlooker cast his eyes over one of the dancers in particular. She was a very attractive, slimly-built and shapely female. He liked them that way. Especially her – he had known her a long time. They had been long-time lovers until he allowed his political and financial ambitions to get between them. When he had enquired around about her it had been brought to his attention that this club had become a regular Saturday night haunt of hers and her whore companions. This, as he had been reminded by that mad bastard Irishman, was strictly against their Belfast employers' wishes of her having to be seen to be a respectable housewife. Due to her unaccountable actions his good health and prosperity had suddenly taken a turn for the worse.

He made his move as her dance partner, a prospective paying client, kissed her hand and fondled her bottom as he returned her to her table to join her companions who were drinking the cheap house red wine and showing signs of giggly inebriation. Arriving at the table he said softly from behind her, 'If I'm not mistaken it's the lovely Delores Castillano.'

Delores jumped up from her seat and threw her arms around his neck and kissed him full on the lips to much hilarity from her drunken companions. Withdrawing her arms from around his neck she then kept him at arm's length with both hands on his shoulders as she replied, 'Eduardo, my dear friend, I thought you were dead. I have not heard from you in ages....' she then turned her head from her companions to confront him directly to add, in a whisper, '...You bastard. Who've you been fucking?' Then returning to her normal voice, said loudly, 'Come, Eduardo, join us and tell us what you've been up to.' Rather than sit beside her drunken companions he extended his hand as the band in a change of tempo segued into a waltz. She accepted his hand and as they glided smoothly onto the dance floor he held her tight and in close to once again have his sense of smell assailed by the delicate fragrance of his favourite perfume, and with the feel of her warm, soft body melting into his own he felt a familiar feeling developing in his groin.

Delores, too, relished having him in her arms. It had been a long time since they had struck the deal and much had gone wrong in this period – all caused by him. Not being the type to let things go she whispered gently in his ear, 'I'm thinking about kneeing you in the balls you rotten bastard. Where's my money? Have you been spending it on that bitch, Estelle?' These being but two of her contentious issues with him.

'And here I am, in your arms enjoying you just like old times....'

Delores, breaking the closeness between them, interrupted, airing another of her contentious issues. 'Old times, indeed! Does that mean you're about to rid me once and for all of that Irish leprechaun I agreed to fuck for you?'

'You agreed to – for muchos money.....'

'Of which I haven't seen another peseta since you deliberately spread it out on the bed to tempt me,' she interrupted again, airing her main issue.

'It just so happens I have your money in my office to give you,' he lied.

On hearing this she gave him her special smile, the smile that she knew he adored, as she renewed their closeness to whisper, 'I love you, Eduardo, even though you're a rat. How much longer do I have to put up with this sham marriage?'

'As I've told you before , Dolly – until the job is finished. I thought you and Curran were getting along famously. In fact I was almost getting jealous,' he lied again. 'So what's the problem?' She didn't reply. She bit her bottom lip instead. 'I know that gesture. Spit it out. What have you done?'

'I think we had better sit down,' she replied, as she took his hand and led him towards the bar. They found a quiet corner away from the band. 'Curran's changed...'

'Why has he changed? What have you done – *this time*?'

'As you know Gib is a small town and certain of my old clients got to hear of my change of address but not my circumstances and came to visit me. Curran, unfortunately, answered the door on a couple of occasions when these visits happened. The men in question apologized and said they didn't know I had married. Curran questioned me about them. I told him they were old boyfriends. He must have become suspicious because he came home early from one of his night shifts, without warning and for no good reason, to catch me fucking one of them.'

There was a silence before Suarez exploded, 'You did what! Don't tell me you didn't contact all your clients to tell them your change of circumstances? The look on Delores' face confirmed his suspicions. 'You stupid.... stupid... bitch. You're about to become as rich as Croesus and you're still fucking people for peanuts. You...you, greedy, *stupid cow*. Do you know what you've done? You've totally fucked my, er, *our* livelihood. Belfast knows about your extra marital activities. My control has threatened to withdraw our funds – or worse.' He made a slit-throat gesture with his forefinger.

'How does Belfast know? It's a long way away.'

'I don't know how they know. They possibly have somebody in this dump watching you and for all I know he could be one of the ones you've been screwing. All I know is, they do know and that you have well and truly buggered things up.'

Delores, behaving out of character, took all the insults in her stride without retaliation and calmly replied, 'Easy, Eduardo – easy. It's not as bad as you're making out. Please let me explain. Curran broke down and cried when he found me in that compromising situation. He told me he had only agreed to the sham marriage for personal revenge reasons. But when he met me he fell in love. He thought that because of my looks and the fact I spoke English I was, believe it or not, from a good family. And *you...*,' her finger stabbed him in the chest. '....just conveniently didn't tell him I was a prostitute and was in it only for the money. When I told him that he burst into tears. But, he is well aware of his situation, too. He knows that if he fucks up that's him dead as well. I don't know who you are both working for, and I don't want to know, for they appear to be evil bastards. So, there you have it. Everything's back to normal, except Curran now sleeps in the spare room.... And I promise to behave. So, your evil bosses have nothing to worry about. Oh! And Curran and me still talk occasionally. In fact he told me when I met him in the kitchen this morning that our upstairs neighbour – that lovely French lady, Yvonne, was asking him if I knew any locals that would know about the sewage system back in 1800's. I said I didn't but I suddenly remembered you telling me years ago about your grandmother's tale of smugglers, so should I tell her you will help?'

A relieved Suarez, who had listened intently to Delores' explanation of the sham marriage break-up, didn't apologize for his outburst. He merely nodded his head in acceptance of her stated facts with a sigh and a shake of the head to indicate his disgust. He did, however, wonder why her upstairs neighbour, Yvonne, an MOD inspector for the new reservoir under construction in "The Rock" should concern herself about ancient sewage and told Delores that if she asked again to tell her it was just an old wives' tale. However, Delores' recollection of his grandmother's tale when he was a youngster came back to him. Whether or not it was true he had no idea but she had told of a tunnel that her great grandfather had used for smuggling tobacco and alcohol out of the bonded warehouses in the dockyard then across the border and into Spain. As he recalled, the entry into the tunnel was through a sarcophagus in a graveyard. He couldn't remember which cemetery but he did remember that the sarcophagus had a knight warrior on its stone lid. It was at this point in her tale that she used to frighten him by telling him in a scary voice that the warrior rose with sword in hand to protect the incarcerated body against thieves. All this would tie in with the1800's date asked of Delores by her neighbour. Could this, he excitedly thought, be the break he needed to get into the dockyard and get that red haired IRA madman off his back? Unfortunately, his grandmother was dead and her tale could not be confirmed. However, an inkling of an idea was forming ....but first he needed to get into Delores' apartment tonight.

Delores interrupted his reverie. 'What are you thinking about, Eduardo?'

'I'm thinking about Curran in the spare room, and having the car outside and you being able to drive me through.....'

'Through the border with you pretending to be a drunken slob sprawled across the back seat for the sake of fooling border control – just like old times when you were first made non persona gratis in Gib,' she interrupted. 'I best go and get my bag off the table.'

'With those whores you associate with you'll be lucky if there's any money left in your purse.' She giggled as she opened wide her already plunging neckline to show banknotes projecting from her brassiere. 'Okay, let's go. You can always steal another bag. Delore's giggled again and snuggled in close with her head on his arm.

With his car parked out of the way of nosey neighbours around the back of the apartments, Suarez spent the night with Delores. He was up in time to see Yvonne mount her bicycle and set off for work. When she disappeared from sight he went up the external stone stair to her apartment gaining entry with the key that Curran, as custodian of the two HMG apartments, kept in a hall cupboard. A quick browse around brought him to a table adorned with an ancient map of Gibraltar and books between bookends about cemeteries and drainage systems. The map had the three principal cemeteries circled in red pencil. Two were crossed out, leaving the Trafalgar cemetery (also known as South Port Ditch) with a tick against it. The book on cemeteries was open at Trafalgar showing a plan of the cemetery. Three quarters of the plan was lightly shaded over in pencil leaving a corner in the north end untouched. That's where he would start. He returned the book to between the bookends and departed for Delores' apartment where he intended to stay until dark before heading for Trafalgar Cemetery. He was now looking for a sarcophagus with a knight warrior in the cemetery's north end.

***

Being anxious to get started, Suarez at the first signs of darkness set off with a tool bag slung over his shoulder for the cemetery. He left Delores' apartment through the back door to reduce the risk of being identified by the police. Electing to walk he entered the side service road from the back court and almost bumped into a cyclist at the junction with the main road but with some nifty footwork managed to avoid the bicycle. He was about to apologize but just in time recognized the cyclist and quickly turned his head away then hurried down the main road. The cyclist was Delores' upstairs neighbour Yvonne, the attractive MOD inspector. He quickened his pace.

Arriving at the cemetery he found its east boundary wall to be part of the Old Town walls. A further inspection proved the north boundary to be formed with densely planted trees overhanging tall spiked iron-railings, offering no access. The west boundary was similar. At the intersection of the west and south boundaries he found ornate cast iron spiked railing gates. The gates were locked with a rusted chain and padlock. With desperation beginning to set in lest Yvonne arrive to continue her search he found to his relief, between the gates and the east Old Town wall, a break in the railings hidden by the overhanging branches. He squeezed between the gap and found himself in knee high grass and weeds. He recalled reading in the book on cemeteries in Yvonne's apartment that the cemetery had not been in use since 1842. This he could now well believe by its unkempt state as he fought his way through the undergrowth until he came to the area not pencil shaded on Yvonne's map. By the light of his torch he noticed the area in general boasted mainly simple ancient weather beaten sandstone crosses or headstones peeping above the unmanaged grass and weeds. After twenty minutes of fruitless effort trying to find a way through the thorny bramble bushes growing between the trees, he found himself facing a dead-end – the ancient stone wall of the Old Town. He about-turned just as a shaft of moonlight peeped through the dark drifting clouds hit upon a silhouette between the last tree and the wall and decided to investigate. With the aid of his torch the beam struck a lichen covered mass some 250 cm long and 150 cm high. As he got closer he realized it was a sarcophagus – a sarcophagus with a knight-warrior lying on his back holding a sword! His heart was thumping. Had he found the burial chamber of his grandmother's tale? Having never seen a sarcophagus before he did not know how you gained entry so he proceeded to scout the structure looking for a door. What he first thought to be a door on one of the gables turned out to be stone mullions 10 cm wide with gaps of 5 cm between. His torch when directed between a gap found the interior to be empty but with a dark shadow on the ground at the far end. This he thought peculiar – he had expected a stone casket. Perhaps the shadow was the grave. The remaining sides were solid. Entry had to be by means of the stone lid. As he turned towards his tool-bag he became aware of a raised inscription on the sarcophagus wall. He brushed the lichen off to disclose an unreadable name eroded with time but a date of 1815 was still readable. He then withdrew from his tool bag a small crowbar and set about trying to move the lid. He could not get it to move. His futile attempts had resulted in damage to the sandstone edge of the lid. He gave the problem some thought before finally settling for four stout and rounded, broken-off branches of the many trees growing in the vicinity. He returned to his task. As he lifted the edge of the heavy lid he inserted one of the rounded branches. He then attacked the other side of the lid in the same manner. Having repeated this operation on both sides, then took up position at the end of the sarcophagus and inserted the crowbar between the newly raised lid and the inside face of the sarcophagus wall and with all his strength heaved upwards. To his delight he had the satisfaction of seeing the lid roll on the rounded branches clear enough to allow him entry into the tomb itself. Exhausted but exhilarated he sat down with back against the tomb's outer wall. After a rest of several minutes he had regained enough energy to hoist himself up to look inside. To his amazement his torch picked out not an embalmed or emaciated body but a brick lined vertical shaft over half of its floor area and inset with rusted iron horseshoe rungs and handholds disappearing into a dark abyss. He presumed that the remainder of the floor had been used for storage due to a coil of old rope lying there. The smell of fustiness and damp permeated his nostrils rather than that of putrefied flesh. He lowered his tool bag to the bottom of the shaft with the aid of a rope withdrawn from his bag. He estimated the depth of the shaft to be approximately twenty feet (6mtrs). Due to care being required because of the rusted iron rungs the descent was slow.

When he reached the bottom he had to crouch low to enter a 150 cm high by 90cm wide arched brick tunnel running in both directions. Having totally lost his bearings in relation to the harbour he guessed and turned right. The ancient brickwork was in a dreadful state of disrepair and leaking water, the result of which he was now ankle deep in watery sludge. After fifteen minutes he was suddenly aware of the tunnel narrowing, the brick wall lining stopped to be replaced with rock. With a sharp decrease in head-height he had no option but to stop. His torch picked out a rough-hewn rock face directly in front. He had reached the end of the tunnel. Disappointed he turned to retrace his steps he knocked his shin on a rusted pick with a well-worn broken handle. With his nerves now a jangle he was thankful not to see the bones of the owner still attached to the pick as he trudged back through the sludge with the rope entwined around his shoulders and hauling his tool bag in one hand and carrying his torch in the other. Twenty minutes later he reached his original starting point where he paused to look at the moonlight filtering down the shaft from the cemetery above. He deliberated as to whether to continue. However, with the Irishman's threat still uppermost in his mind he breathed a deep sigh and moved off again down the unexplored tunnel for what seemed an eternity until his now flickering torch picked out a rusted gate mechanism across the end of the tunnel. Fortunately the gate was rusted-up in the open position. This he figured out must have been the exit for the collection chamber that received all the excrement from the old dockyard sewage system. With the fusty stink suggesting he was correct he crouched low as he scrambled through the opening. Once through and standing upright his torch showed an enormous brick-vaulted chamber then flickered and died. He stood there shivering, realizing too late he did not have the correct clothing to go reconnoitering. It was the adrenaline coursing through his veins at the thought of what he could achieve – the Holy Grail – the breaching of dockyard security, not to mention the Irishman's threat that kept him going as he fumbled inside his thin jerkin for his spare torch. The new torch picked out the old inlet high above his head. A rusted iron architrave set into the wall indicated that an iron gate had been removed and the opening bricked-up. There was a wide brick edge running under this old inlet and once again iron rungs set in the brickwork from floor to ledge obviously for maintenance work to the then used inlet. He knew he had not walked upwards. The sludge he had trudged through had stayed at the same ankle depth therefore the floor of the chamber must be at the same level as the bottom of the shaft. After giving the situation some thought he came to the conclusion that the inlet above him had to be above harbour high-tide level so he started to climb the rungs with the rope now entwined over his shoulder. At the top rung a vertical iron post continued as a handrail for access to the ledge. The ledge was sufficiently wide to stand on comfortably but the drop to chamber bottom was precarious so he tied one end of the rope to the top rung and the remainder in part around his waist. He withdrew a pointed chisel and hammer from inside his leather jerkin and started work on scraping out the mortar joints of the bricked-up opening. To his delight the old lime/cement mortar came away easily. With the removal of each horizontal brick layer he awaited an implosion of water from the harbour but his calculation held as he felt a draft of fresh air between the brick joints. He tentatively removed a brick to find not water but lovely fresh air carrying with it the salty tang of the sea. He stretched his arm through the hole to discover the brickwork was 45cm thick. He now realized that the ledge he was standing on, as well as being the chamber wall, was also acting as the retaining sea wall to the harbour. He had broken through into the harbour. He lowered the wall above the ledge brick by brick until he could hear the lapping of water just below the ledge he was standing on. He had formed an opening two brick courses wide by 180cm high from the top of the ledge. Not daring to use his torch Suarez waited for his eyes to adjust to the dark before he slipped through the gap in the brickwork. Standing on the edge of the new opening with the sea lapping 60cm below his feet he was aware that all around him was the supporting steelwork for the dockyard quay above and tethered to capstans on the quay was the battleship grey hull of a warship. Having seen enough he reset the bricks facing the harbour as best he could to hide the new opening. He knew it wouldn't pass close inspection but at a distance he reckoned it stood a good chance of being undetected. With the cold and dampness biting into his bones he intended to beat a hasty retreat to the shaft and much needed fresh air but not before he sank to his knees and with arms held wide open above his head, let out a resounding whoop of delight that echoed off the chamber walls and arched dome to his repeated chant of, "Haaaallelujah.....Haaaalllelujah, I've found the holy fucking Grail... I'm rich....I'm riiiich....".

Hastily making the sign of the cross he took off as fast as the slippery underfoot conditions would allow, scrambling out of the sarcophagus to enter his new world of untold wealth.

CHAPTER 6

Gibraltar Race Day.

Suarez arrived in Delores' apartment from the sarcophagus shivering, exhausted and frozen but euphoric. He couldn't wait for daybreak to contact that red haired, mad bastard Irishman to claim his pot of gold. However, as it transpired his early morning call from Delores' phone in the hallway to the Irishman in Marbella was met with something initially less than enthusiasm at his news. The Irishman reminded him that today was race day and that the explosives were being taken across the border. He assumed Suarez had had the good sense to carry out his orders for Curran to arrange for the horse-box to have free passage through customs. Suarez, who had forgotten about Curran because of having to sort out Delores' aberration and his nocturnal activities in the sarcophagus, lied that he had, of course, told Curran. With his query confirmed positive the Irishman *then* congratulated Suarez on having found a way to penetrate the dockyard, albeit with a grudging reminder that it was about time there had been a return on the money he had been paid. At the mention of money Suarez nervously cleared his throat and interrupted to remind the Irishman that Belfast had promised him a bonus on successfully finding an entry into the dockyard.

There was a long silence before the angry, bellowed, answer, 'You taking the fucking piss – Suarez? You don't honestly think I'd authorize payment to a lying, thieving eejit like you without you first leading me to the breakthrough... do you?' A weary Suarez, knowing eejit to mean idiot in the Irish vernacular, puffed out his cheeks in a silent sigh of resignation as the Irishman continued, 'Unfortunately, this news now forces me to advance my plans just in case the breakthrough into the dockyard should be discovered by the security guards who I understand constantly inspect the under quay structures. The attack would have to be tonight at the latest. I will supply the task force – *and you Suarez* will lead them to this breakthrough understand?'

Suarez sighed a defeated "Yes" and was told to meet the horse-box at the race track no later than 1-00pm.

When the call finished with a final threat to have Suarez's balls rammed down his throat in the event of any fuck up, a panicking Suarez dropped the phone on its cradle and ran down the hallway to Curran's bedroom. The answered, sleepy, groan to his knock on the door came as great relief to Suarez.

As he entered, Curran sat upright, shock showing all over his face. 'What do *you* want? It isn't my fault that I surprised Delores in bed with a…a… client.'

Suarez held up a hand to stop him and with a shake of head and a sigh, lamented, 'She told me the whole story, Curran. So don't panic. Just do as I tell you and all will be well. Understand?' Curran nodded. 'Today is race day. You have to make sure you're on duty at the border…'

'No problem, Suarez. Due to the expected increase in race going traffic I am on duty from 11-00am,' interrupted Curran.

With a sigh of relief, Suarez said, 'Good. Make sure you, and only you, let through a horse-box with the name "Marbella Racing" on its side. Give it a thorough pretend inspection in case the Brits have any of their Special Branch officers about. It's due to arrive around 1- 00pm. Okay?'

Curran replied, 'Yes. I know the van. I have seen it several times before. It is owned by a very prominent Irish horse owner and businessman….'

'Well, he's our new boss. A real nasty, psycho, bastard,' cut in Suarez.

'I've got the picture, Suarez, I won't rock the boat. I don't want to mess things up before I can avenge my parents… whilst on that subject can I ask, will what I'm about to do help *my* cause?' Suarez nodded his reply. A broad happy smile broke out on Curran's face. 'Good,' he replied.

***

Suarez arrived early at the race track and sat in his car until the arrival of the horse-box. At shortly after 1-30pm he saw Curran stop the van. The driver had a passenger. They showed their passports to Curran. The driver jumped out and went round to the back of the vehicle to open the doors for Curran's inspection. As the doors were opened the horse pawed the timber base of the van and snorted at the intrusion as Curran looked past the horse to observe a giant of a man that he assumed to be the horse's groom sitting on a wooden crate. The groom stared sullenly at him. The driver on Curran's order closed the doors and on further instruction reversed the van alongside Suarez's Auto Union parked near the stables. The driver reopened the back doors of the van and led the horse to the stable area. Curran's assumed groom on an all-clear signal from Suarez slipped out of the back doors of the horse-van with the large wooden crate on his shoulder to deposit the crate and a holdall in the open boot of the Auto Union; the van's passenger had already decamped from the horse-box to the rear seat of Suarez's car. Suarez closed the boot and as the giant groom climbed into the back seat to join the van's passenger he slipped behind the steering wheel. With both of his passengers looking European he spoke to them in English, asking them their names. One of them replied in faltering English that he was German and had just a little English. He informed Suarez his name was Helmut. His colleague, the giant and carrier of the crate, was named Dieter and spoke no English. The introductions had just been completed when a Buick convertible with its hood down parked alongside. The red haired Irishman beckoned Suarez to join him. Once Suarez had settled himself in the comfortable leather front bench-seat the Irishman explained to Suarez that the two sitting in his car were former Kreigsmarine Kommandos. Helmut was a scuba diver and he would place the limpet mines. Dieter was in charge of the explosives and would be responsible for the timers. All Suarez had to do was to lead them to his breakthrough in the chamber brickwork and then leave them to get on with the work. It was highly likely that after the dockyard incursion they would have to make a hasty exit over the border. He was to make sure his car was fuelled and in good running order. Helmut and Dieter were armed, trained killers, and would fight to the end should they be cornered. The preference, of course, was flight – and it would then be every man for himself. Suarez left the Buick to return to his car asking himself what in Christ's name had he let himself in for – and what the hell were *limpet* mines. He hadn't agreed to this heavy stuff. Bonus or no bonus after tonight he would make plans to disappear – possibly to Argentina where he had heard the fascist movement was in its infancy. There was an army guy there called Peron that had shown an interest in his Falangist movement. He could give him the wealth of his experience. With this thought he slid once again behind the steering wheel of his Auto Union, turned the key and pulled the starter, then moved towards the exit. So far, all had gone according to plan except, of course, if you ignored the minor set-backs of the possible loss of his bonus and the fact that he had to physically be in attendance.

The Irishman intended them to lie low in Delores' apartment until darkness with an operational start time as soon as possible after dark. Suarez looked at his watch, 2-30pm. With him being unrecognizable in his beret and moustache, and having arrived directly at the racetrack from Delores' apartment there had been no need for passports, so on departure he was waved through by the local Gibraltar police in their British navy serge uniforms and pointed helmets with their chrome finials. The problem of killing time was resolved when they reached Delores' apartment. Helmut, the leader, enquired about the sleeping arrangements. Apparently as Kommandos they had been trained to rest up before a mission so he gave Helmut Curran's bedroom, and Dieter the front room settee. Suarez tried to sleep in Delores' bed but his nerves wouldn't allow the luxury. Fortunately the front door opened. It was Delores returning from visiting her mother. He arose to meet her in the hall to explain the situation regarding the visitors. She made it quite clear to Suarez that she was not happy about them being in her house – that was until Suarez reminded her they were part of the team that paid her rent. Grudgingly accepting that fact, she then suggested that they too should have a rest period like Helmut and Dieter were having. She then led him by the hand into her bedroom. Suarez awoke from a deep slumber to the German accented voice of Helmut calling out his name. He looked at the bedside clock, 9-30pm. Still groggy from the effects of Delores' voracious sexual appetite he turned over to wake her only to find her gone. In the light of her recent misdemeanours and fearing that she might be making herself available for business with Helmut or Dieter, or even both, he dressed hastily and followed the noise of muted voices to the kitchen. Delores, standing at the stove blew him a kiss and pointed to the table. He sat beside the giant Dieter who was mopping up the last of his gravy with crusty bread. Showing culinary skills Suarez didn't know Delores possessed, she placed in front of him a sumptuous looking, heavily spiced chicken choritzo on a bed of rice. Dieter, to show his appreciation finished with a loud burp. Helmut cleaned the corner of his mouth and thanked Delores for a lovely meal. She thanked Helmut. Then with a loving look coyly said to Suarez, 'There's more where that came from Eduardo dear. Nice and spicy, as you like it.' Being used to her hidden matrimonial innuendoes Suarez, on taking a fork-full, proclaimed, 'It'll certainly take the chill out of the night air.' As they left the apartment Suarez reminded himself not to get downwind of the giant Dieter tonight.

Trafalgar Cemetery 11.00pm

The Auto Union nosed into the main road from its parking spot round the back of Delores' apartment at 10-30 pm precisely. When they arrived at Trafalgar Cemetery, Suarez parked under the shadow of one of the overhanging trees close to the railings. He opened the boot and Dieter moved him gently aside to lift out the heavy crate containing his explosives and Helmut's oxygen cylinders. Dieter then transferred the crate into the arms of Helmut who had clambered through the gap in the railings. Helmut staggered at the weight and immediately transferred the crate to the ground. They set off for the sarcophagus with Suarez, a rope looped over his shoulder, leading the way. Helmut, carried the holdall containing his diving gear, and Dieter, now with the heavy crate on his broad shoulders, followed.

At the sarcophagus that Suarez had already left open from his previous visit they used his rope to lower the heavy crate to the bottom followed by the holdall. They followed using the iron rung foot and hand holds. Reaching the bottom they dragged and pushed the crate through the tunnel until they found the main chamber where Helmut squeezed his way into his wetsuit and applied his oxygen cylinders; then using the iron rungs and the rope Suarez had previously left dangling he reached the ledge. With the oxygen cylinders strapped onto his back he managed, awkwardly, with the aid of the handrail running vertically beyond the ledge, to haul himself safely onto it. Whilst Helmut had been climbing Dieter had been opening the crate with a claw hammer from Suarez's toolbox and withdrew two Limpet mines from the crate. Each mine contained five kilos of high explosives – enough to severely damage the destroyer that Suarez knew to be moored at the quay local to his breakthrough. Dieter, after setting the timers carefully placed the mines into Helmut's holdall which also contained his goggles, flippers and mouthpiece. He then tied the dangling rope to the holdall's handles and Helmut pulled it up to ledge level. Helmut then finished attiring himself in flippers and goggles and finally connected his mouthpiece to the oxygen cylinders. The task complete, he carefully lifted the Limpets. The last they saw of him, he was wriggling his way through the vertical gap in the brickwork.

To the waiting Suarez and Dieter, it seemed an eternity before they were aware of an empty bag thumping down at their feet in the gloom of the chamber. Using a torch to view his watch Suarez discovered it had only been thirty minutes. He trusted Dieter had factored this time-lapse into his calculations for setting the timers for with Dieter having no English he would have to wait until Helmut clambered down from the ledge to have this question answered. At the noise of the bag arriving at their feet they both shone their torches upwards for the beams to catch a jubilant Helmut giving them the thumbs-up success sign and rather than use the rungs he abseiled nimbly down the tethered rope. When he landed, Suarez, who could not control his anxiety, asked how long the timers had been set for. Helmut informed him ninety minutes including the loose rebuilding of outer skin of the wall. As Helmut was confirming the timing to Suarez, Dieter was on his way up the rungs to rebuild the loose wall. Why had the bloody wall to be rebuilt Suarez asked, anxious to depart lest the timers detonated the mines prematurely. The answer from Helmut had been that in the highly unlikely event of the mines not detonating they would require the use of the breakthrough again. *And* the rebuilding of the wall stopped anybody dockside from noticing the opening. Typical bloody Teutonic thoroughness and totally unrequired reckoned Suarez. Another anxious wait of thirty minutes followed during which Suarez, with his nerves now jangling, considered making a break for the exit. Helmut, now back in his coveralls, had uncannily anticipated Suarez's thoughts and was blocking his path with an oxygen cylinder spanner being tapped in the palm of his hand and a smirk on his face daring Suarez to pass. Unheard and unseen in the gloom, Dieter was suddenly in their midst. He said something in German to Helmut who translated rapidly that the ninety minute time was now running tight and that they had best be on their way immediately. Dieter thought there was every chance come the explosion that the ancient brick retaining walls of the chamber would collapse causing a miniature tsunami taking them with it through the tunnels. He figured they had twenty minutes maximum to clear the tunnel and shaft. They left everything, including extra limpet mines, and fled up the shaft and out into the safety of the cemetery in less than ten minutes. A further five and they were waved through Gibraltar customs by Curran and a sleepy Spanish customs official on the other side.

During the flight from the cemetery, Suarez had been waiting for and expecting certain sounds to assail his ears. The sounds of police sirens, emergency service ambulances, and fire engines with bells ringing – the sounds that were usually associated with a disaster. There was none. They adjourned to Suarez's La Linea office. He switched on the wireless to the BBC World Service for news. After thirty minutes listening and there being no mention of any disaster in Gibraltar, he switched off. The recriminations started. Had Helmut fixed the mines' magnets to the hull of the destroyer correctly? Had Dieter set the timers correctly? Or had it actually happened and they hadn't heard the commotion? Not likely thought Suarez as he put through a telephone call to Curran's restricted number at the border. This number, he had been informed by Curran, was only ever to be used in extreme emergencies. He considered this an emergency. In a guarded call he advised Curran that he had information regarding a limpet mine attack in the dockyard. Did Curran know if it had taken place? Curran had replied he knew nothing of any attack but would check with security. He then thanked the anonymous caller and enquired if there was a number he could contact the caller on? The line went dead. Suarez would now await Curran's reply but in the meanwhile sleep beckoned. It had been a long day. As he laid his forehead on his crossed hands at his desk he noticed his watch showing, 2-05am. He was instantly asleep.

He awoke to the office door slamming off its hinges. His initial thoughts were the *"Civilies"*– the dreaded Guardia Civil para-military police force. He turned towards the back door to escape. The escape was brought to an abrupt halt with a retort from a gun as a bullet shattered the frame of the door he was about to flee through. As he turned with hands held high, a wall clock showed 2-35am. Thirty minutes sleep. Helmut and Dieter were still rubbing aching joints from having tried to get some sleep on an uncomfortable settee.

Standing beside the broken door was the red haired giant Irishman with a smoldering .38 Smith and Wesson squat American police issue revolver in hand. He had all their undivided attention. He spread his hands wide and snarled in English, 'Well, fuck-heads – what happened?'

They all looked at each other. Suarez, now realizing the worst – the failure of the limpet mines to detonate – acted as spokesman to reply, 'We did everything as per your instructions. *And* I have contacted Curran to find out if he knows anything and await his reply.'

'In other words – you haven't a fucking clue what happened. So let me tell you what I know *has* happened – The explosives did not *fucking well* detonate. That's what happened. And why did they not detonate? Because...'

Helmut who was translating the English being spoken for Dieter's benefit interrupted, protesting in German, 'But the timers were set exactly as per the Italian instructions. They were...'

'In fucking Chinese for all the good they did. So, shut it, Helmut. I don't want to hear any more excuses,' was the growled reply of the Irishman in German with Helmut once again translating for Suarez's benefit. His anger rising, he snarled, 'The Brits obviously don't know the mines have been planted....as yet. Having said that and knowing the devious ways of the perfidious British it could, of course, be a double bluff. They might have found the mines and are suppressing any news of the incursion. So we will wait and see what happens when Curran reports back to Suarez. If the British security haven't found the mines we try again tomorrow – same time, same procedure. Only we'll do the job fucking well right this time.'

'But surely the British divers *will have* found the limpets by this time and will be waiting,' reasoned, Helmut.

'Bullshit. They don't dive every....'

Helmut, daringly, interrupted. 'But with all due respect, sir, *our* divers dive at no set times. That's the whole point of security. Not knowing when....'

'Yes, yes, yes, Helmut,' answered the agitated Irishman. 'But maybe the British aren't as thorough as the Kreigsmarine, eh? Right. Enough of this shit. You go in again tomorrow – understood ?'

Helmut persisted, 'But they will be waiting....'

'I don't give a fuck. What do you think you get paid vast sums of money for?'

You're going back to finish the job and that's final. The new oxygen cylinders, timers and mines are in the boot of my car. Get Dieter to get them, *now*.'

Helmut replied, 'We don't need the mines. There are two unused in the chamber.'

'Do you honestly think I'm going to let you idiots use mines and timers that failed to detonate and then let you use them again as an excuse for *another* fucking failure? '

As the Irishman turned towards the door Suarez said, 'Now that Helmut knows the way to the cemetery, and since I was only hired by Belfast to find an entry into the dockyard, I assume there will be no further need for me to get involved further – so maybe you could pay me my bonus.'

The Irishman laughed out loud. 'Good try Suarez but you're in this right up to your neck – you chicken-shit little coward. You go. You don't – you die here and now and you'll never see your money...your choice.' As the revolver was raised level with Suarez's heart it did enter his head that either way he was never likely to ever see his money again so as he hypnotically watched the finger tighten on the trigger he, speechless and trembling, vigorously nodded his head in agreement.

The Irishman then stormed out of the office with Dieter following. Suarez took a step towards the back door only to be confronted by a Luger pistol in Helmut's hand. Helmut shook his head.

Argentina and Peron would have to wait.

CHAPTER 7

Yvonne's apartment Gibraltar.

Yvonne awoke to a distant ringing of a bell. A stretched-out arm to quiet her bedside alarm clock had no effect. Shaking her head to clear the early morning cobwebs she discovered it was the phone in the hallway. Her bedside clock showed 12-48 am. It could only mean trouble. She slipped into her robe, rubbed her eyes to rid her of sleep and hurried into the hall to lift the phone. It was an excitable Twomay, the dockyard's Naval Intelligence chief, on the other end. There had been an unsuccessful limpet mine attack on the destroyer HMS Worcester. No one was injured and there had been no damage. She enquired as to who knew of the incident – and was told: only himself, the duty divers and the dive commander. Remembering her chief, Sir James McKay's, axiom towards perpetrators – "The less publicity they get – the more their anxiety – the more mistakes made", she informed Twomay to keep it that way for at least twenty four hours to see if whoever showed their hand further. No publicity. She did not want to draw attention to the situation. Twomay, surprisingly, agreed with her for he had never come to terms with the situation that a female, especially one of part foreign ancestry as she was, should out rank him regarding security at the dockyard. She then requested Twomay to make sure the dive team involved remained incommunicado until she had time to phone Sir James at his SIS (6) headquarters in Whitehall. Sir James abhorred the use of the phone as a means of secure communication except in dire emergency. She considered this situation such an emergency. With pencil poised ready to tap out her call sign in Morse code on the mouthpiece, she lifted the receiver. Sir James was tracked down eventually in Portsmouth where he had earlier in the day been in meetings with the Admiralty but was now relaxing after supper with fine vintage port in the ancient Sally Port Hotel with the First Lord of the Admiralty, Lord Chatham and Winston Churchill. Yvonne's news of the sabotage attempt came as a not unexpected shock to Sir James. He had had intelligence reports from his Irish agent network of a threat stemming from a covert surveillance on Curran before he left for Gibraltar. The surveillance being instigated by him after his suspicions of Curran at his Home Office interview in Belfast. However, Sir James had not expected anything as calamitous as an incursion into the hallowed dockyard by enemy divers and cursed the unfortunate timing of the incident because one of his agents, Scott Rutherford, had been in Gibraltar not many hours previously seeking passage to London. Regrettably, he was already in the air and on his way to the Naval flying boat yard at Lee-on-Solent for onward passage to London. However, because of Rutherford's estimated time of arrival being the ungodly time of one o'clock in the morning and Sir James getting by on little sleep he had decided to forgo bed and stay up to meet Rutherford. He had contacted Yvonne with a return phone call to inform her that the security actions she had taken were appropriate. A relieved Yvonne then informed Sir James of her late evening/early morning sojourns to the cemetery. Sir James on hearing her revelations agreed that she should follow up her sarcophagus hunch as soon as possible. She indicated it was her intention to set off for the cemetery late this evening. Sir James insisted that should she discover anything of interest she was to return to her apartment to await the arrival of Rutherford. She was not, repeat not, to get herself involved with the enemy, if indeed there was an enemy, until he had Rutherford join her. He would arrange with Twomay to uplift Rutherford and take him to his hotel and then again in the morning and deliver him to her apartment. He hoped to have Rutherford in Gibraltar within twenty four hours. What he did not confide to Yvonne was how he could possibly do this, because the only way to get Rutherford there quickly was by flying boat on account of Gibraltar having no landing strip nor runway for conventional aircraft. However, he did have two of the most powerful men in Britain available to discuss this problem sitting at his table supping the vintage port. Surely, together, they would come up with some solution.

Sir James knew Yvonne was capable. At training school he had witnessed her fell seasoned Marine instructors with an edge of hand blow to their larynx and unbelievably place six rapid shots from her favoured Beretta in six different bull's eye targets whilst on the move. However, with this new highly professional attack on the dockyard he needed Rutherford in position to help, he being the only person he knew that could gain the upper-hand of her mentally and physically. He had used them together as a team twice with great success including the mission Rutherford had just brought to completion within the last forty eight hours. He suspected difficult times ahead and, regrettably, there was no finer man for difficult times than that arrogant sod Rutherford.

CHAPTER 8

Portsmouth January1936

As the graceful lines of the Saunders Roe A27 Royal Navy flying boat fought a turbulent buffeting to the north of the Bay of Biscay, agent Scott Rutherford was giving deep thought to his forthcoming meeting with his cantankerous chief, Sir James McKay, of the Secret Intelligence Service SIS section six. Commonly referred to as SIS(6). His mind was turning over the last forty eight hours to make sure he had his facts right for the London debriefing of the Tenerife mission he had just completed. When he had departed from Gibraltar his report seemed to him accurate but now as he neared his destination niggling doubts had begun to set in. Being by nature thorough he wasn't expecting problems with his report but with Sir James one never knew what to expect; it all depended on how badly his war-wounded knee was playing him up. Due to the knee the weather played a great part in his demeanour and unfortunately with the weather being inclement outside it suggested to Scott that he would be met with something less than good humour. However, as unpleasant as the thought of Sir James' mood was, it was of secondary importance compared with the present predicament that had been thrust upon him. When they had taken-off from Gibraltar, apart from a refuelling stop in Oporto, Portugal, he had spent the flight with his knees tucked up under his chin; the result being that every joint ached with cramp. The reason for this predicament had started when he arrived in Gibraltar. There had been a communiqué from the First Lord of the Admiralty awaiting. The message read that Gibraltar station had to make available for immediate, repeat immediate, transfer to Lee-on-Solent for further passage to London of a Mr. Jordan Hill – Rutherford's cover name from his recently completed mission. From experience, Wing Commander Stein of 202 Squadron, Gibraltar, the recipient of the order, knew this to be yet another agent belonging to one of HMG's intelligence agencies seeking urgent transportation. Whatever the reason, it was of little importance because the MAXP (maximum priority) order had been issued by the First Lord of the Admiralty – and that had never happened before on his watch. However, this order had not gone as smoothly as had been expected. Two minutes prior to the order's arrival Stein had given permission for the last flight of the day to take off on its reconnaissance sortie over the Mediterranean. This sanctioned action was unfortunate because he now realized that the unshaven, scruffy individual sitting opposite him claiming to be a Mr. Jordan Hill – and whom he had told that there was no available transport until tomorrow – was, in fact, the subject of the MAXP.

To the bemusement of Rutherford, Stein grabbed a torch from his desk drawer and fled his office with the words, 'Oh my god. Follow me Mr. Hill,' as he dashed towards the A27's anchorage.

It was 5-30pm and the last vestige of the day's evening sun was giving way grudgingly to darkness as Stein, with arms frantically waving the torch overhead, tried to attract the pilot's attention who was in the process of revving the four mighty Pegasus engines ready for take-off. When the engines were cut to idling Stein ran along the floating gangway to engage the pilot in discussion, leaving Rutherford with duffel bag slung over his shoulder standing on the quayside. The outcome of the discussion was that Stein was informed by the not amused pilot that the flying boat had its full crew complement of six. However, Stein, armed with the First Lord's MAXP communiqué, managed to get the pilot to agree to allow the six foot, athletically-honed figure of Rutherford to be squeezed aboard. On disembarking, Stein signalled for Rutherford to clamber aboard.

As they met mid-way on the gangway Stein laughingly commented, 'Pilot's in a bad mood, Mr. Hill. Told me to tell the First Lord where he could stick his communiqué. But not to worry, he'll get you back safely to Blighty. Good chap is Algy. Just not keen on authority.'

Rutherford could well understand Algy's upset – a four hour recce tour of duty, back in time for a late supper, had now turned into a marathon flight. However, this was not shown by Algy and his crew as he was amiably greeted aboard with cheery thumbs-up signs. As he manoeuvred himself into what, at best, could only be described as the craft's storage compartment he wondered why his colleague, Yvonne Rencoule, now on a mission in Gibraltar, had not been there to meet him. He would like to have seen her again – for they had certain unfinished business to attend to.

Thankful for his Royal Marine endurance training, Rutherford managed to set aside his discomfort and concentrate on his debriefing. His main problem was what to tell and what to withhold. The withholding having all to do with the opposite sex – one being Yvonne Rencoule – the selfsame one that had not met him on his departure from Gibraltar. Three weeks previous they both had travelled together on this A27 flying boat from London to Gibraltar after having had an unsuccessful dalliance in London thanks to circumstances beyond their control – the weather and the leaky roof of his Lagonda sports car. Yvonne was returning to Gibraltar to continue her investigation into the threat of dockyard sabotage having spent time with Sir James at headquarters in Whitehall, the Ministry of Defence and the British Library. Rutherford, also having spent time with Sir James, had been returning to implement the final stage of his mission in Tenerife. Unfortunately, with his mission now completed, and her failure to show at his Gibraltar departure, there was a very good chance he was never likely to see her again. Such was the way of "The Service," he had sighed with regret, for she was his type of woman – easy on the eye, intelligent and as tough as they come. You upset her at your peril.

Rutherford came out of his reverie with a tap on his knee from the flight engineer to attract his attention and inform him he had only to put up with his incarceration for another ten minutes. It came as no surprise to him when they broke through the scurrying rain-laden clouds to find the weather dank with sleet-driven hail. Having departed the warmer climes of Gibraltar some sixteen hours earlier he shivered as the sleet rattled off the porthole he shared with the engineer. As the pilot dipped the bi-plane's wings to starboard between the Isle of Wight and Portsmouth it gave Rutherford a murky view of Portsmouth Naval Harbour, boasting its assorted flotilla of British naval strength with an array of warships at anchor on the dull grey water. In the foreground, nearest to him, was an aircraft carrier getting up steam for departure. The thin wisps of smoke taken on the wind wafted from the twin funnels. The view suddenly disappeared as Algy made the necessary adjustments to his rudder controls to bring the plane onto a flight path for a sea landing at the Lee-on-Solent Navy flying boat base. Once it touched down on the choppy Solent water the Pegasus engines roared into reverse to slow the craft before entering its allocated berth to be rope-tethered by the ground crew. With the A27 moored, Rutherford started his awkward manoeuvres to extricate himself from his cubbyhole. Holding his duffel bag head high he thanked each member of the crew as they moved aside to allow him to wriggle past. As he passed, each crew member was aware that their passenger, even though dressed in scuffed camouflage fatigues and unshaven, must be very important to have had a flight redirected from an active service reconnaissance. They correctly assumed him to be returning from a covert mission and by his bearing – definitely special forces. They were not wrong. Rutherford had been recruited by Sir James from a special forces Royal Marine commando unit. His wriggling past the crew completed, he found himself with duffel bag now slung over his shoulder at the cabin door. He wrenched open the door lever, gave the crew a farewell wave and Algy a thumb's up before jumping out as nimbly as his cramped knees would allow into the now freezing hail. His boots on hitting the iced-up floating gangway had to do a circus high-wire balancing act before he, with his acute sense of balance, brought them under control. After a few knee bends, toe-touches and running on the spot to ease his cramped muscles, his joints and circulation returned to something near normal. Readying himself he skipped along the heaving, slippery, floating gangway with a sure-footed gait as it rose with the Solent's swell, until he reached the quayside. Now drenched with the clinging hailstones and a persistent dribble of freezing water running under his collar and down his spine he looked around for a limousine bearing Foreign Office plates for his onward journey but instead of a FO chauffeur to his surprise he encountered his chief, Sir James McKay, leaning on his walking stick with one hand whilst holding a golf umbrella with his other over the head of his trusty, ever-present, attractive secretary, Elizabeth.

As the foul weather intensified Rutherford approached Sir James with an outstretched hand. Sir James grunted a welcome to accompany his firm handshake. Elizabeth stepped forward and kissed him on both cheeks as she squeezed both his hands whilst wishing desperately to throw her arms around his neck. She did not, of course, follow her desire knowing that Sir James scorned such shows of open affection. She reluctantly released Scott's hands to a disdainful look from Sir James. It had been a chance worth taking for she was thrilled at the unscathed return of her favourite agent from a dangerous mission that she knew had carried a large body count.

With no further niceties to be observed Sir James handed Elizabeth the umbrella and slid behind the steering wheel of his slush-splattered S.S Jaguar and pulled the starter as Elizabeth, after shaking the clustered hail from the umbrella, joined him up front. As he opened the rear door, Rutherford, glimpsed at his Omega SA divers' watch, 1-00am. He had been travelling, including his flight from Tenerife, for over twenty four hours non-stop, but fortunately, with Sir James not being an advocate of small talk he looked forward to getting his head down on the journey to London. These were his thoughts as he languidly spread his six foot frame along the back seat. However, with his now soaking fatigues he found it difficult to get comfortable and was still awake when the Super Sports Jaguar cleared the Lee-on-Solent dock gates security to head for the A27 to Portsmouth and then the A3 trunk road to London. It was to his surprise when Sir James turned off the A27 at the Portsmouth intersection. He knew that it should not have surprised him – Sir James was not one given to unnecessary explanations. What did surprise him, however, was when they stopped at the security barrier outside the gates of Portsmouth Naval Dockyard through which he had passed many times to serve abroad as a Royal Marine captain in special forces overseas, before being head-hunted into SIS(6).

As Sir James brought the Super Sports Jaguar to a smooth halt a Royal Marine guard, resplendent in his dress blues with blancoed belt, matching gaiters and highly polished black boots, marched briskly from the guardhouse to Sir James' rolled down window and was shown his documentation. After close scrutiny of the paperwork and a check tick in his hand-held visitors list, a final inspection of the Jaguar interior, he issued passes and gave directions to Sir James. As the window was wound up and the Jaguar's engine restarted the guard snapped a curt salute to Sir James whilst another armed marine exited the guardhouse to raise the security barrier. Taking the guard's directions to where Sir James wished to go they viewed en-route, through a web of scaffolding, Admiral Nelson's flagship HMS Victory in dry dock looking majestic in the black and beige paintwork known as Nelson chequer which after many years of restoration was finally on the verge of becoming a historical monument. Being a Portsmouth lad himself, Rutherford recalled being taken by his father, a naval captain at the time, on a privileged visit to the famous ship of the line whilst the restoration work was in progress. He was aged ten and now some twenty two years later the work was just nearing completion.

Coming out of his musings Rutherford was suddenly aware that they were alongside the massive silhouette he had observed from the air – the aircraft carrier HMS Eagle. Sir James brought the Jaguar to a halt at the foot of the gangway and from the open window handed the armed marine guard their passes. With a final scrutiny of their passes and the car, the guard indicated where to park. Rutherford noticed they had parked alongside a chauffeur-less Daimler limousine bearing Foreign Office plates. A visiting VIP reasoned Rutherford, as he was about to open his door and leave his duffel bag on the seat. However, Sir James, who had been watching his movements in the rear view mirror, half-turned and growled for him to bring the bag and wipe the leather seat which was showing signs of dampness from his waterlogged fatigues. Rutherford recognized the growl of dissatisfaction from the front seat. Sir James was in another of his foul moods, the weather obviously playing havoc with his knee. To Sir James' disgust Rutherford used the tartan travel rug he had been sharing the back seat with to dry the damp patch. The task completed he then used a dry area of the rug to mop a trickle of water that had started to run down his neck. An irritated Sir James, opened his door and when outside and on his feet vented his anger by slamming the door closed as hard as he could. Rutherford looked enquiringly at Elizabeth who smiled sweetly and with an admonishing waving finger mouthed silently that he was being a naughty boy. Rutherford shrugged and laughed.

A still annoyed, trilby-hatted, Sir James, limped and with the aid of his walking stick, led his entourage up the gangway to be met at the top by the duty officer – a young lieutenant and two Royal Marine guards armed with machine pistols. Heavy security so far noted Rutherford as he pondered once again as to whom the VIP could be. The young lieutenant welcomed them aboard and led them below decks to the officers' sleeping and living quarters. The lieutenant halted outside a wash room and suggested that Rutherford might like to take the opportunity to make use of the facility. Sir James added grumpily that Rutherford should also do what he could to stop himself dripping wet all over the place. Rutherford, in need of relieving himself, gratefully accepted whilst thinking: *there's gratitude for you. I've travelled two and a half thousand miles, half of it with my head stuck up my arse, no sleep for over twenty four hours and on arrival been pissed upon from above then frozen through to the bone and all he's concerned about is the back seat of his bloody*

Jaguar and a ship's sodding carpets. The least he had expected was a change of clothing. Meanwhile, the lieutenant had continued along the corridor to a door designated "Captain," which had a plain clothes Special Branch man stationed outside. The lieutenant knocked and ushered Sir James and Elizabeth into the room and returned to the wash room where Rutherford had had to reconsider his earlier objections. Somebody had actually had the foresight to leave underwear, socks, boots, boiler-suit, and a white shirt – all standard Navy issue, in the correct sizes – laid on top of a dresser and marked for his attention. He suspected Elizabeth's hand had been at work. As Rutherford was in the throes of finishing his toiletries – combing his black wavy hair – there was a knock on the wash room door and the lieutenant entered to lead him to the Captain's cabin. Arriving at the Captain's door Rutherford was surprised to see yet more security in the shape of a civilian whose suit was not quite well tailored enough to hide the bulge under his left arm of a holstered firearm. Rutherford guessed Special Branch. The gent asked him for his duffel bag for inspection. Rutherford pre-empted the outcome by confirming that along with his code book, passport, dirty washing and a crumpled Saville Row tailored tropical suit which badly needed cleaning – he had a PPK automatic pistol and ammunition in the bag. The bag was removed by the Special Branch officer....*Who the hell was actually in the room?* he was thinking, as the lieutenant knocked and a throaty voice that Rutherford knew but could not place bid them enter. The lieutenant opened the door wide to allow Rutherford to pass. To Rutherford's surprise, but obviously expecting him, sitting on the edge of a large oak desk was a rotund figure smoking a cigar. Suddenly it became quite clear to Rutherford as to why the excessive security – the person in question under the fug of smoke was.... Winston Churchill.

Churchill rose and strode towards Rutherford to greet him warmly with a pumping hand action before clasping his other hand over Rutherford's shaking hand. The handshake coupling completed Churchill turned towards Sir James who was sitting at a side table adorned with cut glass decanters of whisky and port and in his deep throaty voice, said, 'I take it, James, this is our hero, Rutherford?

'None other, Winston. This is agent Scott Rutherford. Rutherford, please meet my co-planner of your last mission in Tenerife – Mr. Winston Churchill.'

Delighted at meeting the man he respected and whose opinions he mostly tended to agree with, Scott said, 'I am honoured to meet you, sir.'

'On the contrary young man it is I who is indeed honoured to meet you. Been looking forward to hearing from you about your heroics. Had it not been for your excellent work, my meeting yesterday with the First Lord of the Admiralty, Lord Chatham, would have been less cordial than it was. He is over the moon at your results – one of Hitler's U-boats a goner, a gun emplacement destroyed, photographs and location of another gun emplacement and...and a Waffen, SS special forces cell totally wiped out. Great stuff, Rutherford. No wonder I have the Admiralty eating out of my hand. In fact Lord Chatham was so impressed with your mission he had intended to be here with me to congratulate you but unexpectedly had to return to London to meet prime Minister Baldwin.'

'Thank you, Mr. Churchill, but it wasn't just me. I had my fellow agent Miss Yvonne Rencoule, and...'

An obviously briefed Churchill interrupted to jovially finish the sentence, 'And a geriatric pilot and a pleasure boat-captain. Quite a strike force.'

'Not quite, sir. There were many more brave people involved.'

'Mmm. Quite so. I do believe there were many of the gentler sex involved. Come let us hear the whole story,' said Churchill mischievously.

With that Churchill put a hand lightly on Rutherford's back and guided him to the table to sit beside Elizabeth who was sitting opposite Sir James. Churchill then took the vacant seat alongside Sir James and stubbed out the remains of his cigar in the cut glass ashtray. With all seated, Sir James poured out the drinks. Large Glenmorangies for the men and a vintage port for Elizabeth. On Churchill's lead they all stood and raised their glasses to toast the King. The toast over, the men replenished their whiskies. Elizabeth, who had but taken a sip of her port declined. Sir James accepted the offered Havana cigar from Churchill and lit up. Rutherford declined the offer and withdrew a Piccadilly plain cigarette from a soggy packet that he had rescued from his fatigues.

Churchill then began, 'Right-you-are, Mr. Rutherford – let's hear the story. I've been looking forward to this.'

With the withdrawal of a fountain pen and a notebook from Elizabeth's briefcase Rutherford realised his debriefing was about to take place here aboard HMS Eagle and not as he had expected in London. He did wonder why; coming to the conclusion that with Churchill being a co-planner and therefore having a vested interest, and a man with a busy schedule, they had to take the opportunity when it presented itself. So, he began to relate the whole episode taking care to leave out his liaisons with Charley (Professor Charlene Rogers) except for her professional input and Sandy, a randy Texan who had saved his life with her timely intervention just as Colonel Maria von Reus of Hitler's elite Waffen SS was about to pull the trigger of her Luger pistol as he lay on the bed she had just vacated. Throughout the lengthy report, Sir James and Churchill, listened intently with only the odd interruption to clear up points of relevance.

When Rutherford finished he realised how close the friendship of both men was as Churchill, with a glint in his eye, chortled, 'By Jove, James, that tale of derring-do brings back memories of our days together in the war when we infiltrated behind enemy lines with the Royal Scots – does it not?'

Sir James nodded agreement, and said, 'It does indeed, Winston.' For it had indeed brought back memories. It had been during a return from one of these sorties into enemy held territory that he had encountered a German about to lob a stick grenade into the midst of a trench full of young recruits. He had jumped on the Geman's back bringing him to the ground. The grenade, fortunately, exploded in the mud under the German. That was when he had received the shrapnel in his knee – and a VC.

Churchill then brought his nostalgic trip to a conclusion with a heartily guffawed, 'I would love to have seen dear old Adolf's face when he found out about the conning tower of his U-boat – built in disregard to the Treaty of Versailles, I might add – bobbing about in the Atlantic off the coast of Tenerife.' He then removed his fob-watch from his waistcoat, stole a look and exclaimed, 'Goodness gracious, I've been so engrossed with young Rutherford's adventure that I have lost count of the time. My chauffeur is due to take me to London in ten minutes, so it is with regret that I must take my leave. It has been a pleasure meeting you, Rutherford. I would love to have heard more about your way with the gals – but we will keep that for another day.' He rose from the table, thanked Sir James for introducing him to Rutherford and promised him lunch in the near future at Chartwell, his home. He also thanked Elizabeth for her diligent note taking, the copies of which he looked forward to reading. He then offered his hand to Scott with the words, 'I am sure I have not heard the last of you, young man. Keep up the good work – the country needs more like you.' At the door he turned to address Sir James. 'Kindly keep in touch James, and do let me know how your man gets on in Gibraltar. I'm sure he will sort the problem for you.' He departed under the blue-grey fug of a freshly lit Havana.

As the door closed Rutherford was left with mixed emotions: elation at his success being recognised, embarrassment at Churchill's praise in front of Sir James, who he knew expected all work undertaken to be praiseworthy, treachery, at Churchill's knowledge of his "way with the gals", making it sound as if it had been pleasure and not in the line of duty. His suspicion for this fell on Elizabeth but when he had looked across at her she had met his eye with an innocent sweet smile. And finally the realisation that he had been working unknowingly for Churchill and the Admiralty on his last mission. For this he blamed Sir James who did not like explanations. And, of course, confusion at Churchill's last remark to Sir James as he departed – *"let me know how your man gets on in Gibraltar"*. The one thing he knew for certain was that that last remark could not be directed at him, for as far as he was concerned he was due substantial leave, albeit the length of it still to be negotiated with Sir James. He intended to spend his vacation with Charley in New York. However, there was just one thing that had been nagging at the back of his mind – why had Sir James insisted he bring his duffel bag on board the Eagle?

CHAPTER 9

After her phone call from Sir James in Portsmouth, Yvonne was also of the opinion that the escalation in the sabotage attempts had all the hallmarks of a highly professional team at work – certainly not the rag-tag rabble of Suarez's blue-shirted, red-beret-wearing Falangist ruffians. They would not have the skills required to set the complicated timers required of limpet mines. But, she pondered, how were they getting inside the security area? As well as having acted as liaison to Rutherford whilst he was in Tenerife this was the main task Sir James had set her to solve when he posted her to Gibraltar. So far, she was baffled. Naval divers were always present when the anti-submarine nets were raised and lowered to allow entry and departure into the dockyard and the divers were also used at unspecified times to check the hulls of ships for damage or, as of now, the new menace of limpet mines. This morning's inspection of the hulls had been one of those extremely fortunate unspecified times.

Her toast and coffee finished she mounted her bicycle and set off for the dockyard. When she arrived she spoke with Twomay and the dive team to confirm that there should be no leak of information. They were now the recipients of classified information – and she did not have to remind them of the consequences of violating the Official Secrets Act. The meeting over she returned to her office and withdrew from a plan chest a copy of an ancient 1815 map of the Gibraltar sewage system and laid it on a table. The map had been supplied by the Ministry of Defence when she had last been in London being briefed by Sir James on the then, amateurish, but annoying sabotage attempts in the dockyard. When Twomay had rung her apartment phone at 1-48am she had thought at first it to be her alarm clock which she had set for 2-00am for her visit to further investigate Trafalgar Cemetery. The purpose of her nocturnal investigation, apart from trying to keep it secret from prying eyes, was the possibility of finding the source of an unknown tunnel into the dockyard, as gleaned from her ancient map. However, it was now too late in the day to do anything, which was annoying because she suspected she was nearing her objective. With her anticipation level high she realized she would now have to wait until tomorrow to find out if her new findings bore fruit. This is where she could be doing with the help of that male chauvinist, Rutherford, who she loved and hated in equal measures. Obviously he hadn't completed his mission in Tenerife otherwise he would have contacted her for transportation from Gibraltar to London. However, according to Sir James, it shouldn't be too long now before their paths crossed again. And for all his chauvinistic ways and roving eye she still longed to meet him again.

***

Curran, who had been instructed by a phone call from Suarez on his restricted number to find out what the security authorities were doing about the attempted limpet mine attack, had had no wish to ask Twomay who he knew to be suspicious of everybody and everything and thereby become a suspect himself. So, surprised at seeing a light on at this time in the morning in that rather dishy French lady Yvonne's office, who he knew worked for the MOD, he decided to make the enquiries Suarez required from her instead.

There was a knock on Yvonne's door and on her bidding of "come" it opened for Stephen Curran her downstairs neighbour and Chief Customs Officer of the port and dockyard to enter. She enquired, 'And what can I do for you at this ungodly time in the morning, Stephen?'

'Good morning, Yvonne. I was just passing when I saw a light on and thought I would ask you if you knew anything about a limpet mine attack in the dockyard earlier this morning?'

Yvonne sucked in a surprised deep breath as she wondered how he knew of the attack – especially the use of the word "limpet". She was aware that few people anywhere knew about limpet mines. The mines were attached to hulls of ships by powerful magnets and were new on the market. The Italians had beaten the British to the manufacturing stage. She knew of the British involvement because she and Rutherford had recently been assigned to tighten up security at a secret manufacturing plant in the Scottish highlands. She also knew they hadn't been stolen from Scotland for they had "Made in Italy" stamped on them. She was about to ask Curran how he knew of the attack but he would no doubt have a ready answer along the lines of having heard gossip at the border or he could, of course, have said he had received an anonymous tip-off about an attack. However, had he used that excuse he knew she would have asked him why he hadn't gone to Twomay with the tip-off. No. Craftily, he had picked the easy option – a woman. *Wrong move Curran,* she thought but remembering her twenty-four hour security blackout she bit her tongue instead and said apologetically, 'Sorry, Stephen. I haven't heard anything. *How dreadfully awful,* if there is any truth in what you say. However, you've aroused my curiosity. I will try to find out and let you know. Anything else I can help you with?'

'Er, no, Yvonne, thank you. It was just my nose bothering me. The curse of the Custom officer.'

As she bid him goodbye with a promise to keep in touch should she hear of anything warning bells were ringing. As well as the obvious bad mistake he had dropped about the *"limpet"* mine, Suarez, who she knew to be barred from Gibraltar, had almost knocked her off her bicycle outside *Curran's* apartment. Also, Suarez has his demonstrations outside *Curran's* border control: Common denominators – Suarez and Curran. Coincidence or...... So, she asked Curran just as he opened the door to leave, 'Oh! By the way Stephen, do you still see Suarez.... at the border?'

Watching very closely she recognized the flicker of suspicion in his eyes as, caught totally off-guard, he stuttered, 'Er, er, no. Certainly not regularly since his work permit was revoked, other than his very rare visits to his organized anti-British demonstrations.... Why?' he added, with the merest narrowing of eyes whilst a give-away bead of perspiration appeared on his forehead.

This further reaction to the experienced interrogator that she was, confirmed the suspicion she had seen previously in his eyes as she replied off-handedly, 'Oh! It's a something or nothing, Stephen. I just thought I saw him recently near to where *we* live.'

'Not possible. The police are constantly on the lookout for him,' he replied, sharply snatching the door open before closing it firmly behind him. She had, as intended – rattled him. She lifted her internal phone and dialed Twomay to have someone find out the whereabouts of Eduardo Suarez.

***

Meanwhile, an agitated Curran, suspicious about why Yvonne, an MOD inspector of works should be enquiring about Suarez, adjourned to his office to make the promised phone call to Suarez. The call was answered in an angry, gruff Irish accent that asked before he could speak if he was Curran. Taken aback, Curran confirmed that he was and was informed that Suarez was indisposed and that the speaker was, as of now, taking complete charge of the debacle and that once he got to the bottom of the present fuck-up, heads would roll. Now, what did Curran have to say regarding what had been asked of him by Suarez? A shaken Curran explained that there was no obvious panic in the dockyard. Everybody was going about their business in the usual way. The phone at the other end was slammed down on its cradle before he had time to mention his suspicion about Yvonne enquiring about Suarez. On reflection it was perhaps best forgotten – after all Suarez, he grudgingly had to admit, was a good-looking fellow and she being an absolute stunner would no doubt find him attractive. That was his final summation of the matter. No need for him to worry further. He just wasn't cut-out for the world these people he now associated with lived in. How he wished he was back in Belfast.

***

Yvonne returned to studying her ancient plan. She was deep in concentration when there was a loud knock on the office door. Before she had time to answer, the door barged open. She knew the action to be that of Twomay. She found this an annoying trait of his but put it down to age difference and his feeling of superiority being Naval Intelligence in a naval environment and she, in his eyes, a lowly MOD inspector, albeit he had been made aware by Sir James that as his SIS(6) agent in charge she out-ranked him. Otherwise she found him to be of the "old school" – a thorough gentleman, boorish but capable at his job. He was, however, as with all males attached to the intelligence services, a total male chauvinist with the usual attitude – that females were not suitable for intelligence work other than secretarial duties or being bedded. Fortunately for old Twomay, as she thought of him, he was neither. He was worse; a complete war-bore when he managed to tear his lecherous eyes away from her and the typing pool's legs and cleavages.

Looking up from her plan spread out on the desk, she covered it with her elbow and said, 'And to what do I owe this honour, Francis? Please take a seat.'

Tearing his eyes away from her crossed legs he, with jowls wobbling, growled, 'There's a damned Kraut, a *German*, on the payroll – working on that new reservoir you are allegedly supervising in, "The Rock."'

'Yes, I know, Francis. The *British* civil engineering contractor's head office has to notify me of all personnel they have working on site. And I should tell you that the person you speak of is not a German, he is a Slav. *And* Müeller, the gent in question, has been in place for four weeks. *And* London has also checked his credentials thoroughly.'

'Slav, my backside! – Er, pardon my *French*, Miss Rencoule,' he apologized, then realizing his further faux pas, that of Yvonne being part French, he apologized again, 'Er, no offence meant, Miss Rencoule. *Damn* fine people the French,' he lied, having a dislike of all "Johnny Foreigners", as he referred to all people not of British birth. 'But I can assure you he is *definitely* a damned Kraut, Miss Rencoule. I know a Kraut when I see and hear one. I fought the bastards in the war, and before.' She noted no apology this time for his strong language as he boringly continued on his favourite subject – Germans and their dubious birth rights. 'Why, when I was a young rating back in 1896, long before the war...,' Yvonne, having been subjected to his days as a "young rating" on many occasions had to shake her head to stop a glazed look from developing. '...I was seconded to the German Naval yard in Keil and lived in Hamburg where I encountered them every day... so don't tell me I don't recognize a German accent when I hear one – especially when the bastards are endeavouring to mangle English.... So, what are you going to do about it?' His rant finished he sat back with arms folded, challenging her but with eyes never leaving her bosom.

'We are no longer at war, Francis. It was, after all, eighteen years ago.'

'Well, I think it damnable that any German should be allowed near our sensitive installations. The bloody Slavs are just Germans by another name.'

'I don't think the Slavs would be too happy about that description of themselves. However, I will report this possible error to London and have them check his credentials once again.'

'Not a *possible* error. A *definite* error of judgement and you can tell London *that,* Miss Rencoule.'

As he stood up to take his leave, Yvonne said tentatively, 'Er, Francis, about my earlier phone call regarding Suarez?'

'Yes, yes, quite so, sorry, totally forgot. Got Critchley on the job. Good man is Critchley. Eton you know. Could find a lit fart in a gas chamber. Oh! er, I do apologize, Miss Rencoule – slip of the tongue, eh! what?' He departed the office chortling as he slammed the door behind him.

Yvonne also had a giggle. Stupid old duffer she thought as she turned back to her plan. She had been struggling with a detail which, she felt, if resolved could provide access to a hidden or forgotten tunnel which she hoped would lead into the dockyard. The plan for the ancient 1815 sewage system showed the dockyard sewage to discharge directly into the Mediterranean south of the dockyard. However, a dotted line on the plan connected the dockyard to the Old Town's main outlet further north. She reckoned this to be currently where the coaling station was located. A check with the Town's Sanitary Engineer had found no records of there ever having been any connection made between the dockyard and the Old Town's main outlet. The present day system bore, thankfully, no resemblance or use of any part of the 1815 system that had proved to be hopelessly inadequate and downright unsanitary. Even she knew that for a sewage system to work it required running water and that the one commodity Gibraltar lacked in 1815 was water. Even the present day system was none too clever; depending on catchment areas on the east face of "The Rock" to supply interior reservoirs like the one she was allegedly supervising. However, with the 1815 system, until the rains came, the stinking sewage lay in the drains and was no better than the system it replaced. Her recollections over she returned to the detail she had been struggling with – the dotted line – the proposed link between the dockyard and the Old Town was marked with three equally spaced crosses along its length between the dockyard and the Old Town discharge – they were shown as air vents. She had previously discovered that two of the vent locations had been built over leaving only the one nearest the dockyard, the Trafalgar Cemetery vent (Shown on the plan as South Port Ditch Cemetery) still to be located. She had spent the last two late night/early mornings trying to locate the vent in the cemetery. She had chosen her late, dead-of-night/early morning reconnaissance to eliminate unwanted attention.

This morning, prior to Twomay's phone call about the attempted sabotage, she had intended to give the cemetery her final reconnaissance based on knowledge she had gleaned from a library book about Gibraltar cemeteries. The section about the Trafalgar Cemetery had shown grainy photographs of ancient stone crosses, headstones, and sarcophagi. The sarcophagi, it noted, being for the town's wealthy. She had read that the cemetery had fallen into disuse in 1832 and had been, along with St Jagos, the burial ground for victims of the yellow fever and cholera epidemics that had last beset Gibraltar in the period 1804 – 1814. The deaths after this period had forced the cemetery to extend its boundary northwards until 1832 when it could no longer cope and was closed. However, with 1815 being the year of implementation of the sewage system on her plan, it had set her wondering about the actual plan she was studying. For the sewage system to have been designed the plan must have been prepared with the aid of an earlier surveyor's drawing. This earlier plan would not have shown the cemetery extension required to cater for the last victims of the 1814 outbreak nor of any further deaths until its closure in 1832. Therefore the plan she was studying, based on the out of date 1814 plan, obviously did *not* show the cemetery extension. The northern boundary, the only way the cemetery could extend, showed it to be a line of trees. She would, therefore, tonight, try this line of trees to find an entry into the cemetery extension beyond, in the hope of finding the elusive air vent. If this failed she would try the boundary from the northern roadside. She had wondered how the vent would manifest itself above ground. Would it be just a pipe or a brick chimney sticking above ground level? As she was mulling this over her eye caught the grainy photograph of a sarcophagus and in a flash of inspiration she thought – supposing the vent was disguised as a sarcophagus. Why not? You wouldn't want a chimney sticking up in a cemetery. She now couldn't wait to get started on her new theory and spent the remainder of her working day in a state of anxious agitation at her cover job as an MOD inspector of works.

On a whim, at the new reservoir she was "inspecting" inside "The Rock" she enquired from the site foreman who Wolfgang Müeller was. He was pointed out to her but warned to stay behind the safety barrier until he finished his task of setting the detonator charges to remove a tricky section of rock. A wrong setting of the explosive could bring down a dangerous ceiling rock fall. She was aware that Müeller was listed on his work permit as an explosives expert and after a successful detonation she spoke to him to congratulate him on a fine piece of demolition. The outcome of this short conversation was that with her having fluent Berlin-accented German she now knew that Twomay was correct. Müeller *was* German. To be precise, she recognized him as Prussian. As she was departing he asked her if she knew of a Jerry Hill. She replied in the negative and gave it no further thought until he explained he was an old friend and had heard Jerry was possibly working in Gibraltar for a travel company called Cantravel. Yvonne shrugged her indifference and shook her head, but the dormant brain cells at the back of her cranium had received a jolt. She knew that Rutherford had used being an employee of Cantravel as a cover for his assignment in Tenerife – and that his code name had been *"Jordan....Hill"* – J H or Jerry Hill? Could be a coincidence. She would need to keep an eye on Herr Müeller. However, she would not have a lot of time available to do so, for according to the site foreman Müeller's contract was due to end soon. He had been trying to extend Müeller's contract but had been informed by him that he intended to move on. He had a new job elsewhere. She supposed that that was him off the suspect list – but he *was* an expert in the field of explosives. On the other hand an expert would not have used the type of timer that had been used in the abortive dockyard attack. The type that had fortunately been responsible for the failure.

As she exited on her bicycle from the tunnel leading into the new reservoir inside "The Rock" she was suddenly aware of her altitude in relation to the town's ancient walls below. In an inspirational moment she stopped, leaned her bicycle against the wall and looked down. Below her in full view lay the Trafalgar Cemetery. Suddenly her theoretical problem of the cemetery extension was solved. Why, she wondered, hadn't she thought of this viewpoint before. The northern tree lined boundary that she had assumed to be the boundary for the original cemetery and its extension was in fact the boundary of the original *only*. On the opposite side of this line of trees lay four sarcophagi and due to the unkempt condition of the cemetery, innumerable barely visible headstones. This part of the cemetery was in a similar state of neglect as the original. Its boundary consisted of, in part the ancient wall of the town to the east, railings and dense trees with impenetrable looking bushes between them to the north until its north boundary joined the west railing boundary of the original. There was no sign of main gates. The entry for hearses must have been through the main gates of the old cemetery and then northwards along an internal road leading into the extension. Therefore there must be access through the original north boundary into the extension through the trees. As she turned towards her cycle she was in time to witness a Macaque monkey remove her tyre pump from its clip and triumphantly wave it above its head as it loped upwards to join its screeching, thieving mates. Her fault – she had been warned. At this height on "The Rock" it was their home and you left anything unattended at your peril. She supposed she was lucky to still have her cycle. Undaunted, her excitement grew with each furious thrust on her pedals as she headed back to her office.

Yvonne witnessed, as she cycled for home in the gloom at just gone 6-00pm, the graceful silhouette lines of an A27 flying boat rising from the bay and taking to the nightfall skies. She little realized that it had aboard Rutherford who had been disappointed at her failure to meet his turn-around arrival from his completed mission in Tenerife and then departure to London to meet Sir James. A feeling of nostalgia overcame her at the sight, for it was the same aircraft that she and Scott had shared three weeks ago when she had enjoyed clinging to him during turbulent weather over the Bay of Biscay. She knew he had been finalizing a covert mission in Tenerife. That had been the last time she had seen him. Unfortunately, with Sir James now advising her Rutherford was already on his way back to London his mission had obviously completed and she had missed him. This made her sad. However, she perked up at Sir James' claim that he could have Rutherford with her in twenty four hours. Happy at this thought she went straight to bed when she arrived home, arose around 10-00pm and made herself a light snack after which she washed the plates and cutlery, made the bed and kissed the framed photograph on the bedside cabinet of her dead brother; killed in an Alpine skiing accident. She then had a final perusal of the cemetery plan she had taken home from the office. On the plan she added lightly in pencil a question mark on the northern boundary trees. She then departed for the cemetery at 11-00pm with a knapsack on her back containing what she considered essentials for her late evening cemetery reconnaissance.

***

Trafalgar Cemetery 12.10am.

The belted-raincoat figure of Yvonne slid into the shadows of the trees overhanging the rusting railings of Trafalgar Cemetery until it came to the familiar gap in the railings. Removing her knapsack she slipped into the cemetery through the gap. She had been doing this for the last two out of three late evenings/early mornings, having missed one due to the sabotage attempt. However tonight was different. She had two new instinct clues to pursue. Firstly: she intended to find the entrance into the cemetery extension through the trees that she had mistaken for the old *and* extension boundary – the boundary that she now realized lay beyond the trees. This mistake, she knew, could have been averted had she reconnoitered the cemetery in daylight but it would have drawn attention to a fact that she wished to be kept secret until the vent was found. Secondly, to find an air-vent suitably disguised as a sarcophagus. She did appreciate that all her hard work may come to nothing. It was based on pure supposition. She had no proof that the dotted line sewage tunnel shown on her plan had ever been constructed or indeed if it was even a tunnel. It could quite conceivably be a terracotta land-drain pipe. These were her thoughts as she made her way through the unkempt long grass and weeds in wellington boots she had picked out of her essentials knapsack. Graveyards at night did not trouble her. In fact she found the moonlight lighting up the headstones and simple crosses to be calming as she read the names of the deceased. The majority of the ancient headstones she encountered were for victims, she sadly realized, of the yellow fever and cholera epidemics that had struck down thousands of Gibraltarians in the 1800's. She arrived at the tree line division between the old and new cemeteries. To her exasperation the gaps between the trees were overgrown with thorn bushes making passage through the trees impossible. After thirty minutes of fruitless toil she was about to call it a night when as she turned to leave she stumbled over a hidden corner stone in the long, unkempt grass and sank to her knees cursing. Fumbling for her torch she switched it on – the beam picked up, through a narrow slit in the trees, a silhouette against one of the Old Town walls. An overhanging tree had hidden this entrance into the extension and silhouette from her normal upright eye-line. Excitedly, she got to her feet. The beam showed through the slit a very large sarcophagus. On a closer inspection her torch showed the name of the deceased to be worn off the soft sandstone but the date 1815 was still evident – the year *after* the yellow fever and cholera epidemics. She had found the demarcation line between the old cemetery and the new extension. From her earlier overhead survey vantage point on "The Rock" she knew there to be another four sarcophagi available to explore. However, she would start with the one she had found. She squeezed between the tree and the ancient Town wall to stand in front of the stone sarcophagus. All she needed now was to find an entry into the structure. On raising the torch beam she could not believe what she was witnessing – the sandstone lid had been rolled back on broken-off rounded branches. Somebody had beaten her to it – and recently, too, by the look of the newly chipped stone lid. She mulled over her new problem – was there anybody still in the sarcophagus or had they departed? Only one way to find out. She took a run at the five foot high (1.5 m) sarcophagus and leaped high enough to plant her hands flat on the top of the narrow edge and hoist herself up into a sitting position. From this position she swung her legs to dangle inside the burial chamber. It was fortunate she had not leapt inside for her torch picked out the start of a vertical shaft with inset iron rungs. She listened intently for any noise of intruders. There was none. The vertical shaft took up only half of the floor area; the rest was at first glance given to storage as was evident with a rope coil lying on the earth floor. There was also very narrow vertical mullions forming slits in the end wall, presumably the actual shaft ventilation. Thankfully the only smell was that of musk damp. She descended the rungs carefully until she reached the bottom where her wellington-booted feet disappeared into ankle-deep water. She shivered and then found herself with a decision to make as she encountered a T junction at a tunnel. Right or left. She had been halving and quartering the cemetery on the previous two attempts with a small compass carried in her pocket. She removed it and read that south west, the direction of the dockyard, was achieved by taking the left tunnel. Crouching to allow her tall form to fit into the tunnel and with the aid of torchlight she came to a rusted iron door, fortunately rusted in the open position, leading into a main chamber. Stooping near to double she entered the chamber. When she straightened she discovered, by the light from her torch, discarded oxygen cylinders and various pieces of diving paraphernalia lying about on the floor. She also noted the jagged inner skin of brickwork that formed a hole through the brickwork at the higher level and a rope dangling from an iron rung. There was something seriously amiss with what she was witnessing. Something had happened. She sensed she had found the source of the attempt on HMS Worcester. Her sense of direction, which seldom failed, put the dockyard above where she stood. She had to get security alerted immediately. She back tracked as fast as she could travel. At the foot of the shaft she looked upwards; the moon was just scurrying behind a dark cumulus cloud as she started her laborious climb.

***

Trafalgar Cemetery 12.50am same morning.

Helmut and Dieter, with Suarez hidden in the boot, cruised through border control with only cursory glances at their passports by the half-asleep border guards. When they arrived at the cemetery the moonlight was casting eerie shadows off the headstones as they wended their way through the tangled undergrowth with their new supply of oxygen cylinders, detonators and limpet mines. Reaching the sarcophagus they were in time to hear heavy but controlled breathing coming from inside the open burial chamber. They looked at each other and on a silent hand instruction from Helmut sank back into the shadows. They witnessed a female form in raincoat and trousers start to climb out of the sarcophagus. Helmut stepped forward with his Luger pistol to cover the female. Dieter prodded Suarez in the ribs with his pistol to remind him of his presence. Helmut commanded her to stop where she was. He expertly frisked her with one hand whilst covering her with his Luger. On relieving her of her Beretta he signalled with his pistol for Dieter to climb into the shaft and descend. He then instructed the woman to follow. Suarez was then told to lower the crate by a rope gathered from the storage area within the sarcophagus, then follow. It was finally Helmut's turn. When he arrived below, Dieter was covering Yvonne and Suarez with his pistol. With Yvonne leading and Helmut following, Suarez was, with his hands behind his back, helping Dieter to carry the heavy crate as they set off along the tunnel. Up front, Yvonne was considering breaking Helmut's neck and taking back her pistol but thought it unwise not knowing what Dieter was doing behind her. A wise decision as Dieter had positioned his Luger on top of the carried crate for ease of access. So she decided to wait until the opportunity presented itself later when she could take out all three including Suarez who she recognized from her near miss on her cycle when she had glimpsed him leaving her downstairs neighbour Delores' apartment. She was, however, of the opinion that Suarez was a reluctant participant in whatever they were doing. She had noted a gun held by one of the Germans in his back. After they all struggled through the rusted gate of the chamber Dieter covered Suarez and Yvonne with his Luger at a safe distance as Helmut laid his Luger and Yvonne's Beretta on top of the already opened limpet mine crate and once again clad himself in his wet suit. Once dressed, Helmut picked up his Luger from the open crate then covered Yvonne and Suarez as Dieter broke open the newly arrived crate for the oxygen cylinders, limpet mines and detonators. Before Helmut started his climb to the breakthrough opening into the dockyard he spoke to Dieter in German. Yvonne, a graduate of Oxford University who was fluent in German understood what had been said but reacted just a fraction too late to protect herself as Dieter brought the butt of his pistol down on the back of her head. Her slender frame sank slowly to the floor – out cold. Dieter then tied her hands behind her back and secured her ankles with a rope from the crate. Suarez, frozen to the spot, sucked in a deep breath expecting similar but Dieter just smiled at him. They were keeping him for something else. His devious brain figured a frame-up whilst his vivid imagination confirmed the rest. He figured that that red haired Irish bastard would have instructed Helmut and Dieter to finish the job – setting the mines – then kill him. They would then kill the nice looking woman, whom he suspected to be a British secret service agent – and stage-manage the scene – him lying there dead with one of their Lugers' in his hand and her with her Beretta in her hand. A fatal shoot-out. Then that thieving red haired Irish bastard would tell Belfast that *he had* found the entry into the dockyard and claim the bonus that *he had* agreed with the IRA. Well, that's what he would have done albeit getting somebody else to do the shooting. He had to escape somehow or other.

Helmut, his climb laboriously completed thanks to the oxygen cylinders on his back and flippers around his neck, disappeared through the jagged brickwork opening with the limpet mines and detonators clutched in front of him. Helmut was gone no more than five minutes when he returned through the brickwork opening minus his oxygen cylinders and abseiled quickly down the rope. Reaching ground level he started shouting in panic in his native German. Dieter turned to Suarez and asked him something in German. Not understanding him Suarez shrugged his shoulders. Dieter did an impersonation of starting a car. Suarez then understood as he reluctantly handed over his car key. Dieter grabbed the key and scooped-up Helmut's civvies and personal effects from atop the wooden limpet mine crate to join Helmut as he made towards the chamber exit. Suarez noted he had failed to pick up the Beretta. As he ran Helmut shouted to Suarez in English, 'When I started to remove the outer skin of bricks I saw that the area under the quay was swarming with security guards. They've obviously noticed Dieter's previously badly patched-up brickwork and are heading with torches towards the opening. If I was you I'd make myself scarce. If you're caught say nothing – otherwise you're a dead man. Understand? We'll be in touch later.'

As Helmut was just about to   disappear into the tunnel Suarez shouted, 'What will I do with the woman?'

'Kill the bitch, she can identify us. *And* that's an order Suarez – otherwise......' He made a slicing action with his forefinger to his throat.

Finding himself still alive, a relieved Suarez crossed himself and offered a silent prayer towards heaven. He had no intention of killing anybody. Anxious not to be caught he too reluctantly left Yvonne where she lay and followed Helmut and Dieter. He assumed that security would find her when they entered the chamber. This he conveyed to the semi-comatose Yvonne before he fled.

The two Germans having a start on Suarez were through the gap in the railings and into Suarez's Auto Union and well on their way to the border by the time he reached the gap in the railings. He shrugged his shoulders. It looked like he had swapped his Auto Union for his freedom. Cheap at the price.

Meanwhile, as Suarez, Helmut and Dieter were in flight, a conversation was taking place on the dockyard side of the breakthrough. The arc of the torchlight that had blinded Helmut as he had peeped through one of the removed bricks in the badly rebuilt wall, was held in the hand of a naval security policeman on his daily round. He was complaining to his colleague as the torchlight hit the missing brick, 'That brickwork don't half look in a bad state. It's near to collapse, Fred.'

'The whole sodding lot needs taking down and rebuilt if you ask me, Harry. I'll report it to maintenance – not that they'll take a blind bit of notice,' opined Fred as they continued their torchlight inspection, little realizing that the chaos they had caused behind the faulty brickwork had saved the destroyer HMS Worcester from being sunk or if the magazine had caught – destroyed.

Down in the empty chamber Yvonne stirred. Her head ached. Her mouth was dry and she couldn't see. It was pitch black. Her Wellington boots had been removed when her hands and ankles had been secured tightly behind her back by Dieter. She struggled with her bonds to no avail. She had her Swiss army knife in her coat pocket. How could she get to it she was pondering? Would she need it? She was vaguely aware that Suarez had said something about security coming to her rescue. That was when she heard the first scramble of rats' claws on the filthy ancient brick floor. Her skin crawled – she hated rats.

***

As the abandoned Suarez, free at last of Helmut and Dieter, crept in the shadows back to Delores' apartment with fingers crossed that he wouldn't meet any police patrols, he had time to reflect on his life. Firstly, he was not a man given to violence. But regrettably it was turning out that way. Everything had gone wrong since his encounter with that mad Irish bastard. Why, oh why, he asked himself, had he got himself involved with the IRA? He tried to convince himself the reason was "causes". The return of Gibraltar to Spain. And, foolishly, of no real interest to him whatsoever – the reunification of Ireland. But he knew, of course, the real reason was his usual weakness – money. With his Falangist masters in Madrid but mere puppets of Berlin and only interested in Gibraltar for its strategic position to the Mediterranean, it had been left to him to fly the flag for the removal of the British from Gibraltar. And what had he achieved for that? Barred as an undesirable from his rightful country. And now with British security having found his breakthrough into the dockyard any thoughts of future wealth had gone down the drain. So, bugger the lot of them. He had made up his mind – Argentina it was. And just as soon as possible.

At least he still had the welcoming arms of Delores to greet him was his final thought on the matter as he thankfully turned the back door key in the lock. There was no light showing from under her bedroom door. He opened the door and peeped round the edge – the bed was empty. Closing the door he noticed a shaft of light glinting across the hall from under the sitting room door. It was very unusual for Delores to be up at this time in the morning. He opened the door slowly and cautiously to find his day had gone from bad to worse as he found himself looking down the barrel of a Luger automatic machine pistol held in the steady hand of one of Himmler's enforcers whom he had had the misfortune to meet on one of his visits to Gestapo Headquarters in Berlin.

The badly scarred face of Otto Hertzog said in passable Spanish, 'Please to take a seat beside your lady friend, Señor Suarez.' He nodded to Delores who was tied to a chair and gagged. 'Sorry about the gag but she has a foul mouth and I don't like that from whores.' Delores wasn't taking being referred to as a whore lightly as she rocked her chair and struggled with her bonds. Hertzog just cackled. 'Now, Suarez, I believe you are a very busy man.' Suarez found himself involuntarily staring at the dreadfully scarred face. 'Ugly, eh, Suarez?'

'No..no, I was just thinking how painful it must be....'

'Believe me, Suarez, you will get your chance to find out.'

'Why? What have I done?' he asked in panic, knowing the man to be a raving psychopath.

'The ultimate sin, Suarez – you have offended the Führer.'

'But I have never met Herr Hitler.'

'You don't have to meet him to offend. You have been upsetting the British with your futile demonstrations and attempts at child-like sabotage. They stop as of now. Otherwise...,' he growled, leaving the sentence unfinished as he twirled the Luger by its trigger guard whilst a sinister smile developed on the grotesque face. 'Do you understand, Suarez?' The gun stopped twirling and was levelled to aim between Suarez's eyes, resulting in his bowels beginning to loosen for the second time in as many days.

'Absolutely, Herr Hertzog. Consider it done,' grovelled Suarez, as he, with all the willpower he possessed, clamped his rectum closed.

'That's very thoughtful of you, Suarez, but...' said Hertzog condescendingly, as he delved into his leather jacket pocket and brought out a silencer and fitted it to the Luger. All this without taking his eyes off Suarez whose eyes were staring hypnotically at the silencer. '...but I have my own way of solving the problem.' He smirked as his trigger-finger tightened.

The one thing Suarez prided himself on was his quickness of thought and his mind which had been working overtime came up with, 'So you would kill a man that has just discovered how to get into the dockyard without the British knowing.... *And...* captured a British Secret Service agent who has information about the new Gibraltar defences. Information that my command in Madrid have tasked me to gather for the Führer? '

A silence ensued. A silence during which Suarez felt an escaped hot trickle from his rectum run down the inside of his leg as Hertzog gave this new slant on the situation his consideration before asking, 'Where is this British agent?'

'Tied up in a chamber under the dockyard quay. '

'And now Suarez, the reason for the agent being tied up, please. No more lies or...' He swung the gun towards Delores, who shut her eyes expecting to take a bullet as she silently screamed – *this is all your fault, Suarez, you useless arsehole.* This she would have gladly hollered to let the world know had it not been for the stocking gag in her mouth.

Having nothing to lose since he knew Hertzog's preference was to exterminate himself and Delores, Suarez thought it best he tell this psychopath the whole story, or near enough the whole story, and play for time in the forlorn hope of rescue. So, he told Hertzog of his recruitment into the IRA in Belfast and of their need to gain access into the dockyard to cause damage to British war ships. He did not mention that he had done precisely nothing towards this objective other than buy a new Auto Union sedan with their money – that was until the arrival of the deranged red haired Irishman. Instead he embellished his finding of the entry into the dockyard by lying that he had received accolades from Belfast and the red haired Irishman. He told how the first attempt at detonating the mines failed because of faulty timers, nothing to do with him, and of how at the second sabotage attempt he had encountered and captured the British woman agent who was about to go for reinforcements to help her apprehend him and the Irishman's commando task force. That's when they tied her up. Unfortunately, as the diver was about to enter the dockyard through their breakthrough opening to place new mines and timers, he saw that under the quayside was swarming with Navy security forces. They retreated and left the woman agent, finished Suarez delighted with his impromptu tale.

When he finished, Hertzog, who had listened to every word, said, 'That being the case the British will have found their agent by now – so you have nothing to bargain with Suarez.'

Suarez, thinking on his feet again came up with, 'When I said it was swarming with security this was what the diver saw through a brick he had taken out the wall.'

'He-took-a-brick-out-of-the-wall,' Hertzog said, slowly and incredulously with an unbelievable shake of his head. Now why would I ...'

The lack of belief in Hertzog's voice made Suarez interrupt quickly. 'The diver who replaced the brick in the wall said all of the under quay brickwork was in poor condition and the only way anybody could find our breakthrough in the wall was if they were to demolish the whole wall because it all looked alike – a mess.'

'So why did you run if they didn't know of your presence?'

Suarez had anticipated this follow-up question and had his answer ready. 'It was now obvious that security had found the failed timers attached to the ship and were on full alert. So what was the point in trying to place the new explosives? We weren't a suicide mission.'

Hertzog conceded the point with a nod then snarled, 'So, it boils down to whether the British agent is still in the chamber as to whether you and your whore live or die.'

'I suppose you could put it that way, but don't forget Hitler wants to know about Gibraltar's proposed defences – and the female British agent is the only one that knows what and where they are,' prompted Suarez.

'May I also remind you, Suarez, that in the event of your imminent death the Führer will never find out about the British agent.'

In what he knew to be his live or die speech, Suarez, in a trembling voice bravely replied, 'And may I remind *you*, Herr Hertzog, that you will never know what she knows if you don't at least try to interrogate her – which would be a pity, because if you were successful, and I'm sure you will be, I can assure you Herr Hitler would reward you generously. All it needs is for me to show you where she is. But it has to be now, before daybreak. That red haired Irish bastard will have another attempt tomorrow – believe me'.

'Believe *you* Suarez? That would be a first. Tell me, what makes you think the dockyard security will be clear of the breakthrough when we, if we, go now?'

'When we arrive at the graveyard and there are no signs of security activity it means they have not found the breakthrough.'

Hertzog accepted this with a nod before asking suspiciously, 'Do you know what secrets she knows?'

'No. That's why I had her tied up. I was going to interrogate her later. But I don't have your skill in that department,' he lied, with bowels dangerously close to collapse.

Hertzog secured Suarez wrists with handcuffs. He then made sure Delores' bonds and gag were tight and then they left by the front door where his Mercedes was parked. Suarez, by using the back door to enter the apartment, had missed this warning sign. A terrified Suarez directed Hertzog to the Trafalgar Cemetery and the sarcophagus. His main hope of escaping this psychotic despot was the intervention of British security forces. Unfortunately, for him, on reaching the sarcophagus there was no sign of any security activity. Where were the security services when you needed them was his ironic plea. This sad fact he was pondering as still being in handcuffs he climbed awkwardly down the rungs. Hertzog had attached a rope to the handcuffs and looped it through the top rung to feed out with Suarez's descent. Hertzog sat on the edge of the sarcophagus with feet dangling inside watching Suarez's downwards antics in full view of the powerful torchlight. The beam and the gun followed Suarez's every move. When Suarez reached the bottom his hands were yanked violently upwards and the rope through the top rung tied in such a way that Suarez was now dangling on tip-toes with hands in the air. Suarez marvelled at how the great bulk of Hertzog abseiled nimbly down the rope with torch and gun still in hand. Reaching the bottom of the shaft Hertzog removed a pen-knife from a pocket which he used to cut Suarez down leaving enough rope to go between his legs and be pulled tight from behind. They then proceeded through the tunnel with the Luger automatic digging deep between Suarez's shoulder blades until they reached the entrance to the chamber. Hertzog made Suarez go first on his knees with the Luger muzzle fitting snugly between the cleft in his buttocks as a reminder of the consequences of any wrong doing.

Once through the opening Hertzog growled, 'Where is she, Suarez?'

'Over here,' came the weak voice of Yvonne in little more than a whisper.

Hertzog trained his torch towards the voice whilst keeping Suarez in control with the rope between his legs. The beam picked up an open wooden crate. 'What's in that....' Before he finished there was the loud – *werrumph!* noise of brickwork collapsing and a sudden diffused shaft of light dimly lighting up the central area of the chamber. It showed the trench-coated figure of Yvonne lying with hands bound behind her back on the filthy, ancient, crumbling brick floor. 'What the fuck's that, Suarez?' snarled Hertzog, having let go of Suarez's rope but now with the Luger trained steadily on him.

'That's the British agent I told you about...'

'Not her, you stupid arsehole – the fucking noise.'

'It must be the Marines – they've kicked down the bricked up entry into the chamber....run....run,' cried Suarez in mock panic, having no intention of running but with every intention of giving himself up to the Marines.

Hertzog did not run. 'Shut it, Suarez. You're going no place other than your grave,' Hertzog growled as he yanked the retrieved rope from the ground tighter between Suarez's legs. Suarez thought he was going to faint with the excruciating pain. Hertzog's answer to his scream was to tighten the rope further. Suarez's legs gave from under him and he collapsed onto the filthy floor. As he lay there Hertzog stared at him with a malicious, narrow-eyed stare and brought the Luger up to aim at his head. 'You think I'm an idiot, like you, Suarez. Do you *honestly think* the Marines would kick it down to warn us of their arrival, eh?'

'But they don't know we are here,' pleaded Suarez in a high pitched and agonizing scream, still playing for time.

'Your play acting is not working, Suarez. They're not coming to save you. But don't worry I'm not going to shoot you.....just yet. I have a task for you. Move yourself beside the lady and sit on your arse.'

Suarez, still in agony and in fear, not so much from death, but from talking in the future with a high falsetto voice, crawled uncomfortably along the filthy floor, assisted by a vicious kick from Hertzog, to sit beside Yvonne who as Hertzog had stated was far from looking or feeling her best. She had been tied up in the dark for two days without water, food or toilet facilities. As regards sleep she had had to keep moving knowing that such a luxury would result in her death from the rats. She had been trained to suffer degradation – but the rats – how she hated rats. She also had never been so glad to see anybody as when Suarez arrived in the chamber even though she sensed all was not to her advantage. This was proved as Hertzog strode over and struck her with the back of his hand on her cheek to a gasp of incredulity from Suarez who cowered behind Yvonne. As he cowered his hand brushed her coat pocket. The hand felt something solid. He slid his hand into the pocket and came out with a knife. He hid it under her coat tail. The light in the chamber being poor, Hertzog did not see the exchange. Hertzog ordered Suarez to unbutton Yvonne's trench-coat, cardigan and blouse. With his hands still handcuffed it was a clumsy attempt not made any easier with her resistance which she, having expended all her already weakened energy, gave up on the next command. Hertzog ordered Suarez to take her arms out of her coat, cardigan and blouse leaving her naked to the waist except for her brassiere which Suarez was further ordered to remove, leaving her shivering exhausted and bare-breasted. Hertzog then took out a packet of cigarettes and on lighting one up handed it to the handcuffed Suarez.

'I don't smoke.'

'You do now. *Suck!*' Coughing the cough of a non-smoker's first draw on a cigarette he looked aghast at the ember glow in the gloom. He knew what was coming next as Hertzog ordered, 'Now place it near one of the bitch's nipples. We are about to play a little game of questions and *honest* answers regarding

Gibraltar's future defences. If the answers are not honest then...'

Suarez, with a genuine pleading look of sorrow, placed the glowing end of the cigarette with trembling handcuffed hands under Yvonne's nearest nipple.

CHAPTER 10

HMS Eagle Portsmouth Naval Dockyard

With the sound of the door latch engaging as it closed behind Churchill, Scott was brought out of his musing regarding his duffel bag and the reason why Sir James had insisted it be brought aboard. Turning to face Sir James and Elizabeth he expected them to be showing signs of preparing to depart but to his surprise there was no movement other than Elizabeth excusing herself from the table whilst Sir James replenished his and Rutherford's whisky. Task completed, Sir James lit a cigar given to him previously by Churchill and leaned back in his chair to enjoy his first draw of Cuba's finest. Suspecting a forthcoming happening, Rutherford took the opportunity to withdraw a still soggy Piccadilly cigarette packet from a pocket in his new boiler suit to join him. He, too, took a deep draw and exhaled slowly to await the expected revelation. Sir James laid his cigar down in the cut glass ashtray, leaned back in his chair once again and with one arm across his stomach and the other elbow leaning on the arm, he began stroking his chin whilst studying Rutherford. A sure sign of a problem.

Sir James politely cleared his throat and began, 'You did a fine job in Tenerife Rutherford – couldn't have done better myself.' That coming from Sir James was praise indeed, only for it to be short-lived as Scott's suspected revelation started to unravel. Sir James, leaning forward in his chair, continued, 'You are no doubt expecting an extended leave for your valiant efforts....'

Rutherford interrupted, 'Indeed I am, sir. I intend to go to...New York.'

Sir James shook his head and held his hand up in its usual halt position when he wanted a cessation of conversation. 'Kindly let me finish Rutherford. I was about to say – it is with regret that I have to ask you to forego your leave.'

The very slight harmonious vibration of the ship's boilers building up steam for departure were the only sound in the cabin as Sir James awaited the reply. It was not forthcoming instantly as a stunned Scott, not usually short of a reply, struggled with this unexpected announcement. The reply came, but only after Scott had managed to gain control of his disappointment. 'But, Sir James, I haven't had....'

Sir James, who had not relished being kept waiting during Rutherford's contemplation, interrupted and growled, 'There has been a major sabotage attempt in the dockyard at Gibraltar. Limpet mines were found attached to the hull of HMS Worcester...'

Rutherford suddenly realised that Churchill's words to Sir James of, "let me know *how your man gets on in Gibraltar,*" had a meaning. The unnamed *"your man"* in question had a name – himself. Undaunted by Sir James' revelation of the attempted sabotage, he interrupted to finish off where he had been interrupted, 'With all due respect Sir James – I haven't had a break for three months. Couldn't you get one of our other...'

A livid Sir James pounced, snarling through gritted teeth, 'Damn your impertinence, Rutherford. You are not the only one that hasn't had a break – nor has your colleague, Miss Rencoule. You do remember Miss Rencoule? She was a major part of your team. The same team without whom you just informed Mr Churchill you could not have achieved your triumph in Tenerife. *And,* as my memory recalls, she was the same person that was instrumental in locating the operational base of the Nazi divers whilst you were sunning yourself and, no doubt, whoring your way around the island.' He then stretched for his whisky and drained the glass before he slowly enunciated, 'Well – the – same – Miss Rencoule – is – in – need – of – help.' When he finished he sat back with arms folded glowering challenge at Rutherford.

Scott, on hearing that Yvonne was in need of help, immediately changed his conflicting emotions. The safety of Yvonne, a fellow agent, was not a lifestyle choice but a duty and Sir James was, of course, correct – he did owe her a debt of gratitude. So, feeling guilty about putting his own carnal needs before a colleague in need of help, he apologised. 'Now that I know Yvonne, er, Miss Rencoule is in need of help Sir James, I would like to withdraw my request for leave.'

'A wise decision Rutherford, for I have to tell you I am extremely vexed with you, not for seeking leave, for you have every entitlement to it, but because when I told you a colleague needed help you persisted in your prevarications.

However, I am prepared to put the erosion of your brain cells down to an overdose of tropical sun and travel fatigue. That way we will say no more about the incident, other than we will have it attended to immediately – agreed?'

A chastened Rutherford replied, 'Agreed, Sir James.'

As if on cue there was a light tap on the door and Elizabeth re-entered to be greeted by Sir James announcing, 'He has *finally* agreed, Elizabeth, to assist Miss Rencoule in her hour of need.'

Elizabeth took Churchill's vacated seat alongside Sir James and clasping her hands together to form an arch as she laid them on the table replied, 'Of course he has, Sir James,' as she recast the direction of her gaze towards Rutherford. 'Was there ever any doubt, Scott?' This was said with a smile twitching at the corners of her mouth owing to her being privy to Scott's earlier flirtation with Yvonne in London. The liaison being reported to her, at her request, by his landlady Jean, a former SIS agent and friend. And with the encounter being in contravention of Sir James' mantra of "agents having no relationships with each other" it meant she should have reported Scott to Sir James. However, she had said nothing of her beloved Scott's tryst with Yvonne because she approved of her, thinking them an ideal match. Apart from which Sir James' mantra meant little since Sir James was now a permanent fixture in her Chelsea apartment.

Scott, anxious to make up for his earlier outburst, asked, 'Could I not catch the flight I arrived on, back to Gib?'

'No. It will have departed as it was under instruction to refuel, change crew and return immediately to Gibraltar for reconnaissance duty in the Mediterranean. I appreciate it would have been beneficial for you to about turn immediately you landed but the fact is I could not cancel a meeting at which both Churchill and Lord Chatham wished to meet you, especially when Chatham had arranged your transport from Gibraltar with a MAXP at short notice. Thus your debriefing aboard the Eagle and not Whitehall. I trust that clears up the matter, Rutherford.'

However, Rutherford persisted, 'What about the RAF?'

'Impossible. It may have escaped your attention that there are no airfields in Gibraltar. But, because you signed the Official Secrets Act I can tell you that the racecourse is shortly to be turned into a landing strip. Not that that's of any help to us now. Ships or flying boats only. And this is?'

'An aircraft carrier – that more than likely carries a seaplane or a flying boat in its hanger.'

'*Veeery* good, Rutherford. *Veeery* good. Glad to see you are thinking clearly again. The Eagle, being part of our Mediterranean fleet, does have a seaplane – a new Fairey Sea Fox. It has been going through its final catapult trials right here in the Solent.'

'Catapult?' queried, Rutherford.

'Yes. Catapulting the Sea Fox off the Eagle's flight deck.'

'I trust they were successful?'

'Indeed they were. I'm sure the Sea Fox's pilot, Captain Johnson, will explain all to you,' exuded Sir James and being anxious to move off a subject he wished he hadn't mentioned finished, 'Now can I help you with anything else?'

Scott couldn't help but feel that there was a something he wasn't being told about the Sea Fox but with a touch of scepticism replied, 'Not at the moment, Sir James.'

An obviously relieved Sir James in a tone of bon homie said, 'Here is your passport in the name of William Willis.' Elizabeth slid the passport across the table.

Rutherford opened the passport and exclaimed in surprise, 'But this shows me with a pencil slim moustache. It's the one I used in Berlin a year ago.'

'So you shaved the *bloody* thing off. People often do,' retorted Sir James sharply, his bon-homie towards Scott suddenly vanished as a suppressed giggle from Elizabeth escaped from behind her hand. 'Elizabeth didn't have time to get DOC section to make you a new one. Apart from which you're only going to

Gibraltar and the only time you will need it is if you ever cross the border into Spain.' He paused to regain his composure, cursing himself for yet another loss of control. Rutherford had that effect on him. 'Elizabeth has booked you into the Bay Hotel, a small hotel we use in the Old Town. Your cover will be that of a civil engineer.....'

'But I know nothing about civil engineering. In fact...'

The angry palm of Sir James' hand came down heavily on the table bringing Rutherford to a halt mid-sentence. 'If you want to look like something you are not, take my advice and get yourself a clipboard, stick a pencil behind your ear, and walk around as if you know what you are doing. Frankly, *Rutherford,* I don't give a damn how you do it – just do it. You are a civil engineer....*Alright?'* Scott nodded his agreement as Sir James angrily continued, 'Miss Rencoule's cover is that of a MOD inspector of works which she does admirably. So if she can do it...... need I finish?'

'No, sir. Point taken,' Scott answered apologetically, adding, 'May I enquire as to who you think is behind the dockyard sabotage attempt – is it the Nazis?'

'Possibly. We know Hitler covets Gibraltar and would dearly love to get his hands on it come another encounter with us...but,' he stroked his chin, 'I wonder. He has nothing to gain at this stage in his hegemony. He does not wish to antagonise HMG because he still hopes to sway Baldwin to join him in his fight against the threat of communism on his eastern borders. However, his altruism regarding us joining his crusade against Stalin is, in my opinion, a total red-herring. And since you buggered up his chances of using Tenerife as a U-Boat base – wouldn't U-Boats operating out of Gib be a grand prize for him?'

Scott nodded his head in understanding and asked, 'Italy's Mussolini?'

What's he up to with all these questions? He knows the answers as well as I do. He's up to something, Sir James was pondering as he patiently replied, 'A contender, but he wouldn't dare move without permission from Hitler. He's not totally ga-ga.'

'When I was on that rebreather course that you sent me to with the Italian Navy I made a friend, a Captain Enzo di Rossi. I could always contact him and find out if he knows anything that could be of help to us....'

Ah! Finally – the start of his fairy tale, thought Sir James as he said. 'And, how do you know *he's* not a raving fascist? He's an Italian after all.'

'Well, we got to know each other quite well during my two week training. He invited me to his home for dinner and drinks with his wife and friends and they did not have a good word to say about Mussolini, and they absolutely abhorred Hitler and his Nazi party.' Having never met Mussolini Sir James was about to enquire further about him but let it go for he suspected Rutherford had an ulterior motive to this tale he was spinning and no doubt there would be a woman involved. He wasn't wrong. For whilst Rutherford *had* had dinner and drinks with Enzo, wife and friends once, what he failed to mention was that the remainder of his leisure time had been spent in the Grand Hotel in Genoa – with Enzo's secretary Gina whilst Enzo was out on night manoeuvres. He latterly found out that Enzo's idea of night manoeuvres was Ursula a Scandanavian blonde. 'So if there's transport available in Gibraltar I'll just pop along the coast and see if Captain di Rossi knows of anything helpful,' finished Scott innocently.

Oh no you won't. Pop along the coast – indeed. I've rumbled your little game, my lad, thought Sir James as he said smugly, 'Good idea Rutherford. Contact him as soon as you reach Gibraltar – *by phone.* There is no need for you to go personally to Genoa to meet him. Don't forget, you're back on my payroll, not the Admiralty's. Any questions?' finalised a triumphant Sir James as Liz tried to suppress a snigger from behind a hand cupped over her mouth.

A deflated Rutherford, still with Genoa in mind enquired, 'What about my transportation around, Gibraltar? I had the use of motor cycles in Tenerife.'

'Most of the inhabitants of Gibraltar, walk.....'

'That's not very convenient. What if I have to chase somebody over the Spanish border? What do I do? – Hail a taxi....sir?'

'Damn your impertinence Rutherford. Just for once would you please let me finish a sentence. I was about to say, most walk or cycle but we do have a motor pool of two cars and I believe we also have a motor cycle. I understand it to be a BSA. Oh! And they all require petrol chits for the use of – satisfied?' finished Sir James triumphantly.

Ignoring Sir James' threat of accountability for petrol now that he had his Genoa transportation unofficially authorized, a delighted Scott replied, 'Thank you, sir. Most enlightening. May I also enquire as to who is in charge of this operation?'

Suspecting sarcasm Sir James, as he impatiently drummed his fingers on the table, answered tetchily, 'You are. Assisted by Miss Rencoule. The dockyard Navy intelligence officer goes by the name of Commander Francis Twomay. Near to retirement. Eton type – rugger man, intelligent, capable, but with not an original thought in his head. Don't waste your time trying to engage him in any social discussions other than the war and bloody cricket.'

Scott was aware of Sir James' dislike of cricket – associating it with the aristocracy – which he so loathed and blamed for the unnecessary deaths in the war. Deaths that Sir James as a captain in the Royal Scots had witnessed on the front line. His bravery was legendary in the department – his Victoria Cross deserved. And his inflammatory remark, oft vented in the corridors of the War Office of, "Tell me again, what stupid bastard was it that decided to pit horses against tanks," deservedly still sends shudders all the way up to the top brass.

Sir James continued, 'I have made it quite clear to Twomay that everything has to be cleared through you, and I have further instructed him to offer you every assistance including access to all restricted areas. He will meet you when you land tonight and take you to your hotel and will then pick you up in the morning and take you and Miss Rencoule to her office. Tell him nothing of any plans you and Miss Rencoule make except the bare minimum required. Miss Rencoule tends to think he has a loose tongue when around the ex-pats. You know the type. The-Navy-can't-run-without-me-buffoon. Contact with me will be by phone, but only in emergencies and don't forget to tap out on the receiver your mission code name, Willis, in morse. Otherwise reports by coded wireless telegraph straight to Elizabeth for decipher.' He turned to Elizabeth. 'Kindly hand Rutherford the code book.' Elizabeth withdrew a book from her briefcase. 'All the information you need is in a note inside. Start page, start word, date to page number, etcetera. You know the drill.' Rutherford had picked up the book and studied the front cover by the time Sir James finished asking, 'Anything further?'

'Yes. I notice the book's by Walter Scott. Whatever happened to Dickens? I was really getting to enjoy his take on Victorian living. An interesting man.'

Sensing that Sir James was about to have a seizure, Elizabeth intervened, 'Sorry about Dickens, Scott. Unfortunately, I didn't have another Dickens in my library at home so I thought you would enjoy one by your namesake – Scott – Sir Walter. "Ivanhoe" is a grand read, you will enjoy ...'

An extremely agitated Sir James interrupted to bark, 'Enough of this nonsense the two of you. What the bloody blue blazes difference does it make what book he reads. Pay no attention to him Elizabeth you're not a lending library....he's here to work. We have a lot to get through before the Eagle sails. So, I ask you again, Rutherford – do you have any further questions?'

In the satisfactory knowledge that he had stretched Sir James' patience to the limit he seriously replied, 'Yes, Sir James. How far has Miss Rencoule got with her investigation?'

'When she last communicated with me early this morning regarding the security breach, she indicated she might be onto something. Unfortunately, she could not give me a clear picture until she further investigated something tonight that I'm sure she will reveal to you tomorrow morning. Her information is based on plans and books of ancient Gibraltar that she had secured from the MOD and British Library the last time she was in London – at the same time, as I recall, you were in London attending a meeting with me.' He stopped and looked directly at Rutherford for conformation. Rutherford nodded his agreement whilst deliberating as to where this was leading. He was soon to find out as Sir James stated, 'In fact, since both of you lodged in the same safe visiting agents' boarding house I *am* surprised Miss Rencoule said nothing to you about her visit to the MOD and the British Library.'

'I don't see why you should be surprised, sir. Her mission in Gib had nothing to do with me and I would not expect Miss Rencoule, being bound as she is by the OSA, to reveal any of her mission findings to me,' replied Scott, stealing a surreptitious look at Elizabeth who, behind a hand held over her mouth, was trying to contain her mirth at Sir James' blatantly obvious line of enquiry – his endeavour to get Scott to admit to physically meeting Yvonne in London.

However, knowing Rutherford to be the master of the obtuse, and that he would get no further with this line of enquiry, Sir James in a pretence of indifference muttered, 'Mmm. Quite so, Rutherford. I am sure she will update you when you meet her tomorrow. Now, regarding something you might not be aware of. The burial ground in Gibraltar is at a premium.' Rutherford nodded his head in understanding, wondering where this, too, was leading. 'And as I've told you repeatedly...we are not a clearing house for undertakers. Do you follow my drift?'

Leaning back in his chair Scott said amiably, 'Indeed I do, Sir James. But as you must be well aware, I don't instigate trouble – *but I do* finish it.'

'I wouldn't argue with that, Rutherford.' A snigger from Elizabeth broke the hostile silence developing as Sir James, after a withering look at Elizabeth, continued, 'The mention of burial ground reminds me that one of the books that Miss Rencoule bought in the British Library shop is a book on Gibraltar cemeteries.'

'Cemeteries? Whatever for?

'She didn't know exactly. Had a hunch that it was linked to the sewage plans of Gibraltar she had acquired from the MOD. No doubt she will enlighten you tomorrow.' He then lit a cigar and blew a hazy blue-grey cloud of smoke towards the ceiling. Elizabeth coughed politely as she helped to remove the offensive cloud out of her face with a wave of her hand. Sir James was most apologetic but continued his smoke. Scott, taking the opportunity presented, withdrew the last of his damp cigarettes from the bib pocket of his new Navy issue boiler suit. It failed to light. After three attempts with his lighter, he gave up in disgust and stubbed it out in the ashtray. Sir James was not forthcoming with the offer of a cigar so he helped himself to a whisky from the decanter. A cough from Sir James enlightened him to the fact that his glass was empty, too. He replenished the empty glass that was thrust his way. Sir James then sat back in his comfortable chair with his hands clasped behind his neck – his way of showing he had finished his main agenda. With hands removed from his neck he shuffled together the notes he had taken during the debriefing and handed them to Elizabeth. Task completed, and contrary to the tone of the meeting so far, he said in a sympathetic vein, 'I really am sorry to have had to ask you to assist Miss Rencoule – especially after all your hard work. But, unfortunately there is nobody who knows her better. And from what I've heard, given the choice, she would not have chosen anybody other than you.' Scott nodded, more to himself, for he knew he was listening to a load of softening-up waffle as Sir James carried on, 'Tell me again Rutherford, where had you intended going if your leave had not been so abruptly cancelled?'

'New York. I was looking forward to it very much.'

'A very enjoyable experience. Pity about their treatment of the English language,' concluded Sir James and having got his usual gripe about Americans off his chest he then sat back and added, as if as an afterthought, 'By the way, that acquaintance of yours at Harvard University – Professor Rogers...' Scott was suddenly attentive as Sir James finished, 'She and her team have been reinstated by the Tenerife Cabildo (local government) to carry out their monitoring of Mount Teide.'

'Only fair, considering the lies about their work the Cabildo were fed by that Nazi sympathiser in their midst.'

'I'm not sure we hold the moral high ground regarding lies relating to Tenerife....do we, Rutherford?' chuckled Sir James, conspiratorially.

Scott shrugged his shoulders and splayed his hands wide as he replied with another of Sir James' oft used quotes, 'The end sometimes justifies means....sir.' He should know, he reflected, for he had been in cahoots with Professor Charlene (Charley) Rogers, a New Yorker, when they had told one of the great lies of the world; leading the world to believe that the latest Chinyero eruption on Mount Teide had been natural.

Suspecting Rutherford's usual sarcasm, Sir James glowered at him in distaste before continuing, 'However, irrespective of morality, I forbid you to return to Tenerife until all the hoo-ha you caused there dies down.'

'Why?'

'Because Hitler won't take kindly to the annihilation of one of his elite squads – so be on your guard. Especially now, now that we think the Nazis might be involved in the Gibraltar incident.'

'I am quite sure I left no footprints in Tenerife, Sir James,' answered Scott, at the beginning of his defence to get Sir James to change his mind.

'What you learn at training school? There-is-no-such-thing-as-sure. There's always a something...if you look hard enough. Let me give you an example. From your debriefing, a certain Captain Kruger of Hitler's elite squad, gave your Harley Davidson motor cycle the once-over. Easily traceable. I know he's now dead – but supposing he had notified Hitler or Himmler before his unfortunate "accident"....'

'According to his chief, Colonel Maria von Reus, he only reported to her and she had not as yet informed Hitler, to whom she was directly answerable,' Scott's voice trailed off, realising he may not have mentioned his meeting with the Colonel due to its location – his bedroom.

Not being the sort of thing Sir James was likely to miss, he said, 'I won't ask you how you know she hadn't contacted Hitler since you appear to have overlooked stating that very important piece of information to me at your debriefing.' There was a lull in proceedings as Sir James retrieved the notes of Rutherford's debriefing from Elizabeth and scanned through them. 'Yes, here we are. Your only mention of her, as Kruger's chief, was when she was found dead by the police at a notorious diving spot. Apparently another "accident". I have to hand it to you, people at least die imaginative deaths when they come into contact with you, Rutherford. Kruger and his side-kick crushed to death by two tons of gun barrel dropped from a height, Colonel von Reus, a broken neck from diving off rocks. Now there's another reason of a possible slip-up – she might not even be a swimmer. Scott was going to mention that the deaths had saved ammunition but thought better of it as Sir James continued, 'Knowing you to be the master of duplicity and that I won't get a straight answer to where you met her I will put your forgetful memory down to *bedside* amnesia.' Elizabeth could no longer stifle the snigger behind her hand. Ignoring her, Sir James concluded, 'For these reasons I say your safety would be in jeopardy and I, therefore, forbid your return to Tenerife. Hitler will not forgive. You just disposed of one of his mistresses – Colonel Maria von Reus.'

That fact came as no surprise to Scott who just nonchalantly nodded his head in agreement to Sir James' order knowing it was not his welfare he was concerned about...more that of keeping the Tenerife operation a secret.

Elizabeth, who had sat silent throughout apart from the odd snigger that she could not help as she witnessed the sparring between the aggressive Sir James and the recalcitrant Scott, found herself to be slightly jealous of Scott's claimed professional relationships with Maria von Reus and Charley. A feeling that she immediately chastised herself for as she found herself saying, 'Looking on the bright side Scott, Charley, as I believe you refer to Professor Charlene Rogers, has agreed to give lectures at Mr.Crozier's (the entrepreneur owner of Cantravel) old alma-mater, Oxford University. This, we are informed, being part of Harvard University's repayment in kind for his sponsorship funding of the new expedition to Mount Teide.' A wide smile showing his even, glowing white teeth broke out on Scott's face. 'I thought that would cheer you up Scott,' she finished, to a glower from Sir James who took over.

Sir James, looking at his watch said, 'I have a meeting with the Joint Heads of Forces and would like to be in London by breakfast. Is there anything else pertinent that you can think of to ask me?'

'Yes. May I be permitted to enquire why Mr. Churchill was in attendance? It was a bit of a coincidence he and Lord Chatham being in Portsmouth at the same time as my arrival.'

'It was indeed a genuine coincidence. Just as well, otherwise you would not be travelling back to Gibraltar within the hour. To explain – Mr. Churchill had been called to a meeting yesterday with Lord Chatham in Portsmouth. Elizabeth and I had already decided to meet you at Lee-on-Solent and knowing you were getting in at some ridiculous time in the morning we stopped last evening in the Sally Port hotel, Portsmouth.' Scott, with a smile twitching at the corners of his mouth looked penetratingly at Liz. She blushed. 'That's where we met Mr. Churchill and Lord Chatham. It was gone midnight when I received the phone call, via my office in Whitehall from Miss Rencoule, advising me of the attempted sabotage. When, during the course of conversation, Mr. Churchill found out we were here to meet you he too insisted on meeting you. Lord Chatham, who thinks the sun shines out your backside, was also desperate to meet the Admiralty's blue-eyed boy but unfortunately, as you know, an emergency cropped up and he had to cancel his intended meeting. However, when he found out we had a transport problem that's when he organised the Fairey Sea Fox to get you back to Gibraltar. Does that satisfy your curiosity?'

'Yes, sir. You have been *most* helpful. And I *fully* understand my mission.'

Suspecting Scott's reply to contain more than an element of his usual sarcasm, Sir James narrowed his eyes as he replied, 'Good. No more than I would expect from you Rutherford. I know you will do your best. The next I want to hear from you is that you have shed light on the culprits.' Sir James then rose from the table and whilst shaking Rutherford's hand firmly wished him, 'Good fortune, Rutherford. Remember to watch your back.'

Elizabeth also rose and came round the table to hold both his hands which she squeezed hard as she stood on tip toes to kiss him on both cheeks and whisper in his ear, 'It wasn't me that told him about Yvonne and you. I bet it was what's his name at the FO garage that looks after your Lagonda when you're on mission.' Then for the benefit of Sir James she said loudly, 'Please come back safely, Scott, we do worry about you.' Scott ran his hand slowly down her back and patted her bottom. She blushed and hurriedly looked guiltily towards Sir James who in the meanwhile had crossed to the desk and pressed a button on the intercom to issue an instruction. Seconds later the young Lieutenant entered and led Scott to his quarters.

At the door Scott turned to thank Sir James and Elizabeth. From behind Sir James' back a still blushing Elizabeth blew him a kiss which he returned much to Sir James' aghast horror thinking it was directed at him. Scott left the room laughing with an over the shoulder backward wave. As the door closed behind Rutherford Sir James turned to Elizabeth and sighed, 'You know, Liz, I despair about that young man's attitude towards authority. Every time I have a meeting with him it develops into a battle of wits. He's an arrogant, argumentative, sarcastic sod with a ruthless streak behind that sophisticated veneer. Fortunately for us the bugger's gifted with knowing right from wrong in the delicate moral judgements he's required to make for the good of the realm. And it is that quality that separates him from others and makes him, I regret to say, my best operative. What say you, Liz?'

Whilst Sir James had been expounding on Scott's character Liz had been mentally adding to it. He's funny and well-mannered, not like the majority of the bum-pinching, lewd-joke, double-entendre idiots she had to deal with daily from across the far flung corners of the Empire. And he was the most handsome man she had ever met, she finished guiltily. In her wisdom she also knew that the apparent animosity between the two all stemmed from Sir James seeing in Scott a younger version of himself and wishing that it was he that was going on mission to help the lovely looking half-French beauty Yvonne and not sitting behind his desk. With this in mind she replied to Sir James' question, 'He certainly is, without any shadow of doubt your best operative, Jimmy. In fact, doesn't he remind you of somebody in your past that you know intimately and is sitting with hands clasped behind his neck not a million miles from here?'

Sir James had taken up his favourite relaxing position in his chair – hands clasped behind his neck – and with a rare smile on his usually dour countenance laughingly said, 'Modesty, my dear Liz, forbids me to pass comment.'

'Will he be safe?'

'For goodness sake Liz he's only going to find out who tried to blow up one of our ships. I haven't shipped him out to the Khyber Pass....yet.'

'Yes, but, you only sent him to Tenerife to find suitable inlets for our submarines and he came close to death on at least three known occasions.'

'Liz! If you want to worry, worry about the people that come into contact with him.....they seem to have a relatively short life-span. Now come on, pack up and let's be on our way, otherwise we too will eventually end up in Gibraltar.

Meanwhile, further along the corridor, Scott was looking inside a suitcase lying on the bottom bed of a two tier bunk bed. In his hand was a note from Liz advising him that she had taken the liberty of visiting his landlady and picking up a selection of clothing for his mission. She trusted they were to his liking. A further check inside his duffel bag, also on the bed, reunited him with his trusty PPK automatic and additional boxes of ammunition. Good old Liz. She thinks of everything, thought Scott. It was then he punched the air in triumph – he was on active service again. Charley but a memory. Well, for the time being until he checked out her lecture dates at Oxford.

HMS Eagle departed Portsmouth dockyard at 4-30 am with a Fairey Sea Fox sea plane on its flight deck astride a newly installed catapult.

CHAPTER 11

Rutherford, who had had no sleep in the last twenty four hours, was sound asleep in his bunk aboard the HMS Eagle as it eased its way out of Portsmouth harbour into the Solent. However, nine hours later at Brest, off the coast of north-west France, he found himself sitting in the cockpit behind Captain Johnson in a Fairey Sea Fox seaplane ready for take-off. With the sea being unusually becalmed at this time of year Captain Bullard of HMS Eagle had calculated Brest to be the optimum launch location to suit the Sea Fox's range of seven hundred kilometers to Oporto in north-west Portugal for refuelling before completing its similar duration flight to Gibraltar.

Fear was a total anathema to Rutherford but he couldn't help but have reservations about being catapulted off a ship's deck into the atmosphere. It had, however, been beneficial to hear from Sir James before they went their separate ways that the catapult trials had gone well. With the light metal frame and glass cockpit hood in place it allowed him to converse with the bushy moustached Captain Johnson with whom he broke the silence of their new acquaintanceship by enquiring as to how the actual trials off the flight deck of the Eagle had gone. The answer was not quite as he had expected. The captain informed him that the catapult trials had in fact been successful but they had been carried out with the Sea Fox being catapult launched off a jetty into the Solent. At any moment now when the Sea Fox was launched it would be the first time a plane had ever been catapulted off a moving ship, therefore *this* was the official sea trial. They were about to make history. Before he had time to thank the captain sarcastically for putting his mind at ease the bushy 'tashed war veteran gave the ground crew the thumbs-up "ready to go" signal. With the Napier engine at full throttle and straining against the tensioned catapult the ground crew disengaged the restraining mechanism and the Sea Fox lurched forward forcing Rutherford's head violently backwards. By the time his head rocked forward he was suddenly aware of the flight deck disappearing by the second to offer up a great expanse of Atlantic Ocean. Just as he was catching his breath, which had been knocked out of his lungs with the initial inertia thrust, the Sea Fox gracefully glided airborne upwards towards the fluffy cumulus clouds above. He let out an audible sigh of relief as the cockpit echoed to Captain Johnson's whoop of, 'Wow! That was sensational. Better than the big dipper at Blackpool. What say you, my boy?'

Rutherford who had thoroughly enjoyed the adrenalin filled take-off jokingly quipped, 'Suddenly the ghost train on Southsea pier doesn't seem so terrifying anymore.' However, the experience confirmed what he had thought of all the aviators he had ever met – they were all deranged. It must be something in the upper atmosphere.

His climb to seven thousand feet complete, Captain Johnson settled into a helpful downwind air-pocket enabling him to reach the Sea Fox's maximum cruising speed of two hundred kilometers per hour and arrive in Porto three and a half hours later. After refueling they had a leisurely one hour break. As it had been from the start, the remainder of the journey was completed in congenial conversation mostly about the captain's wartime exploits of which there were many. Rutherford was content to let him babble on because for himself to add anything to the conversation would have given away his cover – that of a civil engineer. A job he knew little about to discuss freely. Not that it mattered for Captain Johnson would have had a good idea that he was security or something similar to have been allowed aboard his plane at short notice. This bending of the rules, at a direct order from the First Lord of the Admiralty, was to the chagrin of the Fairey Aviation test engineer who was supposed to have flown with Captain Johnson.

Darkness was falling as three and a half hours later Captain Johnson settled the Sea Fox, as gently as a wafting feather, in Gibraltar Bay outside the harbour walls to await the signal to enter. It was now dark. Rutherford looked at his diver's Omega watch it showed: 10-05pm. Johnson informed him that their arrival was expected and that the delay was due to the navy dockyard divers supervising the lowering of the anti-submarine boom, a procedure Rutherford was familiar with having no more than thirty eight hours previously arrived off a flight from Tenerife by seaplane. Suddenly the green light flashed and the Sea Fox idled slowly to its allotted berth. When it was anchored to the jetty capstans, Captain Johnson raised the cockpit roof to allow Rutherford to extract his six foot frame, step out onto the wing and withdraw his duffel bag and the suitcase Liz had packed and thank the captain for a thoroughly enjoyable flight. As he jumped off the wing on to a floating walkway he thought it only fair considering the lateness of the hour to invite the captain to join him in the officers' mess to have something to eat. The captain with a wink and a mischievous two handed twirl of his bushy moustache declined the invite and gave forth with a twist to the old adage, "It aint only sailors that have one in every port you know, old boy." Rutherford laughed at the reply but in truth he felt a tad envious as he slung his duffel bag over his shoulder and lifted the suitcase to temper his stride to suit the gentle harbour swell affecting the gangway. Once on terra-firma he turned and faced the smiling face of the captain and snapped him a curt Royal Marine salute. He got a pilots' thumbs-up in return.

Rutherford was suddenly aware of a tall, grey-haired, slightly stooped, elderly and distinguished-looking gentleman in full naval uniform bearing the insignia of commander stepping out of the shadows of the overhead dockside lights. His hand was extended ready for a handshake. Rutherford obliged. The handshake was firm. He introduced himself as Francis Twomay, head of naval intelligence Gibraltar station. Rutherford introduced himself as William Willis. Twomay gave a knowingly condescending smile for he had been privy to Wing Commander Stein's discomfort some thirty-eight hours previously when Stein had been instructed from London to secure immediate passage for one – a *Mr Jordan Hill,* to Lee-on-Solent. And if his eyes did not betray him it was the same man. All the security types he had ever met were the same – shifty. He had oft wondered if they even remembered the name they had been christened with. However, he, too, had been instructed from London to give the man every assistance so – so be it. They all came with their big Whitehall security ideas but all went home with their tails between their legs back to their London office desks. They didn't understand the ways of the navy as he did.

They adjourned to Twomay's office. Once inside Twomay made for the drink's cabinet. He poured himself a large gin and tonic and Rutherford, as requested, a large Glenfiddich malt whisky. Twomay then offered him a cigarette from a full packet of Senior Service. They lit up. Twomay then asked if he had had time to purchase cigarettes on his travels. Rutherford answered that he had bought Portugese cigarettes at their refueling stop. Twomay made a grim face and slid the remainder of a twenty pack of Senior Service across the desk which was pocketed gratefully by Rutherford. The pleasantries observed Twomay enquired, 'Now, Mr. Willis, what can I do to help you at this time of night other than drive you to your hotel?'

'Not a lot. I will get my answers from Miss Rencoule when I see her in the morning. Talking of Miss Rencoule, why was she not here to meet me?

'Couldn't rightly say, old boy. I received a very short phone call from Sir James giving me your ETA and instructing me to meet you. You would really need to ask Sir James the reason. It must have been a good one because she was certainly at work earlier in the day.'

'Mmm. I suppose there must be as you say – a good reason. However, there is one thing I need to clear up...has anybody explained to you the line of authority on this operation?'

A petulant 'Yes' was the answer followed by, 'It was made quite clear to me by your chief, Sir James, backed up by no less than the First Lord of the Admiralty Lord Chatham, that Miss Rencoule was in charge of the operation until you arrive.'

'Good, Francis. It's always best to get this point straight...who's in charge, not that I intend to interfere with your methods which I understand are exemplary,' he lied, as he noted Twomay preening himself.

The praise worked, for Twomay immediately lifted the phone and had the operator put him through to the Bay hotel. Whilst he waited to be put through he informed Rutherford that it would be nigh impossible to have a cooked meal at this time of night with the mess and hotel kitchen being closed but he would see what he could do regards sandwiches and beer. A brief conversation ensued, the outcome of which was that the night manager had on his arrival agreed to have roast beef sandwiches and beer sent to his room. Twomay then apologized for not inviting him back to his place but with the memsahib gone to an early resting place his larder was somewhat bare. He ate out but all the restaurants and cafes were unfortunately also closed at this time of night. As Rutherford opened the driver's door to exit the gleaming Austin eight saloon he was reminded by Twomay that he would pick him up at 8-30am.

After his delicious supper of roast beef sandwiches and a large Glenfiddich (a better option on the night manager's part than beer) he retired to bed to finish his sleep that had been abruptly interrupted aboard HMS Eagle. Up at 7-00am he started the day with a much needed bath and from the suitcase changed into one of his superbly cut Saville Row suits to conceal his holstered underarm PPK, crisp new white shirt, matching tie and gleaming black Oxford shoes, all as chosen by Liz. He was back to looking his usual immaculate self and looking forward to renewing his acquaintance with Yvonne. He couldn't wait to get the day under way. He ate a hearty breakfast and was outside the hotel to meet Twomay sharp at the agreed time of 8-30am.

At 8-35am they were outside Yvonne's apartment. At 8-37am they were on the third ring of her unanswered doorbell.

'Damned unlike Miss Rencoule to be late,' opined Twomay. 'If she's over-slept it will be the first time since I have known her.'

'Do you have a spare key, Francis?'

'No but our Mr. Curran who lives downstairs is the key holder of both of these MOD properties.'

Rutherford gave the door several more rapid fist thumps to no avail before turning to Twomay. 'Right, Francis. Below and get the key, please.'

Twomay had been gone less than a minute when Rutherford heard a shout from below summoning him, 'Mr. Willis, would you please come downstairs I fear there is a something you should see.'

Thinking that something untoward had happened to Yvonne he dashed down the stairs to be met at the foot by Twomay who held out his hand to stop Rutherford's progress. 'Something you should know, old boy, about the person inside. She's Mrs. Delores Curran...' With it not being Yvonne, Rutherford heaved an inner sigh of relief. '...The wife of our head of Customs. Not homegrown – a Gibraltarian. An alleged high-class ex-prostitute. Her pimp was, and possibly still is, an unsavoury character named Eduardo Suarez. As we would term back home in Blighty, a wide-boy – a spiv. Local organiser of the Falange Pary. Persona non Grata in Gibraltar. His list of misdemeanours is endless. However, I assume you are anxious to question Mrs. Curran so I will discuss Suarez with you later.' Twomay, on finishing, stood aside to allow Rutherford to enter the apartment. As Rutherford took one step into the apartment he heard over his shoulder Twomay's warning, 'By the way she tends to be foul-mouthed.'

Rutherford entered the front room to find a black-haired, extremely attractive-looking female, scantily dressed, in her early thirties bound hand and foot to a dining room chair and gagged with what looked like one of her stockings. Her dress was wrinkled to half way up her thighs showing flesh and a suspender between the hem of the dress and her remaining stocking top. Twomay, when he entered, sat on the edge of the table ogling her with a grin on his face as Rutherford withdrew a Swiss Army knife from his jacket pocket, cut her bonds and removed the stocking gag and handed it to her. She snatched it from him as her first words set the tone of the interview to follow. 'Where's that bastard, Suarez? I'll slit his throat this time,' she screamed hysterically as she lunged from the chair.

'Oh! No you don't,' said Rutherford as he grabbed her wrists before pushing her forcibly back down into the vacated chair with a force that made it rock on its back legs before tipping her onto the floor where she landed with her legs in the air.

Twomay who was goggle-eyed at the exposure of Delores' skimpy black laced panties stuttered, 'I.. s..say old boy, one doesn't do that sort of..'

Rutherford cut him dead. 'Well just don't stand there – pick her up. And when you've done that get me the keys to Miss Rencoule's apartment.'

Taken aback at the sharp tone of Rutherford he stammered, 'Er, er, certainly. But I don't know where the keys are kept.' This he said as he extended a hand to Delores to help her up.

Once on her feet she re-took her seat to unravel her stocking gag and pull the black-seamed stocking on slowly lifting her skirt to connect it to the free dangling suspender. She then took her time adjusting her stockings to get her seams straight whilst all the time smiling seductively at Twomay who had resumed his lecherous ogling of her shapely legs. Had it not been for the seriousness of the situation Rutherford found himself in he would have burst out laughing at the antics of the old duffer. As it was he was about to bark at Twomay to get a bloody move on and do something about the keys when Delores came to his rescue.

'Thank you Francis...,' she coyly said to Twomay, '...I always knew you were a gentleman not like some I can mention, and just in case that ape...' she nodded in Rutherford's direction, '...tries any rough stuff on you the keys are in a cupboard beside the phone,' she finished, giving Rutherford a look of disdain. The look went unnoticed by Rutherford who was busy staring at Twomay who had gone ashen at Delores' familiarity.

Rutherford had no qualms about the way he was treating her. She had been genuinely hysterical, no doubt with good reason, and had recovered by using what came naturally to her – her sex appeal. However, he sensed her predicament was related in some way to Yvonne's disappearance and that answers from Delores were required fast – very fast. Enough time had been wasted. So as Twomay shuffled out into the hall to attend to the key for the upstairs apartment he drew up another chair, straddled it sitting back to front with his arms folded along the back rail and sat opposite Delores staring at her. She was one attractive lady, just oozing sex appeal. She stared back with fury still blazing from those fiery dark eyes. He found himself contemplating that had things not been as they were he might very well have been tempted to...however, getting a grip of his wanton thoughts he asked sympathetically,

'Now Delores, how long ago did this shocking thing happen to you?' Delores did not answer. He tried again, still no answer. He decided on a different approach. 'Do you like your upstairs neighbour, Miss Rencoule?'

A sullen, "Yes. Yvonne's nice," followed by an inquisitive, "Why?" and a "Who the fuck are you anyhow?

'I am a police officer. And in response to your question "Why" the answer is because she could be in grave danger. Now, you wouldn't like that on your conscience, would you?'

Shouting at the top of her voice she spat-out, 'What the fuck do you mean *my* conscience. It's *me* that's in danger. It's *me* that's been tied up. It's *me* that's been threatened. First by a psycho then by you, and all the while Yvonnes' no doubt at work.'

Unfazed by her outburst Scott calmly continued, 'How long ago were you threatened by this psycho?'

'Look, if I answer your questions will you let me go?'

'Yes. You haven't done anything wrong. I just need a few answers,' lied Rutherford.

'In that case, 'bout two, maybe three hours ago. Which reminds me, my arse isn't half getting numb sitting on this chair – a cushion would help. You wouldn't like to give me one?' she said with a knowing wink.

Ignoring the double entendre that she no doubt had used many times over when in custody, he snarled a reply to try to impress to her the gravity of the situation, 'My patience is running out. Was-the-psycho-that-did-this-to-you-Suarez?'

'No,' she replied adamantly as Twomay reentered the room and handed Yvonne's keys to Rutherford.

'Then why do you want to slit his throat?'

' 'Cos if it hadn't been for Suarez that nasty piece of shit wouldn't have done this to me.'

'So there was somebody else involved. A friend of Suarez?'

'His type, but I don't think so. It looked like it was his intention to kill us both. But Suarez told him something that stopped the man from killing us.'

'What was the name of this man?'

'Don't know but he was a German.....with a horribly badly burned face.'

'Could his name have been Hertzog?' Delore's shrugged her shoulders. Rutherford knew of a Nazi enforcer with a badly burned face from SIS(6) files by the name of Hertzog that he had had a run-in with in Berlin.

'Do you know him?'

'Only by reputation. He's a bad man Delores. A very bad man....evil. Now what did Suarez tell Hertzog that stopped him from killing you?'

'That figures. Bad's the only type Suarez associates with. Rutherford ignored her reply to ask if she had heard any of the deal they had struck. Delores told him that Suarez had told Hertzog he knew where a British agent was that had information about Gibraltar's defences. She was certain it was this that stopped the man from killing them.

When he heard this news regarding the involvement of a British agent, an excited Rutherford enquired, 'Male or female agent?' as he rose to have a quiet word in Twomay's ear. Twomay nodded then left the room.

'I think I heard a *she* mentioned. Look mister policeman, I've helped you, now how about letting me go because I don't want to file any complaint.'

'Just one more question Delores – where is this person being held?'

'I don't know. I think I heard the word "cemetery".'

'Thank you Delores. You have been most helpful. That wasn't so bad was it? Now if I can just ask you to sit there for a moment my colleague has stepped out to do a message for me.'

'Why?' she asked suspiciously. Rutherford didn't need to answer because as she was asking the question there was a tramp of boots in the hall and Twomay along with two Marines entered. Rutherford nodded his head towards Delores and the two Marines lifted her off her chair and frog marched her to a waiting van. She didn't go quietly. Each and every one within earshot had their parentage questioned, spiced up with every other known profanity.

Twomay asked on what charge he was to detain her. Rutherford suggested he should say that he was taking her into protective custody. He was to tell her that Hertzog, after he disposed of Suarez, would then try to kill her because she could recognize him. Rutherford was aware that Delores knew more than she was telling and wanted to interrogate her thoroughly, but only after he crucially attended to his main priority, finding Yvonne – alive. Throughout the discussion he was aware of an edginess in Twomay – it was as if he wanted to be elsewhere – and he had a good idea of the reason as he asked, 'How did Delores know your name? I didn't mention it in front of her.'

To Twomay's credit he did not try to lie his way out of the awkward question. 'Er, er,' he fumbled. 'With the wife dead these past two years, I, I....occasionally feel the urge for company. And yes, I have used the discreet services of Delores in the past. I can't see the problem.'

'Well, apart from the morality of screwing a work colleague's wife I have to inform you that because of your position you have put yourself in an invidious position by allowing yourself to be indicted for treason...'

'What utter tosh. Since when did a bit of "how's your father" become treasonable?'

'Let me explain. You are using the services of a prostitute...'

'She's not a prostitute, she's an escort....a high class escort.'

'Call her what you might. You, in your position as head of navy security, Gibraltar, are privy to navy secrets and are associating with a person whose pimp, this individual Suarez, is possibly involved in the attempted sabotage at the dockyard. How do you think that will look on your file when that is made public?'

'And what pray tell makes you so sure Delores and Suarez are involved in the sabotage? For god's sake man you've only just arrived. You have no proof. You secret service types are all the same. You make things up to suit yourselves. I would never disclose secrets to anybody.'

'Let's hope that's true. But more importantly let's hope for your sake that Delores is not part of the failed sabotage conspiracy....otherwise,' he left the veiled threat unfinished. 'Look, Francis, I believe you and will do what I can to help. Now, if I were you I would distance myself from Delores and...'

'I thought you said I was to tell her I was locking her up for her own safety plus Hertzog's threat...'

'Change of plan Francis. She gets told nothing. Let her sweat it out in the cells until I interrogate her. Give her only the basics, don't want her thinking she's in a luxury hotel, do we? Meanwhile, you do not, I repeat do *not,* make any attempt to communicate with her once she's locked up. I will come to your office once I've had a look around Miss Rencoule's apartment.

Twomay straightened his slumped shoulders and with head held high proudly retorted, 'Your views have been taken on board and will be carried out in ship-shape fashion....but personally I think your views are absolute *balderdash*. I bid you good day, sir.' He snapped a smart salute, about turned on one heel and stalked out of the room. Rutherford had the satisfaction of giving his back the finger.

As Rutherford followed Twomay to lock the front door he was suddenly aware of a small crowd gathered around a black van parked outside. Its thin sheet metal walls were being bashed, he assumed with her shoes, as at the same time a torrent of abuse flowed from within. He laughed to himself as he turned the front door key. Deep in thought, he hoped Twomay realised the seriousness of his situation. If Delores was convicted, the charge would be aiding a treasonable act – a hanging offence. And with Twomay being a head of security with secrets and associating with a proven terrorist...It didn't bear thinking about what decision any jury at the Old Bailey would return. He liked the old duffer but his only hope was Delores being non complicit in the plot.

After Rutherford turned the key in Delores' back door he took the stone steps two at a time upstairs to Yvonne's apartment. There was no sign of the front door having been tampered with as he entered into a small hall and switched on the light. The first room on the left turned out to be the bedroom. The bed was neatly made. The chest of drawers and double wardrobe showed no signs of disturbance. On the bedside cabinet sat an alarm clock which indicated it had been set for 10-00pm the previous evening. Why had she set the alarm for that time in the evening having worked, he was told by Twomay, until almost 6-00pm? He automatically looked at his watch: 10-05am. Delores had indicated during their discussion downstairs at around 9-50am that she had been bound to the chair for three hours. And being convinced that Yvonne was the *she* Delores had heard Suarez mention that meant Suarez and Hertzog still hadn't met her by 6-50am – meaning they had approximately a three hour head start on him. Not insurmountable. However, the critical thing was, where had she got to late evening / early morning? What was open? Bars? Night clubs? Drinking dens? But Gibraltar wasn't Soho. These were the confusing thoughts jumping around Rutherford's brain like a pinball when he happened upon a photograph in a silver frame on the other bedside cabinet of a handsome young man. He felt an unusual pang of jealousy. With no time to dwell on the matter he entered the main living room. It ran from the front to the back of the house and incorporated the kitchen and dining area. He started in the kitchen. There were no dirty plates in the sink. Nor any evidence of a meal having been eaten. Yvonne was one neat person he mused as he turned to survey what he took to be the lounge on the evidence of it having a fireplace, albeit inset with an electric fire. There was a comfortable looking if somewhat threadbare settee adjacent to the fireplace with a matching arm chair and a dining table with chairs. And the first signs of untidiness. Somebody had pulled one of the chairs away from the table and it lay at an awkward angle. The scene being out of keeping with the general appearance of the apartment he headed for the table and switched on a nearby standard lamp. On the table, the corners held in place with books, lay a copy of an ancient plan showing a primitive sewage system of Gibraltar dated 1815. Looking closely at the plan he found light pencil traces of a dotted line drawn to follow a route from the dockyard in the south to the Old Town outfall in the north. He assumed this to have been drawn by Yvonne. The clue being the pencil lying on top of one of the books. Along the dotted line's length there were three X's but no indication of their relevance. However, to the right of the line, the east, and local to the middle X she had printed and circled in pencil the word "Trafalgar?" He supposed it all meant something but it wasn't immediately forthcoming to him. As he was about to carry on his search elsewhere in the room his elbow accidentally knocked the book with the pencil on top to the ground. As he bent to pick them up he caught sight of the name of the book: "The Cemeteries of Gibraltar." It had bookmarks lodged between the pages. He took a seat at the table and opened the book at the first bookmark. The chapter gave the history of Saint Jago's cemetery. This had been one of the burial grounds for the early victims of the yellow fever epidemics and was long disused. In fact it was now an extension to Saint Jago's Royal Marine barracks. The second bookmarked page advised him that the South Port Ditch cemetery had been the main burial ground for the later epidemics of cholera and yellow fever until its closure in 1832. Shortly after the battle of Trafalgar in 1805 the cemetery changed its name to "Trafalgar" to commemorate the battle even though it held only two of the sailors killed in action. The remainder had been buried at sea and Admiral Nelson returned to London to be buried at Westminster Abbey. He noted the new name Trafalgar had been heavily underlined in pencil. There was, however, a plan of the cemetery on which the majority of the cemetery had been shaded lightly in red crayon leaving one area plain. To his delight he

reckoned he had found where Yvonne had spent her evenings/early mornings –
in the cemetery. To be specific – in the un-shaded north-east area and Delores
had, on reflection, thought she heard "cemetery" mentioned between Suarez
and Hertzog. But, for what was Yvonne looking? He checked the remainder of
the book for underlined words or passages that might give him a clue but found
none. Sensing he was on to something he locked-up and jogged back to his
hotel to get dressed for action.

He felt the adrenalin begin to flow. Twomay and Delores would need to wait.

CHAPTER 12

Anxious to set the next phase of his operation in motion Scott had returned to the hotel to dress suitably for what lay ahead and to pick up a few extras. He changed out of his suit and slipped into a black polo neck sweater and black fatigue trousers. He checked the mechanism thoroughly of his PPK automatic and slipped in a new magazine before sliding it into his underarm holster concealed inside a soft black leather Moroccan zipped jerkin. A final check on his additional accoutrements including a torch and a Swiss army-knife and he was on his way by foot.

As he scouted the perimeter railings of Trafalgar Cemetery he hoped that he had encrypted Yvonne's unintentional clues correctly. He recalled that it was the north-east corner of the cemetery that she had not as yet shaded on her plan. With time running out on Yvonne he trusted this was the area she had next intended to explore. He arrived at the cemetery's main gates to the south and proceeded to scout the boundary railings northwards until he came to a dead end at the Old Town wall. Over the railings at this point, he reckoned, was the unexplored area. The only trouble being that growing closely between the trees on the cemetery side were thorn bushes. However, to his advantage several branches overhung the railings. He chose a branch strong enough to take his weight that was hidden from the road by other overhanging branches. After looking around to make sure all was clear he effortlessly jumped up and caught the branch and with a hand-over-hand action manoeuvred along the branch over the railings and bushes into the tree. From this location within the foliage he found another branch that cleared the back of the dense bushes underneath and dropped with a flexed knee action to the ground where he lay motionless in the long grass. Whilst on his knees he checked for any signs of movement before he rose slowly to his feet with his PPK drawn. Apart from a cool breeze rustling through the long grass there was little sound. A glance at his watch showed it to be 11-05am. Hertzog and Suarez now had a four hour head start. A lot of evil could be achieved in four hours. He was beginning to worry for Yvonne's safety. After a few struggling steps through the long unkempt grass he joined a recently trampled path coming from the south and heading north east towards the Old Town wall. He followed the path which led him to a sarcophagus. The heavy stone lid of the sarcophagus was askew. Giving it closer scrutiny he found fresh fragments broken off the stone lid. He moved back a few paces, took a run at it and with palms meeting the edge of the burial chamber he in one fluid motion hoisted himself with a mid-air twist to sit on the lid just narrowly missing being impaled on the relief stone sword of a knight sculpture. By the late morning sun he looked into the burial chamber. He witnessed a black square hole that required further inspection so he lowered himself off the lid and hung by his fingertips before dropping on to a firm storage area alongside the hole. Kneeling he peered in to the abyss. Not wishing to use his torch for fear of warning anybody below he waited for his eyes to adjust. When his vision adjusted he ascertained it to be a brick built manhole with rusted iron access rungs built into the ancient brickwork. With the PPK returned to its holster he cautiously lowered his weight on to one of the rungs whilst holding the edge of the hole. It was then that he discovered a rope tied to the first rung dangling down into the depths. Looking down he could not see the bottom as he started his descent using the rope. When he reached the bottom he encountered a problem. He had to make a decision – to turn right or turn left. The manhole entered directly into a cross tunnel. With all his twisting and turning above ground level he had lost his usual good sense of direction. He could not afford the time to go the wrong way in the tunnel, so remembering the direction of the sun to be over his shoulder as he sat on the lid he related it to a location on the manhole wall with his torch. He then set the hour hand of his Omega divers' watch pointing at the spot on the wall and then bisected the angle between twelve o'clock and the hour hand. This gave him the north/south axis. He knew the dockyard to be south of the cemetery. He turned left. The tunnel being 150cm high he had to stoop his 180cm frame to suit. Silently he shuffled along the ancient brick tunnel, its crumbling mortar joints leaking water from the roof and walls that was seeping into his navy issue boots (compliments of HMS Eagle) at every step in the drainage channel. He kept the beam of the torch low in an endeavour not to draw attention to his presence from anybody ahead. After a short time he became aware of a very faint glimmer of daylight striking across the tunnel. As he was getting over this surprise he heard muffled, indistinct voices echoing along the tunnel towards him. With the PPK in one hand and the torch in the other he made his way to where the shaft of light struck the tunnel wall 450cm ahead. When he reached the source of the light – an opening off the tunnel – he cautiously peeped around the edge of the opening to observe from somewhere above in the enormous cathedral-type, brick-vaulted roof a dim natural light filtering down into the chamber, enough to show a huddle of people from which drifted English spoken but German accented words, *"Now place it near one of the bitch's nipples. We are about to play a little game of questions and honest answers regarding Gibraltar's future defences."*

Scott took a deep breath, switched on his torch and sent its powerful beam shooting towards the group. The beam picked out Suarez who he recognized from a photograph shown to him by Twomay. Suarez was kneeling beside Yvonne with a glowing hot tipped cigarette close to one of her naked breasts. The order had been given by Hertzog who he recognized from his SIS file. He was holding a Luger pistol aimed at Suarez.

Under normal circumstances on seeing Yvonne's predicament Scott would have shot Hertzog without hesitation but unfortunately Suarez was in the line of fire so he growled in anger, 'Put the gun down Hertzog.'

Yvonne took the opportunity as Hertzog fired a short burst of his Luger towards the torch beam to whisper to Suarez, 'Cut my wrists free with the knife you took from my coat pocket...'

A terrified Suarez hesitated but as Hertzog released another short burst of fire in the direction of the vanished torch light he plucked up enough courage to find the knife and wedge it between her wrist bonds. With a downward thrust he felt the bonds give. As they gave way he heard a yelp of pain from Yvonne. The yelp unsettled Suarez's delicate state of bravado to the extent that he dropped the knife.

After Scott had issued his warning to Hertzog he immediately withdrew from the opening and lay prone along the filthy wet floor. Hertzog, he knew would retaliate with a burst of fire aimed at his torchlight. As Hertzog's bullets whined overhead ricocheting off the brick walls Scott took aim and fired at the lick of flame given off from the barrel of Hertzog's machine pistol. He heard a cry, a German expletive and something strike the ground. With any luck it would be Hertzog's Luger. He switched the torch on in time to see Hertzog with blood pouring from an arm wound reach down and grab a weak Yvonne by the hair and pull her onto her feet where he, with his one good arm around her neck, held her as a human shield. The torchlight also showed Yvonne to be holding a knife as Hertzog tried to pull her into the wall shadows of the chamber. Scott noted that Yvonne held the knife in a stabbing hold. He waited in expectation as he allowed the torchlight to follow them. What transpired was worth the wait as his predicted expectation unfolded. Yvonne with tears streaming down her filthy face from having had her hair almost pulled out at the roots, weakly raised her unseen knife hand and plunged it with all the strength she could muster into Hertzog's thigh. He howled in rage, dropped her on the floor in a heap and darted further into the impenetrable darkness of the chamber. Scott also retired into the shadows to take stock of the situation. He had been aware in his peripheral vision of Suarez sneaking around the chamber perimeter heading for the exit into the tunnel. He would no doubt be well clear of the cemetery by now. He had a brave Yvonne lying on the floor, weak from lack of sleep due to the rats he could hear scurrying about and no doubt dehydrated but otherwise unharmed and was likely to remain so with Hertzog now being badly injured. But where was Hertzog's Luger machine pistol? He had heard it fall when he had hit him in the arm. A dangerous unknown. How best to flush him out? Remembering that the safety of Yvonne was of paramount importance, Scott was pondering a solution when his problem was in part resolved.

Hertzog's voice penetrated from the inky darkness of the shadows, 'We have no quarrel Englishman. I am only here to warn off Suarez from continuing his idiotic amateur sabotage attempts and demonstrations in Gibraltar against the British. Herr Hitler does not wish to antagonize the British government for he still hopes to have them as allies against the communists. So I was sent by Himmler to rid you of the nuisance Suarez.'

'If that is the case why were you about to torture the lady?'

'I was only trying to scare her – to get information.'

'For what reason?' persisted Scott feigning interest.

'You think she works for your British Intelligence. Oh! Yes, I know you are an SIS agent because I recognize you from Berlin and hold no grudge. But you should be aware she is a double agent – she works for the Russian NKVD.'

125

Yvonne struggled to prop herself up on an elbow to mutter something that came out too weak for Scott to understand. He took it to be a denial. She then collapsed in apparent exhaustion. Still feigning interest Scott replied, 'Funny enough, we have suspected the same about her and her associate Suarez for some time,' lied Rutherford.

'Suarez is an associate of her?' queried Hertzog.

'Yes. He too is a soviet spy. That's why we made him persona non grata in Gibraltar. Don't tell me you don't know that. Come out and we will discuss what to do about them for our mutual benefit.'

Hertzog had, in the shadows and whilst talking, painfully extracted the knife from his thigh and tucked it in his belt. All he needed was to get close to the interfering Englishman and the bitch lady that had crippled him and he would rip them both apart. What intrigued him was the ready acceptance of his lie about the bitch being a Russian agent and the fact that the British SIS were already suspicious of her. Not that it mattered. *He would kill them both, starting with the arrogant Englishman.* These were his thoughts as he stepped out of the shadows. Holding his thigh as blood seeped through his fingers he beckoned Scott to approach within striking distance of his knife as he said in a quivering voice, 'Please help me. I need hospital treatment before we discuss the fate of the traitors.'

'Sorry, Hertzog. I don't help scum that torture women.' Hertzog, suddenly realizing that all was not going to plan went for the knife in his belt. Practically before his hand had left his blood-soaked wounded thigh he was slumping to the floor with a neat hole drilled dead centre of his forehead. Scott returned his PPK to its holster, closed the dead Hertzog's eyes, removed the knife from his belt, frisked his jacket pocket to recover a wallet, torch and official papers then turned to face Yvonne.

The gun shot had revived her and she was now sitting up with Hertzog's dropped Luger machine pistol levelled at him. He threw his hands up in mock surrender as she in pseudo Russian snarled, 'So, meester Rutherford you av discovered my true identity. For thees you die. Do you av anytheeng to zay befores I pull ze trigger?'

'Yes. What part of Wales are you from, dearie?'

'Ha,ha. Very funny Rutherford – Now, what the hell took you so long?'

'The bus didn't turn up and I had...'

'Enough! Rutherford. Just get me away from here and these bloody rats.'

'First, let's get you respectable and a bit more comfortable before....' Scott's torch picked out a timber crate and on top of it a Beretta that he recognized as Yvonne's. He lifted her bodily to the crate and sat her gently down, then pocketed her gun. She covered her bare breasts with her grubby hands. He found her cardigan, blouse, wellingtons and coat. She buttoned up her cardigan and blouse while he put her raincoat around her shoulders and finished his sentence, '...Before I get you to a doctor....'

'You're not leaving me here alone with the rats. I – hate – rats,' she enunciated slowly but adamantly. 'And I don't need a doctor. I'm not an invalid. I just need a bath and a good sleep. And that's – *final*. And what's more I've found...foun...'

The strenuous effort of sitting and talking finally took its toll as Yvonne's head without warning sank into her chest leaving Scott the dilemma of getting her above ground. He ran through various permutations, all requiring super-human strength and fraught with danger due to the rusted iron rungs in the manhole. He decided that leaving her and going for help was his only choice. The rats he didn't think were a problem. They had enough to feast on with Hertzog. As he was making Yvonne comfortable on top of the timber crate he looked for the first time towards the source of the light coming from above. His torch picked out iron climbing rungs set into the brickwork leading to the light source. He thumped his forehead with the heel of his palm. It suddenly dawned on him what Yvonne's final words "I've found" meant. She had found the way into the dockyard. Arriving at the bottom of the rungs he discovered a dangling rope from above. He gave it a good pull. The hold was secure. With the aid of the rope he was on a ledge in seconds and facing a hole in the brickwork big enough to allow him entry. Around his feet lay collapsed brickwork from the outer skin of the brickwork. He eased himself through the hole. 60cm below was water; above, the ironwork frame of the quayside. And 600cm in front the battleship-grey stern of a ship. He worked his way along a horizontal steel tie beam until the edge of the quay was directly above him. He was looking for a means of getting aloft. He spotted the means 300cm away – a vertical steel ladder. Balanced on the top flange of a steel joist he made his way with small toe-to-heel steps to the ladder before starting to climb. His final step had just got his head above quay level when he encountered a bayoneted rifle in the hands of a Royal Marine motioning him upwards. By the time he had pulled himself up and on to his feet he had quite a reception committee around him. Being operational he did not carry identification. He would just have to assert his authority. He had started by demanding to see Twomay immediately when one of the Marines said that he had been on escort duty this morning arresting a female on this bloke's say so. Apparently he was Twomay's boss. That did the trick. Suddenly it was all action. Four Marines followed Scott below to Yvonne with ropes and a cradle whilst Twomay and a doctor were sent for. Forty five minutes later Yvonne, after strenuously resisting any attempts to have herself removed to hospital, was in her apartment probing Scott about Suarez. She was worried because he knew about the access to the dockyard. Not only that, he was also part of the team that had tried to sabotage HMS Worcester.

The name ringing a bell with Scott caused him to exclaim, 'HMS Worcester? Now there's a funny thing. Did you know that was also the name of the sixty four gun fighting ship-of-the-line some one hundred and fifty years ago that made a young Horatio Nelson aware of Gibraltar's sewage problems?' A blank look came over Yvonne's face as he continued, 'He complained to his uncle who was the Comptroller of the Navy, and who helped instigate more than likely the same sewage system you just found yourself in. Now, wasn't that of interest? Aren't you going to ask me how I knew all this....'

'You know something Scott?' she yawned, 'You can be very boring at times. I only asked you about Suarez – not about Admiral Nelson and his sewage.' Her head dropped onto her chest and light snoring started.

'If you're interested, it was your book about Gibraltar cemeteries that.....' He said his voice trailing off as he realized that Yvonne had fallen into an exhausted sleep.

CHAPTER 13

Suarez arrived at the top rung of the air-vent exhausted and mesmerized at the scenario that had been played-out below. He was thankful for the intervention of the anonymous Englishman but doubted if he was any match against the psycho Hertzog even with him having been stabbed in the leg by that gallant French lady. However, with none of it being his business any more, he beat a hasty withdrawal from the sarcophagus through the now well-trodden path towards the opening in the railings. As he fled, there were only two thoughts playing roundabouts in his brain: First – the need to get to his office floor safe in La Linea and withdraw the considerable amount of IRA money stashed there to enable him to flee to Argentina. And the second – How to get to La Linea? He no longer possessed the Auto Union. He added a third problem as he squeezed through the gap in the railings – his bloody handcuffs. It was daylight and he was persona non grata in Gibraltar. What to do? The police were on constant alert looking for him and his followers. His followers! Not all lived in mainland Spain – some were disgruntled locals wanting Gibraltar returned to Spain. One such being Father Jiminez of The Merciful Provider Catholic church. The church was but a two minute brisk walk away. He ran.

He had been hidden by the good father many times from the police, albeit only for public nuisance offences, usually disorder meetings outside the British Naval dockyard or before being made non persona gratis – the Governor's house. These protests being ostensibly under the guise of the Falange Party but mainly to suit his own agenda – that being the same as Father Jiminez – Brits out. Those were the days, he thought nostalgically, before he had got involved with that mad bastard Irishman. However, he was about to ask of Father Jiminez a favour he had never dared ask before – transport to La Linea. As he worked his way through the back alleys he formulated a plan. He always had a plan, unfortunately, this one would only work if it was a Sunday. Owing to his comings and goings between the cemetery and La Linea in the last few days he had lost all account of date and day. By the time he entered the church's lychgate he had figured it out to be a Sunday. Not only was it a Sunday it was the right time on Sunday. He knew this from the few parishioners that were leaving the church together. He could have kissed them all but instead took refuge in a bush until they passed. He had recognised one as a policeman. The reason for his glee was that that Father Jiminez preached alternate Sunday mornings between his main charge, The Merciful Provider, and a small country church in the hills surrounding La Linea. This was a regular Sunday occurrence at the border that allowed Father Jiminez unfettered passage. As the parishioners departed, Suarez entered the church. Due to the handcuffs he awkwardly lit a candle and crossed himself. This irreverence, from a devout heathen, one that even the good Lord would not touch with a barge pole, was overseen by Father Jiminez with a despairing shake of the head. What did this wayward child of God seek of him this time? He soon found out.

Before they left for his country diocese Father Jiminez prayed to the Almighty to forgive him his transgression for he could not resist the temptation of the money offered to repair the leaking church roof. As he made the sign of the cross he grimaced as his swollen thumb snagged in his cassock. The thumb gained by a wayward strike from a hammer aimed at a chisel whilst liberating Suarez from his shackles. Could this accident, he wondered, be a warning from the Almighty?

Father Jiminez crossed the border unfettered as usual with Suarez in the boot. As uncomfortable as the journey was Suarez was in a state of elation. He was free. His plan had been brilliant. He had been carrying Delores' share of her monthly IRA retainer when he had crossed the path of Hertzog. He knew it would be pointless offering Hertzog a bribe. The swine would have taken the money then killed them both. Fortunately, money had not come into his negotiations with Hertzog and because of that he had been able to offer Father Jiminez all of Delores' money to repair his roof. Well, not exactly all of it. On deliberation he had thought it unfair on Delores and had reduced the amount to half. Still a considerable sum. Still enough to repair the roof and for the good father to take a holiday in Rome. The fact that he had made up his mind not to see Delores again had not entered his financial deliberations.

With him running late for his country church sermon Father Jiminez, dreaming of his new roof and the possibility of seeing the Pope in Saint Peter's square, dropped Suarez on main street La Linea with a warning to behave; preaching the presence of God was everywhere. Suarez gave the departing car the finger. The good Father Jiminez would not be preaching such religious claptrap when he was seeking La Dolce Vita in Rome. Suarez then walked the short distance to his office whistling an Argentine tango.

The first thing he saw as he entered his office was a sheet of paper lying on his desk. It was from his secretary Estelle advising him that she awaited him in the Hotel Fontaine in Algecirus. Things were on the up at last he was thinking as he opened the door to his private office. He moved his heavy oak desk aside to expose the floor safe and dialled the opening combination with a chortle. The withdrawal of a leather bag containing his fortune was the last thing he remembered as a lead filled leather cosh descended on his head rendering him unconscious. As Suarez sagged face down onto the floor, a German accent with a hint of Irish growled, 'Take the thieving bastard back to Marbella, Dieter, and dump him in the dungeon. I'll deal with him later.'

CHAPTER 14

Scott was sitting in Yvonne's apartment with an open copy of Sir Walter Scott's "Ivanhoe" writing the first coded draft of his report for Sir James. The carriage clock on the mantelpiece showed 4-30 pm.   A lot had happened in the eighteen hours he had been in Gibraltar. He had found Yvonne who had on her own discovered how the dockyard security had been breached. All that was required now was for him to find Suarez. He was the key to discovering who the gang was that had attempted the dockyard sabotage. However, first and foremost was the need to check on Yvonne's health. Not wanting to be hospitalised and against medical advice of the dockyard's doctor Yvonne had insisted on returning to her apartment. However, a compromise had been reached; the doctor would call later in the day to see how she was faring.

With the late January day outside turning chilly as it tended to do with the onset of evening at that time of year, Scott rose and switched on the electric fire to make the room comfortable for Yvonne when she finally emerged from the bathroom. She had warned him that she intended to luxuriate in a bath until she felt she had been totally cleansed of vermin. That had been nearly two hours ago. Having virtually given up hope of seeing her again this evening he decided to make himself a coffee. As he strode towards the kitchen he heard movement. The sitting room door opened and she entered looking as beautiful as he had ever seen her. She was glowing radiantly clean, dressed in a white towelling bath robe and a similar belt tied at the waist. Her lustrous brunette hair was shining and bobbing evenly on her slender shoulders, as she glided to the settee in front of the fire. He asked if she wanted coffee. She replied that she did and that there was a bottle of brandy in one of the kitchen cupboards. Scott returned with two coffees liberally laced with brandy and sat opposite her in the arm chair. Her shapely legs were well tanned.

He enquired how she felt. The lovely infectious smile that broke out told him everything – she was back to her old self as she replied, 'Absolutely marvellous, thanks to you. You saved my life – my hero,' she giggled as she extended her hand over towards Scott.

He clutched her hand delicately in his and kissed it, replying as he got lost in her honey gold eyes, 'I know you would have done the same for me.'

The emotional French part of her answered, as she dabbed away a never before seen tear, 'Mais certainement, mon cherie, Scotty.' She apologised immediately for failing to keep her emotions under control and resorted to her usual brisk business tone, 'Have you contacted Sir James yet?'

Scott, whilst appreciating that she was still obviously suffering from her stressful ordeal was wondering how the French could make something as simple as, *"But, certainly, my dear, Scotty"*, sound so sexy as he replied, 'I was waiting until I had a few answers before contacting Sir James...like how did you get the knife? Answer only if you feel up to it,' he added sympathetically.

She nodded, then told him the story about getting Suarez to cut her wrists free with the knife he had picked from her raincoat pocket and her subsequent picking of it up off the ground where Suarez had dropped it when Hertzog had grabbed her by the hair. Scott congratulated her on her bravery of stabbing Hertzog in the thigh. She replied that it had been a lousy miss – she had intended to stab him in his genitals. Scott grimaced at the thought as she finished, 'I hope that answers your question, but before I start my debrief can I ask why you killed Hertzog? He was unarmed.'

'He was a nasty piece of work and if I had arrived five minutes later you would have found out just how nasty. However, I have to tell you...he *was* armed.' He stared at her whilst deciding whether to continue. To do so would be to make her look silly and he didn't want to inflict any more hurt on her than she had already suffered – but, as part of her "in the field" training she had to learn. So as gently as he could, he continued, 'I will put your failure of missing the obvious down to you not being quite yourself. To explain: when Hertzog stepped out of the shadows, the knife you stabbed into his right thigh was missing. He's right handed. You would have expected him to be holding his seeping wound with his right hand to stop the flow – wouldn't you?' Yvonne nodded, knowing what was coming next. 'But he was holding the wound with his left hand. Why?'

'To keep his right hand free to access the knife he had removed from his thigh with a view to killing you....and me,' she answered lamely.

'Exactly. Had I not killed him he would have tried to kill me and get you back to Berlin for interogation....so I had no qualms about killing him.'

Yvonne, with a tremble, was still able to visualize that glowing cigarette-end approaching her breast and realising the stupidity of her question sighed, 'Silly me. I'll try to be more observant in the future.'

Scott, not wishing to lecture her on her lack of "in-the-field" experience nodded his acceptance of her apology but hadn't finished, 'Now it's my turn to ask you a question.'

'Of course – I'm fine now.'

'What were you trying to tell me when you were lying on the ground. I take it you were trying to deny you were a Russian agent?'

'Firstly, I can assure you Scott that had he won his duel with you he most certainly would *not have* taken me back to Berlin. When your shot nicked Hertzog's arm, he dropped his Luger pistol. I then, after he grabbed me around the neck to act as a shield, stabbed him with my knife resulting in him dropping me to the ground. That's when I picked up his Luger. So what I was trying to tell you was to get out of the bloody way so that I could shoot the evil bastard.'

Scott was lost for words as he stammered, 'And you...you... had the cheek to ask me why I had...' He left it unfinished and roared with laughter.

Yvonne joined in the merriment but when it was finished she said, 'As I lay there summoning up my strength to shoot him I heard the two of you talking. I assumed from the exchange that your paths had crossed in Berlin. I was your liaison in Berlin and I don't remember anything regarding him,' she said looking at him suspiciously.

'You wouldn't have. It wasn't our operation. It was a Russian black op. The Gestapo had kidnapped me. The Ruskies fire-bombed Hertzog's car after they rescued me – thus his face scarring. The last I saw of the blazing car convinced me he was dead.'

'Why did the Gestapo kidnap you? And how in the name did you get involved with the Soviets? And why didn't I know?'

'Please don't ask me any more – OSA. (Official secrets act) For Sir James' eyes and ears only. Apart from which I don't want you repeating what I might tell you to your Soviet masters in the NKVD.'

'Oh! You,' she retorted faking a punch at him. 'But I do understand your OSA reluctance. Now, shall I start my debrief?' Scott nodded yes. 'It's a long story. It starts with me having read a book about the engineer Bazagette's upgrade of the sewers of London....'

'Boy, oh boy! That's a real page turner. Whatever made you read that crap – if you'll excuse the pun.'

'Ha. Ha..... As I was saying, I was obsessed by the notion that there was a secret entry into the docks. What better starting point than the old sewers. There were no plans of them in Gibraltar, so I went to London to visit the MOD to have a gander at what they had available. That was when you and I met at your landlady Jean's lodgings where we...well almost...er,' her embarrassment coming to the fore she hurried on much to Scott's amusement. Which reminded him he still hadn't got the up and over hood on his Lagonda repaired. 'Well the MOD's plans dated 1815 were but little more than a route plan. There were no details. There was even doubt if they had been completed as there were no archive records in London or Gibraltar. However, along its length there were three X's from the inlet to the outlet. No reason given as to what they were. So I then took myself off to the engineers' department at London County Council to enquire as to what these X's could be. The LCC engineer explained that they were more than likely fresh-air-vents or as they are apparently commonly referred to – stink pipes. If I could find the vents I was certain I would find a manhole down into the system – if there was one. Of two of the X's, one had an apartment block built over it. And the other, the one nearest the dockyard, had warehouses built over, which was disappointing. The third appeared to be in Trafalgar cemetery. I couldn't believe they would have one in a cemetery....it seemed sacrilegious.'

'Why not? The inhabitants aren't going to complain, are they?'

'That's not even remotely funny, Rutherford. However, that's when I acquired a copy of the Cemeteries of Gibraltar and started searching the graves late at night for signs of a "stink pipe".'

A chastened Scott asked,' What made you think of a sarcophagus?'

'I can only say in all due modesty – a flash of utter brilliance,' she laughed. 'Seriously though, why not? It would not be intrusive, nor sacrilegious. When I eventually found the sarcophagus after several abortive late night/early morning attempts, the lid had been disturbed. Somebody had beaten me to it. I clambered down and eventually found the discharge chamber. To my amazement it showed signs of a breakthrough into the dockyard. I retreated with the intention of getting help from Twomay. That was when the gang, including Suarez, caught me. One of them clubbed me from behind. I came to with wrists and ankles tied just as they were fleeing the chamber. One of them shouted for Suarez to kill me. He didn't. He gave them time to clear the chamber then followed shouting over his shoulder to me that he would tell security where I was.'

'If you believed that, Yvonne, you'll believe anything. That secret was his pension. As long as he knew the secret he could sell it to the highest bidder.'

'But what about the rest of the gang? *They* know.'

'They, too, will be after him to keep him quiet. A popular man our Suarez is turning out to be.'

'That's as maybe, but I believed him about me being rescued. It helped ease my mind off the nightmare of having to stay awake because of the rats....,' she shuddered, '...and the bone chilling dampness. Then the next day I thought my salvation had showed up – Suarez reappeared with Hertzog, only to discover...well, you know the rest.'

'You weren't Hertzog's intended victim. You were valuable to him. No doubt Suarez had told him you were an important SIS agent, and he was using you in the vain hope that by leading Hertzog to you it would save his own life.'

'It did in a round-about way. But what was the connection between them?'

'Ah! The connection? Well, when Hertzog was trying to do a deal with me he claimed that he had been sent by the Gestapo to rein Suarez in for upsetting HMG with his futile Gibraltar demonstrations. And from papers I removed from Hertzog's wallet, signed by Heydrich no less, they proved he was telling the truth. However, we have digressed. Please continue.'

'All I can add is that I have my suspicions about Curran.'

'Why?'

'Well, he asked me if there had been a limpet mine attack on one of our ships in the dockyard. He claimed his interest to be that of a custom's officer. However, as you know, very few of us are security vetted to know about limpet mines – and he certainly isn't one. Plus he always seems to be on duty when Suarez is having his demonstrations at the border. So I've asked Twomay to send one of his security officers to locate Suarez.'

'Good for you, Yvonne. We'll need to check if Twomay's man was successful. Anything more?'

'Finito. That's my unfortunate tale of woe. Haven't exactly covered myself in glory, have I?' Yvonne sighed sadly.

'I certainly wouldn't say that. You found the entrance into the sarcophagus – a brilliant piece of work I might add – and found the saboteurs' entry into the dockyard. That by my reckoning is first class work.'

'But had you not found me my secret would have died with me and left Suarez and gang to run amok. For saving me I shall be for ever in your debt.'

'Think nothing of it Yvonne. Believe me, you will get your chance to reciprocate. It happens to all us agents at some time or other...if we live long enough.'

'I'm sure it does but that doesn't stop me from personally thanking you. Anyway, that's enough about me. How did you find me?'

Scott then went on to relate the tale about studying her ancient sewage plan and the discovery of the book on Gibraltar cemeteries that he had accidentally knocked to the floor and the working out of her shading sequence in the chapter about Trafalgar Cemetery. The following of the well-trampled path to the sarcophagus and the climb down into the tunnels.

When he finished she clapped her hands and congratulated him on his detective work and asked what he intended to do about Suarez.

'If I was him I would be making passage to South America. And I happen to know the next merchantman leaving Algecirus is on Tuesday. This being Sunday gives me two days to find the blighter.'

'Where will you start?'

Arms stretching upwards he yawned, 'It depends if Twomay's man has found Suarez. '

With an outstretched hand Yvonne beckoned Scott over to join her on the settee. 'I have an idea also,' she whispered in his ear as she pushed him onto his back as the loosely tied belt of her bath robe came loose. Scott had got as far as unbuckling his belt when the doorbell rang and a voice shouted – "Doctor."

After the doctor had examined Yvonne and given her the all-clear Scott saw him off the premises. At the door the doctor informed him that he had given her two very strong sleeping tablets advising him that they should take effect fairly quickly and that he had ordered her to go to bed and rest. Hoping to rekindle her lustful approach that had been in full bloom before the doctor's arrival he rushed back into the living room only to find Yvonne sound asleep. He shook his head in utter disbelief as he lifted her bodily and carried her to the bedroom. To the accompaniment of gentle snoring he returned to the table to finish his report to Sir James.

Damn! He had forgotten to ask her about the gentleman in the photograph on her bedside cabinet.

CHAPTER 15

His report to Sir James satisfactorily completed, Scott set off on Yvonne's bicycle for the dockyard leaving her still sound asleep. He showed his warrant card to the Marine guard on the gate and was admitted. With his only previous visit to the dockyard being his early afternoon sojourn via the sewage chamber to get help for Yvonne he had to ask for directions to both Miss Rencoule's and the signals office. On his way he noted the sign for the guardhouse where Delores languished. At the signals office he gave the duty wireless operator his code name William Willis. The operator checked his list found the ersatz name and had him sign-in. Time 9-05pm. He then posted his encrypted report for Sir James to be sent to London. Being aware that his priority now lay with finding Suarez to discover who the culprits were that had threatened the life of Yvonne and the unsuccessful destruction of HMS Wocester he realized that the helpful information he sought from La Spietza would now have to be, unfortunately, by phone; so on arrival at Yvonne's office he unlocked the door and made for the phone. When the operator answered he asked for Captain Enzo de Rossi at the Italian Naval base in Spetzia, on the off chance that he would be in work. A glance at his watch showed: 9-10pm, highly unlikely. He was put through to somebody but not Captain de Rossi. The person he spoke to was an aide of de Rossi and remembered Scott from his time at the rebreather diving course he had attended in Spietza six months previously. The aide regretted the Captain was not on duty but he knew he would be delighted to hear from the Signor again. He gave Scott a number that Captain de Rossi could be contacted on. Scott placed the call with the operator. Whilst he waited for the connection he recalled his time at the rebreather diving course in Spetzia. The captain and he had become good friends. But he had become a better friend of his secretary Gina. He was giving pleasant thought to the last time Gina and he were together in Genoa, when the phone rang.

Captain Enzo's English was good but Scott's Italian was better so feeling that he would get more information if the conversation was conducted in Enzo's native tongue – they spoke Italian. After the usual opening niceties regarding health and family the captain asked what he could do for Scott. Scott enquired amiably if Enzo had lost any limpet mines recently. He received a very guarded and suspicious, "Possibly". Scott of course realized this was a sensitive question and to receive answers he would have to do a trade-off. He hoped to limit his intelligence output by informing his friend that he had possible information about the stolen mines. It was agreed, on an oath sworn on their respective mothers' lives that their conversation would go no further than between themselves. Scott was made privy to the fact that the Italian Navy, on night trials off the coast of Sardinia had had limpet mines, detonators, timers and a Maiale – a manned torpedo – stolen two weeks ago. His friend would also welcome any news regarding the Maiale. Scott regretted he could not help regarding the Maiale but that limpet mines, with "manufactured in Italy" stamped on them, had been used on a failed attack on one of HMG's warships in Gibraltar. The captain had laughed, the laughter implying that once they exploded who was to know where they were manufactured. After apologizing for his flippancy on such a serious matter Enzo explained his reason. The Gibraltar sabotage failure was no doubt because the culprits had used their stolen timers – their own sea trials of these timers had failed and were on board the Maiale when it too had been stolen. To Scott this suggested that if he could apprehend the culprits he would also capture the Maiale which was on the War Office list of enemy secret weapons requiring further authentication. Scott further noted that they too were having problems with the timers. While Britain lagged behind in manufacture of limpets they had solved the problem of the timer. It had been solved with the use of aniseed balls. They had been proved the best solution to resist the acid used to detonate the mine. The more aniseed balls used the longer the diver planting the mine had to get clear. This, of course, he could not divulge to his friend. When asked how the Maiale had been stolen, Scott was told that that was classified information. Scott took that to mean – Enzo hadn't a clue how the Maiale went missing. Scott thanked his friend for his helpful information and told him he was on the trail of the culprits and would keep in touch. Enzo thanked him profusely for any help offered and ended begging him to come to Genoa soon so that his secretary Gina would stop nagging him constantly of news about him. Scott heard a sleepy Italian female voice in the background begging Enzo to come back to bed. He did not recognize it as Enzo's wife's voice. She, of course, being Italian spoke Italian but the sleepy voice summoning Enzo back to bed also spoke Italian but with a *Scandinavian* accent. Knowing each-others peccadilloes they bade each other a laughing bueno sera. Scott was fascinated to find that the Italian Navy had already been sea trialling manned torpedoes – all told a very worthwhile telephone call even though his now aborted visit to Genoa would have been more to his liking.

Scott, formerly of Royal Marines Special Operations, having eaten nothing since breakfast at his hotel, decided to use his still active officer's rank of captain to eat in the officers' mess before they closed and before going forward to the next stage of his operation. As he was standing at the bar ordering, the familiar voice of Twomay joined him and said in its aristocratic tone, 'Do let me get you that, old boy. And, the usual for me, Edward.' The latter reference being to the barman who dispensed a large Glenfiddich malt to Scott and a similar measure of pink gin and tonic to Twomay. Scott offered Twomay one of the Senior Service cigarettes that Twomay had already given him. They lit up and adjourned to a table. This arrangement suited Scott as he needed a favour from Twomay. They opened their discussion with Twomay proposing a toast to the very brave and gallant Miss Rencoule, may she recover soon, to which they clinked glasses. Twomay then asked if he could join Scott for dinner. Scott, not an advocate of dining alone, agreed – not that Twomay would have been his ideal choice of companion but with the favours he was about to ask he thought it prudent to say he was delighted. The meal itself, considering the hour, was pleasant enough British fare of steak and kidney pie, potatoes and veg, but unfortunately, Scott had to suffer reliving Twomay's part in the war. Based on his intimate knowledge of having lived in Hamburg before the war, Twomay was convinced that the dastardly Germans were responsible for the dockyard sabotage attempt – especially the one passing himself off as a Czech working on the new reservoir. He had warned Miss Rencoule about him. Scott on the verge of nodding off, finally after a mind-numbing thirty minutes had had enough. He looked at his watch, interrupted, and asked his favours. First: he required a motorcycle to contact an old friend (Suarez) who he knew (actually suspected) to be in Algecirus. Twomay, an apparently keen motor cyclist, and still in fear of Rutherford disclosing his dalliances with Delores, agreed to let him have his 500cc Triumph. Secondly, he wished access to Delores. Twomay replied that being senior dockyard security Scott didn't need his authorisation. Scott knew this to be the case but had not wished to undermine the old duffer's authority. Apart from which it saved a lot of explanations to the various jailers he was likely to meet. Twomay on hearing of Scott's intended visit to Delores asked, a little too keenly for Scott's liking, if he was required. Scott thanked the lecherous old sod for his offer but said it was best he attended to the matter himself. As they rose to leave Twomay said he would get the Triumph out of the garage and that it and the keys would be at the gatehouse by the time Scott was finished with Mrs Curran. Twomay then introduced him to the duty officer of the guard who, once he had established Scott was there to meet the "woman from hell", took him to her cell with the warning that she was extremely abusive with language that would make the hair on a bald man's head curl. It was nice to hear that Marines' jokes hadn't improved any since he had left the service.

The interrogation that he was about to execute should, on reflection, really have been handled by Yvonne but due to expediency being the order of the day and her unfortunate incapacity, he had had little choice but to do it himself. A large part of his training had been devoted to interrogation techniques from the subtle to the physical. Unfortunately, they had concentrated on the male gender. So, whilst he looked forward to meeting Delores once again, he had no idea how he was going to handle her. However, the decision was made for him for as his Marine escort unlocked the cell door Delores leapt off her bunk towards Scott aiming her long finger nails at his face with the intent of doing harm. He easily evaded her lunge, caught a wrist, twirled her around and with a sense of déjà vu flung her back onto the bunk. The Marine escort moved smartly to handcuff her wrists behind her back. Scott nodded thanks and signalled him to leave, waited for the corridor door to close, leaving them alone.

'Well, that's him out the way. What do you have in mind next, big man – a quick fuck? Now's your chance with my hands tied.'

Scott stood back with arms folded ignoring her taunt before sighing, 'You can play it tough or otherwise, Delores. The decision's yours. If I was you I would cooperate. Now what was that all about?'

Still taunting him she said coyly, 'Surely you know what a fuck is?'

He thought to say: "the last time I heard it was ten bob" but didn't and instead sternly replied, 'You know what I mean – that stupid attack on me.'

'What that was all about was *you*.... *you* bastard. You told me you would let me go when I answered one more question. Well that was hours ago. So what's the question again?'

'Where's Suarez?'

'How the fuck should I know? I told you already, I want to slit the little bastard's throat.'

'Alright,' he sighed. 'The time for niceties are over, Delores. I will ask you for the last time. Where – is – Suarez?'

'What's so suddenly important about a weasel like Suarez?'

'He knows who the gang are. And where they are. So what's your answer?'

Her eyes blazing she spat out venomously, 'Go screw yourself, cop.'

Getting nowhere fast with pleasantness an out of character Scott forced himself to take a step forward and back handed her across the mouth drawing blood from a lip, growling, 'Keep your filthy trap shut – whore.'

Her pride hurt, as well as her cut and bleeding lip, she retaliated, 'I'm not a whore. I'm a high class escort if you must know. And since you appear to like a bit of rough it'll cost you extra.'

Whilst he admired her gutsy replies Scott decided to change tack again. 'Listen, Delores. I got no pleasure out of hitting you. If I wanted to I could do you real harm but...'

'Go pull the other one – you're a fucking bully. I know your sort. You wouldn't try it on with a man – a real man....bastard.'

'As I was about to say, I get no pleasure from hitting you when I can get *real* pleasure from seeing you *hang* – for treason.'

'Hang? It was me that was trussed up like a chicken for roasting and...'

'You still don't get it Delores, do you? This isn't about you being tied up by Hertzog – this is about you being an accessory to a treasonable act against the Crown...the attempted sabotage of one of His Majesty's ships and that's a a hanging offence.'

'What *the fuck* are you talking about – are you mad? What sabotage?

Ignoring her plea Scott lied, 'Sorry Delores, I've ran out of ideas to get you to tell me where Suarez is, so all I can do now is arrange for your deportation.'

'You can't deport me – I'm a Gibraltarian. *A British subject.*'

'And as such entitled to a fair trial at the Old Bailey in London,' agreed Scott as he doubted if she knew what or where the Old Bailey was.

However, the word "deported" had acted like magic as she calmed down and nervously said, 'You're not a dockyard cop. So who are you?'

Scott noticing the absence of her vitriol replied, 'I'm the guy that holds your future in my hands. So I will ask you again, where's Suarez? You owe him nothing. He's landed you right in it.'

He's too handsome to be as he is – an evil bastard. But given different circumstances I wouldn't mind giving him a shot on the swings were Delores thoughts on Scott as she came to the same conclusion as him – that that rat Suarez wasn't worthy of her. So why should she resist this guy? She was just talking her way to the gallows. Having convinced herself that that was the case she said with a heavy sigh, 'Honestly, on my mother's grave I don't know where he is, nor do I want to. You're right I owe him nothing. As far as I'm concerned I didn't do nothing seriously wrong. I thought they were only smuggling booze and cigs big time across the border and that's why they were using a horsebox – and I certainly didn't know Suarez was into the heavy stuff....and...and I didn't mean all those nasty things I said about you. I was angry, shouldn't have been, for after all you're only trying to do your job...and you're really a nice man,' she finished, fluttering her heavily-laden mascaraed eyelashes.

Wanting to laugh at her dreadful acting but knowing it would set her off again he said in a grave tone, 'Smuggling is also a crime and a hanging offence if its explosives that are being smuggled.' Not waiting for an answer from a dumbfounded Delores at that bad news Scott said, 'You've met the gang – who are they?'

'There's three of them. I don't know their names but I think they're all

Germans. One of them is built like a brick-built shithouse.'

'And, of course, Suarez too,' added Scott. Delores nodded her acceptance of the fact. 'What part did he have you play?'

'I was the landlady, cook and general dog's body.'

'Did Suarez stay with you?'

'Yes.'

'What did Curran have to say about his wife sleeping with another man?'

'Upset. But he knew the marriage was a sham. He also knew they just wanted him so they could cross the border unhindered when he was on duty.

'Was Curran being blackmailed or.....'

'No. It was his idea of revenge. *You British* had murdered his parents somewhere in Ireland, in something called the....the Easter uprising.'

Not wishing to break her tranquil mood by reminding her that she had claimed British citizenship to stop her deportation a few moments previously he hoped to throw her with a complete change of subject by asking, 'What do you know about limpet mines and torpedoes?'

The gormless blank look accompanied by an ignorant, 'Eh! What's them?' told him what he wanted to know, so he reverted back to his original questioning. 'This horsebox they used....what can you tell me about it?'

'It was big and painted green and...,' With a furrowed brow she slipped into deep thought before saying, '...and I think it had gold lettering on the side...'

'What lettering?' encouraged an excited Scott. 'Think Delores...think.'

'Er, er.....Yes it was...no...not that, mmm.' Silence while she grappled with her thoughts, before saying, 'I think it said – "Marbella Racing."'

'Are you sure?' She nodded her head. Forgetting himself in his excitement he said, 'I could kiss you Delores.' *That would get us off to a nice start* thought Delores as Scott went to the door and banged on it to attract the duty guard.

'Will I get deported and hanged?' she asked anxiously.

'I shouldn't think so. Lots of mitigating circumstances.'

'Mitigating? Is that good?' Scott nodded. 'Good. Can I go home now?'

'Manyana.' The door opened. 'Sorry about the lip Delores – got to go.'

As the cell door closed Delores bawled, 'You promised to let me go you fuc…….' The corridor door closed to cut off her cursing.

'She has a way with words,' commented the Marine guard.

'Personally, I blame her finishing school.'

'That means most of the women attached to this base went to the same school.'

Scott laughed and said, 'I couldn't really pass comment on such a chauvinistic point of view. Now would you please contact Commander Twomay and arrange for him to arrest Mr Stephen Curran immediately. He's bound to ask, so tell him the charge is treason and I will make contact with him tomorrow. And arrange for a medic to bathe her lip.'

The surprised Marine snapped a saluted, 'Yes Sir. Will notify Commander Twomay immediately, sir.' When the guard's saluting hand fell to his side he said out the corner of his mouth, 'But I'm afraid I'll need to ask for volunteers to carry out your medic order, sir.'

Still laughing as he approached the gatehouse Scott was met by a Marine who handed him the key to the Triumph. He kick started the engine. A touch of accelerator and it growled to his liking. With the security barrier raised he let the clutch engage and less than two minutes later he was setting the Triumph on its parking stand outside Yvonne's apartment. He glanced at his watch. Just gone midnight. It had been a very full day with his physical rescue of Yvonne from Hertzog and his two mind-draining interrogations of Delores he was beginning to feel the oncoming of exhaustion creep over him. To save the embarrassment of Yvonne's mind making promises his body couldn't keep he hoped, as he opened the apartment door, that she was still asleep.

CHAPTER 16

Gibraltar Town

Wolfgang Müeller was finishing the last mouthful of crispy bacon at a café on Main street. He had had breakfast there every morning for the past month before going to work as an explosives consultant for the London civil engineering company awarded the reservoir contract in "The Rock". The job had been fortuitously advertised in the Civil Engineer and having previously worked for them in Africa it only took a phone call to secure the position. But today was his last day. His forged papers showed him to be a Czech mining engineer specialising in controlled detonations. The London civil engineer had declared him to be the ideal man to supervise the setting of the explosives in the tricky, soft, hard-to-manage limestone of "The Rock". Being a foreigner he was vetted by the MOD and found to be a suitable applicant. On site, once he had given permission for detonation, his job for the day was over. This allowed him time to attend to his main agenda – the finding of his nemesis, the elusive Jerry Hill.

Having spent the four week period of his contract looking, asking and getting nowhere he had decided he had had enough. He had either been given wrong information regarding Hill's whereabouts or Hill had been and gone from Gibraltar by the time he had arrived. Downing his coffee he was about to ask for his bill when the café's doorbell tinkled as it opened and in walked somebody from his past. Their eyes met.

The newcomer's eyes lit up as he dashed forward to bear hug the rising Müeller and thump him heartily on the back. The six foot plus red haired giant's voice boomed out in German, 'Commander, it is so good to see you again.'

Müeller looked around surreptitiously to see if anybody had paid attention to the outburst. Fortunately, the main breakfast rush was over and there were only a handful of customers left with their heads stuck inside the morning papers. 'Sh!' said Mueller with his finger to his lips, 'Speak English. I too am delighted to see you. You're looking well Karl. Were you treated well in jail?'

'People, if they have any sense, tend not to pick a quarrel with me,' he chortled. 'However, I heard you were in a spot of bother yourself with Himmler. So what brings you to Gibraltar?'

'I am looking for the man that caused my "spot of bother' he retorted sharply as the neck tic went into convulsive overdrive. His hand dived into an inside pocket of his jacket to produce a photograph of the man he knew as Jerry Hill, that he had stolen from the swimming pool wall of the luxury country club Cantravel based in Tenerife. 'Have you seen him around?'

Karl studied the photograph closely and then shook his head. 'Sorry Wolf.' Karl had been number two in Müeller's elite Kreigsmarine Kommando underwater explosives team until his court-martial for punching an officer that Müeller reckoned needed punching, but who, unfortunately, had been a member of the Nazi party, and worse, a relative of Himmler. Müeller had borne character witness for Karl but in a Nazi-rigged court stood no chance of acquittal. Karl got two years and dismissed service.

'Thank you Karl,' said Müeller as he took his photograph from Karl and returned it to his pocket. 'I am of the opinion that he is no longer in Gibraltar as I was led to believe.'

'And who led you to believe this?'

'Himmler. Well, not exactly. Let's say he pointed me in the right direction.' Müeller, trusting his former number two implicitly, explained fully his situation.

Karl, after giving what he had heard considerable thought whilst biting his bottom lip finally said, 'You do realise what Himmler has done to you, Wolf? He's on a winner, as usual, and you my dear Commander are on a loser...'

'I'm afraid you will need to explain that Karl.'

'If you find this Englishman Hill – Himmler will get the credit from that raving lunatic Hitler for finding the killer of his mistress Colonel vonReus. But should you fail he will have you terminated and tell Hitler you found the killer but both of you plunged to your deaths off a cliff...or some such story he will fabricate. Either way, Himmler's found his scapegoat – you. The outcome? No pressure on Himmler any more from Hitler to find the killer of his mistress – von Reus.'

There was a prolonged silence as Müeller pondered Karl's summary of his predicament before he, with hand to head, groaned, 'I suspected he was up to something. What a fool I've been Karl – I've been so given to seeking revenge on Hill that I couldn't see what that plausible bastard Himmler was up to.'

'No shame Wolf. Himmler's an expert at using people.'

'How do you know so much about Himmler?'

'You mean apart from whacking that Nazi officer who happened to be his brother in law? Tell you later once I've asked you a few questions.'

'Please carry on.'

'What of your lovely wife, Giselle?'

'Left me. Couldn't stand the shame of my demotion.'

'No loyalty. Can't tolerate that. You're better off without her....So you have basically no reason to go home...'

'Especially not now that I am leaving Gibraltar without finding Hill. Why, do you have something in mind?'

'Possibly. However, the one thing you must not do is go home. Himmler will have you assassinated the minute you arrive. You do understand that?'

'That's as maybe. But I still want revenge on this man Hill. It's just I don't know my next best move to find him.'

'Right. I think I can help you. What I have to offer may be of interest. After explaining his plan he finished, 'So, you can do your patriotic duty to the Fatherland – stand with us officers against that megalomaniac Hitler and at the same time we can help you to find this Hill person.' Karl watched with interest his old boss's brain at work as he assessed the offer. He had made his pitch and now awaited the outcome. The acceptance was of vital importance to his immediate plans.

After what appeared to be an eternity to Karl, Müeller said, 'The offer sounds good to me but has the similar ring to it as Himmler's offer.' The unexpected reply over he met and held Karl's stare.

'I can assure you, *my Commander,* that my offer is based on your past help in trying to prove my innocence regards striking that Nazi swine. You placed your commission on the line for me. I have never forgotten that nor will I ever. Loyalty, Wolf. Loyalty. That's what we of the Kreigsmarine brotherhood expect of each other.' He gave the sign of the dagger stab to his hand.

'I do apologise Karl. I meant no offence. It's just, it's just so sudden. I mean – who are you working for? What are you doing?'

'Still the cautious deep thinker, eh! Wolf? I am security to a Marbella business man.'

'Security covers many aspects Karl. Are you a bodyguard? Or do you install house alarms or...'

Knowing that his old boss was devoid of a sense of humour Karl laughed at his unintentional attempt. 'I don't have to tell you Wolf that what I am about to divulge must go no further than ourselves.'

Müller nodded and laid his hand palm down on the table. Karl followed with his on top. Müeller thrust an imaginary dagger through the hands. Karl repeated the thrust. They withdrew their imaginary daggers and looked around for any witnesses to the ritual. Fortunately, there was still no interest being shown in them. They had just carried out the bonded silence of a Kreigsmarine officer. The equivalent of the Mafia's Omerta oath. The imaginary death dagger used being the insignia badge of Müeller's former command, Kreigsmarine Special Unit Kommandos. Trained killers to a man.

Karl nodded his head in satisfaction as they removed their hands from the table and said, 'As I was saying, he is a businessman – a mercenary. Let's call him "Mr X". Everybody thinks he is Irish, which suits him, but he is German. Born Berlin. Why the confusion of his nationality? I will tell you. Straight from university he was recruited into Kreigsmarine intelligence. He was given his first solo mission, aged twenty five, in 1916. We, as you know, were at war with the British as were a faction of the Irish seeking independence for Ireland. In short, an Irishman in Washington by the name of Casement approached our American Ambassador to suggest that our government release those Irish prisoners of war forced to fight for the British, but sympathetic to the Irish cause of freedom, to form a brigade in Ireland to fight the Brits. This was not acceptable to the Reichstag for the obvious reason that all Irish prisoners would claim to be fighting for Irish independence. However, they did agree to offer help in the way of armaments to Casement's volunteers. "Mr X" was put in charge of this operation. We had confiscated a British merchant ship in the Keil canal at the beginning of the war. "Mr X" noticed it bore a remarkable resemblance to the Norwegian freighter, Aud, and had it painted to look like the Norwegian ship. Casement and two other Irishmen were in Lubek, on the Baltic, to witness the loading of the cargo, ostensibly timber, but in fact was twenty thousand rifles, machine guns, explosives, etcetera, etcetera, bound for County Kerry on Ireland's west coast. Casement and his colleagues joined "Mr X" aboard U-boat 19, which had been given instructions by Berlin to land "Mr X" in Ireland. They were to be landed at Bana Sound in Tralee Bay. "Mr X" was to go ashore with Casement and use Casement's contacts to infiltrate the volunteers under the guise of teaching them how to use the cargo's various weapons. Berlin's idea being that come the defeat of the British and with the intelligence gained through "Mr X" of the Irish insurgent movement they would gain total control of Ireland. Britain's United Kingdom would no longer be united and the Irish – out of the frying pan into the fire.'

Müeller, uncharacteristically, burst out laughing. You couldn't make this up, he thought. Between "Mr X" and the Reichstag they had well and truly stitched-up the poor old Irish and the perfidious British. 'Do please continue Karl,' finished an enthralled Müeller.

'During the voyage Casement disclosed to "Mr X" the names of his contacts should they be separated. Unfortunately for the operation our Ambassador in America, von Bernstoff, had had his messages intercepted by British intelligence so they knew of the operation. A waiting British navy destroyer intercepted the Aug and escorted it into Tralee harbour where the captain scuttled the ship. Meanwhile the U-boat landed "Mr X" and Casement at Bana Sound to be met by members of the volunteers – but weren't.'

'Why not?' enquired an agog Müeller.

'Because they arrived a day early. "Mr X" and Casement then hoofed it the seven miles over sand dunes to Tralee where the Aug was to berth just in time to see it sink into the depths of the harbour with the British destroyer in attendance. The area was awash with British soldiers. "Mr X" gave the order to split up. Casement was later arrested. "Mr X" eluded capture and with the names Casement had given him he made the contacts in Dublin and as instructed he helped the volunteers which later became the Irish Republican Army – the IRA. Completely adopting the insurgent way of life he emerged as a commander in the IRA, complete with Irish accented English. He knew everything there was to know about the IRA, after all he had set most of it up. When the war ended, his knowledge of the IRA meant nothing to a defeated Germany. He was recalled to Berlin to set up an elite core of Kommandos loyal to the Kaiser who was having trouble with an Austrian upstart by the name of Adolf Hitler.'

'If he was a Kreigsmarine Kommando why don't I know of him?'

'You do. You were his commander.'

'Never! I knew all my men by name and their background.'

'His background had been well doctored by naval intelligence. You could be forgiven for not knowing the truth. His name I will tell you later. When he was recalled to Berlin he claimed he was homesick. The Irish accepted this excuse, for after all wasn't that what he had been helping them to do – get back *their* homeland. But he still does work for the IRA. They had recently used an idiot named Suarez to find a way into the naval dockyard in Gibraltar. Suarez was doing nothing other than spending their money on the good life. They then commissioned "Mr X" to sort out the situation. By some miracle Suarez found an entry into the dockyard. I have to assume that "Mr X's" threat of removing his balls might have helped. However, the attempted sabotage was a failure, but "Mr X" was still paid a handsome retainer. Ever the patriot he notified Kreismarine intelligence of the dockyard finding. It was of no interest, the Brits would find it eventually. But they told him of a bigger prize that should he undertake and implicate the IRA he would be paid a king's ransom.

'A fascinating story. Your employer is certainly somebody to admire...if you like mercenaries. But how does it affect me?'

He needs an explosives expert. You are one. He needs a sea going captain.

You are one. Working for him you will never need to worry about money again.'

'What do I have to be captain of?'

'Ah! Good. I have aroused your interest.' He stood up. 'Come. Follow me and I will show you. Do you have your passport?' Müeller nodded yes.

As they departed the café a motor cycle had drawn up to the kerbside. The couple wore leather padded helmets and goggles. The driver turned to his pillion passenger and appeared to help unfasten a chin strap. They nodded their good mornings to the passenger and disappeared up the side road next to the café leading to where Karl had parked his Buick convertible. As they walked Müeller asked Karl why he was in Gibraltar. The reply was that Karl had been there to arrange stabling for the next race meeting. The businessman, Mr X, having had a long association with Ireland couldn't help but be interested in horses and in fact has several thoroughbreds in his stables.

As Karl slipped behind the steering wheel of the Buick, Müeller queried, 'What makes you so sure your businessman will find me suitable ?'

Karl turned from the steering wheel to face Müeller. 'No problemos there, Wolf......*I am* that businessman – *Meet Karl Schultz.*'

The declaration was said with such oratory fervour that Müeller thought the only thing missing was a drum roll as he, shell-shocked at the news, stumbled, 'But...but...Karl, you're not long out of jail where did you get the money for....'

'Let me put it to you this way Wolf – what's the point of planning, organising, leading and taking all the chances in bank raids to bolster the coffers of an outlawed organisation if you don't reward yourself occasionally with a bonus? When I got out of jail I decided to retire to sunnier climes. I chose Spain. Drew money from my Swiss account and bought a bar in Estepona. Lived in the apartment above until the stables and the house with it came on the market and bought them. But, you know what, Wolf? I was bored. I missed the action, the dangers entailed in my previous way of life. That's when I got in touch with various people in high places who could not allow either themselves or their countries to be involved in political chicanery. That's when I became a mercenary. It pays well. *Very* well.' He pulled the choke, turned the ignition key and set the Buick in motion.

As he sat at the Gibraltar/ La Linea border with passport at the ready Schultz was thinking it odd that there was no sign of Curran. He had spoken to him on the way in from Marbella and he had said he was on duty until midday. A glance at his watch showed 9-30am.

Little did Schultz realise that Curran, with head in hands and in deep despair, was in a dockyard navy cell charged with treason. Curran's heart was heavy – not for himself but for his failure to avenge his parents. His only salvation now was that Suarez and his friends would be successful in their plan, whatever it was, against the hated British. Ironically, it still hadn't dawned on him that he was British. Not that it mattered, for he had without coercion relinquished his birth right the moment he had started on his path of revenge.

CHAPTER 17

As Scott opened Yvonne's front door any hope of her being asleep were dashed as the strains of "Mozart's flute concerto in G" floated out from a wireless. He found himself humming along to the soloist's flute as he opened the door of the sitting room. She was in the arm chair with her legs curled under her, book in hand, holding a cocoa and warmed by the electric fire.

She looked up smiling, showing her gleaming white, even teeth as she put her book and cocoa down on the coffee table. 'Ah! The return of the wanderer. I read the note you left. How did you get on with Delores?'

Scott screwed up his face as he replied, 'Bloody hard going. She's as tough as an old boot. Even the Marines in the guard house are complaining about her language...' This drew a laugh from Yvonne. '... However, more to the point how's the invalid?'

'I told you all I needed was a good sleep and that sleeping draught certainly did the job.' There was a slight embarrassing lull as she remembered the circumstances surrounding her sudden lapse into unconsciousness – the open dressing gown and the arrival of the doctor – but recovering she continued, 'I feel great and ready for action.'

Because of the tiredness overcoming him he trusted he had the right meaning of her "action" as he yawningly replied, 'Good. Thanks to Delores we now know where to start. We're off to Marbella tomorrow, er, later this morning,' he said as he further explained about the name on the side of the horsebox. 'That's where she says the gang apparently hang out.'

'Does she know the whereabouts of Suarez?'

'She doesn't know...and I believe her. In fact we were possibly the last to see him when he fled the chamber from Hertzog. However, she confirms what I said – he wants to take her to South America so that means he should be leaving from Algecirus.'

'But that's in Spain. We have no jurisdiction there...'

'I'll worry about that when I catch up with him,' Scott interrupted sharply, not wishing to get involved in an argument over the semantics of International Law. 'However, what we now have is Curran under lock and key for treason and once I get to him – he'll talk. Things are beginning to fall into place.'

Having made known to Scott her own suspicion of Curran this did not come as a surprise but she still asked, 'Why?'

'According to Delores her marriage to Curran was a sham. They, whoever *they* are, wanted Curran in his capacity of Chief Custom's Officer so that they could cross the border at will when he was on duty. And, of course, anything else he could pick-up of interest about the workings of the dockyard.'

'What were they taking over the border if it wasn't contraband excise payable goods?'

'The limpet mines they had stolen from the Italian Navy.'

'Of course! The open crates in the chamber,' exclaimed Yvonne in surprise. 'But how do you know about them being stolen from the Italians?'

Scott told her a censored version of his discussion with Captain di Rossi, before asking Yvonne, 'Anything else you think you should know?'

'Plenty – like what's a Maiale? And if you find it, are you going to return it to your Italian friend?'

Making no attempt at describing a Maiale Scott laughed as he replied, 'Are you pulling my leg? Finders-keepers applies. All's fair in love and war Yvonne.'

With a shake of the head she reminded him, 'But we're not at war now – not that that, of course, will worry you any. However, what does concern me is Delores' welfare. From what you've told me it sounds like that creep Suarez has made a fool of her. Do you think she will be charged with treason?'

'I honestly hope not. But the problem is that Suarez is paying her to appear married to Curran, and that doesn't help her cause. What we need to discover is how Curran came to get the job...'

'Sir James would know....All I can tell you is what I heard from the locals – that the previous incumbent, a good swimmer, drowned,' finished Yvonne.

'Something's not right here, Yvonne. But I can't put my finger on it....as yet. Delores doesn't know it but she's got herself involved in some very murky business. For a start who is paying Suarez? Because should she know and they turn out to be an enemy of the Crown – need I go on?'

'No. I think it's time I had a woman to woman talk with her.'

'Do that. Incidentally, do you think she is aware that we have no extradition treaty with Spain? Because once she is released, and let's face it we have no factual evidence at present to hold her, say she accidentally crossed the border into Spain….. '

A smile twitched across Yvonne's lips. 'You know Scott somewhere in that chauvinistic body of yours is a human being trying to escape,' she teased. 'Now what's your plan for later?'

'First we find the address of Marbella Racing...'

'In the Post Office,' she interrupted. 'But it doesn't open until 9-00am...and there's a café next to it where we can have breakfast.'

'Sounds good to me,' Scott yawned. 'Excuse me, Yvonne, but I'm bushed.'

She rose from her chair extended her hand to take Scott's hand and led him to the settee, moved a cushion onto the arm and had him make himself comfortable. By the time she came back with a spare blanket he was sound asleep.

***

In the bedroom Yvonne stood before a full length mirror dressed in in her "in the field" outfit comprising an all-black ensemble of polo neck sweater, leather zip front jerkin, combat trousers and hiking boots. Her Beretta automatic pistol she slid from her shoulder holster to check the mechanism. Satisfied, she clipped in a magazine, replaced the Beretta and zipped up her jerkin. Her sunglasses she wore arched over her head to add, she felt, a female touch to an otherwise drab male-looking outfit. With a touch of lipstick and a well-manicured finger replacing a wayward strand of hair she gave her appearance a final inspection in the mirror then stepped into the sitting room.

Scott, dressed similarly in fatigues was, with legs crossed lounging in an arm-chair, reading the Telegraph whilst sipping a cup of tea. He rose and said cheerfully, 'Good morning, Yvonne. I trust you had a good night's sleep. Make yourself at home and I'll get you a cuppa.' He then adjourned to the kitchen.

Whilst he was waiting for the kettle to boil Yvonne queried, 'Do you think Suarez is already in Algecirus?'

'If he's any sense – yes. Because I've a feeling his paymasters will be fairly annoyed with him the way things have turned out and might have other ideas about his future. Hopefully, the agent you asked Twomay to find Suarez will get to him before he boards ship.' The tea made, Scott said, 'Your tea madam. No sugar if my memory serves me right.'

'Must be your *Harvard* professor you're thinking about. I am milk and one sugar, please,' she replied tartly feeling piqued. A feeling she instantly regretted knowing she had put team harmony in jeopardy once again.

'I was just joking. I know what you take,' he lied, trying to cover up his faux pas whilst letting her jibe pass. Getting quickly off the subject he enquired, 'Do you have our emergency field bag ready?'

'In the hall cupboard. Binoculars, tape, compass, first aid kit etcetera.'

On his return from the kitchen with her milk and sugar he noticed that Yvonne's high fashion accessory, her sunglasses, had disappeared. He had thought them a peculiar thing to wear over goggles – but he was no expert on ladies' biking fashions so he passed no comment instead he headed for the cupboard, checked the contents of the bag and went down stairs to put the bag in the pannier of the Triumph thereby giving her time to finish her tea .

When he returned upstairs Yvonne was ready with her leather helmet in place and goggles in hand. She said, 'Post office is open in five minutes. And I'm starving.'

As Scott buckled the chin-strap of his leather helmet in place, applied his goggles and eased the Triumph off its stand, Yvonne looked despairingly at Delores' empty downstairs apartment and muttered to herself as she shook her head, 'Stupid, stupid girl. Another life ruined because of a bloody man,' she finished bitterly as she suddenly realised she was herself being stupid by still smarting from Scott's ill-timed sugar and milk faux pas.

Less than a minute later an untroubled Scott pulled up outside the café and balanced the bike with both feet on the road to allow Yvonne to get off and enter the post office. Looking casually around he glanced at the next door café as two smartly dressed males were exiting. One was extremely tall with red hair the other short and squat with close cropped grey hair. To Scott the squat one looked vaguely familiar as they both disappeared up a side road on the other side of the post office.

Yvonne, also noticing the two, urgently tapped him on the shoulder. He turned to her and seeing her pointing at her chinstrap pretended to unfasten the buckle. The action masquerading as help hid both their faces. Yvonne whispered, 'I recognise both of them. The short one is the explosives engineer from my reservoir contract and the other I have seen at the border on race days when I was monitoring Suarez's demonstrations.'

Suarez, demonstrations, horse racing – meaning horseboxes, plus Yvonne recognising an explosives engineer and he also suddenly remembering where he had also him before, were just too many coincidences to ignore. Enough for him to urgently ask, 'Where does that road lead to?'

'There is spare ground at the rear that is used for car parking. Exit is one way, comes out up the road there,' Yvonne replied pointing at a road junction some twenty metres distance. 'It joins this road and if they turn north it will lead them to the border.'

'That's for us,' said Scott as he engaged the Triumph's clutch and headed for the road junction. They only had to wait a few minutes until a blue Buick with white wall tyres approached the junction. Scott, parked behind a car, could see, without being seen, the occupants of the Buick. It was the two from the café. He let them turn north for a hundred metres, swung out from behind the parked car and sat at a sedate speed behind until they came to the border.

As they waited in the queue at passport control Yvonne said, 'I take it the plan is to follow them? And to where?'

'If my hunch is right – we're off to "Marbella Racing".

'Bit of a long shot – even for one of your hunches.'

'You got a better idea?' he queried, the tone curt. Yvonne shook her head. 'The only possible roads they can take are for La Linea or San Roque. With La Linea being Suarez's base it's a possibility.' However, as it transpired, once clear of passport control there was no deviation into either La Linea or San Roque on the part of the Buick. With the road being busy in both directions it gave the Buick no opportunity to overtake the slow moving commercial vehicles. This suited Scott. It allowed him to keep several vehicles between him and the Buick to avoid being observed in its rear view mirror. To their right hand side Yvonne was meanwhile enjoying the Mediterranean Ocean sparkling bright in the morning sun with white caps breaking gently against the bows of merchant shipping and pleasure craft. Scott, now convinced that they were heading for Marbella, opened the throttle at the first opportunity just past San Roque. The massive power of the Triumph responded instantly treating Yvonne to a terrifying overtaking experience as Scott with perfect, albeit skin of the teeth, timing slipped between the Buick and an oncoming lorry leaving the Buick in his wake and Yvonne, with eyes tightly closed, clinging onto Scott for dear life. This manoeuvre he repeated several times building up a good time-advantage over the Buick which was bogged down in the slow traffic. He was further aided by road works which with a motor cycle didn't matter, or at least didn't matter the way he ignored them. This allowed him to pull off the road ten miles from Marbella into the fishing port of Estepona for breakfast.

At anchor in the harbour bobbing on the swell was a trawler offloading its catch, a powerful motor launch with its newly varnished oak deck reflecting the morning sun beside a massive catamaran that particularly caught Scott's attention. He parked outside the local harbour café.

An angry Yvonne dismounted and flung her helmet and goggles into the pannier and ranted, 'You sure know how to give a girl a good time – if she likes suicide rides. What the hell was that all about?'

Ignoring Yvonne's rant Scott turned and walked away to choose a table overlooking the harbour. When Yvonne eventually joined him he was reading a menu. She was still raging, 'Why have we stopped here?'

'For breakfast. I'm starving. Aren't you?'

'Breakfast! You're having breakfast whilst they're getting away.'

Scott put the menu down and sighed, 'No they won't.'

Yvonne stubbornly persisted , 'And what if they do?'

'Then, I'll just have to board that catamaran and ask them,' he replied nodding towards the moored quayside catamaran. 'Now, tell me what you see that might be of interest.'

'Oh!' was all a surprised Yvonne could reply as she read the name of the catamaran along its hull – "Marbella Racing One". Recovering, she lamely muttered, 'Clever Dick.'

Scott laughed at her taunt. 'Elementary, my dear Rencoule, elementary. Now please sit down and order.' Scott summoned over a hovering waiter and in his fluent Spanish ordered for both of them. Then in a low voice said to Yvonne, 'Back in Gib the bloke you recognised, the short squat one, your explosives engineer, I too recognized him. He's a Kreigsmarine Kommando.....'

Yvonne, recalling her meeting with Müeller at her reservoir contract muttered, more to herself than Scott, 'Ah! So I was right – he *is* German. I....'

'So, as I was saying,' replied Rutherford peeved at being interrupted, 'I think it peculiar that I find him in Spain when I know for certain he was badly injured in Tenerife and returned to his naval base in Keil....'

Yvonne, smarting at her summation being interrupted said sarcastically, 'And, pray tell, how do you know he was *badly* injured? Could it be that you had anything to do with his injury?'

A now exasperated Scott shrugged his shoulders. 'If you must know It was just a little tap on the head. I wasn't to know he had a thin cranium.' Yvonne grimaced. The grimace meant to convey her scepticism at his excuse as he continued in a pseudo American accent, that she assumed was meant to be Cagney, *'Da mug was fortunate I didn't plug him, baby.'*

Yvonne wearily shook her head, this time at the use of the pure Hollywood "B" movie Americanisms that would have had Sir James hyperventilating. Deciding he wasn't worth remonstrating with she casually remarked, 'Oh, well,

I suppose that's all right then Scott, I hope *da mug* appreciates your generosity.' Suspecting sarcasm Scott stared back at her with arched eyebrows as she wilfully finished, 'I bet he's over here looking for *da mug* that thumped him on the head.'

Scott didn't reply, instead he went into deep thought. Her reply had jogged his memory of Sir James' warning to, "watch your back". He broke his silence with, 'Just thinking what use a man of his underwater explosive expertise would be to the red haired, racing guy. Where was he when the attempted attack on the Worcester took place?'

'Twomay, who was highly suspicious of him, checked him out and his alibi was watertight. He was in jail cooling off. He had got himself into the usual Saturday night drunken brawl in the Victory public house and was incarcerated when the raid took place,' she finished, picking up a napkin to wipe the corners of her mouth of tortilla as she placed her knife and fork together.

'Good for old Twomay,' said Scott as he finished off his carne con papas and poured them further glasses of the house red before, with chin in hand, elbow on table, fingers tapping and deep in thought he proclaimed, 'You know Yvonne, I think there is something more serious to all this than the attempt on the Worcester...'

'You surely can't think there's something more important than trying to destroy the Worcester?' interrupted Yvonne aghast.

'No. Of course not. I meant who is responsible? Who is behind it? It's certainly not Suarez even though he's in it up to his nostrils. What country? Germany? Italy? Or....?'

'I would have thought the most obvious would be Spain. They want the Utrecht Treaty torn up and Gibraltar returned to Spain. Or even Suarez's Falange Party. You said yourself he's up to his neck in.....'

'Sorry to interrupt Yvonne, but take it from me, Suarez is the lackey in all this. A messenger boy. A clever and devious messenger boy, but way out of his depth. He's being paid by somebody. And that somebody might be a mercenary getting paid by a country. So – what country? Regarding your theory on Spain I can't fault it other than they have enough on their plate with a potential civil war brewing. Nor do I suspect Germany either. As Hertzog claimed, and confirmed by the official papers I removed from his wallet, he *was* sent by Berlin to terminate Suarez for his continual upsetting of His Majesty's Government over Gibraltar. Apart from which, for the Jerries to have used limpet mines they would have to have stolen them from Italy – their allies. So that's Germany eliminated. And as for Italy – well, they're not likely to use dud timers that they know don't work underwater and were stolen from themselves in the first place.'

'Albeit your Italian friend could have been telling you porkies...'

'Yvonne! I'm shocked. I can't believe a well-educated young lady like yourself would use words like that. Sir James would have a fit.'

She laughed. 'What? Porky pies. Lies. That's a nothing. He would be shocked rigid if he knew the words we convent educated girls do know. However, even though these are all sound reasons – you've used an awful lot of supposition. So don't you think we should maybe be concentrating on finding Suarez instead of this "Marbella Racing" outfit – I mean Suarez seems to hold all the answers.

'Mmm. Possibly. But please bear in mind that my hunches and suppositions are always based on ratiocination – which has set my mind rolling...'

'Okay. So you're into the process of logical reasoning,' exclaimed the knowledgeable Yvonne adding, 'So what now, *professor*?'

Scott, showing no signs of heeding her sarcasm leaned casually back in his seat with hands clasped behind his neck and in a reply designed to annoy her replied, 'Just playing a hunch – Yvonne.... a hunch.'

'You know something Scott...you can be very infuriating at times. If you don't want to discuss *my ratiocination* about Suarez – what *do you* want me to do?'

'I would like you to call the waiter over please, and use your exuding charm to ask him for directions to "Marbella Racing". Then tell him we're looking to stable our horses. Questions are always better asked by attractive females. I've noticed he can't help looking at you.'

She desperately wanted to stomp her foot or at least kick him under the table for his condescending attitude but remembering a past remark of his she said, 'I thought you were going to ask the crew of the catamaran directions?'

'Too late. They've just set sail. Not that it matters. Once you establish the location of "Marbella Racing" from the waiter I'm sure we will find them again.'

'Good of you to keep me informed, Scott,' she snapped as she waved the waiter over. While he collected the empty plates and glasses she enquired in her fluent Spanish directions to "Marbella Racing". She and her husband were looking for suitable stabling for their horses. They had heard that it was the best in the area. Without taking his eyes off her ample bust he informed her the stables were the best in Spain. She had chosen wisely. He excused himself only to reappear minutes later with a beaming smile. He had what the señora required. He laid a piece of paper in front of her with a freehand map drawn on it. He explained the map. Yvonne removed the correct amount of pesetas to cover the bill and laid them on the table. The waiter, expecting a tip, looked at the uplifted pesetas in his hand disdainfully. She then added another twenty peseta note and slipped it under the ashtray. The waiter's eyes were now focused on the note instead of her bust. She enquired if the owner of the stables would be home at this time of day. The waiter hesitated. Scott added another twenty note to the ashtray. The waiter replied that he must be home or on his way because Señor Schultz's catamaran that had just departed was a sure sign he was going to be picked up at his house. Scott asked if Señor Schultz was the owner of the stables. The answer was yes. Scott asked if he was red haired. The waiter hesitated again. Yvonne slipped another twenty under the ashtray with a beaming smile. The waiter, with a similar smile at her, replied that he was indeed red haired. Yvonne, studying the map, asked what a line that crossed the main road was. It was a deep gorge leading from the Mediterranean through a narrow gap and under a bridge on the main road to Señor Schultz's private bay, jetty and villa. They were to go back onto the main Malaga road, travel approximately ten kilometres until they came to the bridge over the inlet and take a hard first left turn into a driveway. This uphill drive led to the house and stables. The office was in the stables. He knew this because he delivered meals to the stable hands. When Scott asked why Señor Schultz had a catamaran the waiter looked at him suspiciously. Another twenty peseta note loosened his tongue. Señor Schultz was a racer of catamarans. He had two. Scott enquired if they were all as large as the one that had departed. He was informed that it had recently undergone major modifications to be ready for the annual Algecirus to Alboran island race, in two days. To allay the waiter's suspicions Scott told him that he was a keen catamaran racer back home in England. The waiter congratulated him on his fluent Spanish and also on his being a lucky man to have such a beautiful wife. Yvonne received a kiss on both cheeks, Scott a handshake and a cheery adios.

All this had been witnessed from the café door by a small, rotund, bald man wearing a beer stained apron who, when the waiter returned, asked him who he had spent so much time talking to. The waiter replied they were asking the way to the stables as he handed Scott and Yvonne's payment into the fat grubby hands of the rotund manager plus half the tip – five pesetas. "Mean bastards," muttered the manager as he lifted the phone.

As Yvonne was buckling her helmet she said, 'Very enlightening Scott. Worth every penny, er, sorry, the eighty pesetas tip. Wouldn't you agree?'

'Absolutely. You had him eating out of your hand. I'm proud of you.' Then he quoted a Sir James colloquialism, 'Couldn't have done better myself.'

My, my, compliments. Things are looking up mused Yvonne as Scott in his usual fashion took off with rear wheel spin leaving the smell of burning rubber on the road surface.

CHAPTER 18

Marbella Racing Stables

Having cleared the Spanish border control at Gibraltar Karl and Müeller were on the coast road to Marbella. Müeller was passing comment, 'Traffic appears to be busy today, Karl.'

'Yeah. The Spanish and British governments must be speaking to each other again. The border, as you just witnessed, is open and when it's open everybody takes advantage because it might be closed again tomorrow.'

'I gather it's a regular occurrence.'

'A real pain in the arse. Especially on Gibraltar race days.'

'How do you find time to train horses?'

'I don't. Roisin looks after that side of the business. Her father's one of Ireland's top trainers. She's inherited his talent. Not that there's any horse racing in Spain to talk about. It's more gymkhana. She was one of my lieutenants in Ireland. A handy lady with a firearm. She's now my house keeper cum....*Bloody hell!* Wolf, did you see that fucking idiot..?' A motorcycle with a passenger had cut in front of him causing him to brake sharply and throw the steering wheel kerbside. The bike just making it through a gap between the Buick and an oncoming commercial. As soon as the oncoming vehicle passed them the motorcycle started its overtaking manoeuvre again with the lorry in front of the Buick. 'Bloody lunatic,' howled Karl shaking a fist at the bike driven by Rutherford.

After calming down and several unsuccessful attempts at overtaking the lorry in front Schultz settled into the slow moving nose-to-tail convoy giving him time to ask Müeller, 'Are you familiar with the Italian rebreather method of scuba diving?'

'Yes. I recently led a team on a covert mission to Tenerife. That's where I got this.' He didn't have to indicate his affliction – the tic was in full flow with every oncoming vehicle that passed at speed. 'But it doesn't affect my diving.'

'That's excellent news because what I require is a trusty lieutenant alongside of me for something I have planned for tonight – part of my, Grand Plan.'

'Tonight?' queried a shocked Müeller.

'Yes. I have planned it for......*Bloody hell!* What-the-fuck-is-it-this time...?' he cried, slamming on his brakes to bringing the Buick to a slithering emergency stop. The lorry in front had similarly stopped suddenly and a workman wielding a STOP/GO sign appeared between the Buick and the lorry. The lorry moved off on the workman's waved instruction as he turned his sign to show STOP to Schultz who angrily blasted his horn – only to be ignored. The lorry moved out into the oncoming lane, now devoid of traffic, to allow a steam road-roller to advance towards the Buick. The lorry then manoeuvred itself back into its correct lane to allow the oncoming traffic to start passing once again. They were trapped until the sign was turned to Go. Schultz took a deep breath and resigned himself to his fate. He looked at his watch. He reckoned he still had a good seven hours to prepare. 'Now where was I? Yes. I was saying that I have had the operation planned for some time. The drawback was the securing of a manned torpedo. You are familiar with them?'

'I know of them and am aware that the Italians are well advanced in their research.'

'They are actually at sea trials. Or to be precise – were. They're temporarily suspended.'

'How do you know that?'

'Because I suspended them.'

'How the hell did you manage that?'

'The manned torpedo is referred to as the "Maiale", meaning "Pig" in Italian because of the way it handles got *accidentally* caught in the fishing net hung between the newly reinforced hulls of my catamaran. The poor torpedo operators were sailing along one minute with their heads above water in the dark heading for a rust bucket target at anchor when suddenly they found themselves sinking unconscious to the bottom of the Mediterranean,' he finished with a maniacal cackle.

Müeller, at this revelation, began to doubt Schultz's sanity but the thought of his help to find his elusive assailant, Hill, overruled any doubts as he found himself congratulating Schultz, 'Brilliant work, Karl. But how did you get away?'

'I had a fast trawler with crane and nets waiting further down the coast from Sardinia where the Italian trials were taking place. The transfer of the Maiale to the trawler went seamlessly. The trawler then proceeded to its home port of Estepona and the Maiale was transferred into my boathouse. An Italian motor torpedo boat intercepted us after the incident. What could you find on a catamaran? The suspended net between the hulls was at the bottom of the sea. As to what were we doing out at that time of night – we were practising our night time manoeuvres for the annual twenty four hour catamaran race around Sardinia, Sicily and Corsica. A race that I am actually entered for later in the year. The Italian fools believed it and we were on our way.'

'Well planned. So what is it you have in mind for tonight?'

'I intend to....' The ancient road roller levelling the freshly laid tarmac had reached them and started to reverse with several shrill whistles that made Schultz's explanation hard to hear.

Müeller had heard most of what was said but was confirming, 'Christ almighty, Karl. Did I hear you right, you intend to....' The shrill whistle of the road roller sounded again.

The STOP sign turned to GO. As the Buick moved alongside the workman Shultz hit the horn and gave him the middle digit. In his wing mirror Müeller noticed the workman taking a swipe at the Buick with his sign – fortunately for his continued good health he missed.

'As I was saying, I had intended using Helmut, one of my men, alongside me to place the charges tonight but good fortune has brought you to me. (the good fortune being that Schultz on driving past the café the previous day had spotted Mueller exiting the café and on making enquiries discovered that he breakfasted there every morning) You, the top expert in underwater explosives.' Müeller, normally modest about his undeniable talent allowed the praise to go without his usual protest. It had been some considerable time since he had received praise other than that recently from that attractive lady from the MOD. 'So, what do you say, Wolf – are you up for it? Can you imagine that on your CV? The world would become your oyster. When we pull it off we will then concentrate on finding the evil bastard that did that terrible thing to you.'

Thirty minutes later, after a further forced stop for works, the Buick crossed a bridge on the main road and turned into a long uphill tree lined avenue leading to a large two-storey stone built villa. Schultz parked beside a Mercedes saloon and the confiscated Auto Union of Suarez. As Müeller stepped out of the Buick he noticed stone steps carved out of the gorge wall leading far below to a jetty jutting out from a small sandy beach into a bay. The entry into the bay from Mediterranean Sea was through a narrow gap in the gorge walls under the road bridge they had crossed.

CHAPTER 19

Five minutes after leaving the café in Estepona Rutherford crossed the road bridge that had been drawn on the waiter's map and deliberately overshot the turning to the stables until he came to a suitable hard standing at the side of the road. He stopped with legs astride to steady the Triumph as he gazed up at the majesty of the snow-capped peaks of the Sierra Bermeja mountain range in the far distance. The land in the immediate foreground was scrub, strewn with boulders, lava outcrops and various types of flora. This scrub land led sharply upwards to a tree-lined plateau. This he guessed to be the stables. To his left was a copse extending from the road to the plateau – the driveway. This copse he would use as cover. They dismounted, waited for a break in the traffic flow and then free-wheeled the Triumph behind a large boulder. With the machine now out of sight of the main road, he selected from the panniers the accoutrements needed for his reconnaissance. He chose binoculars and black tape to stop lens reflection from the sun which he applied then slung the binoculars around his neck, a water canteen and a sheathed dagger that he tucked in his waistband. A stout hemp rope, a grapnel hook and a camouflage hat he left aside for Yvonne who was gathering foliage from the near at hand yellow broom and false sage bushes to camouflage the Triumph. Chores completed they took cover behind the boulder to discuss their next move.

Scott opened. 'I propose we use the nearside driveway copse as cover to reach the plateau level. From there we should be able to view the set-up and decide what to do. Any questions?'

'Yes. But why the nearside copse? Why not the far-side copse? Surely that's where you would get a view of the jetty – and where the crew of the catamaran will hang out.'

Scott sighed, 'True. But from what I saw when I slowed down to cross the bridge, the far side copse comprises a single row of trees offering no cover and a vertical drop into the gorge of about sixty feet. The copse does widen towards the top of the drive. So what I would suggest is we climb through the nearside copse to the plateau level then cross the drive to the far side copse and descend from there. Surely that makes sense to you....?'

'Yes, yes. I understand,' she interrupted tartly as she realized her error at doubting Scott's ability to sum up situations at a glance.

Scott, laughing at her anguish, cajoled, 'Not to worry – just assume it to be all part of your "in the field" learning curve.'

Yvonne ignored his mocking taunt to reply, 'What, *I assume,* now that we've found "Marbella Racing", is that your *ratiocinating* depends on my assailants being on the premises and me, of course, being able to identify them?'

'Until I get my hands on Suarez that is precisely all we've got to go on Yvonne. But, as you say, if you should recognise any of them that's good enough for me,' he finished in a placatory tone hoping to ease the tension building up between them. It did not make for good teamwork.

Unfortunately, it didn't work as Yvonne angrily queried, 'So what if I do recognize them? Do we go back to barracks and call out the Marines? Spain won't take kindly to us arresting foreigners on their territory. The relationship with Spain is bad enough because of Gibraltar without our adding to the problem. Shouldn't we just wait and follow them until they set foot in Gibraltar?'

Scott, basically annoyed at her ethical stance, knew she was right. But who was to say they would travel by road. It could be a sea-borne attack, especially with Schultz possessing a racing catamaran. However, to stop the build-up of hostilities he said with lied pragmatism, 'Tell you what we will do Yvonne. We will do precisely nothing until we know who we're dealing with. What their strength is and how heavily armed they are. Then we will make a decision. In other words recognition first. Action later. How does that suit your political ethics?'

'You fibber. You've no intention of doing nothing. You don't ever do nothing. You can't wait to get down there and start another, "gunfight at the O.K corral."

Scott shrugged his shoulders and said, 'Look Yvonne, situations like this never end happily. You'll soon find that out when you confront the baddies, they don't do as they do at the cinema throw up their hands in surrender and say, "It's a fair cop buddy. I'll come quietly," he mimicked again in a pseudo Cagney drawl.

This attempt at another Americanism brought a stinker of a look from Yvonne who, undeterred, tried again, 'Oh! You. You're impossible. Won't you even consider going to the Guardia Civil in Malaga and let them sort it out?'

'Yvonne!' Scott replied impatiently, 'You've just gone to great length about the state of diplomatic relations between Spain and HMG being at an all-time low, so what makes you think the Guardia Civil, the *Civilies,* a Spanish para military police force will help you with a Gibraltar problem? They're more likely to help them than us. Apart from which I wouldn't be at all surprised if they're not on his payroll. Now, enough procrastination. Let's go.' He rose from his squatting position and strode into the copse totally discontented at having to explain his every move to Yvonne. She was a top agent, clever, resourceful, diligent, a fighting force you did not tangle with if you valued your life, and above all he trusted her. Unfortunately, she lacked "in-the-field" experience and this is where Scott excelled and operated best on his own.

As Yvonne picked up the rope and wound it over her shoulder she too was reviewing her situation. She knew he hated his methods being questioned and was used to operating on his own but due to unfortunate circumstances the mission had segued into what it now was and he was going to have to accept that this was a joint venture and she was, like it or not, his partner and liaison. It was their first "in-the-field" action together and the way things were going likely to be their last. And she didn't want that to happen. But she wasn't going to be his lackey. Quickening her pace she caught up with him.

Apart from the odd projecting boulder the going between the pine needles was relatively easy and they soon arrived at the extremity of the copse when they reached the plateau level. To their right the copse carried along the perimeter of the plateau through which they heard horses' neighing and hooves thudding. Straight ahead lay a log cabin with an "Office" sign on the door. Parked outside was a motorised horsebox with the logo "Marbella Racing" on the side panel. To their left the view between the pines showed a two-storey stone villa with a Buick convertible and Mercedes and Auto Union saloons parked in a gravel drive. The Buick confirming Scott's hunch about the destination of the two people he had followed from Gibraltar. All they needed now was sight of Yvonne's assailants who should be found somewhere around the jetty area. Unfortunately, from their present location, among the pines on the wrong side of the drive, the jetty lay out of sight in the deep gorge.

Scott, with finger to his lips, whispered, 'This is as far as you go.'

'Why? Where are you going?' she hissed.

Bloody questions again sighed Scott inwardly as he found himself answering patiently, 'Down into the gorge. And before you ask, "why not both of us?" the answer is because I don't know what sort of reception committee awaits us and with you needed to identify your assailants we both can't afford capture. Therefore, I will go first. I should be back, if it's safe, in sixty minutes to collect you. Should you hear shooting – head back to Gib immediately and report to Sir James. On the other hand – should you be discovered, fire a shot to warn me. Meanwhile, stay alert. See you in an hour.' As he turned to leave he put a hand to his ear and then turned back to Yvonne. 'Do you have your silencer?' Yvonne patted the patch pocket in her fatigues. 'Good. Fit it. I heard dogs and I recognise the growl – Dobermanns – at least two. Nasty bastards. My advice – shoot first. Pat heads and wiggle ears later. With that advice he slipped across the drive into the trees opposite.

In the sudden silence Yvonne sank further back into the engulfing darkness of the copse. She looked at her watch 12-30 pm. An anxious hour to kill. She heard the growl of the dogs. Her Beretta appeared seamlessly in her hand to receive its silencer. A projecting boulder afforded a seat and a chance to reflect on his decision to leave her in the copse. She did not approve of his derring-do attitude but understood his reasoning – or as he would have it now – his rationating. In the heat of battle he did not want her safety to compromise the operation, which she knew he would treat as paramount, even though she was perfectly capable of taking care of herself. And he was further correct in that, first and foremost, she was his liaison – his connection, to be free to report back to Sir James should there be a problem. Trouble was it was not the first time he had excluded her from "in-the-field" action and she was dying to prove herself. However, having satisfied herself that his decision was the right one, she looked at her watch 12-35pm. Five minutes gone. It was going to be a long wait.

When Scott entered the trees he found them to be scant of cover for him.

Fortunately, they were staggered. It was this staggering that offered what little cover there was. Straight ahead, at approximately 300cm daylight filtered between the stagger. Edging forward toward the shaft of daylight he found himself at the precipice of a sixty foot drop into the bay. Looking toward the villa he observed pines and bushes growing randomly from the rock walls and ledges of the gorge. They grew in ascending height upwards from the gorge wall. Each tree trying to out-do its neighbour in reaching towards the sun. This was the cover he sought. Unfortunately, it was about another fifty/sixty feet before the trees growing out of the gorge wall rose to join the driveway trees to give cover all the way down to bay level. He pressed on allowing a safety zone of a tree girth between himself and the precipice until he came to the dense area. As he moved downwards into this area it was here that he discovered the going changed from pine needles to rough terrain as he clambered over ankle-breaking rocks and small crevasses. With each step tentative and tested before being taken he eventually arrived at a viewpoint that offered up a vista of the villa and jetty and in return was well concealed. Casting his binoculars towards the jetty he saw a long indiscernible shape covered by a tarpaulin sitting under a small crane and obviously heavy because it took two four wheel bogies to carry the load. At the rear of the jetty was a pass-door and alongside just above water level were double doors set in the vertical rock face which he took to be a boat house/storage cave. To the opposite side of the jetty he noticed steps and landings hewn out of the rock leading from the beach to the villa. Having seen enough he was getting ready to return to Yvonne when a fog horn broke the tranquillity. Looking backwards to the road bridge he saw the catamaran he had seen in Estepona harbour squeeze through the gap with little to spare between the near vertical faces of the gorge. Settling down again he witnessed it being tethered to the jetty's capstans under the crane. Once secured, the four-man crew with drill-precision took their places. Two removed the tarpaulin to expose a manned torpedo. Scott's mouth dropped open in amazement. What he was looking at was the Italian Navy's stolen "Maiale." The same two crew members then slipped the crane's slings around the torpedo as a third member operated the crane to lift the heavy load aboard the catamaran where the fourth member guided it into place between the two hulls. When the load was released Scott noticed the catamaran visibly sink close to its plimsoll mark maximum. Wherever it was heading, speed would not be of the essence. The crew, of which one was a giant was stripped to the waist and showing off his rippling muscles, then disappeared through the pass-door into the storage area. Minutes later two of them returned pushing a bogie loaded with a timber crate and twin outboard motors. The massive, well-muscled crew member took the motors aboard the catamaran to replace the existing ones. Whilst this was on-going a short, squat person with close-cropped grey hair came down the stone steps from the villa. Scott recognised him as one of the two he had followed from Gibraltar — Yvonne's mining engineer Müeller — who then had the other crew member open the timber crate to inspect the contents. One of the items he withdrew for closer inspection Scott immediately recognised as a seventy five kilo TNT mine. And Scott knew where it was going. When primed, it and others would be stored in the nose cone of the Maiale for removal and fixing onto the chosen target. He wasn't wrong. The massive crew member, after completing his assembly of the outboard motors, picked the crate up as if it were a box of feathers and took it on board the Maiale where Müeller set about priming the mines. Scott was aware that in using this size of mine that whatever they were up to was going to be a major attack on something and that something if hit with the TNT stored in the nose-cone would no longer be a something. But what and where? Could it be the dockyard again? It now remained, with all the catamaran's crew being in the vicinity, time to collect Yvonne to see if she recognised any of her assailants. As he took his first tentative step back to Yvonne he heard a noise of an engine starting. He turned to look back towards the jetty. The boat house doors had opened and a speed boat idled out to be tied up to the jetty. An exchange of words between the driver and the mining engineer resulted in Müeller disappearing from the catamaran to head up the stone steps to the villa. Through the open doors he spied another speed boat moored at the inner quay.

***

From the floor-to-ceiling-upper-floor-bay-window of the villa overlooking the gorge and the jetty, the tall red haired figure of Schultz lowered his field glasses and picked up the phone to give instructions. When he returned the phone to its cradle he turned to Müeller who had, at his request, just arrived from the jetty where he had been attending to the mines and said, 'An interesting happening has resulted from that phone call I received on our arrival. It was from the manager of my café in Estepona to advise me that two people were asking the way to the stables.'

'Is that unusual?'

'No. But it is unusual to pay eighty pesetas for something as simple as directions to the stables. My manager saw the waiter receiving notes on four separate occasions suggesting to a suspicious mind like his, four awkward questions being asked. The waiter tried to tell him they had tipped only ten pesetas, which they split fifty-fifty. My manager is a man with a short temper and a violent way. The waiter, shall we say, suddenly remembered about the extra seventy pesetas in his pocket and the questions the strangers asked. Since then the strangers have had ample time upon leaving the café to show up at the office to ask about stabling their horses – but have not as yet arrived. So I have spent the time studying the gorge and the trees leading to the villa through my binoculars and have spotted one of them working his way towards the villa through the gorge trees in a very professional manner. I have instructed two of my men to pick him up and see what he has to say for himself.'

'And the other?'

'Apparently a very attractive female claiming to be his wife. The waiter says she has a hint of a French accent to her Spanish. Of her, there is no trace. However, if she is on the premises we will find her. They are on a British Triumph motor cycle. That should be easy to find. Now, tell me – how did you get on with the Maiale?'

'All in order, Karl. Charges fitted, detonators primed and timers wired and the extra mines you asked for stored in the catamaran's lockers – all ready for the off.'

'Excellent. Come let's see who we have caught. We have still have a lot of planning to finalise before we leave. But we have time.'

Whilst this discussion was taking place Scott had started his return journey by following snapped off branches and bushes that he had deliberately broken off on his descent and had begun the final climb to the driveway when he heard the familiar growl of a Dobermann. He stopped dead, unzipped his jerkin and with his smoothly drawn PPK pointing towards the growl he was ready to fire the instant it appeared. The snarling face with fangs bared and saliva drooling from its mouth and straining on a leash appeared around a tree at the same moment as the barrel of a gun prodded between Scott's shoulder blades and two further gunmen with weapons at the ready joined the party. Scott again recognised the person that had primed the Maiale – the mining engineer Müeller. The other, the giant with the bare torso, he also recognised from the jetty. A German accented voice growled in English from behind him, whilst thrusting the barrel of the gun harder between his shoulder blades, to drop the gun if he wished to live. The odds being heavily against him at present he obliged.

A tall, red haired, muscular and evil-looking individual who had been restraining the Dobermann stepped from behind the tree and in German ordered, 'If he moves a muscle Helmut – shoot the bastard.' Red hair then said amicably, 'Another opportunity to air your photograph, Wolf.'

Wolf delved into an inside pocket and withdrew a well dog-eared photograph. He studied Scott then the photograph. His eyes lit up as he jubilantly cried, 'It's him Karl. It's the bastard from Tenerife that did this to me.' Scott had just noted red hair to be named Karl at the same moment as Schultz nodded his head to Helmut. There was a sudden blunt trauma to the back of Scott's head as Helmut brought the butt of his Mauser pistol down hard. 'You should have let me do that Helmut,' cried a furiously disappointed Müeller as he took a kick at the unconscious Scott.

'Time for that and more later, Wolf. Business first.'

***

Yvonne was sitting on the uncomfortable boulder with the coiled rope as a cushion looking at her watch and was thankful to note that the rendezvous hour was nearly up when she suddenly heard the loud growl of a Dobermman near at hand. As she picked the Beretta up off her lap she heard low voices. She kept perfectly still lest the dog picked up any movement. The voices came from the direction she had expected Scott to appear. They grew louder. She realised they were speaking German. She was, like Scott, fluent in German as she was in

French (naturally), Italian and Spanish. A voice was thanking somebody named Karl for helping him capture the English bastard that.....she didn't catch the finish but it was sufficient that she had heard the words "capture" and "English." She sensed that something was amiss. She had to take a chance on exposure, so she moved as stealthily as she could on the soft pine needles expecting to hear the growl that would reveal her whereabouts. As she got to within a two tree depth of cover from the driveway she heard grunting, heavy breathing, the type associated with lifting a heavy load and a scraping noise. She stole a look around a stout-girthed pine. The sight caused her to draw a deep breath. Scott was being dragged under the armpits with the toes of his boots scraping on the drive by two of the men that she recognised as her attackers in the sarcophagus. She couldn't remember their names, not that it mattered, the recognition of her assailants proved Scott's hunch – that the stables were the operational base of the gang that had attempted to sabotage the Worcester. The voices were coming from the two people that they had followed from the café in Gibraltar. The squat one being the mining engineer, Müeller, that she had spoken to recently with regard to Twomay's suspicion that he was a German. They both were walking behind Scott's limp figure. The other, the tall red haired one with cruel looking eyes, was restraining a Dobermann on a leash as it tried savagely with salivating mouth to get at Scott.

Müeller was speaking, 'Where could the woman be Karl?'

'I don't know. But have no fear Roison will flush her out. They arrived by motor cycle. When Roison finds the bike, she finds her.'

'But if she goes for help – what then?'

'Help? From whom, Wolf? If she goes to the *Civilies* – nothing will happen. They are well taken care of. If she goes to Gibraltar for help – nothing will happen there, either. There is no extradition treaty between Britain and Spain. And what could she tell them anyway? She saw nothing of the catamaran being loaded with the "Maiale". It was her colleague – this guy that saw it all,' he pointed at Rutherford, 'And he's not going to tell anybody. Not now – not ever,' he finished drawing a forefinger across his throat, 'Kaput.' He held his hand up to stop Müeller from interrupting. 'I know I promised you your revenge on your friend from Tenerife and that is still the case – you may kill him but only after we have completed our mission tonight. Meanwhile, we will throw him in the dungeon beside that little piece of 'Spic shit, Suarez, who I have still to have my pleasure with.' Rubbing his chin in contemplation he chortled, 'Yes,I think I'll start with pulling out his nails. We will make it a happy foursome, eh, Wolf? They will pay a handsome price for fucking us around.'

A look of disappointment crossed Müeller's face. He wanted his revenge now. The photograph he carried had confirmed the swine to be J. Hill, and the American girl in Tenerife had told him that his Christian name was Jerry. So, he reluctantly accepted that having waited several months to find this Jerry Hill what difference would another few hours matter? Hiding his annoyance he asked, 'What time do you intend the attack to take place?'

'Not sure. I'm waiting for my contact to inform me when the target arrives. The only thing I am certain of is that it will happen after dark.'

As Müeller was having his revengeful thoughts, Schultz was having similar. The one thing that was certainly not going to happen was the torture or murder of the British agent by Müeller – or if caught, the woman – at least not now. What happened after he offered them to Himmler or the IRA at a price was another matter. Then, suddenly, he had an idea. Supposing, from what Müeller had disclosed about the death of Colonel Maria von Reus, he presented this Jerry Hill to Himmler as the killer of the Colonel his price for Hill would at least treble. And after tonight Müeller would be surplus to his needs also. So he could offer to get rid of him as well for Himmler. He could wrap it up as a package deal. All told, today was turning out very profitable indeed for Schultz as he slapped Müeller on the back with much bonhomie and said, 'The world's our oyster, *Commander* Müeller. Tomorrow, we will be breakfasting in gay Paree.'

***

As Schultz disappeared towards the villa and its dungeons Yvonne realised Scott was in terrible trouble and that she was now a hunted woman. She knew Roisin was an Irish female name. Rose in English. A very thorny one by the sounds of her. Was Roisin searching for her alone or did she have others helping her pondered Yvonne? Either way she decided to get help from Gibraltar. Throwing caution aside she slung the coiled rope over her shoulders as she moved swiftly through the pines downhill to the Triumph which she discovered to her relief was still there. The key was under a nearby stone. Removing the rope from her person she tried to place it in the pannier. It was locked. The pannier key was not on the ignition key ring. Not having time to waste she discarded the rope and on inserting the ignition key and kick starting the machine it instantly roared into life. Opening the throttle she rode onto the main road with a rear wheel spin that Scott would have been proud of.

***

It was fortunate she had decided to move when she did. Ten minutes later an attractive female in her early thirties dressed in jodhpurs and riding boots and carrying a Schmeisser SC28 machine pistol held at the hip broke cover from the driveway pines to investigate a rope lying behind a boulder and discarded branches lying randomly about the ground local to tyre marks of a two-wheeled vehicle. There was also churned up ground where a motor cycle had obviously had a rear wheel spin get away. Angrily, she retraced her steps through the pines to unhitch a horse from a branch, sling the SC28 over her shoulder and head back to report that the quarry had departed. Schultz would not be happy.

The quarry meanwhile had reached the turn-off for Estepona when the words that the red haired guy, Karl, had spoken jolted Yvonne's memory – words that she was already familiar with – *there was no extradition treaty with Spain*. And any help from Gibraltar would be pointless because she knew there were no "Special Unit Marines" of the type Scott once belonged to available in Gibraltar barracks – the nearest units specialising in covert operations were in Egypt. So, on the spur of the moment she decided now was the opportunity to show Scott what she could do. At speed and without stopping she skidded the Triumph on the compacted off road volcanic verge through one hundred and eighty degrees. Less than five minutes later she was crossing the bridge at the stables just in time to witness a horse being whipped into a gallop up the driveway – the rider wearing a machine pistol slung across her back by its shoulder strap. On the assumption that the rider was Roisin and she had already found their old hiding spot vacant, and that with lightning never striking the same place twice, she decided to park there again. Dismounting, she found evidence that Roisin had obviously been there because the rope she had discarded in her hasty departure had been kicked roughly aside. Yvonne recoiled the rope and just in case she had to go mountaineering slung it over her shoulder again. With Beretta in hand she then made her way up through the pine copse she had already explored with Scott, until she came to the area from where she had seen Scott being dragged along the driveway. Checking that the drive was clear she crossed and disappeared into the pines where Scott had entered. She immediately saw a snapped twig. This was the start of his tell-tales of freshly broken twigs or branches. They led her into the dense area and further down into the gorge over threatening ankle-twisting rocks to Scott's hideaway. She was glad to see that Scott, for their expected return, had left his binoculars, sheathed dagger and canteen of water from which she took a much needed swig. With the water, dagger and binoculars still in place where Scott had left them it obviously meant that he had not been snatched by Karl in his hide, so she settled down to take in her new surroundings. She brought the taped-lens binoculars to bear on the jetty. The catamaran was tied up fore and aft to capstans. Between the hulls was a long tarpaulin covered object. This must be the Italian "Maiale" she had heard the red haired Karl discuss with Müeller. Tied up behind it was a speed boat. There were open double doors set in the vertical rock face with another speed boat inside. Obviously the boat house. There was no sign of life. Being outnumbered and with the catamaran looking as though it was ready for departure she decided to do nothing until they set-sail. Whatever it was they were up to she had heard Karl tell Müeller it would not happen until after dark. That meant any time after 5-00pm. A look at her watch showed: 3-15pm. This indicating that it could be a long wait she took out a chocolate bar from a patch pocket in her fatigues and settled herself comfortably in the late afternoon sun between the boulders to contemplate the situation. Uppermost in her thoughts was Scott languishing in the dungeon and with that evil-looking swine Karl intent on finishing him off and nowhere to be seen, she began to worry. So contrary to her earlier decision of being outnumbered and waiting for Schultz's departure she suddenly felt the urgent need to help Scott. She owed him. Even in the sun's heat she shivered at the thought of him saving her from – *those rats*. By crawling flat around one of the boulders and sticking her camouflaged hatted-head out from the gorge face she observed that the pines which were giving her shelter carried on down the gorge to a sandy beach to terminate against a projecting headland, which was part of the garden of the villa 20 metres above. On the opposite side of the headland was the jetty and between these were carved out stone steps leading from the beach and jetty to the villa. Figuring she would set up her next hide where the pines stopped at the headland she started her descent. She was on her own – no Scott clues to help. She started to work her way down the gorge-face keeping at all times within the tree line. The going was tough. Every step a challenge – if she wasn't clinging by her finger tips to drop from one perilous rock onto another, or endeavouring to avoid breaking her ankles on projecting rocks, she was swinging on pine branches from one tree to another over deep clefts. Ninety minutes later with her once immaculately manicured nails broken and her fatigues ripped she reached her destination – a large bush at the point of the headland that offered a good view of the jetty and its environs. As she sat on a rock within the bush her watch showed 4-45pm.

As the sky darkened she had her next decision made for her.

CHAPTER 20

Yvonne had had nothing to fear regards Scott's immediate safety. Schultz had spent the time she thought him to be torturing Scott actually working out his tight schedule. The planning couldn't be finalised until he received a phone call from an informant in Cueta, a Spanish enclave in Morocco and adjacent to the Straits of Gibraltar. This hadn't been forthcoming until nearly 3-45pm during which time he had had to attend to a disgruntled Müeller who had been trying, contrary to his instruction, to get at the Englishman, Jerry Hill, in the old wine cellars below the house. This he couldn't allow – he needed the Englishman alive to collect the bounty on his newly laid plans – but at the same time he desperately needed Müeller's expertise for the job ahead and had had to cajole him to relax and ignore Hill until after the job. Had the situation been normal he would have had Müeller shot for disobeying orders. To help ease Müeller's murderous mood until his expected phone call, he had asked him what he intended to do with Hill. He had replied that he was going to thrust a stick of TNT up Hill's arse and set a slow fuse. This way Hill would have time to dwell on the headache he was about to receive. To defuse the situation Schultz joked that he trusted he was going to do this outside in the garden as he'd just had the decorators in. This was met with a sullen glower. Thankfully, just then, the phone rang with the information he needed. Schultz had the crew gather round a large dining table with a map of the Mediterranean on display. With the aid of Max, his second in command, all were given their instructions. By the time the instructions had been repeated and relevant questions answered it was 5-10pm and darkness had descended outside the bay window overlooking the jetty.

***

Earlier in the old wine cellars below the house whilst Schultz was awaiting his phone call upstairs, Suarez was administering a tin cup of water to Scott's mouth. 'Here you are my amigo. I am glad to see you survived your ordeal with that terrible man Hertzog – but, unfortunately, I fear we are in worse trouble – as you English say, out of the chip pan and into the fires,' he finished proudly.

Scott had recovered consciousness with a thunderous headache. His vision was blurred and his hearing competing with a constant alarm bell ringing in his ears. 'Where am I? Who are you?' he groaned.

'I am Eduardo Suarez and we are being held against our will in the old wine cellars of a villa belonging to a madman a – raving psycho.'

Through the haze and pain it started to come back to Scott. His first thought was for Yvonne as he asked, 'Was there an attractive brunette lady brought in at the same time as me ?'

'Was it the same woman I saved from Hertzog...'

With being slightly concussed the name Suarez hadn't registered but suddenly his brain cleared. '*You? You,* tried to save her? The last I saw of you, you were trying to torture her with a cigarette,' Scott exclaimed as he knocked the hand holding the cup aside and rose unsteadily to his feet. 'In fact, shit face, you had before that left the lady to the rats in the dockyard chamber.'

In panic Suarez held his hand out palm outwards. '*No. No*, señor. You have to believe me, I would never leave a lady in distress. I thought your security would find her. I had been told by one of the madman's henchmen to kill her – I did not. I had been told to torture her by Hertzog – I did not....'

'Only because of my intervention...' interrupted Scott indignantly.

'No señor. It is not as it seems,' he pleaded. 'I do not physically hurt people. It was because that Nazi bastard Hertzog held my wife Delores hostage that I agreed to help him. He threatened to kill her if I did not lead him to your colleague.'

'And why would he want to see my colleague? Could it be that to save your skin you told Hertzog she worked for the MOD and had dockyard secrets he should know about ?....'

'Upon my mother's grave, señor,' he crossed himself as he interrupted, 'I can assure you I would never do such a thing.'

Ignoring Suarez's lie-ridden tale, Scott said, 'That's funny. I thought Delores was married to Curran, not you, for when I last spoke to her yesterday – tied to a chair – she certainly wanted nothing to do with you. I believe her exact words were that she wanted to "slit your throat". She also told me all about her sham marriage to Curran and that you pay her to pretend to be married to him. Her confession being in the vain hope she will be saved execution for treason,' he added as a lie.

'Hah! But *I'm* not a British subject. And there is no extradition treaty from Spain, so you cannot hang me for treason – I am a Spanish national,' he said triumphantly, conveniently omitting to defend his alleged marriage to Delores.

Scott sighed as he replied, 'Okay, you hang as a terrorist then. It doesn't really matter to me Suarez. My government's not going to kill you – the red haired guy will do it for them. Unless....'

Suarez mocked, 'Unless what? What can *you* do? Start a tunnel? Call in your Marines? They can't put a foot in Spain. The League of Nations would not permit the violation of Spain's sovereign territory.'

With arms crossed whilst leaning against the stone wall Scott was looking Suarez over, debating whether to wipe the smile off his smug face. However, pragmatically he decided to wait until he had the information he required. 'That is true, Suarez. But now that I know my colleague hasn't been captured by the red haired guy, the lady will be, as we speak, on her way to get the Marines,' he lied, wishing it were true, adding, 'And for your benefit you should know that not all Marines go into battle in uniform. We have "Special Units." And who's to say when they're not in uniform that they aren't Spanish.'

Suarez gave this some thought before asking, 'Are you offering me a way out of here?'

'No. Why should I save a scumbag like you?'

'Because I know all about the gang....but why should I tell you if you won't...'

'Okay Suarez. Tell you what – you tell me what you know and if it's helpful I'll take you with me when our Marines arrive,' lied Scott, 'So give. What are they up to?'

'I know a lot señor but the one thing I don't know is what they're about to do...*honest*. It could possibly be something to do with the dockyard. I found a way into it and I was forced to tell them. If I hadn't they would have killed me.'

185

'*Honest*, eh? You wouldn't know what it meant, Suarez, even if it bit you on the bum. However, let's see what you know. Who is funding you and Delores? And who is the red haired guy?'

Scott watched Suarez think his way to an answer that would incriminate everybody but himself before he said, 'The red haired psycho's name is Karl Schultz. A German mercenary working for the IRA. He speaks English with an Irish accent. He was a captain in the German Kreigsmarine Kommando before he got court-martialed. His men here all served under him. A real nasty bunch of bastards. And at some time previously he was a commander in the Irish Republican Army in Dublin. Thus his Irish accent. He told Scott the whole story, from his recruitment by the IRA in Belfast who wanted him to find an entry into the dockyard to his recruiting of Delores, with the aid of the IRA's money, to act as if she was Curran's wife. Curran was the IRA's in place mole in the Customs and Excise. They needed an excuse to get him the job in Gibraltar. It was decided that should he marry a Gibraltarian he stood a better chance. That's when Curran's predecessor had his unfortunate accident. Curran had been recruited to allow Schultz and gang free passage across the border to bring explosives into Gibraltar in a horsebox. And, of course, any other inside information that would be deemed helpful. He confirmed Delores' story that she thought they were only involved in smuggling cigarettes and booze. All had gone well until the arrival of the madman, Schultz. Suarez had been instructed by Belfast IRA only to find the entry into the dockyard and to act as a guide afterwards. That was up until Schultz took control. But after Schultz's take-over of the operation and Suarez's surprising find of the entry into the dockyard due to his grandmother's old wives' tale, he had been forced to become a member of the gang. This had been against his wishes – he wouldn't harm the British. He loved the British. It had all been a dreadful error his banishment from Gibraltar. In answer to a Scott question he replied that as far as he knew the gang consisted of Schultz, Helmut, the brain-dead giant Dieter, the Spaniard Pedro and Max. Scott mentally added Müeller to the list making six known in total. Regarding the stolen Italian, "Maiale," Suarez knew nothing and Scott believed him. It was one of the few things Suarez had uttered that he did believe. There were smatterings of truth in Suarez's fairy tale. It was just a question of separating the many layers of lies. However, Scott was satisfied with the main finding: The IRA were responsible for the attempt on HMS Worcester through the auspices of this mercenary, Schultz. Scott figured they were possibly gearing up to finish the job. He just had to live long enough to do something about stopping the assault on the Worcester....and Schultz.

Suarez finished his diatribe with, 'I am innocent. At worst I am naive and have been used. Ask yourself this question, señor – if I was a gang member why am I being held against my wishes?'

'I would guess that you thieved money from the IRA coffers?'

'Why would I do such a thing?'

'Because thieving little toe-rags like yourself can't help it. It's in your genes. And in your case you ended up way out of your league.'

Suarez shoulder's visibly sagged. He knew the Englishman was correct in his summing up of his character. However, priding himself on his ability of obfuscation, he said proudly, 'But I have never used violence....'

'You haven't? In my book had you and your accomplices been successful in detonating the limpet mines attached to HMS Worcester in the dockyard – there would have been many deaths. Murder. Many whom I would have been acquainted with.'

'But it didn't happen and I didn't place the mines....'

'You led them there....'

'Not voluntarily. Against my wishes I was forced at gunpoint.'

'Could that be in case you fled to South America with their money without telling them your little secret?'

'Señor! I am a man of honour....'

Tired of Suarez's lies and whining he approached Suarez, stopped slightly off-centre and said in a friendly tone as he made to delve into his fatigue's hip pocket, 'Oh! By the way, Delores asked me to give you something the next time I met you.' A smiling Suarez didn't realise he had been hit until the fist sank solidly into his midriff causing him to double up to meet Scott's right knee as it came up violently under his chin to a crunching of broken teeth accompanied by the words, 'And my colleague asked me to give you that message also. Unfortunately for you she hates rats.' A senseless Suarez's back hit the stone wall and he began to slither down the wall with his legs opened wide. Scott, figuring that the solid stone walled dungeon with its heavy steel grilled door might prove to be impossible to escape from decided that he might not readily get another opportunity to pass on his friendly felicitations to scum-ball Suarez; so he took advantage of Suarez's open leg invitation.

While he set about removing the handle of the tin cup to reshape it into a lock-pick he wondered if Yvonne had escaped. And if she had, had she managed to reach Twomay for help. For all their disagreements he knew one thing: they would be put aside and she would be doing her best to rescue him. He had every confidence in her, wherever she was. He, meanwhile, tried his make-shift key in the lock. It moved the bolt fractionally.

**

Yvonne was close by, sitting on a boulder in her new hide, pondering her next move when the jetty and the hewn stone steps up to the villa were suddenly bathed in a yellow glow from overhead lighting hung between poles along the jetty's length and lamp standards lighting the steps up to the villa. Something was about to happen. Out through the pass door alongside the open boathouse doors strode Schultz followed by Müeller and three others, all heavily armed. They leapt aboard the catamaran. Another figure vaulted into the speed boat and started it immediately. As it pulled alongside the catamaran it was flagged down by Schultz who was shouting, 'Repeat to me your instructions Max.' Carried on the still night air Yvonne heard every word of the exchange as did the others aboard the catamaran. Max standing to attention saluted. 'I have to proceed to Algecirus to refuel. I then wait for Pedro and Helmut to arrive with the catamaran in Algecirus; thus indicating you have dropped the Maiale and Dieter, Wolf and yourself at the target. Pedro, Helmut and me wait sixty minutes then I pick up – Dieter, Wolf and you, off the Maiale at the rendezvous point. We then scuttle the Maiale and head back to base.'

'Good man, Max. And don't forget the other important matter,' Schultz bellowed through cupped hands above the rising noise of the powerful engines as Max confirmed he hadn't forgotten with a thumbs-up gesture. On

Schultz's acknowledged wave Max roared off through the gap in the gorge walls into the Mediterranean leaving a white-cap wake rocking the catamaran at its mooring. He was Schultz's second-in-command – and after the Gibraltar debacle with the others, the only one Schultz trusted.

Dieter then started the catamaran's newly mounted twin engines and in contrast to the motor launch it lumbered slowly, low in the water with its heavy load towards the Mediterranean.

***

As the catamaran cleared the gorge into the open sea Yvonne broke cover keeping close to the gorge walls to remain hidden from anybody in the villa above. She advanced toward the timber jetty, slipped under it and waded towards the far side. This would give her a good view of the villa above. She shinned up a timber column and peeped cautiously over. There was no sign of life from the villa. To her left were the open doors of the boathouse. The fact that Schultz and crew had arrived at the jetty through the pass-door meant there were steps inside leading up to the villa. The water being shallow but deep enough allowed her to swim underwater into the boathouse and still be out of sight of the house. Once inside she stood up. This put her above the edge of the quay. That was when her troubles began. There was a low growl building up to a snarl accompanied by a scrabble of paw nails on the stone quay. When her eyes grew accustomed to the dark interior she came face to face with a snarling mastiff straining on a lead chained to a wall adjacent to stone steps leading up to the villa. It had to be the Dobermann she had seen earlier guarding Scott. She decided to abandon the stone steps as a way into the villa and its dungeon. A tethered speed-boat caught her eye. It might be an ideal way to escape later, so using the fixed stern ladder she climbed aboard. Once on board she checked the fuel gauge – it showed full and with the ignition key lying on the control consul it was ready to depart. As she was clambering overboard into the water to the constant growling of the Dobermann, she heard a clang of something metallic scraping off a wall. Figuring out that it could be a firearm she, as a precaution, disappeared under the hull as the boathouse flooded with light and an Irish female voice called the beast to heel. The boat rocked – somebody had come on board. She had been dripping wet when she had climbed aboard. Would whoever notice? This became of secondary importance as the water, a metre away from her, suddenly starter to churn savagely. Somebody, and she suspected it to be Roisin, was about to use the speed boat. Yvonne immediately did a somersault underwater and kicked-off against the quayside wall to give her acceleration to clear the boat and its deadly propeller. She took a straight line path to the opposite cave wall. As she rose slowly in the shadow of the wall she heard a bell ringing. The loudness of the bell suggested an extension from the main house. The boat had not moved. By the overhead lighting she saw a female figure with a machine pistol slung over her shoulder dashing up the internal stairs to the villa to answer the continually ringing phone. About a minute later the bell stopped ringing. Roison had obviously made it to the phone before the caller hung up. Taking a deep breath she submerged again and struck out coming up under the jetty. She would have to take a chance with the lit outside steps....but with an armed Roison on the loose she could become a sitting target. Or...she retraced her steps to the base of the gorge wall near to her hide. From memory her new hide put her directly under the villa some 20 metres above. She knew from her earlier survey that the gorge walls under the villa had sharp rock projections. Slipping around the headland that projected into the bay and protected her hide, she returned with a rope and grapnel hook. Spending her holidays and spare time mountaineering in the French Alps, the use of rope and hook was second nature to her as she scampered like a mountain goat up the near vertical face. The final ten feet was an overhang. Once again from her earlier binocular survey she knew the precipice boundary to be a laurel bush hedge to the garden. Adjusting her rope length she twirled it around sideways to gain momentum, releasing it blind in the hope of the grapnel hook catching the roots of the laurels. It caught. She tested the pull. Satisfied, she started the final climb awaiting a burst of gunfire at any moment that didn't materialise. At the precipice she grabbed a stout stem and pulled herself onto a flat area between the hedge and the precipice and started to crawl on her hands and knees towards the villa until she came to the gable end. One of the windows in the gable was open. She was glad she had not chosen the steps, for the window was an ideal position for a sniper to cover the lit-up jetty and the steps. But there was a triangular dark area between the top of the steps and the window...she crawled into this shadow, rose to her feet with back against the gable. There was no sign of anybody. She stood with her back to the gable chimney breast. To her left, around the corner, was the front of the villa. Similarly, to her right, the back garden. With Beretta in hand she slipped round the corner. Looking along the rear wall of the house she noticed the French doors were open. Crouching low to keep below sill height of a large bay window a horrible thought entered her mind: *supposing Roison had taken the Dobermann from the boathouse into the villa.* Some sixth sense forced her to look around in the gloom. She froze – the beast on a restraining lead was cocking its leg against a tree and looking straight at her. She slipped the silencer onto the Beretta. The mastiff snarled and charged. Yvonne held her nerve. With stance wide and Beretta held in a two-handed grip she waited until it leapt before firing two rapid tap shots into the exposed chest. As she stepped aside its chest erupted in a shower of bone, blood and fur as the momentum of the leap carried it past her to hit the villa wall and slide down lifeless. She took Scott's advice and did not pat its head. Assuming there to be staff as well as Roison she was down on the ground before the beast hit the wall and rolling behind a lawn roller. There was no gunfire. Puzzled at the lack of attention she rose slowly and crouching made for the French doors. A look through the dimly lit bay window showed nobody in the room. With her Beretta at the ready she entered a sumptuously furnished through lounge/dining room running the full length of the house to another set of French doors leading to the garden above the gorge wall she had just climbed. Off the dining room was a door, she imagined, to the kitchen. To her right-hand wall there was a smooth, polished-stone fireplace with comfortable settees arranged at right angles to the fireplace and floor-to-ceiling windows giving a panoramic view of the bay. In the middle of the wall to her left was a massive pair of ornately carved oak doors presumably leading to the hall and upper floors. Crossing the polished oak floor of the lounge with its expensive Persian rugs she opened one door cautiously and peeped out. Straight ahead the polished oak floor continued, leading to the main entrance doors through which she could see a Doric stone column portico. To her left were a series of doors which she assumed to be cloakroom and toilets. To the right was a magnificent marble staircase sweeping up to the bedrooms. Between where she stood at the open lounge door and the staircase lay the kitchen. Suspecting that any access to the dungeons would be in the locality of the wine-cellar which was usually adjacent to the kitchen, she expected to find a door leading into the kitchen from off the hallway. Instead in this recess stood a gleaming suit of armour. The knight stood to attention with a lance in one hand, the other hand atop his sheathed sword. Disappointed, but still of the opinion that the door to the dungeon would lead off the kitchen she was about to re-enter the lounge to access the kitchen from the dining room when she noticed a door behind the suit of armour. She approached the door. It was slightly ajar. With the Beretta drawn she hooked the door outwards with her foot and found herself, with the aid of lit wall lights set in the roughly hewn walls, looking at stone steps leading sharply downwards. Her view was restricted in that the steps curved to her right, but given the relative position of the main entrance her innate sense of direction told her that the steps led in the direction of the boathouse and also the dungeon where Scott should be being held prisoner. As she was about to take her first downward step she heard a familiar noise she had last heard in the boathouse – the scraping of metal against a rock wall. *If you were carrying a machine pistol on a shoulder strap, as Roison had as she entered the boathouse, it would be hard not to make a noise due to the narrow width of the roughly hewn walls,* thought Yvonne. As a precaution she back-tracked into the recess behind the knight knowing that the opening-out door would further conceal her. Her precaution yielded fruit – seconds later the door was kicked outwards violently and a tall, blonde female wearing riding boots, jodhpurs and a light tweed hacking jacket with a machine pistol held in position at her hip strode into view. This Yvonne sensed was Roison. There was the choice of three motor cars available outside. Reckoning Roison had the keys to the dungeon Yvonne could not allow her to gain access to any of the vehicles. With this necessity in mind she took aim from behind the suit of armour and fired a warning shot into the polished oak floor in front of Roison with the warning, 'Drop the gun while you've a chanc....'

Any normal person would have acceded to the request but Roison turned spraying a hail of death that ricocheted off the marble stair case and the suit of armour with the snarled reply, 'Go fuck yourself, bitch. You're dead.'

Unfortunately, one of the sprayed bullets nicked Yvonne's arm causing her to drop the Beretta. To try to pick it up meant certain death. To emphasise this point Roison, with a manic laugh, drilled a line of bullets that churned up the oak floor on their way towards the wayward Beretta. Before Roison could direct the next hail of death at Yvonne she lunged her shoulder at the heavy suit of armour sending it lurching towards Roison who, taken by surprise, hastily side-stepped the falling mass of iron only to step onto a Persian rug that slipped on the polished oak floor. As she went down on one knee she lost her hold on the machine pistol as the lance belonging to the suit of armour fell backwards to be caught by Yvonne who grasped it in a throwing hold. Her adrenalin flowing she returned it with a throw that any Olympic javelin thrower would have been proud of. The deathly blow struck with such force that it impaled the shocked Roison to the floor. Lying face up and with blood gurgling from the corners of her mouth and an ugly wound to the chest she defiantly growled, 'You lose... English whore... You're... too.. late.' Then, in agony and coughing up blood she cried in a shrill cackle, 'Your...Eagle...will...not..return...to..its..nest..tonight.' Her head dropped onto her blood soaked chest – dead. Very dead.

A relieved Yvonne wiped the lance shaft clean of fingerprints before rummaging in Roison's pockets to produce sets of car keys and two large iron mortice lock keys on a ring attached to a belt around her waist. The belt also produced a PPK automatic that she recognised as belonging to Scott. Gathering up the dropped Schmeisser P28 machine pistol and her Beretta she ran down the steps until she came to a landing. Facing her were a flight of stone steps leading upwards. She assumed these to lead to the phone that Roison had ran to answer from the boathouse before continuing up to the entrance hall. The landing had steps leading downwards. By her reckoning they must lead to the wine cellar, dungeon and boathouse. Within ten paces she came face to face with a male lounging nonchalantly with arms crossed against an iron grill door. Scott said, 'Took your time getting here, Rencoule. What kept you? It's bloody freezing down here.'

As she unlocked the door with one of the keys she had appropriated from Roison she said, 'Ha – ha, very funny Rutherford. Perhaps if you had shown up for our meeting on time instead of playing hide and seek with your pals in the woods you might not be in the pickle you're in now. *And*, a "thank you for rescuing me, Yvonne," wouldn't go amiss.' Then noticing the battered Suarez lying on the floor in the foetal position she queried, 'What happened to him?'

'Fell out of bed. Who cares?' Scott replied as he accepted his PPK from Yvonne. 'And, of course, I thank you for your brave rescue,' he added as he kissed her on the cheek. 'Now, just watch out, Schultz's lady friend is on the prowl armed with a machine pistol. She just passed this way a minute ago in a hurry. It's a wonder you didn't meet her.'

'*Was,* on the prowl,' interrupted Yvonne as she turned to retrieve the machine pistol that she had left leaning against the wall while she unlocked the cell door. 'Now dead. A raving lunatic. Seemed to think I was some sort of an English whore who had arrived too late for something.'

'Dead? That's going a bit over the top – topping her just because she called you an *English* whore....when in fact you're a half French...'

'Don't you dare finish that Rutherford unless you want to go the same way as she did....'

'Which was?' interrupted an intrigued Scott.

'If you must know she died by the lance.....'

'Lance? Taken up ye olde jousting have we...Rencoule?'

Initially ignoring him she hastily explained the demise of Roison then continued, '*And,* as I was saying before you interrupted with one of your usual inane remarks – she also seemed to think I was a twitcher.'

'A what?'

'A bird watcher. She said my *Eagle* would not be going to its nest tonight. What did she mean by that?'

A silence ensued during which Scott, after a large intake of breath and the release of a hand that had been massaging his chin, exclaimed, 'She said.....*what*? Did you say, she said, *Eagle*?' A surprised Yvonne nodded her head to affirm. 'Pwhor!' he exhaled banging his forehead with the heel of his hand. 'What-a-bloody-fool-I've-been, Yvonne. I now know what they're up to.'

'What, Scott? What are they up to?'

'No time to explain Yvonne. I'll tell you as we go. However, it's essential we get to the dockyard immediately, if not sooner. The question now is – where is Schultz and his gang?'

'Listen Scott, I've been busy since you last saw me and I've a good idea of Schultz's whereabouts.' She, quickly recapping, proceeded to advise him about her covert snooping on Schultz. Advising Scott verbatim of Max's repeated instructions as to where Schultz and gang were all supposed to be located at any given time.

'Brilliant Yvonne. That confirms my theory.' Before she had time to ask what theory he asked, 'Tell me, did Roison have any other keys on her apart from the wine cellar?'

'Yes,' she replied as she withdrew a bunch of keys from a pocket. They are for the vehicles you saw outside. I also have the key for a speed boat in the boathouse downstairs and, of course, I still have the Triumph's key hidden under a boulder.'

'Excellent. We'll travel by the Triumph it'll be quicker than the speedboat but we'll drive one of the cars parked outside the main entrance to where you've hidden it just in case Roison has tampered with the machine.'

Yvonne's heart sank at this news; the thought of another pillion ride with him filled her with terror. She was scared of little but his driving was right up there with her terminal fear of rats. To keep her mind focused and off the ensuing nightmare ride she changed the subject, 'What about phoning Twomay. There must be one upstairs – Roison went to answer a phone.'

'Look Yvonne, I don't have time to explain why not other than suffice it to say Gibraltar is a foreign country to the Spanish telephone system. Now let's get moving – please.'

'But what about Suarez? You're not letting the creep off the hook for all he's done to Delores, are you?' she said pointing to the groaning Suarez who was trying to stagger to his feet whilst clutching his damaged manhood.

An agitated, anxious to get moving, Scott growled, 'Shoot the blighter for all I care...or leave him locked up for Schultz to attend to.'

At those words a panicking Suarez muttered through his mouthful of broken teeth, ' I told you the truth. I'm innocent ...I was...you promised to take me...'

'Sorry Suarez. Now you know what it's like to be lied to.'

At the terrifying thought of confronting Schultz again Suarez, in a surprise move, lunged between Scott and Yvonne. The move took him in the direction of the down flight of stone steps to the boathouse.

Yvonne raised her Beretta and took aim only to find it knocked aside by Scott. 'What the hell did you do that for?' she retorted angrily.

'Listen' he said as he put his hand to his ear. Seconds later a growling noise echoed eerily up the steps followed by snarling and a horrendous human scream followed by a deathly hush and an agonising dog whimper that set Yvonne's nerves on edge. Scott shrugged his shoulders and said laconically, 'Ah! Just as I thought the beast is still there. We could of course kill it and make our get-away in the speed-boat...' At this Yvonne's hopes rose only to be dashed as he continued, 'But the Triumph is still the quickest way to the dockyard – so let's go.'

A stunned Yvonne, her mind a twirl at the events unfolding whispered, 'How was that possible? I just killed a Dobermann ...upstairs.'

'I told you earlier in the copse that there were two of the beasts.'

Yvonne, then with a heavy sigh said, 'Poor Suarez. What a way to go...' She was talking to herself. Scott was already on the move heading upstairs. Slinging the machine pistol over her shoulder she followed. She met up with him in the hall. He was looking at the gruesome impaled mess that had been Roison.

Scott with a screwed-up face showing his repugnance was shaking his head sorrowfully as he growled, 'Christ, Yvonne you made a real mess of her. Couldn't you have just shot her like any normal person would have done?'

'Frightfully sorry Scott – I didn't have time to clean her up – I was too busy trying to rescue an idiot that had allowed himself to be caught napping and who any *normal person* would have left to rot in the dungeon.'

'Well I must say that's a really nice attitude to adopt towards a person who has just been traumatized....'

'Traumatized? *You*?'

'Yes, me. I don't suppose you would consider apologizing for hurting my feelings ?'

'Correct Rutherford – I wouldn't. But what I will say in my defence is that your bad habits seem to be rubbing off on me,' she replied with a chortle as she jumped off the top step of the porch on to the gravel driveway and athletically loped towards the Buick. As he opened the Buick door it nudged her lightly on the shoulder. It was then that he noticed her grimace as a rivulet of blood dripped from her wrist. He stopped to retrieve a handkerchief from a pocket and worriedly said, 'Here, let me attend to that.'

'Don't fuss so, Scott. Keep going, it's just a nick. Roison got lucky.'

'The last I saw of her Roison didn't look too lucky to me,' he chirpily replied as he slipped behind the wheel of the Buick to relocate it to the driveway's main entrance where Yvonne slipped along its bench front seat to keep the engine running while Scott vaulted the low boundary wall to check that the Triumph was still where she had hidden it. Finding it untouched, and on his signal, she wiped the Buick clean of fingerprints, removed the ignition key and vaulted the wall one-handed to take her place on the pillion seat. Scott took off with his customary rear wheel spin in a splatter of mud and turf with Yvonne clinging tightly around his waist with eyes already shut.

Roison's stable manager exited his office to make his daily report. The main door of the villa being open he entered. Two minutes later he was back in his office phoning the Guardia Civil to report a brutal murder. He then phoned an unlisted number in Ireland.

CHAPTER 21

Gibraltar Bay Area

Aboard the catamaran Schultz was bemoaning the sluggishness of the vessel. 'At this rate, Helmut, it will be bloody daybreak before we reach the Eagle. What's wrong with it? The fucking thing's just back from modifications and I don't recall having this problem with it when we relieved the Italians of their Maiale'

'Yes, sir,' replied Helmut hesitantly, knowing that he was already in disgrace for the failed Gibraltar dockyard attack and was, if he didn't choose his words carefully, about to be blamed for the errant nature of the catamaran. So he said guardedly, 'The increased depth of the hulls to accommodate the above deck storage of weapons, diving gear, seat wells and, of course, *your* brilliantly designed release mechanism that allows us to drop the Maiale into the water without a crane, all come at a cost....'

'You don't have to tell me about the cost – they cost me a fortune... And don't think your crawling will help me forget your fuck-up in Gibraltar.'

'Yes sir. But what I meant by cost was the alterations have added weight. Also when we appropriated the Maiale there was only you and me – now there are five of us constituting considerable additional weight.'

'Why do you think I had, not one, but *two* outboard engines fitted to the cat? That bastard boat-builder assured me they would be powerful enough to take care of the additional loads.

Helmut, having worked under Schultz's command in the Kreigsmarine Kommando unit, knew from experience that he would be thinking about who to throw overboard to gain speed, so to safeguard himself he added, 'I mean Dieter alone is the weight of two people.'

'I need Dieter's strength to carry the mines,' was the curt reply. 'However, Helmut, since you and I have worked together for some considerable time I intend to give you a chance to redeem yourself for the Gibraltar fuck-up. Then putting an arm around Helmut's shoulders he said in a comradely and conspiratorially tone, 'Believe it or not Helmut you are the only one I can depend upon. Now we're at sea I intend an alteration to our plans. This is a chance for you to make-up for the Gibraltar fracas. Here's what I propose.' When Schultz finished a twisted smile broke out on Helmut's face.

While this conversation was ongoing Müeller was surveying his surroundings. He had never travelled on a catamaran and was, even as a seaman of long standing, not enjoying the experience. He was sitting in a semi-circular seat-well in the port hull. Sitting in the opposite hull in similar seats sat Schultz and Helmut in deep animated conversation. The craft had widely spaced twin-hulls for stability with a trampoline tarpaulin suspended between them. The sure-footed crew, when in full race mode, would use this to move between the ten metre long hulls to attend to their allotted duties. Today was not one of these days. Under the tarpaulin, he knew, lay the manned torpedo – the Maiale. Causing bother was the large twin motors and rudder mounted on a rigid stern cross tie. He was aware that the craft was not responding as it should considering the power that was being transmitted from the engines. This of course was due to the weight of the Maiale and the heavy alterations. And the sail was not engaged. Whilst not being au fait with catamarans the experienced Müeller reckoned this to be a mistake. He knew every little would help. With Pedro at the tiller it left only the massive Dieter to crew the modified catamaran. Not being the standard of seamanship he expected he rose from his seat to interrupt Schultz's conversation with Helmut. However, Schultz also realizing the engines needed assistance, broke off his covert conversation with Helmut before Müeller reached him. He ordered Helmut, Dieter and Pedro to raise the sail on the giant ten metre mast that was centred on a steel box girder joining the two hulls whilst Müeller took the tiller. Schultz, meanwhile, attended to the various adjustments to the rigging.

With the sail set and the craft gaining more speed from what little wind was available a happier Schultz signalled Pedro back to the tiller and Müeller into one of the hull seats to join him. 'You don't look as though you're enjoying the sail, Wolf...surely not battle nerves?'

'No Karl. No nerves. Just giving some thought to the dive. It's all been a bit of a rush compared with the way I usually prepare for diving. I mean – we meet and within twenty four hours I'm involved in what will become, if we are successful, a major political storm....even to the point of another war. I have no qualms about this, but being unfamiliar with this Maiale worries me...'

'I wouldn't go so far as to say *war,* but it will certainly rack up the tension between Britain and Germany,' Schultz chortled as he added, 'And as regards the Maiale nobody is really familiar with it other than the Italians. So let me tell you what I know in the hope that it will ease your worries. Firstly, it is not as everybody initially perceives – we do not aim it at the target then jump off. It is battery operated and therefore silent running. This allows us to get in close to place the mines from its nose cone. We – that is you, me and Dieter will be dressed, as we already are, in our wet suits. Each of us is familiar with the rebreather method of diving and will be wearing our oxygen cylinders when we take our seats on the Maiale which will be lowered into the water with the aid of my new release mechanism by Helmut when we are within a five hundred metre range of the target. I will be driving. With it being dark the Maiale will not need to submerge until we are close to the target's hull. Say, sixty metres to enable you to fix our umbilical line to the target. Dieter will, whilst you are doing this, be fixing modified lifebelts, fore, aft and amid-ships to whatever projections the target has to offer – the propeller drive shaft, etcetera, etcetera. There being no underwater magnets strong enough to carry seventy-five kilo mines it has to be done the old tried and tested method. Dieter will then unload the mines one at a time from the detachable nose cone of the Maiale to hand to you, to set the timers. You then have sixty minutes to complete the job and get clear. It's really a trial and error situation that I know you can handle without breaking sweat, Wolf. However, once you have checked the wiring, set the timer and climbed back on board we will rendezvous with Max's speed boat at the coordinates I gave him. And, as per our preplanning meeting, the catamaran, crewed by Helmut and Pedro after dropping us, will continue to Algecirus marina to allow Max to register it for the race. Once we have destroyed the Eagle, we will have breakfast in Estepona after which you can meet up with the Englishman, Hill, in the dungeon and blow his brains out. Does that answer your problem, Wolf?' What he had conveniently omitted to tell Müeller was that he had no intention of allowing him back on board. This had been one of the alterations to the planned attack that he had not communicated to Müeller. Once the mines were in place and timers set, Dieter would make sure he became fish fodder.

'Yes. It does answer most of my queries Karl, but there is one I do not understand. I assume the attack will take place near the Gibraltar dockyard?' Schultz nodded. 'Then, how do you propose to get the catamaran within five hundred metres of the Eagle to drop the Maiale with us aboard ? The Eagle will have an escort of motor torpedo boats armed to the teeth with anti-submarine weapons, depth charges and sonar.'

'A very astute question, Commander Müeller. One that I have given you a clue to already. I mentioned that the catamaran after dropping us, was heading for Algecirus to moor up for the race. I expected you to ask – "What race?" For Max, as we speak, is busy preparing our mooring to enable us to take part in the Algecirus annual catamaran race tomorrow – around Alboran a small island over two hundred kilometres from Algecirus in the middle of the Mediterranean. Pedro, being Spanish, will communicate to the Eagle's escort our intentions. They will check this and find my participation in the race to be true. Thus my rush to get you on board. Because with your experience of underwater explosives....need I say more, Wolf? I will, of course, be disqualified tomorrow morning by the race stewards due to my modifications abusing race specifications. But who cares?....the catamaran will have done what it was altered to do, deliver the Maiale to the drop point and then, unfortunately, will have outlived its usefulness. And don't worry about the Eagle's sonar – the Maiale is battery powered and silent running. That's what makes it a formidable weapon.

'Brilliant, Captain Schultz, brilliant,' answered a delighted Müeller, knowing he was now within touching distance of his revenge on that Englishman, Hill, he added quizzically, 'I thought you said we were to breakfast in gay Paree? Schultz just laughed. And gave him a friendly hug around the shoulders. Paris or Estepona , it would make no difference to Müeller's fate.

At the designated drop point for the Maiale, Schultz hung back to shepherd Müeller into position number two behind the driver on the manned torpedo, sitting behind the driver. Dieter sat in position number three. Schultz nodded to Helmut, who slipped into the driver's seat. Position number one. Schultz then held back to find out if there was a reaction from Müeller about the substitution of Helmut for himself. This was the other alteration to the original plan. There was no reaction. Schultz's ploy had depended on the darkness and the fact they all looked similar in wet suits. It had worked. With all aboard the Maiale Schultz took over the tiller of the catamaran from Pedro and gave him the signal to open the release mechanism to allow the Maiale to drop into the cold waters of the Mediterranean whilst they kept moving. Helmut adjusted the buoyancy tanks and they sank to just below water level. Then out of sight. Pedro on Schultz's further instruction took up a forward position on the catamaran to await the expected arrival of a Royal Navy escort boat. They didn't have long to wait before a Royal Navy MTB signalled them to heave-to. Schultz knowing his English was accented Irish let the Spaniard, Pedro, do the talking albeit in broken English and show the MTB officer their entry papers and passports for the Algecirus to Alboran catamaran race tomorrow. They had to hang about for several nervous minutes whilst the MTB used ship to shore wireless to get confirmation of their entry. When notification duly arrived Schultz opened up the two powerful outboard engines and, without the load of the manned torpedo, they surged forward to deposit them five minutes later in their allotted berth in Algecirus marina.

Through the late evening gloom Max watched the catamaran arrive and berth on the opposite side of the marina's jetty from his speed boat which was moored at the bay end of the jetty ready for a quick get-away. Two people in wet suits jumped off the catamaran and made it fast to the jetty capstans then returned aboard. He recognized the tall figure of Schultz and the demure stature of Pedro. Minutes later Schultz appeared shorn of wet suit and now dressed in reefer jacket, wool beanie hat, and American jeans. He watched him stroll down the jetty towards the twinkling lights of the quayside cafés. This he gave no thought to because it was part of Schultz's revised plan. He was to wait his return and then set course for Cueta, the Spanish enclave in Morocco across the Straits of Gibraltar where Schultz had assured him that from there the world was theirs for the taking. He regretted leaving Helmut and poor Dieter to their own fates. Müeller he knew was to be killed by Dieter after he planted the explosives. Of Helmut and Dieter's fate he could not envisage the Maiale's batteries being able to take them to nearest land. A pity for they had all fought together in German West Africa, in fact that was where he had received his wound that had left him with a prosthetic leg. He was now non-combative due to this injury and was respectful of Schultz's kindness in making him the executive planning officer of the group. For this Schultz in his eyes could do no wrong. Of Müeller and Pedro he cared little of their fate.

After mooring, Schultz, out of sight of Pedro slipped a silencer onto his Luger automatic walked up to the Spaniard and shot him through the heart then coolly sat him in one of the semi-circular seats. Changed out of his wet suit he walked along the floating jetty towards one of the cafés along the sea front overlooking the marina. With a lot on his mind, primarily his next move now that he had decided to sever connections with his present set-up, he chose one called El Sol and took an outside table. This location would give him the solitude he sought and a splendid pyrotechnic view of the destruction of HMS Eagle, the pride of the British fleet. He knew that when he departed with Max for Cueta that would be the end of his current empire. He had no feelings regarding the loss of the long association he had had with his men. They had become sloppy – too old for their jobs. Gibraltar, a fiasco, was the turning point; the moment he decided to be rid of them before they brought an end to him. His one regret was Roison – his type of lady, an obedient born killer. Once he had set up his new organisation he would find her wherever she was. With a deep sigh, he did regret the forthcoming loss of the Maiale. He had intended to sell it back to the idiot Italians but the fees he would receive from the IRA and the secret non-Nazi leaning admirals within the Kreigsmarine for the destruction of the Eagle would more than compensate. As the waiter brought his celebratory bottle of Jameson's Irish whiskey he was aware of a motor cycle drawing up outside of the café next door. The driver removed goggles and leather helmet, placed them in a pannier and shook out her lustrous shoulder length hair. He admired her good looks and elegant walk as she entered the next door café. Five minutes later she reappeared. A drunken local thug appeared out of the shadows to stand in her way as she moved towards her motor cycle. Schultz found himself rising to go to her aid when within a matter of seconds the thug was squirming on the ground vomiting and holding his scrotum. As he returned to his seat she calmly mounted the bike without goggles and helmet and drove it across the road until she stopped outside his catamaran's mooring. Intrigued Schultz sat back to await developments.

CHAPTER 22

La Linea area Spain

With cigarette smoke wafting from the open windows of their Mercedes patrol cruiser the two Guardia Civil officers waited at the Estepona junction of the main Malaga to La Linea two-lane carriageway preparing to join the far side lane to La Linea. With the nearside Malaga lane clear of traffic they started to cross on to the La Linea bound lane when they observed through the evening gloom a small, dim, round, yellowish glow. The driver thinking he had ample time made the decision to race the glow which in the blink of an eye suddenly appeared large and blinding; and a very near motorcycle headlight. Panicking at his bad decision he slammed on the brakes bringing the cruiser to a suicidal, skidding, tyre-burning, broadside stop across the carriageway as Scott, with horn blaring and eating up the miles at close to ninety miles per hour, swerved into the fortunately empty oncoming lane. As the bike listed at a gravity-defying angle to the road Yvonne, riding pillion with Roison's machine pistol slung over her shoulder, suddenly found herself gripping onto Scott for her life with one hand whilst the other held the pistol firmly to her back. Terrified, she couldn't believe her ears as she heard a manic chortle of glee drifting over Scott's shoulder. She, on the other hand, had to bite her bottom lip to stop from screaming. She wanted desperately to strangle him but daren't let go. If she survived, she promised herself she would never again, no matter what the circumstances, get on a motorcycle with that...that suicidal maniac Rutherford.

The officers, paralysed with fear, were brought out of their state of shock with their car radio ringing. The passenger answered as the driver straightened the patrol cruiser. The still traumatized passenger, on returning the mouthpiece to its cradle, advised the driver in a shaky voice that control had informed him that they were to proceed to just short of the La Linea road works to help set-up a road block. There had been a frenzied attack on one of the owners of Marbella Racing. The stable manager had informed control that the perpetrators had got away on a motorcycle. Indications were that it was heading in the direction of La Linea. They looked at each other knowingly, set the bell ringing and with headlights on full gave chase. They knew they would never catch the speed-limit breaking motor cycle but should their colleagues at the road block ahead stop it they could extract their revenge for the near miss.

The much maligned Scott, with every upper muscle sinew screaming in torture heaved the Triumph upright in time to notice the full headlights of the pursuing Guardia in his overtaking mirror and gave them no more thought – the reckless idiots would never see him again. That indeed was true until he approached to within a half kilometre of La Linea where he started to bring the Triumph to an enforced halt. Ahead he witnessed a solid single-line mass of red rear reflectors. A traffic jam or possibly an accident. As he moved in on the rear queuing vehicle he noted that to its right-hand side was a narrow gap between it and a high vertical-faced rock wall. A quick glance ascertained the gap was too narrow to allow him passage. Also, the oncoming side of the road that he thought to be clear of traffic, had in fact, given that appearance because of a wide, slow trundling, out-of-sight, behemoth of a tarmac-laying machine. He suddenly realized his plan would need a drastic overhaul, so he stopped with legs astride the Triumph to analyse the situation acutely aware that the clock was ticking. To the left of the rear queuing vehicle was a gap between it and the oncoming tar machine. Unfortunately, this gap was also too tight to accommodate the width of the handlebars. And, unhelpfully, the gap between the tar machine and the low boundary wall separating the road from the Mediterranean was no more than 60cm. It was then that he caught sight in his mirror full headlights approaching fast from behind. It could only be the idiots from the Estepona junction. Any forced interaction with the Guardia could prove fatal to his plans. Evasion was essential. He made the decision to relieve Yvonne of her machine pistol, abandon the Triumph, work their way down the queuing vehicles and hijack a vehicle at the front of the queue, when suddenly there was a toot of a horn from the direction of the tar machine. Fortunately, the driver of the machine had instantly recognized Scott's predicament and gave him the thumbs-up as he proceeded to move his machine over towards the low boundary wall between the road and sea thus increasing the gap between his machine and the last vehicle. This manoeuvre allowed the Triumph's handlebars to pass through the gap with the narrowest of tolerance. Scott, already on the move, shouted over his shoulder for Yvonne to keep her knees and elbows tucked in as he launched the parallel twin valved Triumph at the narrow gap. Trusting that his upper body strength could once again keep the machine upright, he impelled himself at the high speed necessary for stability until he cleared the length of the tarmac machine. Once clear, all he had to do was to keep clear of the freshly laid carpet of un-compacted tarmac. As he passed the cab of the tarmac machine the driver shouted a warning through cupped hands that the *Civilies* were operating a road block. Scott waved his hand overhead in acknowledgement then kept his fingers crossed as he sped down the narrow gap that the queuing vehicles' drivers wouldn't tire of adding their contribution to the deafening cacophony of vehicle horns and decide to open doors to step out of their vehicles to remonstrate, as was the Spanish way. Fortunately, this came to nothing as he, on reaching the front of the queue, encountered a Guardia Civil officer standing in front of a broadside cruiser with hand held out in the commanding stop position. Scott, with no intention of stopping, noticed out of the corner of his eye a low-loader trailer with its ramps still down after delivering the road roller required to compact the freshly-laid tarmac. Still at speed he swerved past the startled officer, drove up one of the ramps, along the empty flat bed of the low-loader trailer and launched the Triumph off the end of the flat bed to land on the roof of a parked Guardia cruiser with a crumpling of metal and a shattering of glass and took off via its bonnet along the road in one fluid movement.

'Woweeee...that waaaas fun.' Yvonne heard over his shoulder. She wished she could agree with the lunatic. They certainly hadn't taught her Scott's kind of mayhem at SIS training school.

As Scott disappeared in the distance towards Gibraltar he reflected on the help he had been afforded by the tar machine driver and came to the conclusion it was because, like most of his fellow truckers, he was either a Republican or a communist – and with civil strife abounding throughout Spain – both parties equally despised the para-military Nationalist Guardia.

Meanwhile, back at the scene of the recent carnage that Scott had caused there had been an additional disruption. Minutes after his dramatic departure there had been a loud shrieking of brakes followed by the grinding of metal then the hiss of steam from burst radiators permeating the eerie silence that followed. Responsible for the cause of the new carnage had been the pursuing cruiser that Scott had evaded. Sitting in their cruiser seething, the Guardia officers had had no option but to wait until the tarmac machine had very slowly, allowed them clear passage to follow Scott. When the gap was wide enough the driver impatiently floored the accelerator not realizing that the machine had been actually laying tarmac. The outcome being they drove onto the slippery surface making their steering uncontrollable and their brakes useless. These defaults they were soon to find out as the off-loaded road roller, heading for the freshly laid tarmac, suddenly appeared in front of them from behind the leading lorry in the queue. To the squeal of panic-applied brakes the cruiser, slithering on the non-compacted slippery tarmac, smashed into the leading steel wheel of the road roller – did a three hundred and sixty degree out-of-control turn before shunting the rear end of the traffic controller's cruiser that he and a colleague had turned to give chase to the Triumph. The shunt ploughed it into the side of the low loader. With both vehicles a total write-off, to add to the one already destroyed by Scott using it as a launch ramp, any thought of pursuit was abandoned by the officers.

Scott looked at his Omega divers' watch. He reckoned it had been ninety minutes since the catamaran with Schultz, his gang and the Maiale carrying at least three hundred kilos of TNT mines, had set sail for the target from his Marbella villa. According to Yvonne who had witnessed the catamaran's departure it was low on its Plimsoll line and slow moving. Scott reckoned from this information it would take them two hours to reach the target – maybe enough time for him to catch-up on the villainous Schultz. He knew he had to succeed – seven hundred plus lives depended on him. Failure wasn't an option.

CHAPTER 23

Gibraltar Dockyard

The carnage of the Guardia Civil's La Linea road block behind him Scott's mind was working overtime as they approached the border. The border guards being the least of his problems. At this time in the late evening the traffic was generally light as it proved with only two small vans waiting at the manned Spanish barrier to enter Gibraltar. Yvonne, aware that Scott had made no attempt to retrieve their passports from the rear wheel pannier suspected something was afoot when he whispered for her to hold on tight. She was right to suspect a happening for just as they arrived and the lead van moved off, Scott, on the blind side of the local custom officer, lurched forward to squeeze the Triumph between the van and the upraised barrier. The Spanish custom officer stood with mouth agape. At the Gibraltar entry the guards who had been instructed by a phone call from Twomay fifteen minutes earlier to allow *his* Triumph entry when it appeared, made a half-hearted attempt at lowering their barrier to hood-wink their Spanish counterparts into believing they were trying to stop him. Once clear of border control Scott was quite clear in his own mind about his modus operandi. However, for a smooth execution he required Twomay to be on duty to organize his needs quickly and efficiently.

Minutes later, with the barrier already in the up position, Scott was waved straight through into the dockyard by a Marine guard. Having expected to be stopped by the Marine guards at the gatehouse Scott looked quizzically at Yvonne – who shook her head and shrugged her shoulders. The marine guard noticing the look explained that the gatehouse had received a message from Twomay five minutes ago to expect Twomay's Triumph and give it unhindered access when it did eventually appear. Shortly afterwards border control had phoned to say it was on its way. This explanation had been relayed by the Marine without taking his eyes off the dishevelled Yvonne.

Scott couldn't blame him, for even in her torn jerkin, ripped fatigues, scuffed boots and filthy face and hands she still exuded elegance and beauty – a feeling that she did not share there and then, for she was still traumatized from her pillion experience. However, taking slow breaths to regain her composure she removed the machine pistol from her shoulder, laid it against the parked Triumph and bent into the pannier to retrieve their passports. Scott, now that he was in the conflict zone, had his mind totally alert meaning that everything from now on had to be positive action. Action which he immediately took by snapping the Marine guard out of his hypnotic stare at the shapely bottom bending to open the pannier by asking him abruptly if HMS Eagle had anchored. The answer was a crisp, 'Yes, sir. Dropped anchor thirty minutes ago.'

Scott nodded his thanks. This was relatively good news. On the assumption that the Maiale had arrived and was awaiting the arrival of the Eagle it would take Schultz another ten to fifteen minutes for the Maiale to fix the umbilical line before Schultz could start to fix his mines. Helmut also had the problem of finding suitable anchorages for his mines. He worked out that Schultz based on his figures had a twenty to twenty five minute start on him plus whatever time it took him to find the location of the mines and disable them. He then abruptly turned, picked up the SC28 machine pistol and whispered out the side of his mouth to Yvonne that it was the Eagle that was Schultz's target as he ran in the direction of Twomay's office. An annoyed Yvonne followed – not best pleased at the way she had been informed it was the Eagle that was in danger, nor his failure to consult her about his immediate plans. Emergency or not she knew he would have a plan. He always had a plan.

Scott and Yvonne were not to know at this stage that it was Twomay's panic phone calls to the gatehouse and border control that had eased their passage through border control. The calls had been primarily to ascertain if his beloved Triumph was still in one piece. This worry had been brought about because an irate Spanish gentleman, twenty minutes previously, had informed him he was Señor Francisco Matello the area Chief of the Guardia Civil. Apparently there had been serious incidents involving a Triumph motor cycle that had been traced, by virtue of its British plates, to Señor Twomay, who he knew to be head of British Naval security, Gibraltar. The incidents included a suspected murder in Marbella, the hospitalisation of three of his officers and the total write-off of three traffic cruisers. Could he throw any light on the matter? Twomay had been about to ask if there was any damage to his Triumph but caught himself in time before denying any knowledge of the incidents. He assured Señor Matello he was, other than being the owner of the Triumph, most certainly not involved. However, he would certainly look into this grave matter and be in touch. Furious at being embroiled in Willis's shenanigans he lifted the phone to contact border control and then the gatehouse ordering them to facilitate the return of his Triumph. If three police cruisers had been destroyed – whatever state must his pride and joy Triumph be in? If this incident became political it meant the end of his gold-plated pension. Bugger those secret service types. Especially this arrogant upstart Willis or whatever his real name was.

Scott, with Yvonne hard on his heels, entered Twomay's office without knocking. Twomay, still outraged jumped to his feet. 'Ah! Miss Rencoule, and *you* Willis. Do you know I've been accused by the local Chief of the Guardia of murder and..and..' Scott thought Twomay was about to have an apoplectic fit as he struggled to bring his temper under control, '...And various other misdemeanours all committed on *my* Triumph. What do you have to say about that, *Mr. Willis*?'

'Lucky for you Francis there's no extradition treaty with Spain...otherwise... you could be for the high jump.'

'How could you..you absolute....*bounder.*'

'*Shut up*, Twomay, and listen,' Scott retorted angrily. 'We've more to worry about than you and your bloody Triumph. There's a ship out there in the Bay with a crew of seven hundred that could blow within the next hour. I want you to declare an immediate evacuation of its crew. Plus all those, both navy and civilian, working in the dockyard.'

Twomay , still in high dudgeon replied angrily, 'Why? I must say that is highly irregular Willis. In fact I doubt if you have the authority to instruct me to do such a thing.'

'Enough of this shit, Twomay. I'm wasting valuable time. You were told by Sir James – and for Sir James read the First Lord, Lord Chatham, that I was in charge of this operation....' Scott retorted angrily, waving the M28 machine pistol menacingly in Twomay's direction. I take it you *are* familiar with standard MOD emergency lockdown procedures?' A nod to confirm from Twomay.

A terrified Twomay stuttered, 'Of..of...course , I am b..but..t..this is..this is another matter all t..to...together. For *god's sake* man lower that weapon you could kill me.'

Ignoring his request a furious Scott growled, 'Don't tempt me Francis....for I don't seem to be getting through to you. So here's the score. You can kiss your pension goodbye when Sir James is informed in my report that you have been making use of the services of a prostitute whose pimp is a known enemy of the Crown and is involved in this immediate emergency.

In a grovelling about turn Twomay harrumphed, 'Frightfully sorry, old boy. Didn't mean to be evasive. It's just I've never been in a situation like this before.'

'I understand fully,' lied Scott, wanting to wring his neck but desperately in need of his assistance. 'Now, this is important. Did a catamaran recently sail near the Eagle?'

'Yes. About thirty five minutes ago.' To Scott that meant the Maiale had already dropped Schultz, Dieter and Mueller local to the Eagle and had started to fix the mines. 'One of our MTB's intercepted it. It claimed to be heading for the start of tomorrow's annual race from Algecirus. Their papers were found to be in order. The delay was twenty minutes.'

'Not true. The papers might be in order but they have no intention of racing. But I still have time. Now, apart from notifying Captain Bullard about the evacuation, I want *immediate* transport for Miss Rencoule in the shape of a motorcycle.'

A glance at Yvonne showed her to be giving him a bad tempered scowl as Twomay, fearing the worst for its recent outing, quivered, 'But you have my Triumph.'

'*Please* Francis, I don't want to hear any more about your *bloody* Triumph or I will personally throw it into the Bay. And you to follow. But what I *do* want is your intimate knowledge of the dockyard urgently. So kindly do as I ask. The motor-cycle for Miss Rencoule immediately, please.' A shaken Twomay nodded and lifted the phone. Whilst he was in conversation Scott explained to Yvonne, 'I need you to go to Algecirus to find Max and get him to take you to meet Schultz at their rendezvous point. With the catamaran passing thirty five minutes ago, and even with its twenty minute delay, it will have made Algecirus by now. And with you having heard Schultz tell Max to wait sixty minutes after the catamaran docked before picking him up, means that we have approximately sixty minutes to do what we have to do – you get to Algecirus and convince Max to take you to their rendezvous point – and me to get Schultz to you. Happy with that?'

'No,' replied a still aggrieved Yvonne. 'What the hell do I tell Max to convince him to take me to Schultz? And there's Helmut and Pedro to consider on the catamaran....And if I'm successful what do I do with Schultz?'

'Ah! I'm sorry I can't help you, Yvonne. My main priority is to make the Eagle safe so I haven't had time to give the fine tuning any thought. Off the top of my head I would say to Max something along the lines of: Roison's father wants to know how this tragedy could've happened to his daughter and wants to see Schultz ASAP. I know you can do better than that. But it's a start. With regards to meeting Schultz: When you meet him, if my plan works out, you will be meeting me also. With both of us wearing wet suits and it being dark make sure you shoot the right one. I'll be the one removing his goggles and waving at you. As regards Helmut and Pedro they will just have to become collateral damage – if you follow my drift?' Before Yvonne could answer Twomay advised them that a BSA motor cycle was available at the gatehouse to which Scott quipped, 'Now, off you go Yvonne. A nice tame little girly's bike awaits you.'

Flicking a wayward strand of hair from her eyes she gave him a stinker of a look before she hurried out of the office muttering to herself in French, 'Ignorant chauvinist pig.'

Before the door angrily slammed shut behind her Scott laughingly reminded the disappearing back that he too spoke French and laughingly pig-snorted. Then turning to face a mystified Twomay he said, 'Right, Francis. Get your dive officer to get the following immediately: wet suits, rebreather units, complete with all the usual paraphernalia, powerful underwater torches, screwdrivers, pliers, etcetera. And an ankle sheath with a dagger for me. Plus as many divers as he can muster. We have a large area of hull to cover.'

'I only have two divers on duty...but I can draw more from the Eagle.'

'Good. Do that. And while you're doing that you can get Bullard to start the evacuation. You have no longer than one hour to clear the Eagle. And, of course, a tender to take us out to the Eagle. I'm now running tight on time. I, too, have less than sixty minutes to sort out the problem – so no more procrastination – let's go.'

'But that's impossible Willis. You can't expect seven hundred people to clear decks in fifty minutes....'

'Then I better not fail to make the Eagle safe – had I? Meanwhile you make sure you get as many clear of the dockyard as possible.'

'Sorry, Willis, before I go, 'What about prisoners?'

'How many do you have locked up?'

'Two. Curran and....'

'Let me guess ...Delores?' Twomay nodded his head to confirm. 'Let her go. We have nothing on her. In fact it was her evidence that put me onto the gang.

'But you told me to have her locked up on a charge of treason, and that's what's down on her charge sheet.'

Scott shook his head in despair. 'No. Francis. No. It was Curran that was to be arrested on the charge of treason. Delores was to be locked up for her own safety. However, may I remind you Francis that you too, if you force me to submit my report to Sir James about your consorting with her, could be facing a similar charge and Delores would be one of the Crown's principal witnesses against you?' With that he turned on his heel and made off briskly towards the dive officer's station. There was no doubt in his mind that the charge sheet would mysteriously disappear.

Ten minutes later Scott and six divers slipped silently over the gunwales of the tender into the inky blackness of the Bay.

CHAPTER 24

Algecirus Spain

Yvonne, as she kick-started the small BSA 250cc motor cycle into life had hoped, after her experience with Scott, never to sit on a motor cycle again. The only saving grace this time was that she held her life in her own hands as two minutes later she turned into the back yard of her apartment and fled upstairs to change out of her ripped fatigues and slip into her new and highly fashionable American jeans she had bought recently in Paris. A further quick change into a black polo neck sweater, a tailor-made black leather jerkin, cut to hide the bulge of her shoulder-holstered Beretta, a little bit of work on the make-up, a look in the full length hall mirror and she felt presentable enough to meet Max. The time taken from leaving the dockyard was fifteen minutes, leaving her forty minutes to reach Algecirus to meet Max with a suitable tale to convince him to allow her to meet Schultz. There was, of course, the other problem that Scott mentioned – the crew that had brought the catamaran into Algecirus namely Helmut and Pedro. A solution to that problem came to mind instantly as some solutions do. One that didn't being a convincing tale to tell Max. She would just have to embellish Scott's suggestion.

Holding the BSA motor-cycle at its top speed along an empty main road Yvonne found herself fifteen minutes later in Algecirus and quickly found the marina. At the end of a line of floating walkways she recognized Schultz's catamaran – tied up on the same walkway but on the opposite side from the polished wood deck of Max's speed boat. For the problem regarding the catamaran's crew, Helmut and Pedro, she needed a phone, so she stopped at one of the many marina cafés. She picked one local to the catamaran and Max's speed boat. As she removed her goggles and leather helmet to a pannier and entered the café the hub-bub of noise ceased as she found the phone and asked the operator in loud Madrid accented Spanish to speak to the local chief of the Guardia. With her deliberately loud mention of the Guardia the rabble assumed, with her Madrid styled clothing and accent, to be attached to the Guardia – as she had intended – and with heads down paid her no further attention. Minutes later after her discussion with the chief she left the café. Outside, waiting in the shadows, was one of the local rabble who menacingly stood in her way. Seconds later he no longer stood – he was sprawled on the deck, vomiting up his evening's quota of cheap red wine and clutching his testicles. She looked around to see if anybody had noticed her accurate and violent knee thrust. There was nobody, apart from possibly the tall gentleman with his back to her in the next door terrace who was returning to his seat. She mounted the BSA and drove it across the street to stop outside the catamaran's floating gangway. As she made her way along the badly lit floating gangway she passed the catamaran and noticed somebody stretched out with hands on lap and ankles crossed asleep in one of the semi-circular seats. By the bad light she thought the slight build suggested Pedro. This she thought peculiar, for as far as Schultz's plan was concerned both Helmut and Pedro should be preparing to leave with Max to meet Schultz, Dieter and Müeller at their rendezvous point.

Taking no chances she un-holstered the Beretta and stepped aboard the speed boat where she found Max below decks with feet up on a coffee table reading the deBild German newspaper and sipping a whisky. Caught by surprise he jumped to his feet, his hand edging towards his shoulder holster stopped at Yvonne's command, 'Gently Max. Remove it with finger and thumb and drop it on the table.' She watched him carefully as the Luger automatic was laid on the table.

'Who the hell are you?' thundered Max in very good English, not taking his eyes off the Beretta whilst appreciating the professional way it was handled.

'Good evening Max,' she replied in a passable Irish accent that she knew would be good enough to fool the German. 'I didn't mean to scare you. The name's not important but my message to you is – where's Schultz?'

Max answered the question with a question, 'Did you get off the catamaran that just berthed?'

'No,' she replied not falling for his trick question whilst keeping an alert ear for any presence of Helmut being aboard. 'I have driven from Malaga by motor cycle with a message from Mr. Walsh,' she replied

'Who the hell is Walsh?'

With everything from now on being a question of thinking on her feet she replied firmly, 'You and Schultz's boss – Roison's father.'

A silence ensued whilst Max gave thought to this new turn of events as Yvonne waited tensely in a state of apprehension having just made-up the name Walsh. Max knew Schultz was the boss but he also knew that Schultz and Roison were partners and that they had worked together for the IRA...and that Roison's father, whose name he did not know, had a say in all matters financial. However, not completely convinced he queried, 'So?'

A relieved Yvonne repeated, '*So*, Roison is dead – murdered in *your* absence and Mr. Walsh wants to know what you and Schultz intend to do about finding the culprit?'

Still proving hard to convince, Max asked, 'How was she killed and how did Mr. Walsh find out?'

Ignoring the first question Yvonne answered, 'The stable manager found her and contacted Mr. Walsh in Dublin and he contacted me. And before you ask why me, I'm on a job for him in Malaga.'

Max knowing better than to ask about the job instead enquired, 'How did you know where to find me?'

Yvonne, showing genuine exasperation said, 'Because Schultz told Mr. Walsh all about the attack on the Eagle. That includes you. Now, Max – enough of the questions. My orders are to bring Schultz back to Marbella. He knows you have made arrangements to meet Schultz after the attack. So let's not fuck around any longer otherwise....I don't want to use this but believe me I will.'

Max, on hearing that she knew about their plans to attack the Eagle had to believe her story but as a precaution pretended to agree to take her to meet Schultz at the rendezvous point so he said, 'I can't leave for another fifteen minutes otherwise I'll arrive at the rendezvous point too early and we don't want to draw attention to ourselves hanging around.' This time lapse he hoped would give Schultz enough time to return to the catamaran from wherever he was and sort out this problem that had arisen.

Yvonne wanting to be away before her phone call from the café to the Guardia was acted upon and the possible arrival of Helmut snarled, 'Tough Max. We leave now. Just take it slowly. And remember I'll be right behind you.'

Max didn't have to be told twice. Not because of Yvonne's threat but because of a near-at-hand screech of brakes and the slamming of car doors. They both looked out to find the catamaran swarming with Guardia Civil police. It was then that she said, 'Oh! And I forgot to tell you that you and the crew of the catamaran are police suspects for the murder of Roison.' A shaken Max, more worried about the proximity of the Guardia rather than the Beretta covering him, indicated the need to untie the boat fore and aft from its mooring and clambered upstairs to scramble over the gunwale, untie the boat and limping, returned immediately to take up his driving position behind the steering wheel where he switched on the ignition and made a hasty departure. It was his awkward movements in carrying out the untethering that drew Yvonne's attention to his prosthetic leg. The wake of the speed boat rocked the catamaran. Max knew Schultz would understand his hasty departure.

Yvonne chortled to herself at the irony of the act being played-out. It had been her phone call to the local Guardia police chief from the café to inform him that she thought the suspects for the Marbella murder were in a catamaran opposite a café called El Sol that had brought about the present situation. She had concocted her fabrication thinking at the time she had to get the known crew of the catamaran, Helmut and Pedro, arrested and out of her way so she could be alone with Max. Now that it transpired the phone call hadn't been necessary it had almost ensnared her due to the police's quick response time and Max's procrastinations. Yvonne sighed silently. She had, so far, got off with her subterfuge. Unlike Scott, lies did not come easy to her. She couldn't wait to come face to face with Schultz.

***

As Max powered the luxury speed boat away from the jetty he realized he had problems. Ten minutes ago he was simply awaiting the return of Schultz to begin their journey to Cueta – now he had the Guardia Civil and an interfering, albeit attractive, Irishwoman to contend with. He had wanted to wait the extra fifteen minutes to allow Schultz time to arrive and sort out the Irishwoman. Even though she was the bearer of Roison's death he knew Scultz would not allow this bad news to interfere with his revised plans. Not that both issues now mattered – the arrival of the Guardia had put paid to that. Knowing that the Guardia's enquiries would extend to him as a member of the Marbella

Racing team, he had had no option but to flee. Schultz would understand. But where would he take the Irishwoman? His title was chief planning executive – but Schultz made all the real decisions. He forced himself to think like Schultz as he steered well away from the Eagle. A quick glance at his watch showed that the Eagle could blow at any time. His course was set for the rendezvous point (RVP) but should he have chosen to go to Cueta? However, the thought of the RVP gave him an idea. With Schultz's revised plan in pieces he decided to start his analysis at the beginning with the original plan. Had it been in operation, Helmut, Pedro and himself would have been on their way right now to the RVP to meet Dieter and Schultz off the Maiale. Müeller, he knew, was to be disposed of by this time. So how, he asked himself, had the revised plan differed from the original? It differed only in that Schultz and himself were heading to Cueta and abandoning Helmut, Dieter and Pedro. But, they didn't know they were to be abandoned, so they would still head for the RVP – and so would he. With Pedro back on the catamaran, no doubt now in Guardia custody he would head for the RVP with the Irishwoman to meet Helmut and Dieter. During the transfer of Helmut and Dieter to the speed boat they would get the opportunity to overpower the Irishwoman, kill her and dispose of her into the sea. With Helmut and Dieter off guard he would gun them both down then return to pick up Schultz. The question was where to pick him up? Algecirus was out – the Bay would be swarming with hostile rescue shipping. The answer came to him – he would head direct to Cueta. Schultz he knew to have contacts in Algecirus that would secrete him over the Straits into Cueta. Minutes later his compass readings showed him to be at the RVP. Ten miles east of the Maiale. He congratulated himself on a brilliant piece of planning. Maybe his title of chief planning officer had been justified after all. Schultz would understand.

CHAPTER 25

Rutherford, who had witnessed the Maiale being loaded aboard the catamaran at Schultz's Marbella headquarters, was convinced that it was going to be used to help destroy HMS Eagle. With Twomay being Head of Navy Intelligence, Gibraltar station, Scott enquired as to what he knew about manned torpedoes? (The official classification of the Maiale.) Twomay informed him that Naval Intelligence knew little about the recent innovation of the Italian manned-torpedo other than it was a silent-running, battery-operated, submersible that acted as the mother supply ship by carrying detachable mines in its nose cone – maximum load 600 kilos – to as near the target as possible to allow divers to fix the mines to the target. Being battery powered meant it would not be picked up on the Eagle's sonar equipment. The combination of these elements meant they were dealing with a fiendish weapon of destruction. Having worked security with Yvonne at the top secret limpet mine research establishment in the highlands of Scotland, Scott was aware that there were no underwater magnets available that could carry loads in excess of five kilos – meaning the saboteurs had to find suitable underwater projections to attach their heavier mines to the Eagle. With every second being precious this problem should gain him a little more time on the enemy.

From the port deck of the Eagle, Twomay's approach was watched carefully through Captain Bullard's night glasses. As Twomay edged the launch near to the pride of the fleet, Scott and six other divers clad in wet suits and rebreather units, on Scott's raised hand signal, flipped themselves backwards off the launch's gunwale into the bay. In single file they made their way downwards through the murky water towards the keel. By the light from their powerful underwater torches they started at the bow and edged their way carefully in five horizontal bands along the hull looking for any irregularities whilst Scott and one other broke away to thrust themselves downwards towards the propellers, an obvious anchorage for mines. Together they noticed a floating object. The object was fixed to one of the four propeller shafts. Upon inspection the floating object was found to be a converted lifebelt, the type you find on a post, for rescue at all coastal resorts. The conversion had buoyancy floats added to assist flotation. Sitting in the middle of the lifebelt he recognized a 75 kilo TNT mine. He checked the timer, it showed ten minutes of used time against a set dial time of sixty minutes; suggesting the saboteurs had a ten minute start. Assuming this to be the first mine set, and with the Maiale's capability of carrying 600 kilos, a quick calculation meant there could be, hypothetically, another seven 75 kilo mines, available. However, with only fifty minutes left on the timer and the Maiale, according to Twomay, only capable of carrying two active divers plus the driver Scott knew it was out of the question the remaining seven mines ever being used. Had it been him and one other, he in Schultz's situation, reckoned they would only have enough time left to set two more mines to allow them time to escape to the Maiale and clear the danger area. With the discovered mine being at the stern he figured Schultz would achieve maximum damage by placing the others amidships and bow. If all three detonated simultaneously Scott knew that was the end of HMS Eagle....and also him and his fellow divers. Regarding the seven hundred crew, Scott trusted Captain Bullard would not put obstacles in the way of his order, issued by Twomay, to evacuate the Eagle immediately. Having spoken to Bullard during his passage en route for Gibraltar, he struck Scott as one who would go down saluting with his ship. However, his main concern with the Eagle was founded on it being a fighting ship. It had a well-stocked magazine. Should that detonate there would be one mammoth explosion. It could very well destroy the dockyard. He had to hand it to Schultz; it was a well-planned operation but it was now up to him to become Schultz's problem.

Shunting the horrible thought of the explosion to the back of his mind he hand signalled his fellow diver to remove and defuse the mine and with a twirling finger he further indicated to his colleague that he wanted him to inform the rest of the team to follow him, still in their vertical formation, so that nothing was missed. Getting the thumbs-up okay he then flipped his way round to starboard. Putting himself in his adversary's position, Scott was convinced that Schultz, knowing that 225 kilos of TNT (75 kg stern 75 kg amidships and 75 kg bow) would do the job, had planned this as a lightning strike – in and out in sixty minutes. Two experienced divers could achieve this comfortably with the assistance of the Maiale near to hand. With every second now vital he put maximum energy into his thrust towards amidships. With the Eagle being 203 metres long this meant swimming a distance of approximately some one hundred metres. Normally, doing the crawl, he would cover this distance in a minute but with full rebreather apparatus on, the main weight being the two oxygen cylinders, he didn't think he could make it in less than two minutes. Unfortunately, this did not apply to the saboteurs who would have the Maiale near at hand to transport themselves thus gaining further time. A glance at his underwater Omega watch showed he had forty minutes left to find and defuse the other two mines. After three minutes of battling his way along the keel line against the inconsistent eddying flow of the current passing under it, he happened upon the amidships mine floating on a lifebelt and tied to a construction eye-bolt welded to the hull. Its timer showed thirty-five minutes to detonation. Snipping the wires to the timer in similar fashion to the first mine Scott returned to his exhausting crawl. He had travelled less than fifty metres when an oscillation in the water at eye level caught his attention. A closer inspection found this to be a semi-taut rope wafting with the current. He immediately realized he had found the umbilical line between the manned torpedo and the divers. Casting his eyes upwards he saw a silhouetted outline shaped like a cigar. The Maile. He followed the line downwards until he came to a luminous yellow glow. He kept to the periphery of the luminosity and observed the two divers. They had just finished setting the timer on a mine sitting in a lifebelt that was tied to the ship through what he took to be an anchor guide welded to the hull. As the pair were breaking away one of the divers, a large bulky shadow, pulled a knife from his leg sheath and raised it to stab his colleague. His intended victim sensing trouble flipped himself sideways at the very last moment out of the path of the deadly strike, managed to grasp his assailant's wrist and turn the dagger inwards and thrust upwards as he turned the blade. Before Scott's eyes a pool of dark stain mixed with the luminous yellow glow as the instantly dead Dieter with arms and legs floating akimbo began his descent into the murky depths. Another quick glance at his watch – thirty minutes left to detonation. A comfortable safety margin depending, of course, on his dispensing with the other diver promptly. As he used the dark cloud of swirling blood to cover the unsheathing of his dagger he was wondering what the hell had happened between Schultz's divers.

The surviving diver, Müeller, had been having similar thoughts throughout his dive. He had allowed his obsessional hatred towards the British agent that he knew as Hill to cloud his better judgment. Looking back on his supposedly coincidental meeting with Schultz and his sudden recruitment twenty-four hours before a major attack – unheard of, without weeks of preparation – promises of riches and, of course, the dangling carrot – Schultz's offer of help to find, torture and kill the British agent Hill. It had all been lies – lies that had made him suspicious of poor thick Dieter. Yes, he admitted to himself, he had been set-up by Schultz who he would make pay for his treachery. However, as he turned towards the umbilical line, little knowing that Schultz above in the driving seat of the Maiale had been replaced by Helmut, he realised that revenge on Schultz might have to wait, for he was confronted by another dagger wielding diver. It wouldn't be Schultz; he wouldn't put himself in danger. It had to be one of Eagles' divers on a routine inspection. He would have to dispose of him quickly, because there would be others following.

Scott, setting aside the surreal act he had witnessed, had borne in mind the very professional way his adversary had handled his previous attacker as he moved in for the kill. With the timer ticking this would have to be quick. Unfortunately, it was not to be. The ensuing fight took on the appearance of an elegant but deadly underwater ballet. With each combatant being trained in dagger attack and defence it became obvious that one or other of them would have to come up with something original. Chance, however, played its part. The undercurrent eddy from the keel of the Eagle had backed Müeller into a position under the floating lifebelt with its ticking seventy-five kilo load of TNT cargo. To break the deadlock Scott decided on a life or death manoeuvre. He dropped his arms to his side and kicked violently with his flippers to project himself like a bullet upwards towards the lifebelt. This action exposed his torso to Müeller who, taken completely by surprise, was slow to react as Scott's dagger sliced through the rope connecting the additional buoyancy stabilisers attached to the lifebelt. Disconnected they floated from the lifebelt towards Müeller. In themselves they posed no threat but with a natural reflex Müeller threw up an arm to ward them off. A reflex action that was to cost him his life as Scott plunged his dagger with a twist into his heart. As the body floated towards Scott, he swore he could see a flicker of recognition and acknowledgment of his stupidity in Müeller's eyes.

What a way to leave the world – a failure. Tricked by Schult and Himmler who had played on his paranoid revenge on the man who had just brought his life to a sudden halt were Müeller's dying thoughts and as he drifted into the abyss his tic stopped. Peace at last.

Scott glanced at his watch – five minutes before detonation. He immediately turned his attention to the explosives. Without its additional buoyancy the modified lifebelt was showing signs of tipping the explosives. Scott, not knowing the depth of water under the Eagle, dared not let them detonate with their timers still set so he, with shoulder under the tipped edge of the lifebelt, trod water to allow him access to the timer. Using his razor sharp dagger he severed all wires. The second hand on the clock stopped with two minutes to spare. He dropped his shoulder to allow the now harmless mine to tip off the lifebelt and sink into the depths for uplift by navy divers at a later date. His anger rising he couldn't wait to follow the umbilical line to Schultz who was, according to Yvonne, driving the Maiale.

***

In a moonless night some 60metres due south of HMS Eagle the driver of the submerged Maiale looked anxiously at his watch. The sixty minutes he had allowed Müeller and Dieter to place the mines had expired. He assumed Dieter to have had trouble disposing of Müeller and decided to allow a further five minutes. Had he not required confirmation that the mines had been set he would have departed without Dieter. This location had been worked out by Müeller as being outside the shock area of the detonation. However, he had his reservations and was anxious to leave for the RVP. With the passing of the five extra minutes he switched on the batteries and set the buoyancy to lift the Maiale up to surface cruising and was just about to cut the umbilical line when a wet suited goggle-wearing head broke the surface giving the thumb-up signal that all was well and clambered aboard to sit behind him. Content in the knowledge that Dieter had rid them of Müeller and that with the mines in place the Eagle would be history any time in the immediate future, he set a course to the rendezvous point to meet Max. What he wasn't aware of was that the person sitting behind him would have slit his throat had he known the location of the rendezvous point with Max....and Yvonne – provided she had played her part deceiving Max.

***

As Max departed the Algecirus marina at speed, Yvonne relaxed. She had successfully convinced Max that Roison's fictitious father needed to meet Schultz. What worried her was the lack of any sign of Max carrying a gun, for there was, without question, one hidden somewhere other than the one she had him deposit on the coffee table. She couldn't in any way frisk him – that would blow her subterfuge, so she kept her Beretta un-holstered with hands in her jerkin pockets. Physically, Max was powerfully built but she knew with his leg problem she could take him easily if it came to the rough stuff. Yvonne had been paying close attention to anything that would give her a clue as to the location of the RVP. When they stopped she could, through the scurrying storm clouds, just make out in the distance a large umbrella-type glow encompassing an area which she assumed to be a small town. Her guess would be Malaga. With that established, her next problem was the arrival of the Maiale at the rendezvous. With it being dark, and with the arrivals being clad in black wet suits, the question of identity arose. If it was only Schultz she would need to take-out Max first, leaving a straight shoot-out between herself and Schultz. She could cope with that. But if it was Schultz and two or more of his gang, she had a problem. She certainly didn't fancy her odds against that ensemble. However, she did have the element of surprise – they would not be expecting a hostile reception and would, with the possible exception of Schultz, be unarmed. Either way it looked like she would have to take out Max first and as it stood he, too, was unarmed which reduced the odds against her slightly. At all costs she could not let them aboard the speed boat. Ideally, it would be Scott only – but that couldn't happen; he didn't know the location. The next best scenario would be Schultz and Scott arriving together. She could take out Max then go for Schultz. But which one would be Schultz? Scott said he would raise his goggles and wave. But in this inky darkness? With these problems still buzzing around her mind she heard a low hum. As Max cut the engine to idle she glanced overboard. Through a brief striking shaft of moonlight filtering between the dark clouds she saw two wet suited heads appear. One of the heads immediately whipped off his goggles and waved. The shaft of moonlight lingered long enough for her to recognise those piercing blue eyes anywhere. Her heart rate increased. It was Scott.

As the other leaned over from his seated position to grab a line dangling from the boat to tether the Maiale to the speed boat Scott unsheathed his leg dagger. He knew that with villains like Schultz there was no "en-garde" moment. You took the opportunity when you could. And having spotted Yvonne looking overboard he knew the time was right, so he raised his arm to strike the deadly blow to end Schultz and his murderous regime. Unfortunately, the Maiale swung outward on a sea surge away from the speed boat, causing Scott's blow aimed at a spot under the oxygen cylinders on Schultz's back to strike one of the cylinders and ricochet off. Schultz was immediately out of his seat and standing precariously on the top surface of the torpedo now with his dagger drawn but still with his back to Scott. The effort taken for Schultz to turn around to face Scott with dagger drawn gave Scott time to scramble from his seat. As they faced each other they were both of a single mind – they dropped their cumbersome oxygen cylinders from their backs and lunged at each other.

Aboard the boat Max had as if by magic procured a Luger automatic from under the boat's consul and was trying to take aim at the moving target that was Scott. *Bad mistake Max you should have taken me out first,* thought Yvonne as her Beretta cleared her pocket to fire a single shot. Max with a hole drilled neatly through his throat staggered, fired off an automatic burst into the air and sagged over the gunwale.

Meanwhile atop the Maiale, Scott and Schultz, locked in wrestling holds, lost their footing and disappeared into the sea to continue the duel. The fall separated them. As they entered the water the fight took on a new dimension. With both men being former marines in their respective navies they were experienced underwater combatants and knew that there was no point in expending energy fighting the choppy waters of the Mediterranean so for ease of manoevrability the fight to the death would take place in the calmer underwater. Being aware of this both took large gulping intakes of air before sinking below water level simultaneously. Without their oxygen cylinders it would be a trial of the strongest lungs. The ensuing fight was similar to Scott's earlier contest with Müeller – evenly matched. After several close encounters with each waiting for the opportunity to strike should a mistake be made by the other the first sign of weakness was shown by Schultz as air bubbles started to leak from the corners of his mouth. He broke away and struck towards the surface but never made it as Scott with his own last fluid ounce of oxygen plunged his dagger with a twisting turn into the exposed stomach of Schultz.

On deck Yvonne had been anxiously scouring the dark surface of the Mediterranean for any signs of life for what appeared an eternity but in fact had been only two or three minutes when she suddenly noticed a movement on the surface. She shepherded the Maiale against the hull of the speed boat towards the dark shadow. Nearing the shadow she took a long, deep breath and gasped as she observed the shadow to be that of a body floating face down. Expecting the worst – the death of Scott – she resumed her search for Schultz with Beretta drawn. It would give her great pleasure to see an end to the evil bastard.

Without warning a head appeared above the Maiale to shout, 'Don't shoot, it's me, Yvonne.' Her heart leapt with joy at the sight of him clambering up onto the Maiale, untying it from the gunwale and then making it fast to the rear of the speed boat, up the ladders and into the speed boat where he, noticing Max drooped over the gunwale, upended him into the sea. He then sank to his bottom and with back to the gunwale and knees drawn up to chin he said in a low voice, 'Christ, I'm exhausted Yvonne. Job done. Eagle saved. Main culprit dead...many thanks for your help. You can be on my team anytime.'

'Well, you will play these stupid games. And let's face it you're not as young as you used to be....' He made a half-hearted attempt at hitting her. It was then that she noticed the sliced wet suit with blood seeping through the rent.

She couldn't help herself as she darted to his side and put her arms around him and kissed him tenderly. 'You're wounded...'

'It looks worse than it is. I think you will find it to be a surface wound. A sticking plaster will do the job. There's bound to be one below.'

They adjourned below deck to find the medical chest. Scott, after stripping off the wet suit, found a pair of plus-four trousers, a shirt and a tweed hacking jacket in a closet near enough to his size to wear. Yvonne, after admiring the finely honed athletic body, cleaned the wound and bound it. It was worse than he made out. She reckoned it needed stitches and expecting him to say "Gibraltar" when she asked him, 'Where to now skipper?

'Set course for Estepona....'

'Is that wise? That wound needs attention and with Roison's death the

Guardia will be all over the area....'

'Not at this time of night.'

'Okay. But more to the point Sir James will expect to be hearing from you.'

'What's there to tell him that won't be in my report. The Eagle's secure, the perpetrators are dead, we're safe and all's well. Full stop. And there's a fat, grubby, little inn-keeper in Estepona that owes us eighty pesetas. So Estepona it is...'

'You're not going there for the sake of eighty pesetas – that's for sure,' interrupted Yvonne. 'So what are you up to, Rutherford?'

'Tell you when we get there...'

'No. Now! I'm fed up being fobbed off with you thinking you're protecting me. I'm a big girl now and can look after myself. I've done my bit so why don't you tell me *now*,' she persisted.

Scott sighed. 'You're quite right. You've been magnificent throughout and I apologise. To explain – Schultz and his gang lie dead at the bottom of the Med. I had hoped to interrogate him but unfortunately circumstances did not permit me that luxury. I had hoped to find out who he was working for.'

'He would never have told you. In any case a man like Schultz doesn't work for anybody but himself.'

'Maybe. But you have to remember he's a mercenary and they work for money. The rights or wrongs of disputes don't matter to the likes of him. It's the prize that counts. In this case the Eagle was the prize. So who wanted it caught? And I think I know a man who might, just might, know...'

'Who?'

'The inn-keeper. Let's call him Fatso.'

'Him? Never.'

'Yvonne. How do you think Schultz knew we were on our way to the stables?

Without waiting for an answer he continued, 'Fatso didn't leave the doorway whilst we dined. He watched every movement we made. He warned Schultz by phone. Believe me he's on the payroll and I intend to find out what he knows.'

'And you're going to walk into the inn dressed in plus-fours and expect anybody to treat you seriously?' she laughed.

'Yes. He would be a fool not too. And after I have my man-to-man with Fatso I was going to suggest that we stop over in the boat and sail for Gib in the morning. How does that appeal?' He asked as he rose to his feet to re-secure the Maiale to the speed boat for towing.

A smile of satisfaction crossed Yvonne's face as in answer to his question she started the engine to begin towing the submersible towards Estepona. They tied up to the harbour wall. Nobody was about.

Lights were on in the inn as the tweed clad figure of Scott resplendent in plus fours and deerstalker hat (compliments of Max's wardrobe) strode towards the inn with a walking stick. The few patrons there went silent as he entered. He paid no attention to them. Fatso was behind the bar and showed no signs of recognition. Rutherford arrived at the bar and slammed his walking stick across the counter and in fluent Madrid Spanish informed the inn keeper that he wanted to speak to him about the illegal titles of his land that the inn stood on. Fatso in panic at being in the company of Spanish land nobility virtually tipped his forelock before he showed Scott into his private quarters. As the door closed Rutherford whacked him across the nape of his neck with the walking stick and as he spun around he was met with a fist on its way to his nose. He staggered backwards into a threadbare arm chair. As he lay with legs akimbo Rutherford fitted a silencer to his PPK and aimed at Fatso who put up both hands to ward off the bullet as he tried at the same time to communicate incomprehensibly through a mashed nose and broken teeth that Rutherford was welcome to the till takings. The shot exploded the front of the chair between the hysterical inn keeper's open legs close to his genitals. A pool of urine appeared at his feet as tears rolled into his fat jowls. Rutherford bid him a "good evening" and enquired for whom Schultz worked. Fatso couldn't give the information fast enough. The information gleaned, Rutherford raised his PPK. Fatso fainted along with a bowel clearance. He then trussed him up with a clothes rope from the kitchen, removed his wallet and flung him into the beer cellar.

Scott re-entered the bar to encounter the waiter he and Yvonne had been served by on their earlier visit. He was sporting a black eye. The waiter recognized him and asked after the health of Scott's wife with a sly knowing smile twitching at the corners of his mouth. The knowing being that they were responsible for the troubles up at the villa but after receiving the black eye from his boss their secret was safe with him. Scott did not miss the unspoken vibe as he asked how the waiter got the black eye. He was told that his generous tip had been stolen from him by his violent boss. Scott opened Fatso's wallet and extracted all the peseta notes – more than enough to cover the waiter's stolen tip several times over and handed them to him with a rejoinder not to let his boss out of the cellar until he had departed tomorrow morning. The waiter shook his hand warmly and assured him that that would be the case. He would organise breakfast. Scott, not having eaten since he and Yvonne's last meal on the terrace here at the inn, suggested the possibility of sandwiches now. The waiter disappeared into the kitchen to return minutes later with a brown bag of sandwiches and a bottle of champagne. And no he did not want the sandwiches or champagne delivered to his "wife" she had retired for the evening. A look of disappointment caressed the waiter's face. *Lecherous sod,* thought Scott.

The following morning the waiter did get his chance to ogle Yvonne as with a champagne breakfast prepared by himself he brought to the speed-boat on a silver salver. The morning El Dia newspaper was also included which Scott read aloud to Yvonne.

'It says here that: *A man has been arrested for the murder of an Irish stable owner in Marbella. He was found in the boathouse of the villa belonging to the deceased. He was identified as the local leader of the Falange – Eduardo Suarez. He is under Guardia Civil guard in hospital having been severely mauled by a Dobermann guard dog. The dog itself was found stabbed to death with an instrument made from a tin cup handle lying alongside Suarez. There was another Dobermann found dead on the villa's back lawn. The mystery deepens because as we were going to press, a late report reached us from the local police in Algecirus from an anonymous source leading the Guardia to a catamaran in berth for today's big race in Algecirus. The source claimed that two of the crew were linked to the murder of the stable owner in Marbella. When the Guardia arrived at the catamaran it found only one crew member and he had been shot dead. Of the other there was no trace. They would also like to interview the owner of a speed boat moored local to the catamaran that left hurriedly when they arrived. No involvement in the incident is suggested regarding the owner of the speed-boat but the police would like to hear from him should he have seen anything suspicious.'* Scott leaned back and looked quizzically at Yvonne before saying, 'An *anonymous* tip-off about two men on a catamaran? I don't suppose you know anything about that – Miss Rencoule?'

Yvonne just smiled, shrugged and winked at him and said, 'I wonder what happened to the second man from the catamaran? That should be Helmut, shouldn't it?'

'It should, according to what you overheard back in Marbella' agreed Scott.

***

The second man from the catamaran had waited long past the due time for the explosives fixed to the Eagle to detonate before he rose from his café seat on the quayside in Algecirus and stamped on his cigarette end in disgust. Helmut and Dieter had once again fucked up. Even Müeller had joined the gang of incompetents. And the trustworthy Max, on seeing the Guardia swoop on the catamaran, had buggered off without him. Not that it all mattered. It had been his intention that on reaching Cueta to rid himself of Max. Schultz's lift pulled up outside the café to take him to Trafalgar Playa for onward transportation to Cueta. With his money safe in Switzerland and a civil war threatening in Spain – opportunities abounded.

***

The navy divers who had accompanied Rutherford on the Eagle's hull inspection had communicated the welcome news that all the mines had been located and that the Eagle was out of danger. Unfortunately, they had found a diver stabbed through the heart entangled in the anchor chain. Of Rutherford there was no sign. Twomay, immediately suspecting the worst, initiated an all-out search of the vicinity that carried on throughout the night.

CHAPTER 26

First to spot Scott and Yvonne was Captain Johnson flying his Sea Hawk. He overflew them with a waggle of wings. They were half way between Estepona and Europa Point, the southern-most tip of Gibraltar, sipping the remains of their breakfast champagne and enjoying the morning's great-to-be-alive rays of sunshine – their large, floppy straw hat brims fluttering in the cooling breeze. However, their idyll was about to be interrupted. When Captain Johnson's report, about the missing person towing what appeared to be an oversized torpedo, reached Twomay's office, he immediately dispatched a motor torpedo boat to intercept what might yet be another attempt on the dockyard.

Scott welcomed the captain of the intercepting MTB aboard and after confirming that he was who the whole of the dockyard and fleet air arm were searching for, he relinquished the Maiale into the care of the dumbfounded captain's custody as he had only ever heard of manned torpedoes, never mind the responsibility now of being in charge of a secret weapon. Especially a secret weapon of another country. He notified Scott that a welcoming reception awaited him in the Bay. During the transfer of the Maiale from the speed boat to the MTB Scott took the captain aside and had a quiet word with him.

When the speed boat rounded Europa Point the Eagle stood proud on Gibraltar Bay with the early morning sun glinting off the captain's bridge where Bullard and his officers stood smartly to attention in their dress uniforms saluting the homecoming heroes. Bullard also had every member of his crew lining the flight deck also in their best dress uniforms saluting whilst they stood to attention to the shrill whistle of the duty officer. A very sentimental moment for the heroes who stood to attention with straw sun hats pulled well down to cover their faces as they returned Bullard and his crews' salutes. They hoped theirs was a sufficient disguise for both to remain anonymous to all the prying eyes and cameras.

***

As the flying boat revved up its mighty engines for departure Scott looked out of a porthole to see Twomay standing on the quayside in his full dress regalia. On seeing Scott he gave him a smart and curt salute. Scott returned the salute. Twomay now had a different opinion of Whitehall wallahs.

Half way over the Bay of Biscay as Yvonne and Scott were finalizing their report for Sir James, Scott asked, 'What do you think of Delores absconding across the border during the evacuation of the civilians from the dockyard.'

'How do you know that?'

'I told Twomay to release her – she had no case to answer.'

'Good for you Scott. I told you there was a human lurking somewhere inside you,' she giggled. 'Regards her absconding, she must have taken the advice of the well-meaning woman who reminded her that the climate in Spain is much better this time of year. And *apparently* there is no extradition with Britain.'

'*Well-I-never. No extradition indeed?* You learn something new every day. Do *I* know who this woman is who offered all this good advice to Delores?'

'Oh, yes. Not too well, but you're about to get to know her better,' yawned Yvonne and with her head on his shoulder muttered sleepily, 'Are you going to do anything about Twomay?'

'No. The old duffer is about to retire – he's done no real harm. Delores promised me he never discussed his work with her. And that's all that matters to save him. All she did apparently was a striptease dressed in a 1918 Wrens uniform and listen as he re-fought the war. So with his pension now safe he can spend his retirement watching his beloved cricket at Lords. And with Delores more than likely in Malaga and the guardhouse carelessly mislaying her charge sheet there seems no point in pursuing the matter. Not that there is anything to pursue – other than her stupidity of falling for a creep like Suarez.'

'Couldn't agree more,' yawned Yvonne, and with her head suddenly falling against Scott's shoulder she was fast asleep.

Gibraltar

On an inspection of the Maiale it was found to have a passenger. He had been knifed in the stomach and had managed to get entangled by his oxygen supply line to the underneath workings of the Maiale. Photographs of the deceased were distributed to Sir James at SIS H.Q. Whitehall.

Algecirus

Navy intelligence agent Sebastian Critchley, who had been instructed by his chief Twomay, at the behest of Yvonne to find Suarez, found himself on the waterfront of Algecirus. From his enquiries he had received a tip-off in La Linea that Suarez was due to leave for Buenos Aries aboard a merchantman. The ship had sailed fifteen minutes ago without him. However, from his position in one of the many port cafés he recognized that gorgeous French lady, Yvonne, who allegedly worked for the MOD but who, he knew, to really be SIS(6), dismounting her motor cycle and head up a jetty gangway towards a speed boat. He noted that she was being watched through night glasses by a red haired gentleman in the next café who had diverted his viewing from HMS Eagle out in the Bay. He took a seat outside and ordered coffee with the intention of seeing what Yvonne did next. Suddenly the arrival, with sirens blazing, of several Guardia Civil cruisers caused the hasty departure of the speed boat that Yvonne had boarded, followed immediately by the red haired gent slipping into a car that had pulled up outside his café then moved off down the Trafalgar Playa road. With the name being synonymous with Nelson's fabled battle off the coast and the cemetery in Gibraltar, Critchley filed it away in the trivia part of his brain. As he was intrigued by the actions of the red haired gent he followed in the dockyard security's Austin eight. By the headlights of his car he saw the red haired gent, with shoes tied by their laces dangling around his neck and trousers rolled up, wade through the incoming tide to board a speed boat. It took off in the direction of Cueta.

CHAPTER 27

London SIS(6) Headquarters – Sir James Sums-Up

Sir James had been delighted at Rutherford and Miss Rencoule's saving of HMS Eagle as had been the First Lord of the Admiralty Lord Chatham. However, Sir James had not been pleased at the press knowing of the incident, and further annoyed that Rutherford had allowed Yvonne and himself possibly to be compromised even though the photographs appearing on the front pages of the world press were faint and grainy. He had to admit that having studied the photograph he could not recognize the two people saluting the Eagle. These had been his niggling worries before he began Rutherford's debrief. Elizabeth(Liz), Sir James' faithful secretary was as usual at his side taking notes.

Rutherford had finished his report. A report that had been interrupted many times by Sir James. Elizabeth, knowing Sir James better than most, felt there had to be a hidden agenda behind the unusual number of tetchy interruptions. Rutherford, also aware of the increased interruptions had put them down to Sir James' war-wounded knee playing him up. All told an unhappy debrief summed up Liz. They were usually played-out with each man trying to out-best the other. Sir James the righteous interrogator and Scott the supplier of as near to the truth as possible, all intermingled with sarcasm and humour but convened in a pleasant atmosphere. Today had been different. Sir James the being the guilty party. Liz had expected Sir James to close his note book thank Scott for his diligence and her for her note taking thus confirming the meeting closed. Instead he sat there deep in thought twirling a gold Mont Blanc fountain pen between his fingers. Suddenly, his decision made he reached out to a bundle of newspapers at the end of his desk and removed the top copy. Elizabeth, having read the morning editions and being responsible for the daily gathering of the world press suddenly had an inkling as to the cause of Sir James' unusual demeanour as he unfolded the Daily Telegraph to expose its front page. In an unexpected mood change he congratulated, 'You did a grand job, Rutherford. A grand job indeed. One you should be proud of but, unfortunately, there is often more to an operation than a successful finish....there is this.' Scott thought this a peculiar choice of words given they were coming from a firm believer of an "end justifying the means" man as Sir James. He was pointing to two figures standing in a speed boat saluting the crew of HMS Eagle. The paper's banner headline heralded: THE SAVING OF HMS EAGLE BY UNKNOWN HEROES. Suddenly Scott and Liz had an inkling as to where this was now heading. Sir James cleared his throat gently and proceeded, 'Well Rutherford, you and Miss Rencoule have certainly caused a stir in the world press. They all carry the same theme: "Who are the heroes?' and: "The mystery deepened when they were whisked away on a fleet Air Arm flying boat". To solve the mystery for the papers I hope you aren't both expecting an open top bus parade around London.' Well at least sarcasm has returned to the fore mulled Liz as she looked across the table at Scott who she noticed had perked-up at the sarcasm.

'No sir. I suspect it was done to appease the Admiralty. Captain Bullard couldn't have made the decision on his own. He had to have had sought permission from high up the Admiralty tree of command. In which case to have ignored Bullard's welcome home reception would have been considered bad form.....especially by Lord Chatham.'

With Sir James oft depending on the Admiralty's war-chest monies for his covert operations, provided they were helpful to the Navy, and with Rutherford being Lord Chatham's blue-eyed boy he had little option but to grunt his acceptance of Rutherford's facts. However, undaunted, Sir James was determined to press home the folly of such an action, 'You do realize that by returning that salute you exposed Miss Rencoule and yourself to being compromised – and what good are compromised agents to me?' There was a sharp intake of breath from Elizabeth on realizing he had finally got to the nub of the matter as he continued, 'The fact that the photographs are grainy doesn't matter. With these new German Leica camera zoom lenses one can never be certain that the negative was not crystal clear. In other words the lack of clarity in the newspaper doesn't necessarily mean that there isn't a clear print somewhere. And with this comes another dilemma – how did the press *know* about the Eagle – Rutherford?'

'I can only assume Sir James that the local newspaper, The Gibraltar Guardian, would have had to be blind not to notice the Eagle in the Bay.'

Suspecting sarcasm Sir James narrowed his eyes as he angrily retorted, 'You

know perfectly well Rutherford that is not what I meant. I meant how did the press know the Eagle had been saved ?'

'I would also have to assume the arrival of the Eagle caused the Guardian to keep a watchful eye on it for a photographic opportunity. And when the opportunity presented itself they sent a photographer with his Kodak box-brownie to take the photographs that they then syndicated to the world press.' He couldn't help adding, 'Nothing unusual about that, Sir James, unless they had Leica lenses fitted to the box-brownie.' The first snigger of the day emanated from Elizabeth. 'Regarding how they got to know about the saving of the Eagle I would hazard a guess that the return of the evacuated Eagle's crew, many from the Victory public house, would have given them a clue.'

'Alright, since you seem to have all the answers, answer me this – why did you do it? Risk being compromised?'

There was a long pause before Scott answered with a smile twitching at the corners of his mouth as he answered, 'We didn't do it, Sir James. We weren't even there. When the *heroes* welcoming was taking place, Miss Rencoule and I were already in the air and on our way home.' There was a silence in the room, broken as Liz let out a joyous whoop that drew a stinker of a look from Sir James. Scott and Yvonne hadn't been compromised and Sir James' worries of having to rid the department of Scott because of this assumed security breach were at an end.

An apoplectic Sir James, not appreciating that his worries had ended, growled, 'Why didn't you tell me that sooner Rutherford? And how the *bloody hell* did you manage the subterfuge ?'

'Firstly, you didn't ask me the right questions. And secondly, regarding our compromise problem – when the MTB intercepted me mid-way between Estepona and Europa Point to relieve me of the Maiale the captain let it be known that there was a welcome awaiting us at the Eagle. Realising that there would be photographs that might well compromise us I arranged with the MTB captain to replace us aboard Max's speed boat with two of *his* crew. I gave them our floppy straw hats as a disguise and instructed them what to do; basically, waving, saluting and keeping their faces hidden. We then clambered aboard the MTB. The captain radioed Twomay to tell him we were on our way. On our arrival Twomay covered our heads with blankets and we boarded the flying boat. We saw the welcoming ceremony from the air. Looked good. Pity we missed it.' The last said to further annoy Sir James.

Sir James snapped shut his note book and with the words, 'Trust you Rutherford to have an answer for everything.' He then stomped out the front office into his inner sanctum and slammed the door of his private fiefdom.

Liz ran to Scott, hugged and kissed him. He was home again safely and things between Sir James and he had returned to normal hostilities.

***

That had been last week. Setting aside Rutherford's debriefing file Sir James lit a cigar and leaned back in his leather swivel chair to ponder a problem that had arisen since then. The problem needed to be resolved before he advised the Heads of Joint Forces on the final outcome of what had become known as the "Gibraltar Incident". He laid down his cigar and picked up a photograph and an accompanying memo from SIS(6) archives. The memo informed him that the photograph of the body found attached to the Maiale in Gibraltar had been identified as that of an ex Kreigsmarine Kommando – a Captain Helmut Kaymer and not Karl Schultz as had been expected. Unfortunately, Rutherford had in his debrief stated he had killed Schultz and seen him floating face down in the Mediterranean. Being as it was unlike Rutherford to get anything as seriously wrong he needed to investigate further before submitting his findings. To prepare his memory for his plough through of Miss Rencoule's debriefing file for corroboration or otherwise of Rutherford's actions, he bent down to the bottom drawer of his desk and withdrew a bottle of his favourite tipple Glenmorangie and a crystal glass, poured a stiff measure and opened Miss Rencoule's file. Satisfying himself that the malt nectar had helped to ease his near to constant knee pain he commenced his deliberations.

Miss Rencoule had stated that on the night of Schultz's death it had been inky dark and was concerned about her capability of recognizing Rutherford from Schultz in their black wet suits, even though she had agreed a recognition signal with Rutherford. Sir James remembered that he had asked her why only the recognition of Schultz? Miss Rencoule had replied that Rutherford acting on her intelligence knew the operational team to attack HMS Eagle to be Schultz, as the driver of the Maiale, with Helmut and Müeller as the divers also on the

Maiale there to place the explosives. She explained that Rutherford had hoped to dispose of Helmut and Müeller whilst they were in the act of placing the mines on HMS Eagle. He then proposed to climb on the Maiale behind Schultz in his driver's position and wait to be picked up by Max in the speed boat at the Maiale rendezvous where he would terminate both. He had hoped that Miss Rencoule would have inveigled her way onto Max's boat to aid him. Sir James sighed and shook his head at Rutherford's audacious plan. However, in the light of Archives identification of Helmut being the driver of the Maiale and not Schultz there had obviously been a change in their plans. But why? He would need to give this serious thought whilst concentrating on what he knew. Miss Rencoule, after convincing Max with her subterfuge, had stated that he on witnessing the Guardia Civil storm the catamaran on her false tip-off, immediately made a hasty departure from Algecirus to the rendezvous point to meet Schultz and Helmut – this she knew from overhearing Max and Schultz before Max left Marbella for Algecirus. She added that this, of course, depended, on Rutherford managing to terminate Dieter and Müeller and take his position on the Maiale pretending to be either one or the other of them. She explained further that on arrival at the RVP the moon glinting occasionally between the racing storm clouds had helped to alleviate her recognition concern by giving off a flashing beam that broke, as if on cue, over the two black rubber-clad heads as they surfaced alongside Max's speed boat. Rutherford, with the pre-arranged signal removed his goggles. Suddenly, without warning, both men were standing on the swaying Maiale wielding daggers. Rutherford made the first move with a thrust that was parried off Schultz's oxygen cylinder that resulted in both men falling off the Maiale to continue their struggle underwater. Miss Rencoule lost contact with them for several minutes before a head appeared and shouted "Rutherford", at which cry a gun appeared in Max's hand. He made the fatal mistake of firing off a shot that missed Rutherford before he dealt with Miss Rencoule. Without hesitation she shot him through the throat. Rutherford, on clambering aboard the speed boat informed Miss Rencoule that he had won the dagger duel. He had killed Schultz. This she had seen for herself as she witnessed the body floating face down bump into the stern of the Maiale before disappearing under the propeller.

A relieved Sir James now understood why Rutherford thought he had killed Schultz. Obviously in Schultz's changed plan he had substituted Helmut for himself aboard the Maiale with the intention of using the catamaran to get into Spain and thus distancing himself well away from the impending disaster. But why had Schultz killed Pedro and abandoned his men? A deep in thought Sir James came to the conclusion that Schultz had become disillusioned with his men as proved by their successive dockyard failures for the IRA. It certainly couldn't be money or his influential contacts, because Rutherford had discovered from the Estepona inn-keeper that the attack on the Eagle had had nothing to do with the IRA. It was being funded by the non-Nazi supporting Admirals of the Kreigsmarine and the similar minded army generals, referred to as "The Generals". What Sir James further knew was that Rutherford had gleaned his information from the inn-keeper who, under the threat of losing his genitals in a hail of Rutherford's PPK lead, had told him his information came from the Marbella Racing stable's book keeper, an elderly German widow with whom he was having a dalliance. She knew the monies were paid into an account in Switzerland – "The Grand Plan". But she had no account details. That was handled by Roison – gruesomely killed by Miss Rencoule.

He used to think of Rutherford as being the patron saint of undertakers but it looked like he would now have to add the angelic Miss Rencoule who no doubt had fallen under Rutherford's influence. All the lassies did. Their brains seemed to go AWOL when in his company. Managing to get control of his divisive, verging on the jealous, thoughts he had to admit that Rutherford's information from the inn-keeper, and being aware of how he had achieved them, led him to deem them reliable. With what little further evidence he had available he also came to the conclusion that the collective German "Admirals/ Generals" believed that by destroying HMS Eagle, Britain would assume it to be an act of provocation from Hitler and join their coup d'état to overthrow the dictator. It was worth noting that they were prepared to send to their deaths the seven hundred men aboard the Eagle to achieve their aim. Whilst these facts were based on his suppositions they would have to remain a state secret – because, regrettably, to thwart Hitler HMG may actually, sometime in the future, need the assistance of the German "Admirals/Generals". Finally, even though Schultz initially had been working for the IRA to find a way into the dockyard he believed that being the epitome of a mercenary Schultz would take the highest offer for his "Grand Plan" and could not see the IRA matching the combined wealth of the German "Admirals/Generals." However, having had experience of his type, he wouldn't put it past Schultz to have hoodwinked the IRA into believing that they, and not the "Admirals/Generals," were going to be the main benefactors of his audacious plan and thereby relieve them of their Irish punts also.

So what was Schultz planning next? With a civil war in Spain looming Sir James was prepared to bet that Schultz had already laid plans to make personal gain. Men like Schultz always benefited from others misfortunes, greed or deluded hegemony. He had no doubt that he had not heard the last of Schultz.

Sir James elected not to inform Rutherford about the non-death of Schultz for with Sir James' mantra of the end always justifying the means – all was well with the world.

AUTHOR'S NOTE

Those who know Gibraltar well may not recognize it. Towns do change over time but I needed to make certain changes to fit my story line. The Trafalgar Cemetery, for example, one of the story's main locations, does exist but I have taken the liberty of tweaking its whereabouts as indeed I have with other locations. With regards to the protagonists involved – the appalling atrocity of the Easter uprising in Dublin did take place, but the Irish Republican Army in 1936 was in its infancy and did not, as the story suggests, show any antagonistic revenge interest in Gibraltar. However, the Spanish fascist Falange party and the Spanish Government wanted the reunification of Gibraltar to Spain. This would have violated the 1713 Treaty of Utrecht that had ceded Gibraltar to Britain. Given that a civil war in Spain between the Nationalist Spanish Government and Republicans was looking inevitable the government did not want direct conflict with Britain so they resorted to such disruptive methods as closing their border regularly with Gibraltar whilst the Falange carried out demonstrations at the border. But the main danger lay with the German dictator Adolf Hitler. As part of his rising hegemony he had given aid to the Nationalists to quell local revolts in the northern Oviedo region and as a reward expected unhindered passage through Spain to the sovereign British state of Gibraltar.

Therein lay the bones of the story. I trust my liberties in no way detracted from your enjoyment of the yarn.